COMIC SAGAS AND TALES FROM ICELAND

VIÐAR HREINSSON grew up on a farm in Northern Iceland and studied Icelandic and literary theory in Iceland and Copenhagen. He is an independent literary scholar at the Reykjavik Academy and has taught and lectured on various aspects of Icelandic literary and cultural history both in Iceland and abroad, in Canada, USA and Scandinavia. General Editor of *The Complete Sagas of Icelanders* I–V (1997), he has also authored a two-volume biography of Icelandic-Canadian poet Stephan G. Stephansson, published in Iceland in 2002 and 2003. An English version, *Wakeful Nights. Stephan G. Stephansson: Icelandic-Canadian Poet*, was published in Canada in 2012.

GEORGE CLARK is Professor Emeritus, Queen's University at Kingston, Canada. His fields of expertise are Anglo-Saxon (Old English), Old Norse-Icelandic sagas, Medieval English literature and history of the English language. He has written a book and a number of critical and papers on Beowulf and papers on Icelandic sagas.

RUTH C. ELLISON studied Old Norse at London University and taught it, among other subjects, for 37 years at the University of York. She became fluent in modern Icelandic during 20 summers of fieldwork at Gilsbakki, Mýrasýsla, researching later periods of Icelandic history and literature.

FREDRIK J. HEINEMANN is retired from the University of Duisburg-Essen, Germany. His fields of expertise were Old English, History of the English Language, Old Icelandic. He has published numerous articles and book reviews on Old English and Old Icelandic literatures.

JUDITH JESCH is Professor of Viking Studies at the University of Nottingham, and Director of its Centre for the Study of the Viking Age. She has published extensively on sagas, skaldic poetry and runic inscriptions.

ROBERT KELLOGG (1928–2004) received a PhD from Harvard in 1958; his doctoral dissertation was a concordance of Eddic poetry. He taught at the University of Virginia for 42 years. He was specialized in Renaissance and medieval literature on which he published extensively. His best known book is *The Nature of Narrative* (1966) co-written with Robert Scholes. He wrote the Introduction to *The Complete Sagas of Icelanders* (1997).

After completing graduate studies in Old Norse-Icelandic literature at Berkeley, TONY MAXWELL moved to Odense, Denmark, where he has worked as a copywriter and business communications consultant for 15 years.

MARTIN S. REGAL is an associate professor of English at the University of Iceland. His research is mainly in the field of drama and adaptation studies. He is the author of the forthcoming Routledge Critical Idiom volume on tragedy and the translator of *The Saga of Gisli Sursson* (Penguin 2003).

JOHN TUCKER is Professor in the Department of English, University of Victoria in Canada since 1979. His field of expertise is Medieval studies, especially Old Icelandic and Old English. He has edited the Old Icelandic *Plácidus saga*, which is a translation of the Medieval legend of St. Eustace.

Comic Sagas and Tales from Iceland

Edited with an Introduction and Notes by
VIÐAR HREINSSON

PENGUIN BOOKS

PENGUIN CLASSICS

Published by the Penguin Group
Penguin Books Ltd, 80 Strand, London WC2R ORL, England
Penguin Group (USA) Inc., 375 Hudson Street, New York, New York 10014, USA
Penguin Group (Canada), 90 Eglinton Avenue East, Suite 700, Toronto, Ontario,
Canada M4P 2Y3 (a division of Pearson Penguin Canada Inc.)
Penguin Ireland, 25 St Stephen's Green, Dublin 2, Ireland (a division of Penguin Books Ltd)
Penguin Group (Australia), 707 Collins Street, Melbourne, Victoria 3008, Australia
(a division of Pearson Australia Group Pty Ltd)
Penguin Books India Pvt Ltd, 11 Community Centre, Panchsheel Park, New Delhi – 110 017, India
Penguin Group (NZ), 67 Apollo Drive, Rosedale, Auckland 0632, New Zealand
(a division of Pearson New Zealand Ltd)
Penguin Books (South Africa) (Pty) Ltd, Block D, Rosebank Office Park,
181 Jan Smuts Avenue, Parktown North, Gauteng 2193, South Africa

Penguin Books Ltd, Registered Offices: 80 Strand, London WC2R ORL, England

www.penguin.com

Translations first published in *The Complete Sagas of Icelanders*, volumes I, II, III and V,
edited by Viðar Hreinsson (General Editor), Robert Cook, Terry Gunnell,
Keneva Kunz and Bernard Scudder. Leifur Eiríksson Publishing Ltd, Iceland, 1997
This edition first published in Penguin Classics 2013

015

Translations copyright © Leifur Eiríksson, 1997
Introduction, Further Reading and Notes copyright © Viðar Hreinsson, 2013
All rights reserved

The moral right of the translators and editor has been asserted

Leifur Eiríksson Publishing Ltd gratefully acknowledges the support of the Nordic Cultural Fund,
Ariane Programme of the European Union, UNESCO, Icelandair and others.

Set in 10.25/12.25pt PostScript Adobe Sabon
Typeset by Jouve (UK), Milton Keynes
Printed and bound in Great Britain by Clays Ltd, Elcograf S.p.A.

ISBN: 978-0-140-44774-3

www.greenpenguin.co.uk

Contents

Acknowledgements

The translations of the sagas and tales in this volume were originally published in the *Complete Sagas of Icelanders* by Leifur Eiríksson Publishing, Reykjavík, which contributed to the production of this volume. Bernard Scudder wrote 'A Note on Poetic Imagery' for *Complete Sagas of Icelanders* and Diana Whaley compiled 'Outline of Medieval Icelandic Literature', originally for *Sagas of Warrior-Poets* (Penguin Classics, 2002). The Notes are partly based on various Icelandic editions of the sagas and the Glossary is from *Complete Sagas of Icelanders*, vol. V. Jón Torfason compiled the Index of Characters.

Thanks are due to Emily Lethbridge, Bergljót Kristjánsdóttir and Sverrir Tómasson for reading and kindly commenting on the first draft of the Introduction and to Örnólfur Thorsson for stimulating discussions on comic sagas.

I am grateful to Jóhann Sigurðsson, publisher of the *Complete Sagas*, for support and Jessica Harrison at Penguin for her cheerful cooperation and insightful help with the Introduction.

Introduction

Humour is a key element in the Sagas of Icelanders, and even the most tragic ones, such as *Njal's Saga* and *Gisli Sursson's Saga*, feature comical characters and incidents lightening the cycles of violence and vengeance. In *Njal's Saga*, for example, Njal's son Skarphedin abuses some chieftains with the memorable insult: 'You really ought to pick from your teeth the pieces from the mare's arse you ate before riding to the Thing' (chapter 120). In *Gisli Sursson's Saga*, Gisli seeks refuge from his enemies in the house of the farmer Ref, who hides him under his bed with Ref's wife, Alfdis, lying on top of him. When the noisy warriors come in, Alfdis reacts with a 'flurry of foul language that they were unlikely to forget', thereby ensuring Gisli's escape (chapters 26 and 27). However, these are single comic episodes in sagas that are essentially tragic, unlike the sagas collected in this volume. The term 'comic saga' is in fact a recent one, partly replacing the nationalistic and romantic notion that these late sagas were essentially degenerate and escapist, lacking the tragic depth of their classical predecessors. Rather than maintaining this old view of the development of the sagas, in a pattern of rise and fall, it is more fruitful to regard a number of the late sagas as representing a new stage in saga-writing. In these works – which contain strong parodic elements and are fundamentally comic – the traditional world view and values of the classical sagas are challenged, scrutinized and, in some instances, turned completely upside down.

THE SETTLER SOCIETY

The Sagas of Icelanders did not emerge fully developed from a vacuum in the first half of the thirteenth century; rather, they were shaped by two important factors. First, they are the cultural product of a settler society whose experiences were initially recorded orally and then written down in a series of exceptionally varied texts. And secondly, in terms of intellectual context, they are rooted in Iceland's conversion to Christianity in the year 999 or 1000.

According to national myth, Iceland was first settled by independent chieftains who had left Norway in order to preserve their freedom after the country was united under the rule of one king. (This myth of the Icelanders' love of freedom and independence would later become an ideological cornerstone of the country's struggle for independence in the nineteenth and twentieth centuries.) The settlement of Iceland was, first and foremost, part of the general expansion of the Nordic world towards the end of the Viking Age, as the Norsemen travelled along rivers far into Russia in the east, to the Mediterranean and Istanbul in the south, and to Britain and Ireland, the Faroe Islands, Iceland, Greenland and eventually Vinland (America) in the west and north. According to written sources, they first arrived in Iceland in the second half of the ninth century, and the country was fully settled within a few decades. In Iceland, the Norsemen encountered a place quite different from what they had left, a land of volcanoes and hot springs, glaciers, vast lava fields and sands cut by unpassable, even sulphurous, glacial rivers. It was also a country without an indigenous population, meaning that the settlers would adapt their own traditions in order to establish and develop a new, functioning society.

A general assembly, the Althing, was instituted in 930; this was the legislative body and the supreme court. A system of local assemblies also developed, serving as lower courts. The country was divided into thirty-six (later thirty-nine) domains ruled by godis, chieftains who protected and were supported by free farmers and their households (see also Glossary). The weaknesses of this system were the absence of an executive power and that it fostered the conditions for fierce power struggles between clans. After 1000, following Iceland's conversion to Christianity, this lack of a central executive power became increasingly problematic as political control began to be concentrated in ever fewer hands. The country was more or less in a state of civil war for long periods in the first half of the thirteenth century, which culminated in its subjection to the Norwegian king in 1262. Although this event has traditionally been regarded as marking the beginning of decadence and decay in Icelandic society, the arrival of the king in fact brought peace to the country, stabilizing what was a rather abnormal situation for a medieval society. Significantly, most of the best sagas were written after this time.

RELIGIOUS AND LITERARY CULTURE

Although the official implementation of a Christian world view after Iceland's conversion may have caused heathen customs to become an undercurrent or subculture for a long time, they remained in circulation in oral lore. The dialogical relationship between Christianity and paganism is apparent in an Icelandic translation of the second part of Nicodemus' Apocryphal Gospel (*Niðurstigningar saga*), in which Christ's descent into Hell is described using heathen imagery: Norse giants inhabit Hell, and Satan resembles the serpent of Midgard from Norse mythology.[1] This was not the clumsiness of an ignorant translator but an artful device intended to amplify the cultural resonance of the story.

The conversion to Christianity had been politically motivated and decided on by the leading chieftains; consequently, there was a particularly close relationship between the chieftains and the Church. They hired priests and administered individual churches as if they were their own property, and their sons often received clerical educations. As Christians brought books and writing to Iceland, the chieftains probably also began to realize the political benefits that could be gained from writing down history. Latin books were imported and Icelandic translations of scriptures, homilies, saints' lives, and theological and encyclopedic works soon appeared, with the aim of nurturing the faith and maintaining the Church as an institution.

Around 1100, literary culture began to be utilized for secular purposes too, initially in records of laws and genealogies. *The First Grammatical Treatise*, written in the mid-twelfth century, was an attempt to adapt the Latin alphabet to the Icelandic language. Between *c.* 1122 and 1133, Ari Þorgilsson the Learned wrote *The Book of Icelanders* (*Íslendingabók*), a work dealing with early Icelandic history; he may also have been involved in writing the first version of *The Book of Settlements* (*Landnámabók*), another historical work assumed to have been composed about 1150. Around that time too, Eiríkur Oddsson wrote the first kings' saga, *The Back Piece* (*Hryggjarstykki*), which is now lost. Significantly, all these works were written in the vernacular, not in the Latin of the Church and the learned world.

In establishing the importance of the settlement of Iceland, these texts helped to create a new narrative way of representing past history and society, and laid the foundations for the Icelanders' understanding of history – that would be recorded and redefined in an exceptional variety of texts in the ensuing centuries.

THE SAGAS

Despite the small size of the population, literary production in Iceland was extraordinarily active and varied; indeed, extant texts dating from 1100 to 1400 are but the tip of the iceberg. By around 1200, the literary variety was already considerable: law codices, historical works such as *The Book of the Icelanders* and *The Book of Settlements*, *The First Grammatical Treatise*, encyclopedic translations, bestiaries, geographical descriptions, travelogues for Rome and Jerusalem, an original domestic time-reckoning, a few kings' sagas, the first bishops' sagas, and a number of foreign histories translated or rewritten (probably as school textbooks), including *Universal History* (*Veraldar saga*), *Sagas of Romans* (*Rómverja sögur*), *Sagas of Britons* (*Breta sögur*) and *Saga of the Trojans* (*Trójumanna saga*). Distinct saga genres also began to emerge soon after the turn of the century (although it should be noted that the division into genres is largely a modern construction): bishops' sagas, contemporary sagas, Sagas of Icelanders, legendary sagas, romances.

The reasons for the emergence of the Sagas of Icelanders before 1250 are unknown; however, it is likely that they relate to the chieftains' desire to tell the stories of the first settlers in Iceland in order to connect themselves to their forefathers. Richard Tomasson has suggested that 'no greater stimulus exists, it seems, to the development of epics than great overseas migrations',[2] and perhaps it was this stimulus that caused the Icelanders to become the historians of the Nordic expansion. Settler societies can be characterized as blending conservatism and progressiveness: preserving knowledge, customs and social forms from the old countries, but at the same time, adjusting to challenging new circumstances by fostering a flexible and creative mentality.[3] Such a developing settler society needed storytelling in order to create a myth of identity and collective memory, and the sagas perhaps developed from this need.

Some scholars have argued that the chieftain Snorri Sturluson (one of the few assumed saga-authors known by name and traditionally regarded as the most prolific) wrote *Egil's Saga* and thereby 'invented' the genre, but this is an anachronistic oversimplification: it is impossible to prove that Snorri composed this saga – or anything at all. Rather than looking for a clear, linear, evolutionary progression, it is more rewarding to approach saga literature contextually. Many cultural changes may have taken place simultaneously, affecting the development of the sagas; and the skill and maturity of the individual writers would naturally have impacted on the quality of their sagas. In addition to the problems of dating and authorship, there is some, albeit vague, evidence of narrative forms that may have been in circulation before the extant Sagas of Icelanders. Did earlier historical writings exist, which became obsolete as soon as better stories appeared? There are certainly references to, or indications of, at least twenty lost Sagas of Icelanders, some of which were older versions of existing sagas.

Short narrative forms such as the tales (*þættir*) may have also existed, as well as annals and even biographical sketches (*exempla*), one of which is preserved, *Life of Snorri Godi* (*Ævi Snorra goða*). The saga-writers, influenced by translated works, may have then combined these short forms with their abundant oral traditions, which provided a great stock of narrative material. Once they had written down such stories, the writers had a concrete basis on which to develop further narratives, with increasingly sophisticated and self-conscious designs. It is significant that such narrative self-consciousness is less apparent in many of the sagas that are deemed the oldest, which are somewhat confused in plot and detail and often uneven in terms of style and composition.

The stories the Icelanders told had an extraordinary geographical reach, stretching from the Near East and the Mediterranean in the south to the Arctic Ocean in the north and North America in the west. The narrative pivot of the Norse world, however, was Iceland. The sagas were also vast in literary scope, integrating both poetry and oral narratives, with different genres and themes emerging in order to serve the shifting demands and interests of the ruling classes. However, they share certain structural patterns and characteristics, as well as a similarly terse style. Most begin with a variation of the settlement legend; they are often concentrated around family feuds; and they frequently recount a cycle of revenge, counter-revenge and ultimate reconciliation. There is usually a strong affinity between the tale and the supposedly true events it relates: the time of events reported is close to the time of writing; the saga-heroes and contemporary chieftains supposedly share kinship ties; and, of course, there is geographical proximity, as most sagas take place in real and familiar surroundings.

The sagas' extensive use of the extensive stock of oral material available made it difficult for writers to deviate greatly from stories familiar to everyone, and the sagas' realistic qualities have, over the centuries, led people to believe in their literal truthfulness. However, it is wise to keep in mind philologist and poet Jón Helgason's comment on a sorcery-based episode in *Egil's Saga*, that a saga hardly becomes more truthful if we remove the sorcery from it.[4] Besides, the medieval conception of truth – as something God-given which couldn't be tampered with – was different from the modern one. On this understanding, the stories were confirmations of truth, material or spiritual, and the better a story was told, the truer it was. The stories could thus be regarded as exempla, revealing and proving the God-given truth.

It is generally accepted that the Sagas of Icelanders peaked in the second half of the thirteenth century, with such works as *Njal's Saga*, *The Saga of the People of Laxardal*, *Gisli Sursson's Saga* and *Hrafnkel's Saga*, to name but a few. These works were generally more fluent than most of the presumed oldest ones, and are quite long and complicated, revealing a more conscious and deliberate design. Their authors skilfully fused an abundance of oral material from the ninth and tenth centuries with the painful experience of decades of civil war in the mid-thirteenth century, and the resulting works contain a kind of surplus of meaning, a significance that by far surpasses a simple retelling of past events.

In the period following this classical era of saga-writing, from around 1300 onwards, writers seemed to be increasingly aware of the untapped potential of the saga narrative and began to innovate, breaking free from the established conventions. For example, sagas such as *Hrafnkel's Saga*, which is regarded as among the best, can be seen consciously inserting ideas explicitly and telling the story with a particular instructive or ethical aim. The fourteenth century used to be regarded as a phase of increasing decadence and degeneration into escapist fantasy. However, in many cases, the new emphasis was the result of a more premeditated design and self-conscious sense of authorship, and it is even possible to argue that this movement towards greater self-consciousness is comparable to the development in Middle English literature that led to Chaucer and Malory.

The later saga-authors were completely comfortable with

the form, structure and style, so they were increasingly able to subsume diverse and dissimilar material within it, as is exceptionally evident in *The Saga of Grettir the Strong*. This also occurred when, for instance, characters began to resemble the non-native medieval rogue and trickster Reynard the Fox. The older sagas had contained an abundance of humorous episodes and incidents: for example, *Morkinskinna*, the oldest compilation of kings' sagas, includes a number of short episodes about Icelanders at the king's court, some of which are grotesque and comical, but humour and irony began to play increasingly important roles in fourteenth-century sagas. In earlier sagas, humour is confined to single occurrences or episodes within the narrative; in later ones, it becomes an intrinsic feature of the work as a whole, directed critically towards society, the saga genre and its heroic ideals. The comic sagas included in this volume exhibit this fundamental ironical sense, and also reveal an increasingly self-conscious sense of authorship and design.

The Saga of the Sworn Brothers

The Saga of the Sworn Brothers (*Fóstbræðra saga*) is incomplete in all three of the oldest manuscripts (see A Note on the Translations). The narrative has three main parts: the various adventures of the sworn brothers, the (mock-)hero Thorgeir and the poet Thormod; Thorgeir's adventures in Norway; and Thormod's protracted revenge in Greenland for Thorgeir's death.

The Saga of the Sworn Brothers was once thought to be one of the oldest sagas, but in 1972 Jónas Kristjánsson argued convincingly that it was written near the end of the thirteenth century. The previous acceptance of an earlier date was based on its stylistic irregularities being seen as signs of a primitive stage of saga-writing. In particular, a few peculiarly wordy, learned sections called '*klausur*' were regarded as anachronistic, so earlier scholars had claimed that these passages had to be later insertions. Kristjánsson demonstrated that the *Flateyjarbók* manuscript, which preserves most of these *klausur*, is closest to the assumed original version, meaning the saga as a whole dates from a later period.[5] We can perhaps interpret the unusual *klausur* as a self-conscious authorial intrusion, serving as an ironic counterpoint to the more conventional descriptions of the saga. This means conceiving of the authorial or narratorial voice entirely differently from previous assumptions. Here is the best-known example, from chapter 23:

> When Egil heard the great blow that Thormod dealt Thorgrim, he ran back to Skuf's booth. Some people saw him running and believed him to be the man who had wounded Thorgrim. Egil was terrified when he saw them chasing after him, armed, and when they caught him, he shook from head to foot with fear.

> [From *Flateyjarbók*]

> Every bone in his body shook, all two hundred and fourteen of them. All his teeth chattered, and there were thirty of them. And all the veins in his skin trembled with fear, and there were four hundred and fifteen of them.

> As soon as they saw Egil they realized that he could not be the man who had slain Thorgrim, and the fear left him like heat from iron.

The comical numbering of Egil's bones (based on common encyclopedic knowledge in the Middle Ages) introduces a new, ironic tone into the narrative, thereby breaking with the terse, realistic style which has traditionally been regarded as the ideal saga style. According to the old, romantic conceptions of saga-writing, one sign of the sagas' degeneration was their declining realism, and these famous *klausur* in *Sworn Brothers* were regarded as examples of this increased 'subjectivity' and authorial commentary. But this saga is actually quite realistic, with its descriptions of humble houses, daily chores, and the darkness and bad weather in which Thorgeir usually carries out his heroic feats.

Helga Kress's groundbreaking 1987 essay on *The Saga of the Sworn Brothers* shows how heroic ideals had always been taken for granted as a key feature of the sagas, and argues that this saga inverts the convention.[6] Indeed, the saga makes a mockery of such ideals, as an examination of the hero, Thorgeir, and his sworn brother, Thormod the poet, reveals. The narrator's comments on these two men are often ironic and presented in humorous, mock-eloquent clauses, especially those in praise of Thorgeir (who won't 'stoop to women' because it is 'demeaning to his strength', chapter 3). In fact, some of the men's quarrels with their opponents show them as being more like small boys in a playground than great heroes. Kress also highlights the grotesque aspects of the saga, such as the episode when Thorgeir chops the head off a shepherd, and when Thormod has a fierce fight in the sea in which his opponent's ugly rear is seen bobbing up out of the water just before he drowns. Overall, Thorgeir is far from being a convincing hero: although he is supposed to be utterly fearless, many of his killings are very unheroic, and carried out in embarrassing or shameful circumstances. The famous 'angelica episode' in the *Flateyjarbók* manuscript (chapter 13), where Thorgeir grabs the stem of an angelica plant and thus avoids falling down a cliff before being rescued by Thormod, undercuts heroic ideals and probably indicates homosexual love.[7] Kress links this parodic quality with popular medieval carnival and interprets the saga as a kind of lower-class revolt against the chieftains' ideals. It is also possible, however – particularly since written literature was principally a vehicle of the chieftains and the learned – that this was simply a way of gently poking fun at the now anachronistic old heroic ideals, not least since peace had been established in society by this time.

No good saga is completely unambiguous. While Thorgeir is clearly a grotesque, parodic character, Thormod is more complicated. A slightly tragic tone is discernible when Thorgeir, at the peak of his hubris in Iceland, indicates that he wants to find out which of them is the stronger fighter, and in doing so destroys their friendship. And although Thormod's dealings with women are depicted parodically and in Greenland he is presented as something of a trickster, in the final episode (which tells of his death together with that of King Olaf the Saint) he is portrayed as being genuinely heroic. This might have been due to the fact that the episode was well known in other places, making it difficult to change its tone drastically. It may, however, have been a conscious authorial intention: having parodied heroic ideals throughout, the author now deliberately deflates the expectations he himself has set up by portraying true heroic spirit and genuine loyalty to the king, given that the Icelanders were, by the time of writing, subject to the Norwegian king. If intentional, the diffuse, counterpoint character of the saga as a whole might then be taken as a signal of an author in full control of his medium, rather than as a reflection of stylistic clumsiness or lack of skill. In this reading *Sworn Brothers* appears to be pushing against the boundaries of traditional saga expectations.

Olkofri's Saga

Olkofri's Saga (*Ölkofra saga*), written late in the thirteenth century, is very short and sometimes labelled generically as a tale. It tells of the farmer Thorhall, known because of his clothing as Olkofri or 'Ale-hood', who sells ale at the Althing and is thus acquainted with most of the leading men of the time. Far from resembling a traditional saga-hero, Thorhall is a wealthy merchant, described as small and ugly, close-fisted and cowardly. After accidentally destroying an area of woodland owned jointly by six powerful chieftains (all of whom appear in other sagas: see note 2), Thorhall appears doomed to be sentenced to outlawry. On account of his pitiful appearance at the Althing, however, he gains the support of the young and noble Broddi Bjarnason and his powerful brother-in-law, the chieftain Thorstein Sidu-Hallsson. They manage to defend Thorhall, and Broddi scolds the chieftains at the Althing, accusing them of greed, cowardice and sexual perversion.

This well-written short saga is quite different from conventional sagas in its representation of the main protagonist, a wretched miser who becomes a kind of trickster and reveals the vices of the ruling chieftains in lively scenes with witty dialogue. One such is when Ale-hood enters the Law Council to find that only two of the country's most dignified chieftains remain: 'After the other men had left Gudmund and Skafti stayed behind and talked law.' This is a subtle, ironic comment in the light of what, subversively, happens later in the story, when their knowledge of the law comes up short. At this point, the narrative takes the form of a flyting (a contest consisting in the exchanging of insults), and resembles grotesque old Eddaic poems such as *Loki's flyting* (*Lokasenna*).

If *The Saga of the Sworn Brothers* marked the beginning of a new phase in saga-writing by ironically twisting the available material and mocking heroic conventions, *Olkofri's Saga* displays a similar departure from its oral foundations by moving towards greater fictionality. It is true that the characterization of the chieftains is simply taken from the common stock of oral and written material – their description is in accordance with how they appear in other sagas. And the saga's style is realistic, demonstrating familiarity with the Althing, its location at Thingvellir and the law of the Commonwealth. Nevertheless, the story is pure fiction: it can be read as a kind of moral allegory in which vanity and greed are criticized through storytelling that deliberately loosens the ties to the oral backbone of the sagas and the alleged 'truth' of tradition.

The Saga of the Confederates

The Saga of the Confederates (*Bandamanna saga*) was written late in the thirteenth century and takes place in Midfjord in north Iceland and at the Althing around 1050 (i.e. shortly after the so-called 'Saga Age', a relatively peaceful period in Icelandic history). It tells the story of self-made man Odd Ofeigsson, who, after a disagreement with his father, Ofeig, becomes rich from trading and fishing. Odd entrusts his farm to the villain Ospak but Ospak steals his sheep and kills Odd's best friend, the noble Vali. Odd then has Ospak outlawed at the Althing but fails to observe certain legal formalities, allowing eight of the country's greatest chieftains to take advantage of this and sue him, intending to get hold of his wealth. Finally, Odd's wise and shrewd father, Ofeig, appears in order to help Odd out of trouble. Odd had purchased a godord (the domain belonging to a godi), and was thus a kind of an intruder in the chieftain class, but at the end, his entry is consolidated by his marriage to one of the chieftains' daughters.

The Saga of the Confederates clearly resembles *Olkofri's Saga* in its mocking of wealthy chieftains at the Althing, and scholars agree that it is modelled on the latter. However, unlike other sagas, *Confederates* is less concerned with heroism, killings and vicious cycles of revenge and counter-revenge than with the moral and legal aspects of power. In fact, the 'historicity' of the saga is very doubtful, although the confederates bear the names of well-known, powerful chieftains and are ascribed their characteristics, just as in *Olkofri's Saga*. Odd's disagreement with Ospak is mentioned in two other sagas, so he may have existed, and it is possible that some oral tales might lie behind that relationship. The fact that the events of the saga take place after the Saga Age also indicates some deviation from tradition, towards greater fictionalization. As in *Olkofri's Saga*, the *Confederates*'s author utilizes the saga form to express a social or moral message, with similar criticism of the vain and avaricious chieftains as a social class. Nevertheless, the deeply realistic style characteristic of the sagas is rigorously maintained here and *Confederates* does not contain any supernatural elements.

The Saga of the Confederates is brilliantly written and composed, setting up a subtle tension between the success of Odd and the power of the chieftains on the one hand, and the wisdom of old Ofeig on the other. Ofeig dominates the scenes in which he appears with his eloquence, psychological insights and keen understanding of social power. This is subtly conveyed by the author, who uses dialogue in a manner never seen before in a saga, and only exhibited later in chapter 19 of *The Saga of Grettir the Strong*, when Grettir manipulates twelve berserks in order to kill them.

The ability to imagine oneself into another's situation in order to manipulate and gain power over him was, according to Stephen Greenblatt, first seen in the Renaissance, a famous example being Iago's manipulation of Othello.[8] However, in *Confederates* and *Grettir*, such manipulation is staged brilliantly through dialogue, so that the reader sees, word for word, how the agents gain power over their victims and entrap them through verbal stratagems. Manipulation of this kind also takes place in *Njal's Saga*, when Mord Valgardsson incites Njal's sons to kill Hoskuld, but this is not represented through dialogue as it is in *Confederates* and *The Saga of Grettir*.

The Saga of the Confederates is thus a clear example of the genre's development from a simple attempt to represent reality towards greater fictionalization with the aim of conveying more sophisticated meaning. The saga-author here shapes the available material in order to express a particular message: the idea takes precedence over the material, and the result is brilliant, satirical comedy.

The Saga of Havard of Isafjord

The Saga of Havard of Isafjord (*Hávarðar saga Ísfirðings*) may have been written as late as the fifteenth century and can be considered a parody of a typical saga. There are some indications that an older version of the saga existed (referred to in *The Book of Settlements*), and while it is impossible to say what that might have been like, it does suggest that Havard and some of his adversaries existed. The extant saga has been criticized for a number of inaccuracies with regard to history, kinship, personal relations and geography; nevertheless, some critics concede that it is fluently written and amusing.

Although chapters 1–4 are a straightforward account of the villain Thorbjorn's killing of Havard's son, Olaf, the rest portrays events, characters and situations that are surely not intended to be taken at face value. Halldór Guðmundsson has argued that the saga displays certain novelistic characteristics which also appear in other late sagas: a conscious play with appearance and reality, for example, and an apparent parodying of heroic ideals. Instances of this include the 'real' hero being killed before the story really begins, and a former hero getting up from his bed and recovering enough from his grief in order to avenge his son. That the truly victorious heroes of the saga are children, women and elderly people can also be seen as parodic.[9]

The vengeance that Havard and his companions take upon their enemies, his conduct before, during and after taking revenge, and the antics of his cohort (especially the comic miser Atli) all smack of hyperbole, burlesque and pastiche. Havard, who resembles no other single saga character (except perhaps the comic figures Ale-hood and Ofeig), is actually a composite of three distinct types: the decrepit Viking, the versifying warrior and the avenging hero. Aided by his wife, he enjoys a rebirth as a kind of *miles gloriosus* (braggart warrior), but one who can fight as well as boast. In this fairy-tale world, absolute good triumphs over absolute evil and exacts a richly comic revenge, with a romance-like feast in the end and gifts distributed between friends.

There is a clear sense of an authorial voice in *The Saga of Havard of Isafjord*, as exemplified by the initial description of Vak: 'He was small and puny, abusive and foul-mouthed, and repeatedly goaded his uncle Thorbjorn, who behaved even worse. Vak became unpopular because of this, and people spoke of him as he deserved' (chapter 1). The description of this comic villain suggests the narrator's humorous intentions and also his moral stance. Here is an author who does not care about historicity, whose intention is to shape his material in order to communicate a moral message in comic form. Thus *The Saga of Havard of Isafjord* can be seen to have taken one more step away from tradition, breaking free from convention and exploiting, as Robert Kellogg puts it, 'the narrative potential of authorship'.[10]

The Saga of Ref the Sly

The Saga of Ref the Sly (*Króka-Refs saga*), about the strange adventures of Ref Steinsson, was most likely written late in the fourteenth century. It has come down in complete form in only one manuscript (AM 471, quarto), written in the second half of the fifteenth century, which contains two other Sagas of Icelanders (*The Saga of Thord Menace* and *The Saga of the People of Kjalarnes*), one chivalric romance and three legendary sagas. The manuscript context provides a clue to how the saga was perceived by its medieval audience: it belongs partly to the world of romance.

Gest Oddleifsson the Wise is the only 'celebrity' to appear: he is said to be Ref's maternal uncle, and encourages his nephew to have his saga written because Ref is the second wisest man in the family. This comment has been interpreted as a narratorial trick to persuade the audience to believe the truthfulness of the saga, but it could equally be understood as an ironic manifestation of the author's literary self-consciousness. Since the seventeenth century, scholars have agreed that saga is more or less pure fiction, with some condemning it for this reason, and others acknowledging the artful composition and style. Despite this, *Ref the Sly*'s saga has also been discussed in terms of its historical and geographical verisimilitude: for instance, the saga's inaccurate chronology of Nordic kings, the wrong physical distance between the two farms mentioned in the saga, Kvennabrekka and Saudafell, and conditions in Greenland at the time in which the saga is set.

The Saga of Ref the Sly opens in Breidafjord, west Iceland, but Ref Steinsson's adventures take place in foreign lands, including Greenland, Denmark, Italy and France. Ref is a *kolbítur* (literally, a 'coal-biter' but often translated as 'ashlad' or 'unpromising hero'), which suggests that he is a sort of male Cinderella figure, a distinct character type in the sagas. The typical *kolbítur* lay on the floor by the fire, and was disliked by his father but loved and supported by his mother. Usually at the age of twelve or eighteen, he got up, performed some deeds and then became a hero. In the sagas, the *kolbítur* type is usually more colourful and provocative than other characters. Some of the best-known saga-heroes, such as Egil Skallagrimsson and Grettir the Strong, have traits that belong to this type (although they never actually lie by the fire).

After bullying by a neighbour contributes to the death of Ref's father and then the killing of the family's cow-herder in a dispute over grazing land, Ref's mother incites her son to action and tells him that even a daughter would have been more use in defending their farm. Ref answers sarcastically that 'The rest will make hard hearing, mother, if your scolding begins like that' (chapter 3); following this, he gets up and kills the neighbour, in a rather unheroic manner. Ref's reply and the saga's free variation of the *kolbítur* type – with the mother scolding her son – is evidence of the author's independence from the saga tradition, which the entire work more or less subverts. After fleeing to Greenland, Ref never returns home and thus has no connection to the subsequent history of Iceland, except that one of his sons is said to have returned and had many remarkable descendants there (none of whom is mentioned further). Ref is said to have been buried in a French monastery, which distances the saga from a traditional ending linking the story with later times. The 'historical' frame of the saga is carelessly artificial, and this lack of attention highlights the anachronism of conventional saga ideals, perhaps suggesting that the author does not share the same concerns or aims as previous saga-writers.

After his first killing, Ref goes to his uncle Gest Oddleifsson the Wise, who discovers that he is a master craftsman. This turns out to be his greatest asset, and is, of course, an ironic deviation from the traditional heroic ideal of the sagas, according to which it is unthinkable that such skills would make someone admirable. In another deviation, Ref's identity is ambiguously compound: he is not only a 'hero' but also a fox (the meaning of *'ref'*). In this sense, he is probably partly a literary import, an Icelandic incarnation of Reynard the Fox or Reinhard Fuchs from Continental literature. This literary identity is underlined by the nickname that King Harald gives him, 'Króka-Refur', which loosely translates as Trickster-Fox or Sly-Fox. Compound or ambiguous identities, as well as disguise, became increasingly prominent features in later sagas as the world in which this literature was written down grew more uncertain – in part because the traditions that lay behind saga narratives no longer had any direct bearing on contemporary problems within society.

Ref is not aggressive, but his reactions to physical and verbal attacks are fierce. In Iceland, he kills the neighbour and Gellir, who had insulted and injured him; in Greenland, he kills four brothers and their father in one night after being slanderously accused of homosexuality; in Norway, he kills the rampant Grani. Most of these killings are in fact murders and therefore immoral according to saga standards, since they are committed in the darkness of the night (*náttvíg*, murder at night) and by means of ambushes. Ref is an anti-hero, but above all he is a clearly literary creation, a fox thrown into the strange world of the sagas against his will.

Turning everything upside down in such a playful manner demands profound knowledge of the world and traditions of the sagas, as well as familiarity with Continental literature such as the Reynard traditions. The saga-author's own mastery is underlined by Ref's craftsmanship, which extends beyond mere boatbuilding skills to include technological brilliance. Ref's fire-proof fortress in Greenland might be regarded as a parody of the tendency to burn houses in other sagas, but it is both a technological masterpiece and a fox's den at the same time.[11] This practical form of craftsmanship is then transformed into literary craftsmanship when Ref kills the king's man in Norway and confesses to the king by means of a riddle. This is a prose parody of the kennings in court poetry (*dróttkvætt*) that were traditionally composed in praise of kings and quoted throughout the sagas (see 'A Note on Poetic Imagery'). King Harald is portrayed as very wise in the saga – he is able to work out from a distance how Ref's fortress in Greenland was designed – but it takes him such a long time to solve the riddle that Ref is able to escape easily. Ref thus defeats the king through his unbeatable literary craftsmanship. As well as demonstrating the saga's profound literary self-consciousness, this episode perhaps suggests the saga's metaphorical resistance to royal power. Indeed, such instances were not uncommon in the fourteenth-century sagas, the best example being the legendary saga *The Saga of Aun the Bow-bender* (*Áns saga bogsveigis*).

The Saga of Ref the Sly is a self-conscious fictional masterpiece in which the connection with the traditional oral background of the sagas has totally disappeared, to be replaced by a variety of strange external elements. It has no direct textual relationship to the historical world of the sagas other than a chieftain's name dropped here and references to a few kings there. The realistic, terse style is maintained, however, and the saga does not contain any of the marvellous, supernatural elements that are so common in other late sagas. Nevertheless, it is evident that the old saga world has come to an end in *Ref the Sly*'s saga, a fact underlined by the hero's final departure to a French monastery. By the time of its composition, the social and cultural dynamics that formed and influenced the Sagas of Icelanders as a genre had disappeared. Indeed, it is even possible to claim that *The Saga of Ref the Sly* had entered the precursory phase of the modern novel.

THE TALES

The 'tales of the Icelanders' are short, anecdotal narratives, generally concentrated on one event and featuring relatively few, mostly Icelandic, characters. It is impossible to trace precisely how oral material found its way into these tales, but they do perhaps indicate the existence of older, smaller narrative forms, such as *exempla*. Scholars have assigned the tales to seven groups: on kings and Icelanders, religious conversions, feuds, skalds and poetry, dreams, journeys to other worlds and mythical heroes. Although it is open to debate, the tales are regarded by some scholars as being a distinct genre in saga literature. As Joseph Harris has observed, a clear six-part structural pattern emerges in many: an introduction in which the Icelandic protagonist is presented; a journey from Iceland; alienation from or a conflict with a king; reconciliation or recognition; a journey back to Iceland; and a conclusion.[12] Some elements may be missing, but the central themes of dispute and reconciliation are always present. Finally, many of the tales are pure comedies (hence the four in this volume), presenting characters who resemble the medieval fool, clown or trickster. The presence of such characters adds an ironic or ambiguous twist to the overall work within which the tales are preserved.

The tales are often described by the word *þáttur*, meaning 'strand', which suggests that the individual tales are part of a larger narrative whole; indeed, many of them were preserved within larger works in manuscript collections. When the tales appear in the context of kings' saga compilations, such as *Morkinskinna* and especially *Flateyjarbók*, they can be interpreted as serving the plan of these works. Yet the tales were not necessarily originally composed to be read in this way, and this tension between a tale's individual presentation and context may affect how we read and understand it today.

The earliest extant manuscript with tales is the kings' saga compilation *Morkinskinna*, poorly preserved and damaged (as indicated by the name, which means 'rotten skin'), from *c.* 1280, which derives from an older original, compiled or written around 1220, probably not long before the first Sagas of Icelanders (family sagas) were written. A double or ironic vision is often at work in the tales in *Morkinskinna*, which to some extent is comparable to the late Sagas of Icelanders, for it is not confined to a single event or episode but is an integrated element within the overall design. Another characteristic is the presentation of the rural Icelanders' eccentric stubbornness at the king's court; some of them are poets, and some get into quarrels with the king or his men. Other significant features are the authors' self-conscious interest in storytelling, and the tales' close concern with the reputation of the king. Ármann Jakobsson has demonstrated how individual tales in *Morkinskinna* have close thematic relations to the surrounding narratives, for example, adding or highlighting particular traits in their portrayals of individual kings, thereby foregrounding the theme of kingship.[13]

In *Hreidar's Tale* (*Hreiðars þáttur*), for instance, Hreidar is a *kolbítur*-type, regarded as garrulous and utterly stupid, who manages to force his brother to take him on a journey to the king's court in Norway (a travel motif that also appears in *Egil's Saga* and *The Saga of Aun the Bow-bender*). When he meets King Magnus, Hreidar walks around him in order to observe him carefully from all sides; Hreidar's behaviour is, according to Ármann Jakobsson, symbolic of the saga's aim to portray the king from all sides.[14] Through subtly brilliant dialogue, the tale depicts Magnus's gentle wisdom and even his prophetic skills, highlighting the difference between him and King Harald, who was traditionally depicted as a ruthless ruler. In this reading, the role of Hreidar, the fool, is to reveal the truth under the surface and expose the kings' characters in order to discredit Harald. However, the tale also conveys Hreidar's development from rustic foolishness to escalating success; as Anthony Faulkes notes, Hreidar 'wants to experience the whole range of human emotions, especially anger', in order to 'become a whole man'.[15] His encounter with King Magnus triggers and will sustain that development, symbolized in the poem Hreidar composes for him and acknowledged by the king in his gift to Hreidar of an island.

The other large compilation of kings' sagas containing tales is *Flateyjarbók*, written 1387–94, the largest of all Icelandic manuscripts. To some extent, this is based on a number of older kings' sagas (*Morkinskinna* among them), but it is considerably amplified, including sagas and other works. The Reverend Jón Thordarson, who initiated the compilation of *Flateyjarbók*, included around sixty tales, from long and fantastical stories to short and concise narratives. He also interpolated additional material from other sagas to underline what may be seen as a distinct theme in the work: the greatness and grace of the tenth- and eleventh-century Norwegian kings Olaf Tryggvason and St Olaf. The whole work may have been intended as a compilation of advice for the young Norwegian king Olaf Hákonarson, but he died long before it was completed. The religious and political context of the tales in *Flateyjarbók* is very different from that of *Morkinskinna*, with the emphasis here being on religious typology rather than secular kingship.[16]

The Tale of Thorleif, the Earl's Poet (Þorleifs þáttur jarlaskálds), in *Flateyjarbók*, is set at the court of Hakon, Earl of Lade, before Olaf Tryggvason came to power in 995. It is about the dealings between the Icelandic poet Thorleif and Hakon, a heathen. Descriptions of Hakon's evil reign function as an antithetical prologue to the account of Olaf Tryggvason, who in turn prefigures St Olaf, credited with completing Iceland's conversion to Christianity.[17] (From a modern perspective, however, Hakon and Olaf Tryggvason seem equally brutal in their conduct.) The religious context is evident from the way in which the tale is framed: an intrusive prologue and epilogue in which the compiler attacks Hakon for the witchcraft and sorcery that prevent him from gaining access to God's mercy. But the story itself is not delivered in religious terms and the religious context is only sporadically visible. Earl Hakon is a completely detestable figure but Thorleif is more ambiguous, despite being called a sorcerer and thereby affirming the religious logic of the tale. The narrator follows him with some sympathy and shows him enjoying success in Iceland until he is killed by a wooden figure raised by Hakon's witches. The tale must have been intended to reflect God's will but perhaps a small detail escaped both God's and Jón Thordarson's attention: in the final chapter when Thorleif pulls the shepherd Hallbjorn's tongue in order to turn him into a poet, there is the suggestion that in Hallbjorn, Thorleif lives on, despite his pagan conduct.

The Tale of Thorstein Shiver (*Þorsteins þáttur skelks*), probably originally written around 1300, is also a part of King Olaf Tryggvason's saga in *Flateyjarbók*. It is a short anecdote about the dealings between the wise king and Thorstein, a stubborn, strong-willed Icelander who disobeys the king by going alone at night to the privy where he has an entertaining encounter with a loud demon from Hell. This scatological tale both mediates between and plays humorously on the opposition between Heaven and Hell by means of the grotesque combination of the demon and the outhouse. While following the motif set in *Morkinskinna* of the king and the self-willed Icelander, the tale is also intended to demonstrate God's grace through the example of King Olaf and the fate of well-known pagan heroes who burn in Hell.

The final tale in this volume, *The Tale of Sarcastic Halli* (*Sneglu-Halla þáttur*), is found in both *Morkinskinna* and *Flateyjarbók*. The version here is from *Flateyjarbók*, a longer and more self-contained narrative, which includes the sexually grotesque puns that King Harald and Halli direct at Queen Thora. It is difficult to find any deeper intention than pure entertainment, and it might appear surprising that it was added by a priest. But the tale of the bold and talkative clown Halli is preserved in *Flateyjarbók*, a compilation of sagas and stories which range from the typological to the annalistic.[18] This was the time of the innovations of Boccaccio and Geoffrey Chaucer elsewhere in Europe, and perhaps *Flateyjarbók* reflects a similar shift in literary taste from previous generations.

Most of the comic sagas and tales in this volume, then, represent a new stage in saga-writing, one that is characterized by increased narratorial self-consciousness and an ironic, critical stance towards the genre. Humour is a vital part of this new authorial position, and to a certain extent this points towards the emergence of the modern novel, in a similar manner to Cervantes's *Don Quixote*. However, the modern novel did not subsequently emerge in Iceland, and it can equally be argued that these sagas are as much about the literary past, marking the end of medieval saga-writing in Iceland. The conditions that created the sagas – the settlement of a virgin country and the establishing of a new society – had disappeared. In a fairly balanced peasant and completely rural society, dominated by the king's officials and wealthy landowners, there was no stimulus for a further development of the sagas towards the end of the fourteenth century. They were copied in large numbers in the following centuries, but only very few new works emerged, and those are not included in the medieval canon. Indeed, *Flateyjarbók*, whose compilation had been arranged by a rich landowner, was the last one on such a grandiose scale. And so the comic sagas are poised at a crucial moment in Icelandic literary culture, gesturing towards future narrative developments and innovations, and at the same time marking the end of the extraordinary era of the medieval sagas.

NOTES

1. G. Turville-Petre, *Origins of Icelandic Literature* (Oxford: 1953), pp. 126–8.
2. Richard Tomasson, *Iceland: The First New Society* (Minneapolis: 1980), p. 13.
3. Ibid., pp. 14–17.
4. Jón Helgason, 'Höfuðlausnarhjal', in *Einarsbók. Afmæliskveðja til*

Einars Ólafs Sveinssonar 12. desember 1969 (Reykjavík: 1969), pp. 156–76.

5. Jónas Kristjánsson, *Um Fóstbræðrasögu* (Reykjavík: 1972).

6. Helga Kress, 'Bróklindi Falgeirs. Fóstbræðrasaga og hláturmenning miðalda', *Skírnir* 161 (Fall 1987), pp. 271–86.

7. Sverrir Tómasson, 'Rímur og aðrar vestfirskar bókmenntir á síðmiðöldum', *Ársrit Sögufélags Ísfirðinga* 43 (2003), pp. 150–52.

8. Stephen J. Greenblatt, *Renaissance Self-Fashioning: From More to Shakespeare* (Chicago and London: 1980), p. 225.

9. Halldór Guðmundsson, 'Skáldsöguvitund í Íslendingasögum', *Skáldskaparmál* 1 (1990), pp. 62–72.

10. Robert Kellogg, 'Varieties of Tradition in Medieval Narrative', in *Medieval Narrative: A Symposium*, ed. Hans Bekker-Nielsen et al. (Odense: 1979), pp. 126–7.

11. For more on this, see Sverrir Tómasson, '*Króka-Refs saga*', in *Sígildar sögur 2: Skýringar* (Reykjavík: 1989), pp. 195–212; Örnólfur Thorsson, 'Refur', in *Lygisögur sagðar Sverri Tómassyni fimmtugum* (Reykjavík: 1991), pp. 100–106; and Kendra Willson, 'Króka-Refs saga as Science Fiction: Technology, Magic and the Materialist Hero', in *The Fantastic in Old Norse/Icelandic Literature: Sagas and the British Isles; preprint papers of The 13th International Saga Conference, Durham and York, 6th–12th August, 2006*, ed. John McKinnell, David Ashurst and Donata Kick (Durham: 2006). See also www.dur.ac.uk/medieval and www.sagaconf/willson.htm.

12. Joseph Harris, 'Genre and Narrative Structure in Some *Íslendinga þættir*', *Scandinavian Studies* 44 (1972), pp. 1–27.

13. Ármann Jakobsson, *Staður í nýjum heimi: Konungasagan Morkinskinna* (Reykjavík: 2002), pp. 78–92.

14. Ibid., pp. 87–8.

15. Anthony Faulkes, *Two Icelandic Stories: Hreiðars þáttr, Orms þáttr* (London: 1968).

16. Elizabeth Ashman Rowe, 'Cultural Paternity in the Flateyjarbók *Ólfáfs saga Tryggvasonar*', *Alvíssmál* 8 (1998), pp. 3–28.

17. Ibid., pp. 13–14.

18. The tale is part of *The Saga of King Magnus and King Harald*, from the section of *Flateyjarbók* compiled by Magnús Þórhallsson, who, according to Rowe (ibid., pp. 7–8), was annalistic in his choice of material rather than typological like Jón Þórðarson. This might explain the absence of any religious context for the tale, which appears in a succession of tales that have no apparent thematic connection.

Further Reading

THE SAGAS AND TALES
OF ICELANDERS

The Complete Sagas of Icelanders (Including 49 Tales), 5 vols,
ed. Viðar Hreinsson (Reykjavík: 1997).
*Morkinskinna: The Earliest Icelandic Chronicle of the Norwe-
gian Kings (1030–1157)*, trans. with introduction and notes
by Theodore M. Andersson and Kari Ellen Gade (Ithaca,
NY: 2000).
The Sagas of Icelanders: A Selection, ed. Örnólfur Thorsson
(London: 2000).

SINGLE VOLUMES AVAILABLE
IN PENGUIN CLASSICS

Egil's Saga, ed. Svanhildur Óskarsdóttir (London: 2004).
Gisli Sursson's Saga and *The Saga of the People of Eyri*, ed.
Vésteinn Ólason (London: 2003).
Njal's Saga, ed. Robert Cook (London: 2001).
The Saga of Grettir the Strong, ed. Örnólfur Thorsson (London:
2005).
The Saga of the People of Laxardal and *Bolli Bollason's Tale*,
ed. Bergljót S. Kristjánsdóttir (London: 2008).
Sagas of Warrior-Poets, ed. Diana Whaley (London: 2002).
The Vinland Sagas, ed. Gísli Sigurðsson (London: 2008).

SELECT BIBLIOGRAPHY ON
COMIC SAGAS AND TALES

Amory, Frederic, 'Pseudoarchaism and Fiction in *Króka-Refs saga*', *Mediaeval Scandinavia* 12 (1988), pp. 7–23.

Faulkes, Anthony, *Two Icelandic Stories: Hreiðars þáttr, Orms þáttr* (London: 1968).

Harris, Joseph, 'Genre and Narrative Structure in Some *Íslendinga þættir*', *Scandinavian Studies* 44 (1972), pp. 1–27.

—, 'Theme and Genre in Some *Íslendinga þættir*', *Scandinavian Studies* 48 (1976), pp. 1–28.

Jakobsson, Ármann, 'King and Subject in Morkinskinna', *Skandinavistik* 28 (1998), pp. 101–17.

—, 'The Individual and the Ideal: The Representation of Royalty in Morkinskinna', *Journal of English and Germanic Philology* 99 (2000), pp. 71–86.

Lindow, John, 'Old Icelandic þáttr: Early Usage and Semantic History', *Scripta Islandica* 29 (1978), pp. 3–44.

—, 'Hreiðars Þáttr heimska and AT 326: An Old Icelandic Novella and an international folktale', *Arv* 34 (1978), pp. 152–79.

—, '*Þorsteins þáttr skelks* and the Verisimilitude of Supernatural Experience in Saga Literature', in *Structure and Meaning in Old Norse Literature*, ed. Lindow, Lönnroth and Weber, pp. 264–80.

Rowe, Elizabeth Ashman, 'Cultural Paternity in the Flateyjarbók *Óláfs saga Tryggvasonar*', *Alvíssmál* 8 (1998), pp. 3–28.

GENERAL

Andersson, Theodore M., *The Problem of Icelandic Saga Origins: A Historical Survey* (New Haven and London: 1964).

—, *The Icelandic Family Saga: An Analytic Reading* (Cambridge, MA: 1967).

—, *The Growth of the Medieval Icelandic Sagas (1180–1280)* (Ithaca, NY: 2006).

Arnold, Martin, *The Post-Classical Icelandic Family Saga* (Lewiston, NY: 2003).

The Book of Icelanders, in *The Norse Atlantic Saga*, trans. Gwyn Jones (Oxford: 1964).

The Book of Settlements (Landnámabók), trans. Hermann Pálsson and Paul Edwards (Winnipeg: 1972).

Byock, Jesse L., *Feud in the Icelandic Saga* (Berkeley: 1982).

—, *Medieval Iceland: Society, Sagas and Power* (Berkeley: 1988).

—, *Viking Age Iceland* (New York: 2001).

Clover, Carol J., *The Medieval Saga* (Ithaca, NY and London: 1982).

—, and John Lindow, *Old Norse–Icelandic Literature: A Critical Guide, Islandica* 45 (Ithaca, NY and London: 1985).

Hallberg, Peter, *The Icelandic Saga*, trans. Paul Schach (Lincoln, NE: 1962).

Hastrup, Kirsten, *Culture and History in Medieval Iceland: An Anthropological Analysis of Structure and Change* (Oxford: 1985).

Íslendingabók (The Book of Icelanders), trans. Halldór Hermannsson (Ithaca, NY: 1930).

Jesch, Judith, *Women in the Viking Age* (Woodbridge: 1992).

Jochens, Jenny, *Women in Old Norse Society* (Ithaca, NY: 1995).

—, *Old Norse Images of Women* (Philadelphia: 1996).

Kellogg, Robert, and Robert Scholes, *The Nature of Narrative* (Oxford: 1966).

Ker, W. P., 'Epic and Romance', in *Essays on Medieval Literature*, 2nd edn (London: 1908; repr. New York: 1957).

Kristjánsson, Jónas, *Eddas and Sagas: Iceland's Medieval Literature*, trans. Peter Foote (Reykjavík: 1997).

Meulengracht Sørensen, Preben, *Saga and Society: An Introduction to Old Norse Literature*, trans. John Tucker (Odense: 1993).

Lindow, John, Lars Lönnroth and Gerd Wolfgang Weber (eds.), *Structure and Meaning in Old Norse Literature: New Approaches to Textual Analysis and Literary Criticism*, The Viking Collection 3 (Odense: 1986).

Miller, William Ian, *Bloodtaking and Peacemaking: Feud, Law and Society in Saga Iceland* (Chicago and London: 1990).

Nordal, Sigurður, *Icelandic Culture*, trans. Vilhjálmur T. Bjarnar (Ithaca, NY: 1990).

Ólason, Vésteinn, *Dialogues with the Viking Age: Narration and Representation in the Sagas of Icelanders*, trans. Andrew Wawn (Reykjavík: 1997).

Pulsiano, Phillip, and Kirsten Wolf (eds.), *Medieval Scandinavia: An Encyclopedia* (New York and London: 1993).

Ryding, William W., *Structure in Medieval Narrative* (The Hague: 1971).

Schach, Paul, *Icelandic Sagas* (Boston: 1984).

Sigurðsson, Gísli, *The Medieval Icelandic Saga and Oral Tradition: A Discourse on Method*, trans. Nicholas Jones (Cambridge, MA: 2004).

Steblin-Kamenskij, M. I., *The Saga Mind*, trans. Kenneth H. Ober (Odense: 1973).

Tucker, John (ed.), *Sagas of Icelanders* (New York: 1989).

Vinaver, Eugene, *The Rise of Romance* (Cambridge, 1971).

A Note on the Translations

The texts in this volume are reprinted with minor revisions from *The Complete Sagas of Icelanders (Including 49 Tales)*, 5 vols, ed. Viðar Hreinsson (Reykjavík: Leifur Eiríksson Publishing, 1997).

The Saga of the Sworn Brothers (in vol. 2 of *The Complete Sagas*), translated by Martin S. Regal, follows the text published in *Íslendinga sögur* (Reykjavík: Svart á hvítu, 1987), apart from an apparently incongruous insertion from *Konungsbók* (*Poetic Edda*). The saga is poorly preserved, being incomplete in all three of the oldest manuscripts, which differ from each other. The text here uses all three: *Möðruvallabók* (chapters 1–20), *Hauksbók* (most of the remaining four chapters) and *Flateyjarbók*, which accounts for eight sections of varying length and a variant ending: these are all identified and – except for the ending – are in a smaller font. One verse (no. 35) and its brief introductory text are taken from *Hólmsbók*. Several verses are repeated almost exactly in the two main manuscript sources, and are also found in Snorri Sturluson's *Heimskringla*, while verses nos. 1 and 6 occur in *The Saga of Grettir the Strong* as well.

Olkofri's Saga (in vol. 5) is translated by John Tucker from *Íslenzk fornrit XI*, based on the text preserved in the principal codex of the Sagas of Icelanders, *Möðruvallabók*.

The Saga of the Confederates (in vol. 5) is translated by Ruth C. Ellison from Hallvard Magerøy's edition of 1981, which is mainly based on the text preserved in *Möðruvallabók*. There also exists a later, shorter version.

The Saga of Havard of Isafjord (in vol. 5) is translated by Fredrik J. Heinemann from the text in *Íslenzk fornrit VI*.

The Saga of Ref the Sly (in vol. 3) is translated by George Clark from the text in *Íslendinga sögur*.

Hreidar's Tale (in vol. 1) is translated by Robert Kellogg from *Íslendinga sögur*.

The Tale of Thorleif, the Earl's Poet (in vol. 1) is translated by Judith Jesch from *Íslendinga sögur*.

The Tale of Thorstein Shiver (in vol. 1) is translated by Anthony Maxwell from *Íslendinga sögur*.

The Tale of Sarcastic Halli (in vol. 1) is also translated by George Clark from the *Flateyjarbók* version in *Íslendinga sögur*.

The Notes are to some extent based on the explanatory material in Icelandic textbook editions: *Íslendingaþættir: Úrval þrettán þátta*, introduction and notes by Bragi Halldórsson and Knútur S. Hafsteinsson (Reykjavík: Mál og menning, 1999); *Fóstbrœðra saga*, introduction and notes by Bragi Halldórsson and Knútur S. Hafsteinsson (Reykjavík: Mál og menning, 1995); and *Sígildar sögur II: Skýringar*, ed. Örnólfur Thorsson et al. (Reykjavík: Svart á hvítu, 1987).

As is common in translations from Old Icelandic, the spelling of proper nouns has been simplified, both by the elimination of non-English letters and by the reduction of inflections. Thus 'Þorsteinn' becomes 'Thorstein' and 'Þormóður' becomes 'Thormod'. The reader will soon grasp that '-dottir' means 'daughter of' and '-son' means 'son of'. Place names have been rendered in a similar way, often with an English identifier of the landscape feature in question (e.g. 'Hvítá river', in which 'Hvít-' means 'white' and '-a' means 'river'). A translation is given in parentheses at the first occurrence of place names when the context requires this, such as Svidning (the Singed). For place names outside Scandinavia, the common English equivalent is used if such exists; otherwise the Icelandic form has been transliterated. Nicknames are translated where their meanings are reasonably certain.

On the translation of poetry, see A Note on Poetic Imagery.

A gap in the manuscript source ([. . .]) is indicated where the reading of the missing text cannot be conjectured.

SAGAS

THE SAGA OF THE
SWORN BROTHERS

I

In the days when Saint Olaf[1] was king he had many chieftains under his rule, not only in Norway but in all the other lands over which he reigned, and God gave honour to all those whom the king favoured most.

At that time there was a most excellent chieftain, named Vermund, in the Isafjord district[2] of Iceland. Vermund, who was the son of Thorgrim and the brother of Killer-Styr,[3] lived on his farm at Vatnsfjord and was a wise and well-liked man. He was married to a woman named Thorbjorg – known as Thorbjorg the Stout – the daughter of Olaf Peacock.[4] She was a wise and magnanimous woman. Whenever her husband was away from home she governed the district and its people, and each and every man was satisfied that his matters were handled well under her charge.

It so happened that on one occasion when Vermund was not at home, Grettir Asmundarson[5] came to Isafjord. He was an outlaw at the time, and wherever he went he managed to have people give him what he wanted. However, what Grettir called gifts would not have been regarded as such – or been so readily given away – had people not felt that they had a troll on their doorstep. It was this that eventually led to the farmers gathering their forces, capturing Grettir, condemning him to death and building a gallows on which they intended to hang him.

When Thorbjorg heard about this she set out with her men to the place where Grettir had been tried. When she arrived, the gallows had been raised, the noose attached to it and Grettir already placed in position. The sight of Thorbjorg's approach was the only thing that stood between Grettir and his death.

As she reached the gathering, she asked the farmers what they meant to do. They told her what they had planned.

She said, 'I would advise you not to kill him. Despite his general lack of good fortune, he comes from a high-ranking family and is greatly respected for his many physical accomplishments. His kinsmen will take his death badly, even though he is regarded as overbearing by many.'

They said, 'We feel he is rightly condemned to death. He is an outlaw and a proven thief.'

Thorbjorg said, 'His life will not be forfeit on this occasion if I have any say in the matter.'

They said, 'Right or wrong, you have the power to prevent him from being executed.'

Then Thorbjorg had Grettir released, gave him his life and told him to go wherever he wished. Grettir marked the occasion with this short verse:

1.
I would have stuck
my own head
in the baited snare
before its time,
if Thorbjorg,
woman so fair,
had not saved
this poet's life.

It can be seen from this incident that Thorbjorg was a woman of firm character.

2

There was a man named Havar, the son of Klepp, who lived at a farm called Jokulskelda. Havar originally came from Akranes in the south but had left there on account of some killings. He loved fighting, and was a boisterous and overbearing man.

He had a wife named Thorelf, from the Breidafjord area, who was the daughter of Alf of Dalir – an excellent and well-respected man. Havar and Thorelf had a son named Thorgeir, who developed early into a large and powerful man with a fighting temperament. He learned at a young age to defend himself with a shield, and was skilled in the use of arms.

There was a man named Bersi who lived in Isafjord, on the farmstead known as Dyrdilsmyri. He was married to a woman named Thorgerd and they had a son named Thormod. The lad was of average build with black, curly hair and was a man of vigour and courage.

At that time, Thorgils Arason[6] lived at Reykjaholar in Reykjanes. He was a great chieftain – powerful, honest, wise and well-liked. He had a brother named Illugi, who was a follower of King Olaf the Holy. Illugi was a great merchant, who usually spent alternate winters at Olaf's court and Reykjaholar. He brought timber to Iceland to build a church and a hall.

The brothers Thorgils and Illugi were the sons of Ari, the son of Mar, the son of Ulf the Squinter who settled Reykjanes, the son of Hogni White, son of Otrygg, son of Oblaud, son of King Hjorleif. Their mother was Thorgerd, the daughter of Alf of Dalir. Alf's mother was Thorhild, daughter of Thorstein the Red, son of Oleif White, son of Ingjald, son of Frodi. Ingjald's mother was Thora, the daughter of Sigurd Snake-in-the-eye. Sigurd's mother was Aslaug, the daughter of Sigurd Fafnisbani[7] (Killer of the Serpent Fafnir). Thorgeir Havarsson was the cousin of Thorgils Arason.

Thorgeir and Thormod grew up together in Isafjord, and since they were so alike in temperament they quickly became fast friends. Both also felt early on – and it later turned out to be true – that they would die fighting, since neither was the kind of man to back off from or give in to anyone he came up against. They were more concerned with success in this life than glory in the life to come.

They thus swore that whoever survived the other would avenge his death. Though people called themselves Christians in those days, Christianity was a new and very undeveloped religion and many of the sparks of heathendom still flickered, manifesting themselves as undesirable customs. It had been a tradition among men of renown to become bound to each other by a law that stated that whoever outlived the other would undertake to avenge his death. They had to walk underneath a triple arch of raised turf, and this signified their oath. The arch was made by scoring out three lengths of turf and leaving them attached to the ground at both ends, then raising them to a height whereby it was possible to walk under them. Thormod and Thorgeir undertook this rite as part of their sworn agreement.

Thormod was a little older than Thorgeir, but Thorgeir was the stronger of the two. Their rise to fame was fast. They roamed far and wide about the land but were far from popular. Many deemed them not to be fair-minded men but, as one might expect, they had the support and trust of their fathers – and many believed it was they who were actually encouraging the lads to do wrong.

Those who felt they had been cheated by the sworn brothers went to see Vermund and asked him to rid them of this trouble.

Vermund invited Havar and Bersi to meet with him and told them that people were little enamoured of their sons.

'You, Havar, are not from this district,' he said, 'and have settled here without leave from anyone. So far we have made no complaint about your dwelling here but now it seems that your son, Thorgeir, is unruly and aggressive and we want you to move your home and your goods away from Isafjord. Bersi and his son may stay because they are from this area, and it is our hope that Thormod will be less unruly if he parts company with Thorgeir.'

Havar said, 'Vermund, you have the power to make me leave Isafjord with all my belongings, but I expect Thorgeir will want to decide for himself where he stays.'

As a result of this decision, Havar moved south to Borgarfjord and lived on an estate now known as Havarstoftir. Thorgeir stayed either with his father or in the west at Isafjord with Thormod. Yet, despite his youth, he was an unwelcome guest at most places he visited. He was at Reykjaholar for a long time with his cousin Thorgils, who favoured him greatly. Thorgils's son, Ari, and Thorgeir were close friends from a young age and remained so for the rest of their lives.

There was a man called Jod who lived at the farmstead of Skeljabrekka. He was a chieftain and a great champion, but he was difficult to get along with and had a reputation for being generally unfair in his dealings with others. He had authority in the district, but was ambitious and slew many men while rarely paying compensation for the lives he took.

One winter, it happened that Jod and his men went out to Akranes to buy some flour, and on the way Jod stopped at Havar's farmstead and asked him to lend him a horse for that purpose.

Havar lent him the horse and said, 'But I'd like you to return the horse to me on your way back and take it no farther.'

Jod agreed to this. Then he went out to Akranes and bought the flour as he intended and left for home as soon as he had dealt with what was most pressing. As he rode along Grunna-fjord, past Havar's farm, his companions mentioned that they had to stop off at the farmhouse to return the horse.

Jod said, 'I won't trouble with that now. I'll use the horse to carry back its load and return it to him when it's served my purpose.'

They said, 'You can do that if you wish, but Havar has never looked kindly on broken agreements.'

'There's nothing to be done about that now,' said Jod.

Havar saw the men riding along and recognized them.

He went out to meet them, and greeted them, saying, 'This is as far as you may take my horse.'

Jod said, 'Surely you'll lend me the horse to get home to Skeljabrekka?'

Havar said, 'I don't want the horse to go any farther.'

Jod said, 'We shall have the horse with or without your consent.'

Havar said, 'That remains to be seen.'

Then he ran at the horse, pulled off its load, took it by the reins and led it towards home. Jod had a barbed spear[8] in his hand, and he turned suddenly to Havar and drove the spear through him, wounding him mortally. Jod then took the horse

and journeyed on until he reached home. Havar's men thought
he was late coming home so they went out to look for him.
They found him dead where he had been slain. They thought
these ill tidings indeed.

Thorgeir was staying in the west at Isafjord at that time.
News of Havar's death spread quickly, yet when Thorgeir
learned that his father had been slain he showed no reaction.
His face did not redden because no anger ran through his skin.
Nor did he grow pale because his breast stored no rage. Nor
did he become blue because no anger flowed through his bones.
In fact, he showed no response whatsoever to the news – for his
heart was not like the crop of a bird, nor was it so full of blood
that it shook with fear. It had been hardened in the Almighty
Maker's forge to dare anything.

3

It is said that Thorgeir was not much of a ladies' man. He said
it was demeaning to his strength to stoop to women. He seldom
laughed and was harsh and rough in his daily dealings with
other people. He was a large man, brave in appearance, and
of enormous physical strength. He had a broad axe, a mighty
weapon, keen-edged and sharp, with which he had sent many
a man to dine in Valhalla.[9] He also had a barbed spear with
a hard point, a large socket and thick shaft. In those days, very
few men were armed with swords.

When Thorgeir learned of his father's death, he went to
Thorgils at Reykjaholar, told him that he wished to travel south
to Borgarfjord to meet his mother and asked him for some
means of crossing the fjord. Thorgils did as he was asked, and
Thorgeir went south to Borgarfjord, though there is no mention of where he spent the nights. Travelling was easy since
there was no snow in the district, and all the rivers, lakes
and streams were frozen over. After crossing south over the
Hvita river, he made his way to Skeljabrekka. The weather was
mild, but fog made the night even darker than usual. Thorgeir
reached Skeljabrekka late in the evening and the farm doors
were closed. The people in the house had just finished feeding

the livestock and gone into the main room, where a light was burning. Thorgeir knocked on the door.

Jod spoke, 'Someone's knocking on the door. One of you go and attend to it.'

Then one of the farmhands opened the door. He saw an armed man standing there and asked him who he was.

The man answered, 'My name is Vigfus.'[10]

The farmhand said, 'Come in. You may stay the night if you are so disposed.'

Thorgeir said, 'I accept no offer of lodging from a slave. Go tell Jod to come out.'

The farmhand went back in while Thorgeir stood outside.

When the farmhand came back into the main room, Jod asked him, 'What man is out there?'

The servant replied, 'I have no idea who he is, and I suspect he doesn't know himself, either.'

Jod said, 'Did you offer him lodging?'

He answered, 'I did.'

Jod said, 'And how did he answer?'

'He would not accept an offer of lodging here from a slave, and asked you to come out.'

Jod picked up a spear, put his helmet on his head and went to the door with two of his men, where he saw a man standing in the doorway. He turned his spear down and stuck the point into the threshold. Then he asked who the man was.

The man said, 'My name is Thorgeir.'

Jod said, 'Thorgeir who?'

'The son of Havar,' he replied.

Jod said, 'Why have you come here?'

The man replied, 'I don't know what the outcome will be but I've come to find out whether you will compensate me for slaying my father.'

Jod said, 'I don't know whether you are aware that I have killed many a man and never once paid compensation.'

'I did not know that,' said Thorgeir, 'but whatever has been the case, it is my duty to seek compensation from you now since I stand closest to the man you have slain.'

Jod said, 'I'm not averse to giving you some pittance, but

I will not pay you compensation for this slaying, Thorgeir, or others will think they can make similar claims on me.'

Thorgeir answered, 'It's for you to decide how much you pay, and it's for me to decide whether I accept or not.'

They continued to discuss the matter while Thorgeir stood some distance from the doorway. He had a spear in his right hand and turned the point forward. In his left hand was an axe. Having come from the brightness inside, Jod and his men had some trouble seeing out into the dark, whereas it was easier for Thorgeir to see them from where he stood away from the doorway. When they least expected it, Thorgeir moved forward and drove his spear straight through Jod's middle, so that he fell into the arms of his servants.

Thorgeir turned away into the darkness of the night while Jod's men tried to administer to him. Thorgeir was fifteen years old at this time, as Thormod says in a long memorial drapa he composed after Thorgeir's death.

2.

The slayings started when the wealth-giver   *wealth-giver*: generous
brought doom to Jod,   person, Thorgeir
Klaeng's son and heir;
the wave-horse's launcher was brave.   *wave-horse*: ship; its *launcher*:
Havar's vengeance was won   seafarer, Thorgeir
when the sea-steed's god   *sea-steed*: ship;
was fifteen years of age;   its *god*: seafarer
resolute, he wrought that deed.

Thorgeir walked the whole night, not halting until he came to his father's farmstead. He knocked on the door, and a long time passed before someone came to open up. His mother, Thorelf, called out to one of the farmhands to answer. The man woke up, rubbed his eyes and was evidently displeased at being roused.

'I don't see the need to get up just because men choose to travel by night,' he said.

Then Thorelf said, 'Only a man in great need would have to travel by night in such great darkness.'

'I don't know about that,' said the farmhand.

He rose to his feet slowly and went to the door where he saw a man standing outside, but offered him no greeting. Instead, he returned to his bed, lay down and drew the bedclothes over him. Thorgeir came in, closed the door behind him and walked into the main room.

Thorelf asked, 'Who is it?'

The servant replied, 'I don't know who he is, and I don't care.'

She said, 'You show a distinct lack of curiosity.'

Then she called out to one of the servant women: 'Get up, go into the main room and see who is in there.'

The woman got up, went into the main room, opened the door a little and asked whether there was anyone in there.

'There most certainly is,' was the reply.

She asked who he was, and he answered, 'My name is Thorgeir.'

Then she closed the door again and went back to the hall.

Thorelf said, 'Who is it?'

The servant woman answered, 'I believe it's your son, Thorgeir.'

Thorelf got up, lit a lamp and went into the main room where she greeted her son warmly. She asked if there was any news.

Thorgeir said, 'A man has been wounded this evening at Skeljabrekka.'

'Who was responsible?' she asked.

'I cannot deny my part in this,' he answered.

Then Thorelf asked, 'How bad was the wound?'

And Thorgeir replied, 'I don't think the wound he suffered at my hands will need binding. I saw my spear pierce him through and he fell back into the arms of his men.'

Then Thorelf said joyfully, 'This was no child's deed. May your hands always serve you this well, my son. But why didn't his men pursue you?'

Thorgeir answered, 'They had other, more immediate, matters to attend to – and soon afterwards they lost sight of me in the dark.'

Thorelf answered, 'That may be so.'

Then Thorgeir was brought some supper, and when he had his fill, Thorelf said, 'I think you should get some sleep now, but be on your feet again before daybreak, then get on your horse and ride west to Breidafjord. My farmhands will accompany you as far as you wish. Tomorrow, men will come here looking for you and we don't have the strength to protect you against a large party. If this thaw continues, the rivers and lakes will unfreeze and it will be harder to travel. You have done what was required. Take word to your cousin Thorgils that he must find me somewhere to live close to him in the west. I will sell my lands here and return to my birthplace.'

Thorgeir did as his mother advised. He went to sleep, arose before daybreak and then rode off. There is no other report of his journey until he reached Breidafjord in the west, where he got a boat and set sail west to Reykjanes. It was there that he announced that he had slain Jod.

Everyone who heard these tidings thought it remarkable that one young man on his own should have slain such an experienced fighter and chieftain as Jod. And yet it was no great wonder since the Almighty Creator had forged in Thorgeir's breast such a strong and sturdy heart that he was as fearless and brave as a lion in whatever trials or tribulations befell him. And as all good things come from God, so too does steadfastness, and it is given unto all bold men together with a free will that they may themselves choose whether they do good or evil. Thus Jesus Christ has made Christians his sons and not his slaves, so that he might reward all according to their deeds.

Thorgeir spent his time either at Reykjaholar or at Isafjord in the west country. In the spring following these events, Thorelf rode west to Reykjanes with all her livestock and goods. That summer a settlement was concluded regarding the slayings of Havar and Jod, and after that Thorgeir spent a long time with Bersi. Thorgeir and Thormod were the best of friends. They obtained a small ferry boat and took seven other men along with them. They moved from place to place that summer, but were welcomed nowhere.

There was a man named Ingolf, who lived in Jokulsfirdir at

a farm called Svidinsstadir, and was known as Ingolf Svidin. He had a son named Thorbrand, a great champion, but overbearing and generally unpopular. Both he and his father were aggressive troublemakers, obtaining money and goods from others by bullying and stealing. They were both thingmen of Vermund the chieftain, and he took great pains to protect them because they always gave him valuable gifts.[11] They were safe from reprisals for riding roughshod over so many men by virtue of their oath of allegiance to Vermund.

There was a widow named Sigurfljod, who lived in Jokulsfirdir. She was wise and well-liked and had proven to be an invaluable friend to many. Her farm and Ingolf's lay on opposite sides of the fjord, and Ingolf and his son caused her considerable trouble.

Thorgeir and Thormod prepared to set sail to hunt and fish at Strandir in the north, but just as they were ready to start out the wind turned against them and made it impossible for them to leave the fjord. For the rest of the summer they caused considerable trouble among the people there.

When winter arrived, a fair breeze allowed them to set sail out of Isafjord in good weather. However, it was too calm for them to make much headway, and when they had sailed for a while the weather first began to thicken and then it started to snow. By the time they were out of the fjord, the weather turned against them. They were so beset with squalls that blustered and blew around them in the freezing cold that they could no longer see their course and great darkness surrounded them, made thicker by the night and the storm. Then the wind was behind them and great waves broke over the ship, drenching them and making their clothes freeze to their bodies. The daughters of the sea-goddess, Ran,[12] tried to embrace them, but they managed to make their way into a fjord and then along the coast to the bottom of the fjord where they found a boathouse with a boat inside. There they tied their vessel down and went ashore to look for a farmstead.

They found a small farm dwelling and knocked on the door. A man came out and greeted them, then invited them in out of the storm, and they went into the main room where a lamp was

burning. There they seated themselves on one of the two
benches[13] and were welcomed by the people on the farm. Then
a woman asked them who was the leader of their party.

She was told that it was Thorgeir and Thormod who had
arrived.

'But who wants to know?' they said.

They were told that it was Sigurfljod, the mistress of the
house, who asked.

'I have heard of you,' she said, 'but I have never seen you
before. What has brought you here today, fair weather or fair
friends?'

They replied, 'Many would say that there's not much difference between the two, but there again that depends on who's
talking.'

Sigurfljod answered, 'That may well be true.'

4

She had them take off their garments and a fire was kindled to
warm up the men and thaw out whatever clothes were frozen.
Then they were given some food, accompanied to their beds
and covered up well. They soon fell asleep. The storm blustered
through the freezing night. The wind, like a wild cur, howled
constantly and with relentless force the whole night long, and
gnawed at the ground with its cold and savage jaws. When
daylight came, someone was sent to look outside, and when he
returned Thorgeir asked him what the weather was like. He
replied that there was no change from the previous evening.

Sigurfljod said, 'You need not fear the storm. You are welcome to remain here and accept whatever we have. You don't
have to leave until the weather improves.'

Thorgeir answered, 'Thank you for your offer, mistress, but
the storm does not alarm us. We have no women, children or
livestock to take care of.'

Then the storm began to die down and the bays and fjords
became covered with thick ice.

One morning, Sigurfljod rose early, looked outside and then
hurried back in. Thorgeir asked how the weather was out there.

She said, 'Much improved. The sky is clear and there's no wind.'

Thormod said, 'Then let's be up and away, men.'

Sigurfljod said, 'What are your plans?'

Thormod replied, 'We'll go north to Strandir and see what we can catch. We'll leave our boat behind here.'

Sigurfljod said, 'What strange men you are. You're ready to go whaling at Strandir while there's a much better and braver catch to be made close by.'

Thormod asked, 'Where is this catch to be found?'

She said, 'I think it would be a greater deed to kill the bad men who steal around here than to go whaling.'

Thormod said, 'Of what men do you speak?'

She said, 'I'm talking about Ingolf and Thorbrand who have brought harm and destruction to so many. You would be avenging many a man if you killed them, and many a man would reward you handsomely for the deed.'

Thormod said, 'I don't know whether you are giving us good counsel. They are friends of Vermund and there will be consequences if any harm comes to them.'

She said, ' "Best to know bad company by report alone",[14] as the saying has it. You think yourselves great fighting men while you bully crofters, but you grow fearful when a real test of manhood is before you.'

Then Thorgeir sprang to his feet and said, 'Stand up, lads. Let's pay the woman for our stay.'

So they stood up and armed themselves, and when they were ready they travelled across the ice-laden fjord, reaching Ingolf's farm before anyone there had arisen. Ingolf awoke and heard men walking around outside by the buildings. There were quite a few of them and their shoes were frozen. Thorgeir and the others went up to the door and knocked on it. The men in the hall woke up at the sound and jumped to their feet. Ingolf and his son, Thorbrand, always slept in their clothes because they had many enemies. They had two farmhands with them. All four men armed themselves. Each took his spear, then they went to the door and opened it up. There they saw eight men, all armed, and they asked who was their leader.

Thorgeir spoke up, 'You may have heard report of Thorgeir Havarsson or Thormod Bersason – now you can see them for yourselves.'

Thorbrand replied, 'Of course we have heard of you both, but rarely anything good. Why have you come here?'

Thorgeir answered, 'We come to lay down conditions and redress an imbalance. We will give you a choice. Either you hand over all the property you have wrongfully taken, and thus buy your lives, or defend that property to the death like men.'

Thorbrand replied, 'What we have taken we took like men, and bravely too, and we would not part with it in any other manner. As for you, Thorgeir, I think you'll sooner be breakfasting on my spear than on my property.'

Thorgeir said, 'Like others in my family, I can prophesy from my dreams and I have dreamt a good deal about myself, but very little about you. But what I have dreamt will happen – your Lady Hel[15] will embrace you and all your property will become forfeit. Ill-gotten gains never come to any good.'

5

When these words had been spoken, Thorgeir and Thormod attacked Ingolf and Thorbrand, and forbade their companions from doing the same since they wanted to defeat them alone. The house was dimly lit, and it was therefore difficult for Thorgeir and Thormod to see inside. Outside, however, it was much lighter and that gave the defending party an advantage over their attackers. Ingolf's men rushed out occasionally and exchanged blows with Thorgeir's party, but ultimately Thorbrand fell at Thorgeir's hand and Ingolf was slain by Thormod. Ingolf's men were badly, but not mortally, wounded. As Thormod said in his drapa composed on Thorgeir's death:

3.
I tell how the master
of the awning-horse   *awning-horse*: ship;
took the life of Ingolf's son –   its *master*: seafarer, Thorgeir
word of his death spread wide.

At the hand of the famed mover
of mast-stallions Thorbrand fell,
others lost their lives there –
actions speak louder than words.

mast-stallions: ships;
their *mover:* seafarer

Thorgeir and his men took two horses and loaded them up
with food, and then herded three of the fattest bulls and drove
them back with them across the fjord. Sigurfljod was outside
when they arrived. She greeted them and asked what news
there was. They told her what had happened.

She said, 'You have done well since you left here and cut a
good piece of flesh from the whale, and by this action taken
reprisal for many a man's harm, disgrace and dishonour. I will
now go to Vatnsfjord and meet with Vermund to tell him the
news, but you must remain here and wait for me.'

They told her to go, and she set out with some of her farmhands. They took a six-oared boat that she owned and rowed
along Isafjord, not stopping before they reached Vatnsfjord late
in the evening.

She said to her men, 'Now you keep silent. Not a word from
you about what has happened. Let me do the talking.'

They consented to this. Then they went to the farmhouse to
speak to the people there. Vermund greeted them warmly and
when he asked what news they had, they replied that they had
none. They stayed the night and were well looked after. When
morning came, Sigurfljod said that she would return home.

Vermund tried hard to dissuade her.

'You come here so rarely,' he said. 'Why rush off again so
quickly?'

She said, 'I don't get away from home too often, but the
weather is so good for travelling right now that it would be
unwise not to set out while it lasts. I hope, though, that you
will accompany me as far as my boat.'

He replied, 'Let us go then.'

So they went off to the boat.

Then Sigurfljod said, 'Have you heard about the slayings at
Jokulsfirdir?'

'What slayings?' replied Vermund.

She said, 'Thorgeir Havarsson and Thormod Bersason slew Ingolf and his son Thorbrand.'

Then Vermund said, 'They go too far, these sworn brothers, killing our men like this. I will not have them killing any more of our people.'

She said, 'It was to be expected that you would react like this, though some would say that they have not killed your men but done this slaying for you. Who else should punish crimes such as plundering and robbery if you, as chieftain of this district, choose not to? It seems to me that Thorgeir and Thormod have carried out a task that you should either have carried out yourself or employed someone to do, and you would understand what I mean if you weren't blind. I came to see you in order to purchase immunity for those responsible for the slayings, though not as compensation for the slain – they have long since forfeited their property and their lives – but because I wish to show you respect in all matters, as is my duty. I want to give you these three hundred pieces of silver as a settlement price[16] for Thorgeir and Thormod.'

Then she took the money from her belt and poured it into Vermund's lap. It was good silver and Vermund opened his eyes wide at the sight of it. Then his anger was assuaged and he promised this would grant Thorgeir and Thormod a degree of security, though he added that he did not want Thorgeir to stay long in Isafjord.

Then they parted. Sigurfljod returned home to her farm and told Thorgeir and Thormod what had been settled between herself and Vermund. They thanked her, too, for the counsel she had given them and stayed on there for the winter. When spring came and the weather began to improve, they launched their boat and made ready to sail. Just before they departed they thanked her for her hospitality, for all the good things she had done for them and for the superior integrity she had displayed. They parted as friends.

Thorgeir and Thormod travelled north to Strandir and stayed there for the summer. The fishing was good and so was the quarry. They had whatever they desired of the locals, all of whom were as frightened as lambs are of the lion when it prowls among them.

Bersi moved to Laugabol in Laugardal since Vermund did not wish to have Thorgeir and Thormod sheltered so close to him. That autumn, they travelled south to Isafjord, brought their vessel ashore in a good spot and covered it over. Thormod went to his father while Thorgeir intended to go south to his cousin at Reykjanes. Their companions also returned to their respective homesteads. They decided on parting that all would meet at the boat when spring came and go north to Strandir again to hunt and fish. Having agreed on that, they said their farewells and took leave of each other.

6

There was a man named Thorkel who lived at Gervidal. He was wealthy but not generous, preferred his own company and was rather faint-hearted. He had a wife and three servants, one of whom was a woman.

There was a man named Butraldi, a loner of no fixed abode. He was a large, powerfully built man with an ugly face, quick-tempered and vengeful, and he was a great slayer of men. He worked as a hired hand during the summers and wandered about during the wintertime with two other men, staying at various farms for a few nights at a time. He was a distant relative of Vermund at Vatnsfjord and thus escaped the payment he so richly deserved.

Butraldi came to Thorkel's farm in Gervidal with his two companions one evening and wanted to stay there. Even though Thorkel was miserly about his food, he dared not refuse them lodging and so he led them into the main room and lit a lamp. There they sat, armed, while the house-servants were in the hall. There were scattered snow drifts in the mountains, but lower down the ground was bare. The rivers, streams and lakes had frozen over as a result of the great cold, and small snow-storms came and went.

Thorkel came into the main room to ask them a number of

things that excited his curiosity. He asked Butraldi where he was headed and the latter replied that he was going south across Breidafjord. Thorkel said he was not certain that the weather would allow such a journey over the moors the following day. Here his courage failed him; for he did not want them to stay but did not have the strength of character to stand up to them.

At that moment he heard a knock on the door, and that certainly did not improve matters for him. He left the room, went to the door, opened it up and saw an armed man standing out there. Thorkel asked the man's name. It was Thorgeir. Thorkel asked whose son he was, and the man told him he was the son of Havar. This put great fear in Thorkel's breast, and his heart began to beat faster.

Then Thorkel said, 'Butraldi is here with two other men and I don't know how warmly he feels towards you, though I expect he wishes you ill since he is a friend of your enemy Vermund. But I cannot bear the sight of bloodshed and I will surely faint if you two start fighting.'

Thorgeir said, 'Rest assured, farmer, my presence here will bring you no harm.'

Thorgeir went into the main room, followed by Thorkel and his wife. Thorkel took a table and placed it in front of Butraldi.

'I don't have much to offer,' said Thorkel, 'but come, Thorgeir, sit here beside Butraldi.'

Thorgeir did so. He walked across the room and sat down at the table beside Butraldi. There is a detailed report of what they ate: two platters were brought in; on one of them was some old short-rib mutton and on the other a large quantity of old cheese. Butraldi made a brief sign of the cross, then picked up the mutton ribs, carved off the meat and continued to eat until the bones were picked clean. Thorgeir took the cheese and cut off as much as he wanted, though it was hard and difficult to pare. Neither of them would share either the knife or the food with the other. Though the meal was not good, they did not bring out their own provisions for fear that it would be seen as a sign of weakness. Food was also brought to Thorkel and his wife, where they sat by the fire. Occasionally, they went to the main room, opened up the door and timidly looked in.

When the guests had eaten their fill, Thorkel came into the main room with his wife and she cleared the table.

Thorkel said, 'In return for my hospitality, I only ask that you show each other no aggression while you stay in my house. It would cause me great trouble if you were to start fighting here. I think it best that Thorgeir rest with us in the hall while Butraldi and his companions sleep here in the main room.'

This is what they did, and they slept through the night. When it started to get light, Butraldi and Thorkel rose early, and so did Thorgeir. A lamp was lit in the main room, and a table placed there with food just like the evening before. This time, Thorgeir took the mutton ribs and began to carve off the meat, while Butraldi chewed away at the cheese.

When they were full, Butraldi left with his companions and followed the trodden path up the valley. A little later, Thorgeir left and took the same route. A river flows through Gervidal Valley and the steep heath ridge leads up from the valley to the high road. There was a good deal of hard, frozen snow on the ridge at the time. Thorgeir watched where Butraldi and his companions went and saw that it was a difficult route and that they were going to have a hard time ascending the ridge, so he turned and crossed the river and made his ascent from the other side, reaching the high road while the others were still on the ridge. Butraldi reached the patch of hard snow and used his axe to cut footholds in it. Thorgeir could see all this since he was now on higher ground.

Then Butraldi said, 'So the hero ran off, did he?'

Thorgeir said, 'I didn't run off. I simply took a different route so as not to have to cut my way through the snow. There'll be no running away from you now, though.'

Thorgeir stood at the edge of the ridge while Butraldi continued to cut his way through the snow. When Butraldi was about halfway up, Thorgeir placed his spear underneath him, with the spearhead facing forwards, raised his axe to shoulder height and slid down the snow towards Butraldi. He heard the sound of Thorgeir whizzing down and looked up, but before he knew what was happening Thorgeir struck him full on the chest with his axe and cut right through him, and he fell back down the slope. Thorgeir continued down past him until he reached flat ground, and moved with such speed that the other two men rushed off. A verse commemorates this incident:

4.
Fitting work to tell how
flashing weapons showered down
and silenced Butraldi –
the grey eagle often flies from battle,
but there is no denying that
the reddener of the sword-strap's   *sword-strap's path*: sheath, scabbard;
                            path   its *reddener* (with blood): warrior
will earn thanks all the less
for spilling this man's blood.

Butraldi's companions did not dare take revenge, nor even confront Thorgeir since they had no desire to be sent off to rest for the night by his weapons. They fussed around Butraldi's body while Thorgeir climbed up on to the moorland and continued his way south until he reached Reykjaholar. He received a warm welcome, stayed there for the winter and was well looked after.

The winter was exceedingly harsh far and wide across the country. Livestock died and farming conditions were difficult. Many men went north to Strandir to hunt whales.[17]

7

The following spring, Thorgeir went to Isafjord where their boat was laid up. Thormod and their shipmates arrived, and they set out north to Strandir as soon as the wind was favourable.

There was a man named Thorgils who lived at Laekjamot in Vididal. He was a big, strong man, skilful in the use of weapons and a good farmer. He was a kinsman of Asmund Grey-locks, the father of Grettir, and related to Thorstein Kuggason. Thorgils's father's name was Mar.

Thorgils also went off to Strandir with some companions to where a whale had been washed ashore on common ground.

The hunting was poor where Thorgeir had landed, and there

was neither whale meat nor any other food to be had there. He inquired as to where Thorgils was engaged in cutting up the stranded whale and then went there with Thormod.

When they arrived, Thorgeir said, 'You've already cut quite a lot from that whale. It would be best now to allow others a chance at it while there's still something worth having. We're all equally entitled here.'

Thorgils replied, 'Well said! Then, let each keep what he has already cut.'

Thorgeir said, 'You have cut away a large portion of the meat and may keep what you have cut. Now we want you either to leave the rest of the whale to us and take with you the meat you have cut or to divide equally with us both what is taken and what remains.'

Thorgils replied, 'I'm not inclined to leave the carcass, nor do I plan to give you the meat I have already cut from it – not while we've still got the whale.'

Thorgeir said, 'Then you will have to see how long you can hold us away from it.'

Thorgils answered, 'That seems like a good solution.'

Then both sides armed themselves and prepared to fight. And when they were ready, Thorgeir said, 'It is best, Thorgils, that you and I fight each other since you're a seasoned, hardy and experienced fighter and I'd like to see how I fare against you. Let the others stay out of our fray.'

Thorgils answered, 'I fully approve of that.'

Their parties were of even strength, and they attacked each other and fought. Thorgeir and Thorgils exchanged a few quick blows. They were both skilled fighters, but Thorgeir was the deadlier of the two and he therefore prevailed over his opponent. Three of Thorgils's party and three of Thorgeir's were also slain in this fight.

After the fight, the remainder of Thorgils's men returned north from where they had come, overwhelmed with grief. Thorgeir took the whole whale, both the portions that had been cut and the carcass. He was outlawed for slaying Thorgils – a judgement brought into effect by Thorstein Kuggason and Asmund Grey-locks.

Thorgeir and Thormod spent the summer at Strandir. All the men there were frightened of them, and they prevailed over all things like weeds overtaking a field.

People say that at the height of their tyranny, Thorgeir spoke these words to Thormod: 'Do you know of any other two men as eager as we or as brave, or indeed anyone who has stood the test of his valour so often?'

Thormod replied, 'Such men could be found, if they were looked for, who are no lesser men than us.'

Thorgeir said, 'Which of us do you think would win if we confronted each other?'

Thormod answered, 'I don't know, but I do know that this question of yours will divide us and end our companionship. We cannot stay together.'

Thorgeir said, 'I wasn't really speaking my mind – saying that I wanted us to fight each other.'

Thormod said, 'It came into your mind as you spoke it and we shall go our separate ways.'

And that is what they did. Thorgeir took the boat and Thormod took the larger portion of the movable goods and left for Laugabol. Thorgeir stayed on at Strandir for the summer and remained a threat to many. When autumn came he brought his boat ashore there in the north, covered it over and made arrangements for his goods. Then he went to Thorgils at Reykjaholar and spent the winter with him. Thormod refers to this division between them in the following verse from his memorial drapa to Thorgeir:

5.
People have heard we had many
slanderers who tried to come
between us – but I enjoyed
advice from the wound-snake's reddener.   *wound-snake*: sword;
Though men's hatred I have felt,   its *reddener*: warrior, Thorgeir
I will remember nothing
but good between me and him,
the steerer of wave-beasts.   *wave-beasts*: ships; their *steerer*: Thorgeir

8

There was a ship laid up in the river Nordura near Floi, a common place for putting ashore. Thorgils and his brother, Illugi, had secretly bought a share in this vessel for Thorgeir and had goods brought aboard to the same value as that share. Thorgils and Illugi did not ride to the opening of the Althing that summer since they did not want to cross the Breidafjord valleys before Thorstein Kuggason had left the district to attend it. The reason for this was that they meant to accompany Thorgeir, the man Thorstein had had outlawed, to the ship.

[From *Flateyjarbók*]

Thorgils and Illugi learned that Thorstein had ridden off to the Althing, and they set off from home with sixty men. Among them were the sworn brothers, Thorgeir and Thormod.

The party rode on ahead of them, and when these two reached the river Drifandi in Gilsfjord, Thorgeir said, 'Do you know of two other sworn brothers who are our equals in exploits and valour?'

Thormod said, 'I expect they could be found if one looked far enough.'

Thorgeir said, 'I don't think you will find any in Iceland. But which of us do you think would prevail if we fought each other?'

'I don't know,' said Thormod, 'but I do know that this question of yours will break up our companionship and our share.'

At that moment Thorgeir rode out past the cliff face. The tide was so high that his horse was almost forced to swim. When he reached the shoal water in front of the cliff, he dismounted and saw that Thormod had turned his horse around farther up the fjord. He called out to him to come back and ride past the cliff.

Thormod replied, 'We will part ways for a while. I bid you farewell.'

Then Thormod rode back along Gilsfjord and did not stop until he came home to his father, Bersi, at Laugabol.

When he had gone, Thorgeir remounted his horse and rode after the others, but when he reached Saurbaer the party had already ridden off to Svinadal. Thorgeir rode on at a great pace.

There was a man named Hlenni, who lived at Maskelda, and
he had a man lodging with him, known as Torfi Bundle. Torfi had
gone up to the stream to cut some faggots and carry them home.
He had just put a load on his back when Thorgeir rode by below
him along the riverbank, and as Thorgeir came towards him, he
called out and asked the man his name. But because the wind was
rustling through his burden of faggots, Torfi did not hear him call
out. Thorgeir wanted to inquire about his party and he called out
to the man several times, but Torfi never heard him call. Thorgeir
grew tired of calling out and his already bad mood turned to
anger. He rode across the stream at Torfi and plunged his spear
through him, killing him instantly. Since then the stream has been
called Boggullaek (Bundle stream). Thorgeir rode on his way
until he reached Illugi and the rest of the party at Mjosund, where
he told them he had slain Torfi. They were not pleased with this
deed.

There was a man named Skuf who lived at Hundadal in
Dalir. He was a good farmer and helpful to others. He had a
son named Bjarni who lived at home with him, and a man who
looked after the sheep in Hundadal who was also named Skuf.

People began to leave for the Althing, including Thorgils and
Illugi who left Reykjaholar in the west, having sent some men
ahead of them to hang their booths with cloth. They had an
evening meal at Saurbaer then rode east through the night from
Dalir, intending to stop for breakfast in Hundadal. By morning
they had come as far as Middalir, just beyond the woods at
Thykkvaskog, and it was there that they ate and then slept.

Thorgeir had a beautiful, large russet horse, good for riding.
Towards late morning, the men were asked to get the horses
and they got up and went off to round them up. Thorgeir's
horse was not among the others, so they went on to the heavily
wooded slopes to look for it – but to no avail. The horse was
nowhere to be found. So they took one of the packhorses, after
dividing its load among the others, and gave it to Thorgeir.
Then they noticed a man mounted on a fine-looking russet
horse, coming along the gravel banks from Saudafell, driving
some sheep ahead of him. He was driving them hard because

he had a swift horse, and it seemed to Thorgeir that the animal was very much like his own. He showed no reaction, but nevertheless kept an eye on where the man rode and saw him chase the sheep up to a farm in Hundadal. Some ewes from Laxardal in the west had been given to Skuf in payment for a debt, but they had run off, and it was Skuf's son, Bjarni, who had taken Thorgeir's horse to go off and look for them.

Illugi, Thorgils and the rest of the party rode up to the farm at Hundadal and the two brothers told their men to unload their horses before they reached the farm and to make sure they did not graze on the hayfield. Then the brothers rode up to the farmhouse with a few men. Thorgeir rode off to the sheep pens where he thought he recognized his horse. Bjarni was mounted on the horse after having driven the ewes he had found into the pens.

Thorgeir asked, 'Who is it who sits on this horse?'

'His name is Bjarni,' was the reply.

Thorgeir said, 'That's a fine-looking horse. Who does it belong to?'

Bjarni replied, 'Quite true, it is a fine-looking horse, but I don't know whom it belongs to.'

Thorgeir said, 'Why did you take the horse?'

Bjarni answered, 'I took the horse because I preferred to ride rather than walk.'

Thorgeir said, 'I think it would be a good idea for you to get down off that horse and give it back to its owner.'

Bjarni said, 'I won't be riding it much longer because I have no farther to go than the front door of my house.'

Thorgeir said, 'I want you to get down from the horse immediately.'

Bjarni said, 'It's not going to hurt the horse if I ride up to the house.'

Thorgeir said, 'I must insist that you ride it no farther at this present time.'

Bjarni tried to turn the horse towards the gate to ride back to the house. Thorgeir struck at him with his spear and it pierced him clean through, so that he was already dead when he fell from the horse.[18]

Skuf the shepherd was closing the gates to the sheep pens when he saw Bjarni fall from the horse. He ran out, grabbed his axe, held it with both hands and lunged at Thorgeir. Thorgeir used the shaft of his spear to divert the blow and then, wielding his axe in his right hand, he struck Skuf on the head and split him to the shoulders. He died instantly.

Thorgeir's companions returned home with great speed and told the chieftains what had happened, and they regarded it as bad news indeed. They sent some men at once to escort Thorgeir from the place before the dead man's father or any of the rest of his family saw him, and after that they related the news to Skuf [Bjarni's father] themselves. He saw no better alternative than to accept their suggestion that he name the compensation price himself for the slayings, especially since the brothers were men of such standing, but even more importantly because the man responsible for them had already been outlawed. A settlement was thus reached.

These slayings are referred to by Thormod in his drapa on Thorgeir:

6.
Fate favoured the warrior
when the swords rained down:
Mar's son paid for his pride,
ravens tore at raw flesh.
Then the rider of the waves,   *rider of the waves*: seafarer, Thorgeir
the skilled battle-worker,
gladly lent his hand
to kill Skuf and Bjarni.

Thorgils and Illugi breakfasted at Hundadal and then rode south to Borgarfjord where they put Thorgeir aboard a ship.

[From *Flateyjarbók*]

Thorgeir had ridden south ahead of the others and when he came to Hvassafell there were some men there standing outside. The shepherd had just come home from the herd and he stood in the hayfield, leaning forwards on his staff, talking to the other men. It was a short staff and the shepherd was tired. Thus he was rather hunched over, with his tired legs bent and his neck sticking out. When Thorgeir saw this he drew his axe in the air and let it fall on the man's neck. The axe bit well and the head went flying off and landed some distance away. Then Thorgeir rode off and the rest of the men in the field stood there helpless and amazed.

Shortly afterwards, Illugi and Thorgils came by. They were told what happened and were not pleased. It is said that they provided compensation for Thorgeir's deed and then rode on to meet him. He greeted them warmly. They asked him why he had slain the man and what possible fault he had found with him.

Thorgeir replied, 'He had committed no wrong against me. If you want the truth I couldn't resist the temptation – he stood so well poised for the blow.'

'One can see from this,' said Thorgils, 'that your hands will never be idle. We have already paid compensation for the man's life.'

After that they all rode together to the ship.

A man named Gaut came down to the ship. He was the son of Sleita and a close relative of Thorgils Masson, whom Thorgeir had slain. Gaut was a large, powerful and overbearing man and a hard fighter. He had been taken aboard by the skipper and had no idea that Thorgeir was along for the journey. He grimaced with anger when he saw Thorgeir arrive, and both men saw that being aboard the same vessel was bound to be difficult on account of their temperaments. The ship was ready and the hold secured, with Gaut's goods inside it.

When Thorgeir heard the Norwegians grumbling about having both him and Gaut aboard, he said, 'Travelling along with Gaut might well come in useful to me no matter how angry he gets about it.'

But despite what Thorgeir said about himself and Gaut, they decided to open up the hold and put Gaut's goods ashore, after which he rode off in a northerly direction.

The Norwegians sailed along the river up to Seleyri, but Illugi and Thorgils did not leave the area until the ship was out at sea. Then they rode to the Althing with a large group of men and made a settlement, on Thorgeir's behalf, for the slaying of Thorgils Masson, and pleaded for him to be acquitted.

Thorgeir and his shipmates were tossed about on the open sea for a while, then finally sighted land ahead. The Norwegians recognized it as being Ireland and felt that putting ashore there was likely to mean trouble.

Thorgeir said, 'I think if we put up a stand that we can send a number of them to dine in Valhalla before we ourselves are slain. That's the best defence we have.'

So they cast anchor some distance from shore, took their weapons from the hold and made themselves ready to fight if need be. Then they saw a great host of men ashore with so many spears that it looked like a forest. But though the Irish had long-shafted spears, they could not reach them. In this way they managed to hold on to their lives and their goods, and they sailed off as soon as a favourable wind arose. From there they went to England, where they stayed for a while and, as Thormod has said in his verses on Thorgeir, he received good gifts from the chieftains there.

After that Thorgeir went to Denmark and, according to Thormod's verses, he was held in such high esteem that the Danes revered him almost as a king. From there, Thorgeir went to Norway to see King Olaf. He went before the king and greeted him warmly. This pleased Olaf, and he asked who he was.

He replied, 'I am an Icelander and my name is Thorgeir.'

The king said, 'Are you Thorgeir Havarsson?'

Thorgeir answered, 'The very same man.'

The king said, 'I have heard of you. You are a big man and have the look of a champion, but are not endowed with great luck.'

The king invited Thorgeir to stay and become one of his followers. He held Thorgeir in high esteem since he proved himself to be a brave and hardy champion wherever he went. Thorgeir went south to the land of the Wends[19] to trade at a time when northern merchants had little hope of a peaceful reception. He proved his excellence on this journey and obtained all he asked for. From that time on, he spent alternate winters with King Olaf in Norway and at Reykjaholar in Iceland. He usually sailed into Borgarfjord and then proceeded up to Floi on the river Nordura, where he laid up his ship for the winter on the west bank of the river. That place is now called Thorgeirshrof,[20] south of the heights known as Smidjuholt.

Thorgeir set sail seven times from Iceland, and as Thormod says:

7.
Six[21] times he set forth
on his sea-charger hence,   *sea-charger*: ship
tree of the valkyrie's gusts,   *valkyrie's gusts*: battle; their *tree*: warrior
bold to deliver the wound-snake;   *wound-snake*: sword
hurtful to wealth, he led   *hurtful to wealth*: generous
his black ship to the sea,
and wrought great deeds.
This I learned at home.

9

Now the time has come to tell of what Thormod was doing while Thorgeir was travelling abroad. When the two of them parted ways, Thormod went to his father Bersi at Laugabol and stayed there for a number of years, but he found the place dull because there were so few people there.

There was a woman named Grima, who lived at the farm known as Ogur. She was a widow of some considerable wealth, and it was said of her that she had dabbled in many things and people believed she was skilled in the ancient arts. Since Christianity was new to the country and had not fully taken hold, many considered such skills quite an advantage. Grima had a daughter named Thordis, who lived at home with her. She was a good-looking girl, and skilled in many tasks but was rather loud-mouthed. Grima had a slave named Kolbak. He was a large, strong man with a pleasing appearance. He was also a good fighter. Thormod visited their farm often and sat there for long periods of time, talking to Grima's daughter, Thordis, and as a result of these frequent visits and long conversations a rumour grew up that he was seducing her.

When Grima heard word of this she went to talk to Thormod and said, 'A lot of people are saying that you are seducing my daughter, Thordis, and I am not at all pleased about the effect you are having on her reputation. I'm not saying that you would be a bad choice, it's just that any man who might be thinking about proposing marriage to her will regard you as a troll on his doorstep.[22] But if you ask to marry her I will give her to you.'

Thormod replied, 'You put the matter very well and I shall take due notice of what you say, but marriage does not suit my temperament. If it did, I would look no further than to ask for your daughter's hand. But even so, this will not come to pass.'

Having spoken thus they parted. Thormod went home and stayed there for the rest of the summer. When winter came, the lakes, rivers and streams were covered with thick ice, which made it easy to travel. The lake at Ogur was also frozen. Thormod once again found life at Laugabol dull since there was so little there in the way of amusement, so he renewed his visits to Thordis at Ogur. The same problem arose and rumours arose again concerning the friendship between Thordis and Thormod. Thormod armed himself with shield and sword whenever he made his way to Ogur because he expected trouble from some quarters.

Grima discussed the matter again with Thormod, telling him to stop coming, 'So that my daughter will not be scorned,' she said.

Thormod answered her eloquently but did not stop visiting.

One day while Thormod was at Ogur, Grima spoke to Kolbak, 'I want to send you to a farm with some weft for some cloth that is being woven there.'

As Kolbak got ready to leave, Grima opened a large trunk, took out some coils of yarn and an old short-sword with a sharp cutting edge, and placed the sword in his hand, saying, 'Keep hold of this and you'll not lack a weapon.'

Kolbak took the short-sword. Then Grima stuffed the coils of yarn inside his long coat, and passed her hands first over his body and then over his clothes. After that Kolbak went on his way. The weather began to thicken then thaw, thus dispersing what snow had fallen.

Later that same day, Thordis spoke to Thormod, 'I want you to take another route than the one you usually take. Go to the near side of Ogur bay and then make your way from there along the slope to Laugabol.'

Thormod replied, 'What makes you desire me to take this particular route?'

Thordis said, 'It's likely that the ice in the bay has thinned since the thaw started and I don't want you to have an accident.'

Thormod said, 'The ice is solid enough.'

Thordis said, 'I'm not in the habit of making requests, Thormod, and I shall take it badly if you don't do as I ask.'

Now Thormod saw that what she asked mattered to her and he promised to take the route she suggested. Late that night Thormod left Ogur, but as soon as he was a short distance from the house it occurred to him that it would not make any difference to Thordis what route he took. So he changed his mind and took the quickest route across the bay over the ice.

There was a sheep house in a hayfield down by the bay, and just as Thormod walked past the door of the house, a man ran out wielding a short-sword and struck at Thormod. The blow caught him on the arm, just above the elbow, wounding him badly. Thormod threw down his shield, drew his sword with his left hand, then held it with both hands and dealt Kolbak a few quick blows, but his sword had no bite. Kolbak was made so powerful by the charms that Grima had poured over him that no weapon could harm him.

Kolbak had only struck Thormod once.

He said, 'I can do whatever I choose with you, Thormod, but I shall refrain from doing anything more now.'

Then Kolbak returned home and told Grima what had happened. She felt that Kolbak had been too gentle with Thormod, yet she acted as if it were not she who had betrayed him.

Thormod tore a strip from his breeches, bandaged up his wound and then walked home. One of his servant-women was waiting for him in the main room and there was a lamp burning

there, but the rest of the household had gone to bed. When
Thormod came into the main room, a table was set before him
and food brought in, but he had little appetite. The woman saw
that he was bleeding so she left the room and told Bersi that
Thormod had come home and that his clothes were covered in
blood.

Bersi rose from his bed and went into the main room, where
he greeted his son and asked him what had happened. Thormod told him how he had met with Kolbak and of the bloody
wounds he had been dealt.

Bersi said, 'Your weapons had no effect on Kolbak, then?'

Thormod replied, 'I struck at him often enough with my
sword but it had no greater effect than my striking him with a
piece of whalebone.'

Bersi said, 'Grima's sorcery was at work there.'

Thormod composed a verse:

8.

I parried the furies' blows,   *furies*: valkyries
the furious assault,
but cast my shield away,
suffered wounds from the war-king's song.   *war-king's song*: battle
When will I see a chance,
giver of wave's beacon,   *wave's beacon*: gold
of vengeance on that clumsy
launcher of wave-riding ravens?   *wave-riding ravens*: ships; their
                                         launcher: seafarer, Kolbak

Bersi said, 'It is as I thought, but it's not clear how this out-
rage is to be avenged if we have to deal with sorcery.'

10

Bersi bandaged Thormod's wound again, for he was skilled in
the art of healing, and the following morning he set out for
Ogur with a large number of men.

But before he reached the farm, Grima said to her men-
servants, 'Now, all of you go into the main room and sit on the
lower bench while Bersi is here.'

They did as she asked, went into the main room and sat on the lower of the two benches. They were fully armed. Grima told Kolbak to sit in the middle of the bench and she made a gesture with her hands above his head. Then Bersi came to the house and knocked on the door. Grima went to the door and greeted them.

Bersi said, 'You greet us warmly but we suspect you have little concern how we fare. Well then, know this – finding that you fare badly would hardly upset us.'

Grima said, 'What you say surprises me greatly. I thought you were our friends as we are yours. Do you bring any news?'

Bersi replied, 'What news we have you already know.'

Grima said, 'But we haven't heard any news lately. What is it you have to tell us?'

Bersi said, 'We have come to tell you of the bloody wound that your slave, Kolbak, inflicted on my son Thormod.'

Grima replied, 'That is bad news indeed, but even worse if it's true since it was I who sent Kolbak off with some weft and he didn't return last night. I expect he didn't dare face me because he knows how I value Thormod as my friend. I have long suspected Kolbak of having pretensions towards Thordis and now he has shown great folly in attacking Thormod – that excellent man – out of jealousy. This deed has heaped scorn on my daughter and brought shame and dishonour upon us. It is my responsibility to do what is in my power to put this right.'

Bersi said, 'Some people say, Grima, that you're quite capable of feigning on occasion, but we'll find out how close this is to the truth.'

'I should be grateful, and it would give me great satisfaction, if you came into my house and searched all the rooms, thus quashing any suspicion that I have been party to the malicious deed Kolbak has done.'

So Bersi went into the main room with his companions and sat down on the upper bench. He remained seated there for a while, but he did not see Kolbak who was sitting directly opposite him because Grima had hidden him with a magic helmet, making him invisible to the sight of men. Bersi left the room and searched the farmhouse, but he did not find Kolbak.

After that, he formally accused Kolbak of grievously wounding his son,[23] Thormod, and so left.

Thormod's wound healed badly and he had to rest for a long time. For the remainder of his life he was left-handed. Kolbak stayed at Ogur that winter where Grima secretly looked after him. The following spring a case was brought against him at the assembly and he was declared an outlaw for life. A ship was moored at Vadil, and its skipper was a Norwegian named Ingolf. It was ready to set sail at about the same time as the Althing began, but the weather prevented them from setting out.

When men all over the country had ridden off to the Althing, Grima spoke to Kolbak: 'I expect you will be found guilty and outlawed for life for giving Thormod a bloody wound, but because I am responsible for this I want to give you your freedom – you are no longer a slave. Now, go and get four horses without anyone seeing you, two for riding and two others to carry some goods and provisions that I will give you. I will secretly accompany you to the ship at Vadil and see if I can arrange a passage for you aboard it.'

Kolbak was pleased to obtain both his liberty and the goods that Grima gave him. He secretly prepared to leave Ogur that night without anyone noticing. Then he and Grima rode across the Glamuheidi moorland to Arnarfjord and took the mountain route to Bardastrond until they reached Vadil. The merchants were asleep on board ship, but the skipper was ashore in a tent, Grima opened the tent, while Kolbak looked after the horses, and then went inside to wake Ingolf the skipper, whom she knew by sight.

Ingolf greeted her and asked what errand she had there.

She told him, 'I have come to see you because I want you to take a man aboard. He is here now.'

Ingolf said, 'Who is the man?'

Grima replied, 'His name is Kolbak.'

Ingolf said, 'The one who attacked Thormod Bersason?'

Grima said, 'The very same man.'

Ingolf said, 'It would mean quite some trouble taking aboard a man who is bound to be outlawed this summer, or having to deal with fighting men as tenacious as Thormod and his father, Bersi. We've been moored here for quite a while with our load and Bersi might well return before we are able to set sail, in which case it would be unlikely that we could keep Kolbak's presence here a secret from him.'

Seeing that Ingolf was reluctant to comply with her request, Grima pulled a purse out from under her cloak and poured two hundred pieces of silver into his lap, saying, 'I will give you this money if you take Kolbak aboard and look after him.'

Ingolf said, 'That money's a fine sight, but too dearly earned if Bersi and Thormod discover us with the man they had out-lawed before we are able to leave.'

Then Grima said, 'I can see terms we'll agree to. You will take Kolbak and this money which I've offered you and get him out of Iceland and look after him – but only if you set sail tomorrow.'

Ingolf said, 'It shall be as you wish.'

So Ingolf took the money, stood up and accompanied Kolbak to the ship with his goods. Grima stayed ashore and recited some old chants that she had learned in her childhood. At that very moment, the wind that had been blowing inland for so long suddenly dropped. Ingolf had their leather sleeping sacks taken on to the ship and all of them hurried aboard. By dawn everything was ready to set sail. As the sun stood in the south-east and a good breeze began to blow, Ingolf and Kolbak went ashore to bid Grima farewell. She made ready to return home and had someone accompany her, but there is no other report of her journey until she reached Ogur, well before people had returned from the Althing. As soon as she had left, Ingolf went aboard his ship and had the sail hoisted. A good breeze sped them on their way across the ocean and they arrived in Nor-way. Kolbak was taken in by a group of Vikings and proved to be a hardy man in all tests of strength.

Thormod returned to Laugabol from the Althing and stayed with his father for several winters. There is no report of Thor-mod having had any other recompense for the bloody wound than having Kolbak outlawed.

11

Thormod felt that living at home with his father was dull. After the Althing that summer, he set out with some of his father's farmhands to collect a cargo of stock-fish that Bersi had out in Bolungarvik. They took a small ferry boat that belonged to Bersi and sailed out along Isafjord on a good breeze. Just past Arnardalir, the wind turned against them and they were swept off course. They cast anchor, went ashore and set up a tent. They were forced to stay there for some time since the weather prevented them from continuing on course.

In Arnardalir was a woman named Katla, the widow of a man named Glum. She had a daughter named Thorbjorg, who lived at home with her. Thorbjorg was a courteous woman, but hardly a beauty. She had black hair and dark eyebrows and was therefore nicknamed Kolbrun (Dark-brow). She had an intelligent look about her, a good complexion, and was of medium height with a slim and well-proportioned figure, but she was a little splay-footed.

It so happened that Thormod left his tent one day and went up to the farmhouse. He went into the main room and saw some women there, but no men. Katla greeted him and asked him his name, which Thormod told her. Then she asked whose son he was, and he told her that, too.

Katla said, 'I have heard of you, but never seen you until now.'

Thormod stayed there for the rest of the day and the women were well pleased to have his company. He glanced occasionally at Katla's daughter and liked what he saw. She looked him over, too, and he was pleasing to her. When night came, Thormod returned to his tent. He then made regular visits to Katla's house and recited occasional love songs,[24] which the women there liked very much.

One day, Katla said, 'Thormod, what made you decide to go along to Bolungarvik with your father's farmhands?'

He replied, 'No other reason than to amuse myself. It is so dull at home.'

'And what would amuse you more, going with them to pick

up the stock-fish at Bolungarvik or staying here and enjoying yourself? You have full leave to remain here if you wish since we take much pleasure in your company.'

Thormod answered, 'Thank you for those kind words. I shall accept your offer because I would much prefer to stay here with you.'

Then Thormod went off to see his companions and told them that he would be staying behind in the valley while they went off to Bolungarvik for the stock-fish, and that he would rejoin the crew on its way back. They parted, Thormod going to the farm while they waited for a good breeze to set sail again.

Thormod remained in Arnardalir for two weeks, composing poems of praise to Thorbjorg Kolbrun, and he called them the Dark-brow Verses. When he had completed them, he recited them where many a man could hear.

Katla took a large and beautiful ring from her finger and said, 'I would like to give you this ring, Thormod, as a reward for those verses and in token rename you Thormod, Kolbrun's Poet.'[25]

Thormod thanked her for the gift, and he became known by the title that Katla gave him. His father's farmhands returned to meet him and he went aboard ship, after thanking Katla for the hospitality she afforded him. Katla said he should not pass by her house without visiting if he came that way again, and they parted with those words. Then Thormod went home to Laugabol and remained there for the rest of the summer.

When winter arrived and the lakes, rivers and streams were covered again with ice, Thormod remembered his relationship with Grima's daughter, Thordis, and he set out for the farm at Ogur. Grima received him joyfully, but Thordis was stiff and haughty and held him at a distance, as women do with men whom they dislike. Thormod quickly saw how she looked away and treated him coldly, so he thought he might try to draw her in a little by reminding her of how close they had once been.

Thordis said, 'I've heard that you have a new love and that you have composed a poem of praise for her.'

Thormod replied, 'Who is this love of mine for whom you say I have composed poems?'

Thordis answered, 'Thorbjorg at Arnardalir.'

Thormod said, 'It's a lie that I wrote poetry about Thorbjorg. The truth is that I composed a poem in praise of you while I was staying in Arnardalir because I realized how much more beautiful and courteous you are than she. And that's why I came here – to present those verses to you.'

Thormod recited the Dark-brow Verses, turning most of what he had written to Thorbjorg into praise for Thordis. Then he gave the poem to Thordis so that they might be fully reconciled and that her affection and love for him be re-established. And like the dark mists that are drawn up out of the ocean, dispersing slowly to sunshine and gentle weather, so did these verses draw all reserve and darkness from Thordis's mind and Thormod was once again bathed in all the brightness of her warm and gentle love. Thormod visited Ogur often from that time on and was made very welcome.

One night, some while after this, Thormod was at home at Laugabol and he dreamt that Thorbjorg Kolbrun came to him and asked him whether he was awake or asleep. He said he was awake.

She said, 'You are asleep, but what appears to you now will take place when you are awake. What have you done? Have you given another woman the poem you wrote about me?'

Thormod replied, 'It isn't true.'

Thorbjorg said, 'It is true that you gave the poem in praise of me to Thordis, daughter of Grima, and altered what you composed about me because you're a cowardly little man and dared not tell the truth about which woman you had wrought them for. Now I shall repay you for your treachery and lies. You will experience such great and terrible pain in your eyes that it will seem as if they are about to burst out of their sockets – until you publicly admit that you betrayed me and gave the poem you had composed for me to another woman. You will never be well again until you remove those verses you have now turned to Thordis's praise and replace them with what you once wrote to me. And you shall not dedicate them to anyone except the person for whom they were originally intended.'

Thorbjorg appeared fierce and angry to him, and he was almost sure he saw her face as she left. He awoke with such a great pain in his eyes[26] that he could hardly refrain from crying out, and he could not sleep for the rest of the night. The next morning, he stayed for some time in his bed. Bersi rose at his usual hour, and the rest of the men were all on their feet before Thormod. Then Bersi went to his son and asked him whether he was ill since he had not risen from his bed as he would have usually.

Thormod recited a verse:

9.

Grievously I erred when on Thordis,
maiden of the ring of islands,   ring of islands: sea, fjord
I bestowed all the Dark-brow Verses –   ('Ogur' means fjord)
in a dream doom's goddess came to me.   doom's goddess: Thorbjorg
I took the punishment she dealt –
Thor's splendid daughter is versed   Thor's ... daughter: i.e. Thorbjorg
in those wily arts, and I would rather
make amends with that goddess.

Bersi said, 'What has come to you in your dream?'

Thormod told him his dream and the whole story concerning the poem.

Bersi said, 'These women of yours are no good for you. One has given you such a bad wound that you will never recover from it, and now you can fully expect to have your eyes burst from their sockets. My advice is that you alter the poem back to its original state and rededicate to Thorbjorg Kolbrun the poem you composed for her.'

Thormod said, 'I submit to your judgement.'

Then Thormod publicly confessed how he had changed the poem, and in front of many witnesses he gave them back to Thorbjorg. His eyes improved quickly and he fully recovered from the pain.

Now we shall leave for a while the account of Thormod Kolbrun's Poet and say a little about Thorgeir.

12

Now the story turns to Thorgeir Havarsson, currently a follower of King Olaf. One summer Thorgeir took his ship up the river Hvita, sailed from there to the river Nordura and then stowed it for the autumn at the place at present called Thorgeirshrof. He spent the winter in the west at Reykjaholar with his cousins, sold his goods there and then early in the following spring he went south to Borgarfjord and made ready to sail out again.

Just before the assembly, he went back west to Reykjaholar to fetch some goods he had bought with the proceeds of what he had sold the previous winter. He moved these goods to Skogarstrond, got some horses and then went south to Borgarfjord. He had a man with him who rode in front, leading a spare horse, while he made up the rear behind the packhorses. He rode armed with shield, spear and axe. And that is how they proceeded.

There was a man named Snorri, known as Haekils-Snorri, who lived at Hvitstadir. He was a large, strongly built, fine figure of a man but had a cruel face. He was not well-liked, lost his temper easily and was of a vengeful nature. He had a son named Helgi, who was quite young at the time. The living quarters of the farm were farther down on the spit than now and the farm was called Mel. A large sheep house stood in a hayfield to the west, now known as Snorratoftir.[27]

Thorgeir and his companion passed by the place. But as the latter rode by the farmhouse, the packhorses that Thorgeir was driving ran off into the hayfield. Snorri came out of the house at the moment that Thorgeir was chasing the packhorses and trying to get them out of the hayfield. But they obviously liked grazing there, and one of them stopped to do so as Thorgeir pursued the other.

Snorri went indoors, took a large barbed spear, and came out again swearing and cursing at the horses and then at Thorgeir. Then he struck out at the horses and wounded them. Thorgeir, seriously concerned that Snorri might kill the animals, jumped down from his mount, holding his shield in front of him and an axe in his left hand. In the other hand, he had a spear with which he attacked Snorri, forcing him back towards the sheep house where the fellow tried to defend himself with his spear. Two of Snorri's farmhands had seen their master run out angrily, clutching his spear, and each picked up an axe and went out to help him. Thorgeir defended himself deftly and then attacked with the strength and sureness of a lion. They were soon wounded because they had only short-shafted axes while Thorgeir had a spear with which he lunged at them fiercely again and again. Snorri and his two men retreated back into the sheep house. The doorway was low and narrow and it was therefore harder to attack them there. Thorgeir ran up on to the roof and began to tear off some of the turf, but Snorri's spear met him where he made an opening and he was wounded, though not seriously. Then Thorgeir threw down his spear and took up his axe in his right hand. Snorri attacked him fiercely through the opening in the roof. Thorgeir deflected the blows with his shield and axe, seeking only to cut the shaft from Snorri's spear and he did not stop until he had succeeded. As soon as he had broken Snorri's spear, he jumped in through the opening with both axe and shield and struck him such a hard blow to the head that he cleaved it right through and killed him instantly. Then Thorgeir turned to Snorri's farmhands and attacked them with great agility, defending himself with his shield and striking at them with the axe that had bid many a man goodnight. By the time he was done, he had slain both of them.

After that he returned, remounted his horse and rode up to the farmhouse to talk to the people there. He told them that Haekils-Snorri wanted to meet them and was waiting down at the sheep house. Then he rode off to meet up with his companion, who had driven the packhorses out of the hayfield while Thorgeir was fighting, and the two of them went to the ship. Thorgeir made ready to sail and then set out for Seleyri. There he waited for a fair breeze and then sailed out into the ocean.

He was not long at sea. Good winds brought him swiftly to Norway, where he immediately went off to meet King Olaf and was well received by him. This event was mentioned by Thormod in this verse from his drapa about Thorgeir:

10.

Warrior of the bloodied sword,   *Warrior*: Thorgeir
who repays in kind the harm
he suffers, made all haste to Snorri,
son of Haekil, and there did battle.
Three men he slew outright, aspiring
to an even braver show.
Of this seafarer's deeds
I have heard the proven truth.

Snorri's son, Helgi, lived at Hvitstadir for a long time. He was unlike his father and his family both in appearance and temperament. It was he who moved the farmhouse to where it now stands. He was nicknamed Helgi Hviti (the White), not to belittle him[28] but because he was a handsome man with plenty of white hair. That is why the farmhouse is called Hvitstadir. Helgi was a good farmer, and he was well-liked and helpful to his neighbours. He was involved in a dispute with Thorstein Egilsson[29] over the marshlands known as Gufufitjar which Thorstein wanted to buy but which Helgi did not wish to sell.

One winter, Helgi went with his men out to Gufufitjar, driving his oxen laden with hay south through the marshes as usual. Thorstein pursued him with some of his farmhands and came upon Helgi by some islands, south of Hvitstadir, known as Langeyjar. Helgi and Thorstein fought, and Helgi was badly wounded. Knowing where both parties had gone, some other men arrived on the spot. They had good intentions towards both men and after they had separated them, they had them agree that Thorstein purchase the marshlands and compensate Helgi, as the law dictated, for the bloody wound he had dealt him.

13

There was a man named Thorir who lived at Hrofa in Steingrimsfjord. He was a loud and overbearing man and much disliked. He fell out with one of King Olaf's men at the market in Steingrimsfjord and wounded the man badly. There was no settlement, and when the king heard news of what had happened he was not pleased.

He spoke to Thorgeir Havarsson: 'I want you, Thorgeir, to avenge the wounding of one of my men in Iceland, so that the people there will think twice before attacking my men.'

Thorgeir answered, 'I expect I will be able to avenge this offence against you.'

The king said, 'I am asking you because I believe you will do my will in this matter.'

Thorgeir replied, 'I am obliged to do as you bid me.'

Thorgeir prepared his ship to sail to Iceland early that summer, and good winds brought him to Vadil. From there, he went west to Reykjaholar and began to build a hall. There was a man named Veglag engaged in building the hall with Thorgeir, and each of them took one side of the construction. The hall was panelled throughout and floored with boards, but there were no divisions or chambers. The interior was intact right up to the time when Bishop Magnus Gizurarson lived at Skalholt.[30]

Early in the following winter, Thorgeir went north to Hrofa in Steingrimsfjord, and Veglag the carpenter went with him. They came to the farm late in the evening and knocked on the door. A woman came to answer, and she greeted them and asked them their names. Thorgeir told her their true identities, then asked whether Thorir, the farmer, was at home. She said he was.

Thorgeir said, 'Ask him to come outside.'

She went in and told Thorir that some men were outside and 'want to meet you'.

He said, 'Who are they?'

She answered, 'I believe Thorgeir Havarsson is here.'

Thorir stood up, picked up his spear and went to the door. He rested the point of his spear on the threshold and greeted the two men.

Thorgeir ignored the greeting and said, 'The reason I am here is to find out what you intend to do to repay King Olaf honourably for the shameful deed you have committed on his follower.'

Thorir replied, 'Are you party to this matter?'

Thorgeir answered, 'I have become party to this matter on the king's behalf.'

Thorir said, 'It may well be that you are here as the king's representative, but I seriously doubt that these are the king's words you speak.'

Thorgeir replied, 'It is true that you do not hear him speak personally, but it may well be that you feel his power.'

Then, without warning, Thorgeir thrust his spear at Thorir's chest and it pierced right through him. Thorir fell backwards into the house, dead. Shortly afterwards, Thorgeir and his companion left and there is no further report of his journey until he reached home at Reykjaholar.

Thormod composed the following verse about this incident:

11.
Long I remember how Thorgeir,
skilful thane of the board's raven,   *board's raven*: ship
speared Thorir's worthy son   *Thorir's ... son*: Thorir in the saga
so beautifully to death.
This steerer of the board's stallion   *board's stallion*: ship
avenged the wounds of Odd   *Odd*: in the saga, Thorfinn or Bergfinn
and left the eagles sated.
Glory and dignity in this deed.

That winter there were a great number of thefts at Reykjaholar. Numerous articles disappeared from people's trunks, and the thievery was so widespread that almost everyone had something taken no matter how strong the locks placed on them. And yet none of the locks was broken.

Illugi Arason was at home at Holar that winter. Then, after Yule, he and his brother, Thorgils, gathered together all their servants.

It was then that Thorgils spoke: 'Everyone knows that a great many items have been stolen here this winter, and much of what went missing was under lock and key. We intend to make a thorough search, and it shall begin with going through my and Illugi's trunks and then everyone else's. If nothing is found at home then we shall go to other farms and search there.'

Then they searched through each man's trunk, but nothing they looked for was found.

Veglag, the carpenter, had a large trunk which had not been searched, and Thorgils said that it must be opened up so that they might see what it contained.

Veglag said, 'I have never been subjected to being searched like a thief and I will not open the trunk.'

Thorgils said, 'You're not the only one in this. Our chests have been searched. You'll have to comply like everyone else.'

Then Veglag said, 'I don't care whether you have searched all the others, I'm not opening up my trunk.'

Illugi jumped to his feet. He was holding a hand-axe.

He went over to the trunk and said, 'I have here a master key that opens all chests and locks, and I'm going to use it to open this one if you don't give up your key.'

Veglag saw that Illugi would hack up the trunk if he did not open it, and he handed over the key. Then Illugi opened it up and found a number of keys that fit all the locks at Reykjaholar, as well as many of the items that had gone missing. Everyone now knew that it was Veglag who had stolen the missing valuables and he was forced to speak. He admitted to many thefts and then showed them where he had hidden the stolen goods in various places about the farm.

Then Illugi said, 'I reckon Veglag deserves to die for this, and I suggest that he be hanged.'

Thorgeir said, 'You wouldn't dispose of your own farmhand in this manner.'

Illugi replied, 'In my opinion it would be wrong to let such a great thief get away with this.'

Then Thorgeir said, 'Despite what you think is the right course of action, in this instance the man's price will be too costly for you. He will not be executed if I have any say in the matter.'

Illugi said, 'You're a great defender of thieves, but this one will cause you grief – and your pledge will not always be enough to save him even if he escapes justice this time. He will leave Reykjanes now and never return.'

Thorgeir said, 'Let it be as you say.'

Then Thorgeir went with Veglag west to Laugabol in Laugadal

to Bersi and Thormod and asked them to put him up until they sailed out during the Moving Days.

'Then put him aboard at Vadil,' said Thorgeir and promised them he would get the man out of the country.

Bersi and Thormod took Veglag in for Thorgeir's sake and he stayed there for the winter. Thorgeir returned to Reykjaholar and remained there for the same period of time.

[From *Flateyjarbók*]

The following spring Thorgeir and Thormod set out north for Strandir as far as Horn. One day they went to the cliffs to gather angelica, and on one grassy ledge, known since as Thorgeir's Ledge, they cut a large bundle. Thormod carried it up to the top while Thorgeir remained where he was. Suddenly the loose ground began to give way under Thorgeir's feet and he grabbed at the base of one of the angelica plants close to the roots to prevent himself from falling. It was some sixty fathoms down to the rocky beach below. He could not make his way back up, so he hung there and refused to make any attempt to call out to Thormod even at the risk of falling to certain death below.

Thormod waited up on the cliff top, thinking that Thorgeir was bound to get himself back on to the ledge. When he saw Thorgeir hanging there much longer than he expected, he went down on to the ledge and called out to him, asking him if he had enough angelica now and when, if ever, he was coming back up.

Thorgeir replied, his voice unwavering and no trace of fear in his heart.

'I reckon,' he said, 'I'll have enough once I've uprooted this piece I'm holding.'

It then occurred to Thormod that Thorgeir could not make it up alone and he stepped down on to the ledge and saw that Thorgeir was in grave peril of falling. So he grabbed hold of him and pulled him up sharply, by which time the angelica plant was almost completely uprooted. After that they returned to their hoard.

One may conclude from this incident that Thorgeir was unafraid as far as his own life was concerned, and that he proved his courage in whatever dangers he encountered, either to his body or his mind. People say that all three men – Thorgeir, Thormod and Grettir Asmundarson the Strong – had stayed at Reykjaholar at the same time, and that the combined strength of the two sworn brothers almost equalled that of Grettir.

People also say that Thorgils was asked one time at the Althing whether the men he had taken in for the winter were not the bravest in all Iceland, men who hardly knew the meaning of fear.

He replied that it was not true: 'Because Grettir was afraid of the dark and Thormod feared God.'

Of Thorgeir, however, he said that he feared absolutely nothing, and least of all sudden catastrophe.

The sworn brothers went south from Strandir with the hoard they had gathered, Thorgeir returning to Reykjaholar while Thormod went back to Laugabol.

That spring, Thorgeir made ready to sail, took Veglag aboard when he arrived, and then set out to sea with him. They stopped at the Orkneys, where Rognvald Brusason[31] had made ready for battle. There were Viking raiders all over the islands, stealing from farmers and traders, and Rognvald wanted to punish them for their evil deeds. Thorgeir sold his ship and joined forces with Rognvald.

Veglag went to Scotland, where he became a notorious thief and was later killed.

Rognvald and his companions liked Thorgeir because the more his courage was put to the test the greater it proved to be. As Thormod said:

12.

The god of sword-play, I shall tell,
fearless in battle, went
on the wave-horse with Rognvald,
when he wanted to do battle:
the son of Havar, dauntless warrior,
spared little the lives of men,
threw himself into the fray eagerly –
his deeds will live all the longer.

god of sword-play: warrior

wave-horse: ship

In fighting, Thorgeir proved to be an excellent man, brave, skilful in the use of arms and in every test of courage. Earl Rognvald also won fame in this battle against the Vikings both because he was victorious wherever he fought that summer and also because he brought peace to the farmers and merchants in the Orkneys.

14

Later that autumn, Thorgeir went to Norway and spent the winter with King Olaf where he was shown great respect. The king thanked him for redressing the wrong that Thorir had committed against him. Illugi Arason was also at court that winter.

When spring came, Illugi made ready to sail to Iceland and Thorgeir said that he wanted to go with him.

Illugi answered him thus: 'I don't think it wise that you come to Iceland. You have been very busy in many parts of that country and can expect plenty of trouble there. Here you have the respect of the king himself and no man wishes you harm. I will not take you away from the peace you enjoy here to where there is none to be had. You will not find in Iceland the great honour you are shown here daily at court.'

'It might be,' said Thorgeir, 'that I make my way to Iceland even though you do not take me there.'

Illugi prepared his ship to leave and set out to sea as soon as a good breeze was blowing. One day, some time after Illugi had left, Thorgeir went to the king and asked his permission to leave.

King Olaf said, 'It seems to me that you enjoy less good fortune in Iceland than you do here with us. Therefore, staying here, where you are in favour, seems the wiser choice.'

Thorgeir pressed the king hard on this matter, and when the king saw how much this request meant to him he said, 'What I said to you the first time we met will now come to pass – you will not be fortunate in all you do. I shall grant you leave to go to Iceland, but we will not meet again if we part company now.'

Thorgeir answered, 'I thank you for granting me leave to go, and I fully intend to return to meet you next summer.'

The king said, 'You may well intend it, but it will come to pass.'

They parted after these words. Thorgeir obtained passage to Iceland with a Norwegian named Jokul. The ship put ashore at Vadil and Thorgeir went from there to stay at Reykjaholar.

Illugi was at sea for a long time that summer, and he finally put ashore in late autumn in the north at Hraunhofn in Melrakkasletta. He brought his ship in, covered it over and employed some men to guard it for the winter, then went south into the country on his way home to Reykjaholar. Gaut Sleituson, who was mentioned earlier, came to meet Illugi before he left and obtained a place aboard his ship for the following summer.

One day, while Illugi and his companions were resting their horses, a man wearing a white hooded cape came riding over to where they had stopped. He greeted Illugi, who acknowledged the greeting and then asked who he was.

He said, 'My name is Helgi.'

Illugi said, 'Of what family are you and where do you live?'

Helgi answered, 'My family are spread all over the land, though mostly in the north. I have no home nor the good fortune to be employed all year round, but I usually find work during the summer, as I have this year. Many people recognize me when they hear my nickname.'

Illugi asked, 'What is it?'

Helgi answered, 'I am known as Helgi Selseista.'[32]

Illugi said, 'A highly unusual nickname that, but I have heard you mentioned.'

Helgi said, 'I have come here to see whether you will take me aboard next summer.'

Illugi said, 'Are you in trouble, and can you pay for your passage?'

Helgi replied, 'I am not in any trouble and I have no money or goods, but I might lighten your work because I'm quick on my feet.'

Illugi said, 'Are you highly accomplished?'

Helgi replied, 'I never compete but I have great faith in my legs and I have good lungs – no one can outrun me.'

Illugi said, 'That's useful for people who are greatly prone to fear.'

Helgi said, 'I've never had the experience of being prone to fear. But will you take me aboard or not? I need to know.'

Illugi said, 'Come and see me next spring, help me load my goods on to the ship, and I'll give you passage abroad.'

'I'm very happy with that arrangement,' said Helgi.

They parted after this. Illugi went west to Reykjaholar and remained there for the winter.

15

Two brothers lived in Garpsdal. One was named Kalf and the other Steinolf. They were young, wealthy and well-liked.

There was a woman named Thordis, who lived in Olafsdal. She was a widow, a good housewife and generally helpful. Her son, Eyjolf, lived with her. He was a promising and popular man. Thordis had a relative named Thorgeir, whom she had fostered and raised. He was an energetic man and was known as Thorgeir Hofleysa (Boundless). He was given this nickname because whenever he had any money he always extravagantly exceeded his needs.

The two foster-brothers, Eyjolf and Thorgeir, were great friends from an early age. Both were loud, full of energy and always up to something. They often upset an old woman, whom Thordis had taken in, with their rowdiness and wrestling, and the more distraught she became the more they taunted her.

One day, they were wrestling on the floor and making a great row, and they kept bumping into the woman and trampling on the work she was doing.

She said to them, 'You'll get nowhere by spoiling my work or taunting me. I shall predict what will become of you – as well as you get on with each other now, thus badly will your friendship come to an end.'

They said, 'You don't seem much of a seer to us.'

The woman said, 'No matter what you think of me, what I have spoken will come to pass.'

That spring, after Illugi and Thorgeir Havarsson had spent the winter at Reykjaholar, Thorgeir asked Illugi if he would take him aboard when he sailed from Iceland. Illugi did as he asked. Kalf and Steinolf from Garpsdal were also aboard Illugi's ship.

As they made their way to the ship that spring, Illugi said to Thorgeir, 'Cousin, I want you to go north to the ship with my men and get it ready while the Althing is in session. I have to go there to meet some friends of mine, and I'll ride north from there to join you. I want the ship fully prepared to sail when I arrive.'

Thorgeir said he would do as he was bidden. Then he rode north to the ship at Melrakkasletta while Illugi made ready to go to the Althing. Steinolf, Kalf and Helgi Selseista accompanied Thorgeir, having sent their things on ahead of them. Thorgils Arason, his son, Ari, and his brother, Illugi, rode to the Althing with a group of men from Breidafjord.

When Thorgeir came north to the harbour, he set the ship afloat and made it ready to sail. Gaut Sleituson had already arrived and mucked in and ate with a different group of men from Thorgeir. There was very little firewood in the area, and each party went out daily to collect what kindling they could – Thorgeir with his companions and Gaut with his.

One day Thorgeir went out to get some firewood while Gaut remained at camp. Gaut's cooks had set up a pot and just as the contents were about to boil, they ran out of firewood. They reported the problem to Gaut and he went over to Thorgeir's tent, took out his spear, cut off the spearhead and tossed it into his bed. He kept the shaft. Then he took Thorgeir's shield as well and went back to the fire, where he hacked up both shield and spear-shaft and burned them to heat the pot. It proved sufficient to cook the meal.

Thorgeir returned that evening and quickly noticed that his weapons were missing.

He asked who had taken 'my shield and spear'.

Gaut said, 'I took your shield and your spear-shaft and broke them up to heat our pot. We'd run out of firewood so we couldn't finish cooking – and we didn't like the idea of eating our food raw.'

There was no indication from Thorgeir that he was upset by what Gaut had done.

The following day, Gaut and his companions went out to gather some firewood and Thorgeir stayed behind to see to the ship. Thorgeir's cooks did not have enough firewood, and when they were ready to prepare the meal they told Thorgeir about the shortage. He went to Gaut's tent, took his spear and shield, hacked off the spearhead, broke up the shield and put them both under the pot. There was no longer a shortage of fuel to cook the food.

Gaut came home that evening and asked whether anyone knew the whereabouts of his spear-shaft and shield.

Thorgeir answered, 'I broke up your shield and spear-shaft today to put under our pot – my cooks were running low on firewood.'

Gaut said, 'You never tire of testing our patience.'

Thorgeir replied, 'The run of the game is decided by the first move.'

Then Gaut struck out at Thorgeir, who deflected the blow with his axe and in the process took a slight wound on the leg. Some men ran between them, grabbed hold of them and held them fast.

Thorgeir said, 'You don't need to hold me back. I have no intention of making a fight of this.'

Then they were separated, and each returned to his own tent, had his supper and lay down to rest for the night. As soon as everyone was asleep, Thorgeir rose to his feet and picked up his axe and went over to the tent where Gaut lay. He opened the tent flaps, then went over to his bed and roused him. Gaut awoke, sprang to his feet and tried to grab for a weapon, and in the very same moment Thorgeir struck at him and split him to the shoulders, wounding him mortally.

Thorgeir left and went back to his own tent. The rest of the men in Gaut's tent were woken by the sound of the death blow and they huddled round the body and covered it over. Thormod composed this verse about the incident:

13.
Gaut, the sword-brave son of Sleita,
I know from life he banished –
the bold-minded man
with his troops in the fray.
The fated man was paid with groans
in the howling of battle-swords –
he who does such deeds
often reaps a just reward.

16

One day after this event Thorgeir saw a ship sailing across the
water and into the harbour, where it docked and cast anchor
some distance from his own vessel. He boarded a small boat
with his companions and went out to the merchant ship to ask
who owned it. He was told that a Greenlander named Thorgrim Einarsson, known as Thorgrim Troll, owned it along with
a northern Icelander, Thorarin Thorvaldsson the Overbearing.
They asked who owned the other ship in the harbour and were
told it belonged to Illugi Arason, but that it was in Thorgeir's
charge at present. Thorgeir asked how many men they had on
board and was told that they had a crew of forty. Thorgeir saw
that they would be ill matched if there was any trouble since he
had only thirty fighting men of his own.

Thorgeir said, 'I want to bring this to your attention, skip-
pers. Many people say that both parties here are troublemakers
and not slow to take the offensive. So I'm going to ask you that
our valour and our courage turn not to foolishness and fighting, and that we make a peace pact between us to that end.'

Thorgrim and Thorarin took this well and they made a pact
between them. As Thormod says in a verse:

14.
Seeing he had no choice
with fewer men, Thorgeir
in his wisdom demanded
a truce of the gold-trees.

                                                        gold-trees: men

That brave man was quick
to believe all the words of those
who gave their pledges of peace
– just while they plotted against him.

Now that the truce was agreed upon, Thorgeir went back to
his ship. He had everyone's goods and valuables loaded up and
let the vessel lie anchored some distance from the shore with
the whole crew aboard, for he did not believe that Thorgrim
and Thorarin would keep to the pact they had agreed on.

Some men came across country to Thorgrim and told him of
the slaying of Gaut Sleituson, which had taken place in the harbour there but which Thorgeir had not mentioned to him.

And when Thorarin heard this news, he demanded that
Thorgrim speak to him privately and said, 'I would not have
made any pact with Thorgeir if I'd known about the slaying of
my kinsman, Gaut. Now, I want to know what support I can
expect from you if I were to avenge Gaut's death.'

Thorgrim answered, 'I will not let you stand alone in this,
but I think that Thorgeir is going to be a difficult man to
take on.'

Thorarin said, 'We'll choose a day to carry all our fine clothes,
linen and other valuables ashore and spread them out to dry
there. Perhaps some of Thorgeir's men will come to admire
them and then we'll kill them and so reduce the opposition.'

Thorgrim said, 'You can try that if you wish.'

Thorgrim and Thorarin, who were partners in both ship and
crew, were on their way to Greenland and had therefore not
brought their goods ashore.

One day when the weather was fine, Thorarin and Thorgrim
carried their cargo of fine clothes, linens and valuables ashore
and spread them out to dry. On the same day, Kalf and Steinolf
went ashore with ten other men to get some water, and when
they saw the goods laid out there, three of the men ran off to
take a closer look. They were killed as soon as they arrived.
Then Thorgrim and Thorarin and their men pursued Kalf, captured him and Steinolf, and bound them in fetters. After that
they killed three other men by the water. At the outset, Helgi

Selseista dealt one of the attackers a death blow, then ran off. Some of them ran after him but they did not manage to catch him. He ran day and night across the highlands and did not stop until he came to the Althing at Thingvellir, where he told Thorgils and Illugi of what had happened at Hraunhofn at the time of his escape.

17

After the events related here, Thorgrim and his men took the trading vessel on which Kalf and the others had come ashore and rowed out to their own ship. Thorgeir was aboard his ship with eight men and had no knowledge of what had taken place on land since their view was barred by a hill which lay between them and the watering place. Before Thorgeir knew it, Thorarin and his men had arrived alongside his ship in their main trading vessel and two smaller boats, all armed for battle.

Thorgeir and his men took to their weapons and set up a strong defence. Then Thorgrim's men moved their ship up against Thorgeir's ship and a hard battle ensued. The attacking party boarded Thorgeir's ship quickly and exchanged a few quick blows. Thorgeir wielded his axe with both hands. For a long time no one managed to strike back at him since none desired to be laid to rest for the night by his axe – yet that was the fate that many of them suffered. All of Thorgeir's men were soon slain, while Thorgeir himself ran back to the prow and defended himself from there, for he was greatly outnumbered. As Thormod says in his drapa:

15.
This hardy ruler of riches
made his stand on the stream-deer's prow   *stream-deer*: ship
and fought two score men, mightily
– famed for his strength since a youth –
before the battle-tree   *battle-tree*: warrior
was laid low on his ship
with no small show of valour –
wounds were dealt, for sure.

16.
Thorgeir taught how a fighter must stand
fast by his kinsmen's side
boisterous though it be
to follow such a man.
From the north came news
of the spreader of hand-rock,   *hand-rock*: gold; its *spreader*:
I heard how Thorgeir's heart   generous man, Thorgeir
was brave beyond compare.

   All who knew how valiantly he had fought praised the stand
he made, and they all said the same of his brave defence. None
thought his equal had ever been found. Thorgeir struck hard
and fast with great power, his courage never wavering – and
this courage was both his shield and his armour. No man was
known to have put up such a fight as he. It was the Almighty
who touched Thorgeir's heart and put such fearlessness into his
breast, and thus his courage was neither inborn nor of human-
kind but came from the Creator on high.
   Now Thorgrim and his party's attack upon Thorgeir proved
to require greater manhood than patting their wives' bellies.
Indeed, they could hardly get near him and his demise cost
them dearly. As Thormod said in his poem Thorgeir's Drapa,
Thorgeir slew fourteen men before he fell, two of whom are
named in those verses.[33] One was a Norwegian named Mar,
the first to inflict a wound upon Thorgeir. He struck at Thorgeir's hand, and as he wounded him, Thorgeir struck him his
death blow. The other man named was also a Norwegian,
called Thorir, who plunged his spear into Thorgeir. But Thorgeir, though wounded, closed in on him and slew him, too.
   Thormod wrought the following verses on this event:

17.
I heard how he who gave   *he*: Thorgeir
the hawk its prey was never   *hawk*: raven; its *prey*: carnage
dismayed by the bandiers
of bickering swords.

Mar was one, and Thorir,
whom the nimble-tongued one slew.
I learned that this came about
after their truce was broken.

18.
Unflinching, the warrior dealt
death by sword, before he fell,
to thirteen men – himself
a mighty guardian of ships.
Here I end the tally of foes
that he slew with bold deeds.
Now my tripping verse
draws to its close.

Though Thorir had fallen and his spear remained in Thorgeir's flesh, piercing him clean through, Thorgeir did not fall. Instead, he exchanged a few quick blows with Thorarin and Thorgrim, who bore down on him and overcame him so that he was finally cut down and lost his life. Thorarin the Overbearing cut off Thorgeir's head and took it away with him.

Some people say that he had shown such courage that they cut him open to see what kind of heart lay there, and that it had been very small. Some hold it true that a brave man's heart is smaller than that of a coward, for a small heart has less blood than a large one and is therefore less prone to fear.[34] If a man's heart sinks in his breast and fails him, they say it is because his heart's blood and his heart have become afraid.

18

After that battle, Thorgrim and Thorarin broke up their partnership, for Thorarin thought he had won a great victory and expected it to bring him honour here in Iceland. Thorgrim took the ship and Thorarin the valuables. Thorgrim went to Greenland and prospered there.

Thorarin obtained some horses and men and rode south

from the harbour with a party of eleven. He had Thorgeir's head in a leather bag tied to his saddle straps to show off his great victory.[35] Whenever they stopped to rest, they would amuse themselves by taking the head out of the bag, putting it on a mound and laughing at it. When they came to Eyjafjord, they stopped close to Naust and, as usual, they took out Thorgeir's head and set it on a mound there. But now the head seemed ghastly with its eyes and mouth open and its tongue hanging out, and the sight of it appalled and terrified them. So they dug a hole beside the head with their axes and pushed the head into it and covered it over with turf.

The people at Sletta carried ashore the bodies of all the men who had been killed on Thorgeir's ship, and buried them in the harbour. It would have been too great an effort for them to take the bodies to a church because in those days there was no church anywhere near the harbour.

Kalf and Steinolf were released from their fetters after the battle and they helped the men at Sletta to bury the bodies, and stood guard over the goods that were aboard until Illugi arrived. Even though Christianity was still new in Iceland at that time, it was not common practice to take goods and valuables of those who had been slain. Illugi sailed north to Sletta that summer.

Thormod Kolbrun's Poet grieved for a long time after Thorgeir's death, and that summer he left Vadil and went abroad. Eyjolf from Olafsdal and Thorgeir Hofleysa, his foster-brother, sailed out from the Grimsa estuary and came to one of the islands at Lofoten in Norway.

Thormod Kolbrun's Poet went to see King Olaf to pay his respects and was well received. The king inquired from which family he came and whose son he was.

Thormod replied, 'I am an Icelander. My name is Thormod, son of Bersi.'

The king said, 'Are you the man they call Kolbrun's Poet, sworn brother of Thorgeir Havarsson?'

'Yes,' said Thormod, 'that's exactly who I am.'

The king said, 'Then you shall enjoy our favour for his sake and are welcome here. And you shall know that I account myself deeply offended at the slaying of my follower Thorgeir and would be grateful to have him avenged.'

Then Thormod spoke this verse:

19.
King, he who long shall dwell
at your knee needs take heart –
and the king weighs word for word
with his careful answer.
Few of my kin have dared address
a king, though never reproached
with lack of courage – I'd rather
discuss my other task.

The king said, 'I think we shall enjoy your poetry.'

Thus Thormod became one of King Olaf's men.

A ship sailed to Norway that summer from Greenland, captained by a man named Skuf, who was a Greenlander by origin. Skuf was a great merchant, and a wise and well-liked man. He was a friend of King Olaf and in his paid employ. Skuf went to court and remained there for the winter. Illugi Arason, Steinolf, Eyjolf, Kalf and Thorgeir Hofleysa were also there for the same period of time.

The following spring, when one year had passed since Thorgeir Havarsson was slain, Thorgils Arason and his son, Ari, started a case against Thorarin and the others in his party for the killing of Thorgeir, and they made much of the deed that had been done there. The matter was settled at the assembly, and Thorgils demanded that the compensation for slaying Thorgeir be two hundred pieces of silver and that it be paid there on the spot. Thorgils also determined that Gudmund the Powerful[36] be paid one hundred pieces of silver. That summer, Thorarin was slain at a gathering in Eyjafjord.

That same summer, Kalf and Steinolf sailed to Iceland and arrived at Vadil on Bardastrond. From there they went home to their farm in Garpsdal.

Eyjolf and Thorgeir Hofleysa bought a ship in Norway and set out for Iceland as soon as they were ready to sail. They were tossed about at sea for quite some time and finally arrived at Borgarfjord late that autumn, but were divided in opinion as to where to put ashore. Eyjolf wanted to sail to Straumfjord because the winds favoured it, while Thorgeir Hofleysa wanted to let the ship drift and see whether the winds might carry them past the glacier and on to Dagverdarnes. They went to the mast and asked how many of the crew were in favour of sailing towards land and how many wanted to let the ship drift, and since the men were tired of being at sea the majority elected to sail towards land. The foster-brothers were so angry that they went for their weapons, but the crew made sure that they did not fight. Then they sailed towards Straumfjord.

When the ship put ashore, Thorgeir Hofleysa obtained a horse and rode until he reached Garpsdal in the west, where he stayed with the two brothers, Steinolf and Kalf. Eyjolf stayed with the ship until it was put up and covered over, and then went home to his mother in Olafsdal and stayed there for the winter.

19

The old fortune teller, mentioned earlier, fell ill that winter and was laid up for a long time before she finally passed away the night after Palm Sunday. Her body was moved by boat to Reykjanes since there was no church near Olafsdal. The closest was at Holar, and it was there that Eyjolf and his farmhands took her. After the burial, the weather worsened. It became very cold and snow started to fall. Ice covered a large part of the fjord and no ship could approach Olafsdal.

Thorgils said to Eyjolf, 'My advice is that you do not return home until Easter has passed. Then I will lend you some men for your ship to get there, if you can get past the ice. If you cannot make your way through, I will lend you a horse to ride there. If the need arises, your farmhands may return earlier.'

Eyjolf answered, 'I will accept your offer.'

Eyjolf's farmhands returned home by land, making their way around Kroksfjord. Eyjolf himself stayed at Holar till almost the end of the week after Easter, and on the fifth day of that week he told Thorgils that he wanted to leave. Thorgils said that the choice was his, and he had a horse shod for him and offered to send a man with him if he needed one. Eyjolf said that he preferred to ride alone, and he left Reykjanes, making his way around Berufjord and Kroksfjord.

As he approached Garpsdal, Kalf and Steinolf were standing outside by one of the walls talking, when they thought they saw some men making their way across the fields. It appeared to them that it was Thorgeir Havarsson and the nine men who were slain on the ship with him. All the men were covered in blood, as they walked along the fields and away from the farm, disappearing again as they came to where the river flowed past the farm. The brothers were amazed at this sight and they went back into the house.

There was a man named Onund who looked after the cattle at Garpsdal. He came out of the cattle shed after the brothers went into the farmhouse and saw a man riding at the outer edge of the fields, mounted on a fine horse. The man was armed with a sword and a spear and had a helmet on his head, and as he came closer to the farmhouse, he recognized the man as Eyjolf. Onund went into the main room, and there was hardly anyone in there – only Thorgeir Hofleysa and a few women.

Onund spoke, 'Eyjolf is riding through here.'

When Thorgeir heard this he ran outside with a spear in his hand. By this time, Eyjolf was riding past the house. Thorgeir ran after him, but Eyjolf rode on, not seeing a man chasing him. Eventually, he came to the river at Garpsdal, saw that it was in spate and looked for the best place to cross. Thorgeir called out to him and told him to hold up if he dared. Eyjolf heard him call out, looked round and saw Thorgeir running towards him. He jumped down from his horse and ran towards him. The two men clashed swords and ran each other through, and both died in the same instant. Thus the old woman's prophecy came true.

Kalf and Steinolf came into the main room of the farmhouse, after the faintness they felt had left them.

'Where is Thorgeir?' they asked.

And they were told that he had left armed with a spear after

Onund the cattle-minder had said he had seen Eyjolf passing
by. The brothers left quickly and made their way across the
farm to the river where they found the two men. Both were
doomed but still breathing. Steinolf and Kalf sat by them until
they breathed their last and then took their bodies to the
church.

20

When Thormod Kolbrun's Poet had been with King Olaf for
one winter, Skuf made his ship ready to leave for Greenland.

Thormod went to see the king and said, 'I would like your
permission to go to Greenland this summer with Skuf.'

The king replied, 'What business have you in Greenland.
Do you intend to avenge the death of your sworn brother,
Thorgeir?'

Thormod answered, 'I don't know what fate awaits me in
that matter.'

The king said, 'I will not forbid your leaving because I
believe I know what you want.'

After these words, they parted company and Thormod
obtained passage with Skuf. When they were almost ready to
leave, they went to see the king to thank him for all the friendship he had shown them. The king wished them well and gave
Thormod a gold ring and a sword at their parting. Then Thormod and Skuf went off to the ship.

As they reached the ship, a man walked out on to the gangplank. He was a big strong man with broad shoulders and was
wearing a hood that prevented them from seeing his face. He
called out his greetings to Skuf, who accepted them and then
asked the man his name. He said he was called Gest.

Skuf asked, 'From where do you hail?'

Gest replied, 'My folk are spread far and wide. But the
reason I've come to see you is to find out whether you will take
me aboard to Greenland this summer.'

Skuf said, 'I don't know you, so I'll have to ask my crew
whether they accept you as one of their number or not.'

Gest said, 'I thought it was the skipper who gave the orders, not the crew. You can count on me to do what is required of me – I'll not be a burden to the others.'

At the end of this exchange Skuf promised the man passage. Then Gest went up to the settlement and returned shortly afterwards with baggage so large and heavy that two men would have had difficulty lifting it. He took a place behind the hold, had little to do with the other men and kept himself to himself.

Then Skuf put out to sea, and met with such winds that the ship was in dire peril from the crashing waves. But when trouble came Gest proved his real worth, and it seemed to many of the crew that he had the strength of two men. Despite this, Thormod and Gest were at odds with each other in all they did.

Then, one day, Gest and Thormod happened to be bailing water together – in those times they used buckets rather than bilge-gutters. Thormod was down in the keel filling buckets while Gest was up on deck emptying them overboard. Thormod was not a strong man and often he did not lift the buckets high enough. Gest told him to hold them up higher, but Thormod made no answer and continued as before. Then, when it was least expected, Gest let a bucket of seawater fall back into Thormod's arms. Thoroughly drenched, Thormod leapt up from his bailing and reached for his weapons. Gest did the same. They wanted to fight.

Skuf spoke: 'On board a trading vessel in the middle of the ocean is not the right place for men to have differences. Indeed, it may cause much harm, for seldom will a voyage go well if the men are at odds. Now, I'm going to require both of you to refrain from fighting while you are still at sea.'

They both complied.

The ship was tossed about on the ocean for a long time and encountered constant bad weather. One storm sundered the sail-yard and the sail was thrown overboard. The men grabbed it and dragged it back aboard, and here Gest's effort was by far the most effective.

Skuf knew that the men he had brought from Greenland were not very skilled at crafts, but he had noticed that both Thormod and Gest had some ability in carving wood, so he spoke to Thormod and asked, 'Will you put our sail-yard back together?'

Thormod answered, 'I don't have the skill. Ask Gest to repair the sail-yard. He's so strong that he could simply ram the two ends together.'

Then Skuf went to Gest and asked him to repair the sail-yard.

Gest answered, 'I don't have the skill. Ask Thormod to do it. He has such a way with words he could charm them together with verse. That should hold them tight. But since necessity calls, I will shape one end if Thormod takes the other.'

Then each was given his axe and each carved one of the ends. Gest glanced over his shoulder at Thormod, who had finished his end of the sail-yard and was sitting on the hold. Gest carved his piece of wood a little longer, and when he was done he placed the two pieces together and saw that neither needed any more work. So, he put them together and then fastened the sail, and they were able to sail again.

They reached Greenland late in the autumn, and sailed into Eiriksfjord. At that time Thorkel, the son of Leif Eiriksson, was head of the Eiriksfjord settlement. He was a great chieftain, both powerful and well-liked, and a good friend of King Olaf. Thorkel quickly came down to the ship as soon as it had pulled ashore and bought what goods he needed from the skipper and the crew. Skuf informed Thorkel that one of King Olaf's followers was aboard, a man named Thormod, and told him that the king had sent him there to provide assistance if the need arose. These words resulted in Thormod staying at Thorkel's farm, Brattahlid.

Skuf lived at Stokkanes, on the opposite side of Eiriksfjord to Brattahlid. A man named Bjarni lived at Skuf's farm, a wise and well-liked fellow who was an accomplished and skilled worker. He looked after the farm while Skuf was away travelling. They owned the farm jointly and did well together. While Thormod went to stay at Brattahlid, Gest stayed at a farm called Vik in Einarsfjord, which belonged to a man named Thorgrim.

21

Thorgrim Troll, the son of Einar, lived in Einarsfjord on Longunes. He was a godi,[37] a great and powerful chieftain and an excellent champion who had many men under his command. With him lived his sister, named Thordis, who had been married to a man named Hamund. Thordis's four sons also lived at Thorgrim's farm: the first was named Bodvar; the second, Falgeir; the third, Thorkel; and the fourth, Thord. All of them were good and agile warriors. Thorgrim Troll had another sister, Thorunn, who also lived in Einarsfjord at a farm called Langanes. She had a son named Ljot, who was a large man. All of Thorgrim's nephews were aggressive and overbearing.

A woman named Sigrid lived at a farm called Hamar, which was a good and profitable homestead. Her son, named Sigurd, lived with her. He was an agile man and well-liked, but though he was not loud and unruly he did not show the same friendliness to all.

There was a slave named Lodin at Brattahlid, a good worker, and he shared his bed with a woman named Sigrid who was assigned to work for Thormod. There was a separate building at Brattahlid, quite close to the farmhouse, where Thorkel and his men slept and where a lantern burned each and every night. All the other folk slept at the farm. Now Lodin felt that Sigrid spent far too long in the men's building at night and that she was paying him less attention than she once had. Then he remembered the short verse that had been composed about loose women:

20.
On a turning wheel
were their hearts shaped,
and filled with treachery.

He spoke to Sigrid and told her that he did not want her to stay long in the men's building during the night, and she answered him in her own way.

[From *Flateyjarbók*]

He felt that she did not twine her fingers around his neck as she used to and that made him angry. A man's anger resides in his gall, his lifeblood in his heart, his memory in his brains, his ambition in his lungs, his laughter in his spleen and his desire in his liver.

One evening, Thorkel and Thormod were about to go out to where they were housed, and Sigrid was with them. Lodin grabbed hold of her and she tried to pull herself loose. When Thormod saw this, he took Sigrid's hand and attempted to tug her free from Lodin's grasp, but it was not to be done so easily.

Thorkel watched them struggle, and then said, 'Let Sigrid go where she wishes. She has nothing to hide about staying late where we are put up, and I shall see to it that no shame befalls either one of you. You can watch over her while she's not in my charge.'

22

As Yule drew near, Thorkel had some ale especially brewed for the occasion. It was also to show his generosity, for such festivities were a rare occurrence in Greenland. He invited all of his friends to his home and the place was full of people. Skuf and Bjarni from Stokkanes were there at Yule and they brought furniture, tapestries and goblets with them. And everyone drank and celebrated Yule with great gladness and enjoyment.

On the last day of Yule they all got ready to leave, and Lodin handed them their garments, as well as the swords and gloves he had been looking after. Then he brought out Skuf and Bjarni's boat and the farmhands loaded the goblets and tapestries into it. Lodin was wearing a sealskin coat and sealskin breeches.

When he and three other men went into the main room, only Thormod and Bjarni were there. Thormod lay on a bench at the front end of the raised platform, and as they came in Lodin grabbed hold of Thormod's feet, tugged him down to the floor and dragged him across it. Bjarni leapt up, took hold of Lodin round the waist and threw him down hard. Then he cursed the others, who were still dragging Thormod, and told them to let him go, and they obeyed him.

Then Thormod stood up and said to Bjarni, 'We Icelanders think nothing of such pranks. We're used to doing such things in skin-throwing games.'[38]

Then the men left as if nothing had happened.

When Skuf and Bjarni were ready to set off, Thorkel came out to the boat with them along with his men. They had a ferry boat and a plank led from it to the shore. Bjarni stood by the ferry and waited for Skuf while the latter spoke to Thorkel. Lodin was quite close to the ferry boat and handed over their garments. Thormod was also close by.

And when it was least expected, Thormod drew out an axe from under his cloak and struck at Lodin's head so that he fell to the ground, dead.

Thorkel heard the noise and turned around to see Lodin lying there. He ordered his men to go and kill Thormod, but they were too taken aback. Bjarni said that Thormod should go aboard the boat – which is what he did – then Bjarni and Skuf followed him. Once they were aboard, they drew in the gangplank. Thorkel urged his men to attack them, and was ready to fight Skuf and Bjarni if they did not hand Thormod over to him. But they would not surrender him.

Then Skuf said, 'Wanting Thormod killed is a grave mistake, Thorkel. He is your guest and the king's follower and poet. His life would cost you dearly if King Olaf heard that you had him killed, especially since he was sent to you to help if the need arose. This proves, as so often before, that anger is blind to the truth. We are prepared to offer you compensation for the man Thormod has slain and the loss it has caused you.'

Thorkel was calmed by these words. A good many people helped them come to an agreement, but in the end it was Skuf who awarded Thorkel the right to decide on the sum. After that Thormod went to stay at Stokkanes.

23

Skuf and Bjarni had a farmhand named Egil. He was a large, strong man with an ugly face, and he was clumsy and stupid. He was nicknamed Egil the Fool.

Thormod was unhappy for long periods of time. Skuf and Bjarni asked him if there was anything they could do to relieve his sadness.

Thormod answered, 'I would like you to give me a man who could accompany me wherever I wanted to go.'

They said they would do this, and asked him to choose whichever of the farmhands he wanted.

Thormod replied, 'Then I choose Egil the Fool. He's a big, strong fellow and stupid enough to do what he's told.'

They agreed, but were very surprised at his choice.

[From *Flateyjarbók*]

So Egil became Thormod's companion and the daughters of Stupidity – Conceit and False-reckoning – tricked him so often that he hardly knew who he was.

Thormod had Bjarni make him a special broad axe and told him what he wanted. It was hammered right down to the cutting edge, had no weal to obstruct it and was thus extremely sharp.

The summer after these events, people gathered at the Gardar Assembly in Einarsfjord.[39] Those who came from Eiriksfjord had covered their booths, and they were separated from the place where the Einarsfjord people had their camp by the higher ground that lay between them. Most of the people had their booths ready, but Thorgrim had still not arrived. Then, a little later, he was sighted. He sailed in on a splendid ship, with a fully armed crew of fighting men. Thorgrim was so overbearing that no one even dared to exchange words with him. As always, the Greenlanders had their hunting and fishing gear aboard.

When Thorgrim's ship reached land, people went down to the shore to look at the magnificent vessel and its well-armed crew. Thormod was there, and he picked up a seal-hunting spear that they had cast ashore to look at it.

Then, one of Thorgrim's crew grabbed at the spear and said, 'Let go of that spear, man! Holding on to it won't do you any good, and besides I don't expect you know how to use it.'

Thormod replied, 'I'm not sure you can use it with more skill than I.'

'There is no doubt about the matter,' said the man.

Then Thormod spoke this verse:

21.

He thinks he knows better than I
how to wield this seal-spear
– the shield of Balder boasts –   *shield of Balder*: warrior
the sea-steed's tree races over rocks.   *sea-steed*: ship; its *tree*: seafarer
I remember more clearly whom
the brave-hearted king placed first
in his wall of shields; upon me
he who had gold bestowed it.

Then Thormod went to Thorgrim's booth, which was being covered and furnished magnificently.

It happened that one fine day at the assembly all the people at Skuf and Bjarni's booth had left except Thormod, who remained behind and slept. He had covered himself over with a double-layered fur cloak, black on one side and white on the other. He had been asleep for some time, and when he awoke he saw that everyone had gone. This surprised him since there were so many there when he fell asleep.

At that moment, Egil came running into the booth and said, 'You're too far away here. There's some excellent entertainment going on.'

Thormod asked, 'Where have you come from? And what entertainment are you talking about?'

Egil answered, 'I was at Thorgrim Einarsson's booth. That's where most of the others at the assembly are too.'

Thormod said, 'And what kind of entertainment is taking place there?'

Egil said, 'Thorgrim's telling a story.'

Thormod said, 'This story he's telling, who is it about?'

Egil answered, 'I couldn't tell you who it's about, but I can tell you one thing – he certainly knows how to tell a good, entertaining tale. He's sitting on a chair outside his booth and people are sitting all around, listening to him.'

Thormod said, 'Surely you can name someone in the story, especially since you say it's so enjoyable.'

Egil said, 'There's a man called Thorgeir in the story, a great warrior. And it seemed to me that Thorgrim himself was in it quite a lot and did quite a bit of the attacking, as you might imagine. I wish you'd go over there and listen to the entertainment.'

'Perhaps I shall,' said Thormod, and he stood up and put on his fur cloak with the black side turned outwards.

Then he picked up his axe, put on his hood and walked over to Thorgrim's booth, taking Egil with him. They stopped by the wall of the booth and listened from there, but they could hardly hear what was being said from that distance. It had been a bright day with a good deal of sunshine, but as Thormod reached the booth the weather began to thicken. Thormod looked by turns up at the sky and then down at the ground in front of him.

Egil said, 'What are you doing that for?'

Thormod answered, 'Because both the sky and the earth indicate that a great crash is imminent.'

Egil said, 'And what does such a great crash usually mean?'

Thormod replied, 'Such crashes always portend important tidings. Now, should you hear such a sound then you must do what you can to keep out of harm's way. Run back to the booth as fast as you can and take refuge there.'

As they were speaking, there was a great shower of rain, a downpour that no one had expected, so that they all ran off to their booths. Some of them went into Thorgrim's booth and crowded the entrance. Thorgrim stayed in his chair and waited for the throng to disperse.

Then Thormod said to Egil, 'You wait here while I go to the front of the booth and find out what's happening. But if you hear that great blow, then you run back to our booth as fast as you can.'

Then Thormod went to the front of the booth, to where Thorgrim was sitting and said, 'What story were you telling earlier?'

Thorgrim answered, 'It can't be told in a few words. It's a story of great import. But what is your name?'

Thormod replied, 'My name is Otrygg (Unreliable).'

'Whose son are you?' asked Thorgrim.

'The son of Tortrygg (Untrustworthy).'

That made Thorgrim rise from his seat, and then Thormod struck him on the head, splitting him to the shoulders.

Then he hid his axe under his fur cloak and sat down and held up Thorgrim's back and shouted, 'Come out here! Someone has cut Thorgrim down!'

A great many people came over and saw the wound, and they asked Thormod if he knew who had wounded Thorgrim.

Thormod answered, 'I saw him here just a moment ago, and I rushed over to hold him up after he was wounded, but I didn't see where his killer went. Now, some of you come and hold him while the rest go and look for the man who slew him.'

So some of them supported Thorgrim's body while Thormod went off. Then he walked along the coast until he passed a small headland, and there he turned his cloak inside out so that the white fur was showing.

When Egil heard the great blow that Thormod dealt Thorgrim, he ran back to Skuf's booth. Some people saw him running and believed him to be the man who had wounded Thorgrim. Egil was terrified when he saw them chasing after him, armed, and when they caught him, he shook from head to foot with fear.

[From *Flateyjarbók*]

Every bone in his body shook, all two hundred and fourteen of them. All his teeth chattered, and there were thirty of them. And all the veins in his skin trembled with fear, and there were four hundred and fifteen of them.

As soon as they saw Egil they realized that he could not be

the man who had slain Thorgrim, and the fear left him like heat from iron.

Then they went off to the booths to search for the man, but they did not find him. They went down to the sea and round the headland that jutted out into the water, where they met a man wearing a white fur cloak. They asked him his name. He said it was Vigfus (Eager-to-kill). Then they asked him where he was going.

He answered them, 'I'm looking for the man who struck Thorgrim.'

And since they were moving at quite a pace in opposite directions, they were soon past each other.

Skuf and Bjarni found that Thormod was missing, and thought it not unlikely that he had made the attack since they had heard what the king of Norway said about avenging Thorgeir Havarsson. And when the fuss had died down a little, they stole away into a boat, filled it with provisions and rowed out past the headland where the man named Vigfus had been spotted in his white fur cloak. When they reached the place, they saw that the man was Thormod and they put ashore and told him to get into the boat. He did so. Then they asked him whether he had struck Thorgrim, and he told them he had. They asked him to tell them what happened and how great a wound he had dealt him.

Thormod spoke this verse:

22.
My left hand is no hindrance.
Many instances I recall:
the poet's fame would have been
dashed to the ground had I dealt
a soft blow to the black head
of that bringer of piercing storms,   *piercing storms*: showers of
for I aimed death at the god   arrows or spears, battle
of the life-benighting sword.   *god of the . . . sword*: warrior

'It probably wasn't such a great blow,' said Thormod, 'since it was struck by a left-handed man, but I thought it was enough to finish the job so I left it at that.'

Then Skuf said, 'You were fortunate they didn't recognize you while you held his head or when they ran into you on the headland.'

Then Thormod spoke a verse:

23.
Great wonder that the trees
of steel-hail knew me not,   *steel-hail*: battle; its *trees*: warriors
nor my full crop of black hair;
much marks my speech too.
But I escaped far, for a longer
lease of life was fated
for the god of sweeping   *god of sweeping sword-storms*: warrior
    sword-storms,
but death for those gold-trees.   *gold-trees*: men

'I'm an easy man to recognize,' said Thormod, 'with my dark, curly hair and my stammer, but it was not my time to die. Perhaps there was some reason for my being spared. Perhaps some of Thorgrim's kinsmen are fated to be laid low before I am.'

Then Bjarni said, 'You should let this suffice as revenge for Thorgeir. You have done what was required of you.'

Then Thormod spoke a verse:

24.
I did not vie for vengeance
with the many but fed the raven's
maw through clash of steel.
I slew the god of sword-beds.   *sword-beds*: shields;
I, the swarthy man, made my axe   their *god*: swordsman, Thorgrim
sing out and fulfilled my duty.
May more of Thorgeir's friends
avenge him further still.

'I don't think,' said Bjarni, 'that you need go any further in avenging Thorgeir. You have already done a great deed in slaying the second most important chieftain in the whole of

Greenland. You're a foreigner here and alone, and it's not certain that you'll be able to escape. Thorgrim leaves many able kinsmen behind him, and they're good fighting men, too.'

So they took Thormod to Eiriksfjord and went with him to a cave, which now bears his name, in the sea cliffs on the opposite side of the fjord to Stokkanes. With the cliff both below and above it, the cave is hard to approach from either direction.

Skuf and Bjarni said to Thormod, 'Now stay here in this cave and we'll return here when the assembly is over.'

So they left and went back to the assembly. Thormod's absence there led people to suspect that it was he who had slain Thorgrim. Bodvar and Falgeir initiated a case against him and he was deemed guilty and made an outlaw. When the assembly was over, all returned home.

Skuf and Bjarni went back to Thormod and gave him some food and other provisions that he needed. They told him he had been outlawed, and that he would have no peace at all if anyone knew of his whereabouts. Then they said they would come back every once in a while to see him. There was a large grass ledge in front of the cave on to which a man, if he were nimble enough, could jump down to from the top of the cliff.

Thormod found the cave dull for there was little for him to do to pass the time, and one fine day he left. He climbed up the cliff face, taking his axe with him, and when he had gone a short distance from the cave he met a man journeying there. He was a large man with an unpleasant and off-putting appearance, one who would have been hard pressed to find a companion. He wore a cloak sewn from all sorts of rags and tatters, which overlapped each other like the folds in a sheep's stomach. On his head, he wore a hood made in the same way, and it was covered with lice.

[From *Flateyjarbók*]

Since the sun shone down hotly, the fully fed lice kept their distance from him and nested not in his skin. Instead, they bedded down in the reaches of his tatters and baked themselves there in the sunshine.

Thormod asked the man his name.

He answered, 'My name is Oddi.'

Thormod asked, 'Of what kin?'

He replied, 'I'm a vagabond, though bound to this district, and they call me Oddi Louse. I wander about mostly. But I'm not dishonest and I know a thing or two – and good people deal fairly with me. And what is your name?'

Thormod answered, 'My name is Torrad (Abstruse).'

Oddi asked, 'And what do you do, Torrad?'

Thormod replied, 'I am a merchant. Would you like to trade with me?'

Oddi said, 'I have little to trade. What would you have of me?'

'I want to buy that coat of yours.'

Oddi answered, 'There's no need for you to poke fun at me.'

Thormod said, 'I am not poking fun. I will trade you the cloak I'm wearing for yours if you can get a message to Stokkanes for me by this evening. Tell Skuf and Bjarni that you have met a man today named Torrad and swapped clothes with him. That's all I ask of you. Do this and you may keep the coat.'

Oddi replied, 'Getting across the fjord is no easy task. You need a ship for that. But perhaps there's some chance that I can board one and reach Stokkanes by evening.'

So they exchanged cloaks. Oddi took the black cloak and Torrad put on the rag cloak.

Then Thormod went to Einarsfjord where he met a shepherd who worked for Thordis at Longunes. He asked him whether Thordis's sons were at home.

The shepherd answered, 'Bodvar is not at home. His brothers were here last night, but they've gone off to fish now.'

Thormod answered, 'I see.'

The shepherd assumed Thormod was Oddi Louse. They parted ways and Thormod went to Thordis's boathouse and stayed there, and at dusk he saw the three brothers row into land. Thorkel was at the prow, Thord amidships and Falgeir at the stern. As they put ashore, Thorkel stood by the prow and was about to fasten the boat. Then Thormod came out of the boathouse, and they thought he was Oddi Louse. Suddenly, Thormod turned to Thorkel and dealt him a two-handed blow to the head, and cleft him through. He died on the spot.

Then Thormod turned and ran, throwing off the rag cloak as he went. Thord and Falgeir chased after him, but he ran at great pace to the cliff edge above the cave, then jumped down on to the grass ledge that lay in front of it. As Thormod landed on the grass, Thord was right at his heels and leapt after him, but he twisted his knee and fell forward. Then Thormod struck him so hard between the shoulder blades that the axe sunk in up to the shaft.

Before he could remove the axe from the wound, Falgeir leapt down on to the ledge and struck out at him, catching him between the shoulder blades and wounding him badly. Having no weapon, Thormod grabbed hold of Falgeir and wrestled with him, but he could feel that his opponent was stronger than he. Things did not look good. He was sorely wounded and weaponless. Then his thoughts turned to King Olaf and he hoped that the king's good fortune would assist him. At that moment, the axe fell from Falgeir's hand down over the rocks and into the sea. Thormod was encouraged since neither of them had a weapon now.

Then both fell from the cliff into the sea below, and tried to swim and to push each other under. Thormod felt his strength waning. He was badly wounded and had lost a good deal of blood, but he was not fated to die then. Suddenly, Falgeir's belt snapped and Thormod pulled at his breeches, making it difficult for him to swim. Falgeir kept going under and swallowed a good deal of water. His buttocks and back rose up out of the water, and then his face suddenly turned upward. He was dead. His mouth and eyes were open and from the look on his face it seemed as if he was grinning at something. Thus their struggle ended with Falgeir drowning.

By this time, Thormod's strength was much depleted. He made for some rocks that stood up out of the water, crawled up on to them and lay down. He had no other expectations than to die there, since he was wounded and weary and a long way from the shore.

Now, to return to Oddi Louse. He did as Thormod instructed him and told Skuf and Bjarni that he had met a man called Torrad on his travels that day, and that the man had swapped cloaks with him and asked him to come to them at Stokkanes and tell them about this. They recognized Thormod's cloak and suspected that he had sent Oddi Louse to them because he had planned something momentous.

That evening, they secretly took a boat and rowed across the fjord through the night. As they approached the cave, they saw something moving on one of the skerries and tried to determine whether it was a seal or something else. Then they rowed out to the skerry, went up on to it and saw a man lying there whom they recognized as Thormod. They asked him what had happened and he told them what had taken place during the night.

Skuf said, 'It wasn't for nothing that you left the assembly at Gardar. You've slain three warriors in one night, and all of them from a prominent family.'

Thormod said, 'Before you arrived, the only thought that passed through my mind was that I would die here on these rocks. But now it seems there is hope that I will recover, and therefore my escape will have been worthwhile.'

When they asked him about his fight with Falgeir, Thormod spoke this verse:

25.
I dodged and darted
in the salty brine, and strangely
Falgeir's arse bobbed up
and down, and gaped at me.
The fool died a shameful death.
I saw the depths of depravity   *depths of depravity*: i.e. backside
on that base god of sword-storms, then   *god of sword-storms*: warrior
he swung his eyes on me and grinned.

Since Thormod could not walk, Skuf and Bjarni carried him to their boat in a piece of cloth that they held at the corners. Then they went up to the cave to fetch his clothes and provisions, for they realized that he could not stay there now, and they rowed into Eiriksfjord with him.

There was a man named Gamli who lived at the end of Eiriksfjord, just beneath the glacier. He was rather poor and kept himself to himself. He was an excellent hunter and fisherman, and was married to a woman named Grima, an ill-tempered woman but one with many talents. She was a good healer and quite well versed in the ancient arts. Just the two of them lived there. They rarely went to see other people and other people just as rarely came to them.

Skuf and Bjarni landed their boat a short way from Gamli's farmhouse, then Skuf went up to the house while Bjarni waited in the boat with Thormod. Skuf received a warm welcome and he was offered refreshment.

'We have a wounded man travelling with us,' he said, 'whom we would like you to heal.'

Grima said, 'Who is the man?'

Skuf replied, 'Thormod the poet, follower of King Olaf, is the wounded man.'

'Who wounded him?' she inquired.

Skuf told her what had taken place.

'This is no small matter, and he has brought considerable trouble upon himself. Taking in a man brought to justice by Thorgrim's family is quite a responsibility – especially since he did all this after he was outlawed.'

Skuf said, 'I will pay the full price should you be accused of any complicity in this matter, and I will make sure that you lose nothing by helping him in any way you can.'

After they had talked, Grima took Thormod in. He was moved up to the farmhouse where he was attended to and his wounds bandaged. After that, his pain eased somewhat. Skuf and Bjarni returned home to Stokkanes.

Everyone regarded the news of the slayings as very serious, but what actually took place could not be confirmed. Many believed that Thormod had drowned where Falgeir's body had been found.

Thormod's wounds were slow to heal and he was laid up with them for twelve months. At the end of that time, he was

able to move between the fire room and the main room but was
not completely recovered.

One night it happened that Thordis at Longunes tossed and
turned and called out in her sleep, and the household wondered
whether they should wake her.

Then her son, Bodvar, said, 'Let my mother finish her dream.
Perhaps it contains something she wishes to know.'

So they did not rouse her, but when she did wake up she was
breathing quickly.

Then her son, Bodvar, said, 'You have slept badly, mother.
Has your dream told you anything?'

Thordis answered, 'I have ridden my staff far and wide this
night, and learned of matters I did not know before.'

Bodvar said, 'What matters?'

Thordis answered, 'Thormod, who slew my sons and your
brothers, is still alive and is staying with Gamli and Grima at
the far end of Eiriksfjord. I want to go there and capture Thormod and repay him with a cruel death for the great harm he
has done to us. We will go first to Brattahlid and ask Thorkel
to come with us, for he has extended his protection to Gamli
and Grima for a long time and will take it badly if any harm
comes to them.'

Bodvar said he was ready to leave as soon as they wished. So
they arose in the night and took out one of their boats, went
aboard with fifteen men and rowed out to Eiriksfjord. It was at
that time of year when it is light enough to travel by night.

It is said that on the same night that Thordis set out with her
party, Grima slept badly. Thormod told Gamli to wake her.

Gamli answered, 'Grima will not want to be woken. She
usually discovers something important in such dreams.'

They stopped talking, and soon after that Grima awoke.

Then Gamli said, 'You have been tossing and turning in your
sleep, Grima. What have you seen?'

Grima answered, 'What came to me was this – I know that
Thordis from Longunes has set out with fifteen of her farmhands, and she's on her way here because her witchcraft has
told her that Thormod is staying with us and because she
intends to kill him. Now, I want you to stay in the house today

and not go hunting or fishing. Two of you are hardly too many if fifteen men turn up here, especially since Thormod is in no condition to fight. And I don't want to send you up on to the glacier. It's best you stay here.'

Thordis travelled through the night until she came to Brattahlid, where Thorkel welcomed her party warmly and offered them refreshment.

Thordis said, 'This is how the matter stands. I'm on my way to two of your thingmen, Gamli and Grima, because I have reason to believe that Thormod, whom we had outlawed, and whom many believe to have drowned, is staying there. I want you to come with us and make sure that we bring them to justice. You will know what is spoken if you witness our conversation.'

Thorkel answered, 'It seems unlikely to me that Grima would shelter a man you have had outlawed, but I'll go with you if you wish.'

While Thordis and her party breakfasted, Thorkel gathered some of his own men because he did not want to have to be ruled by Bodvar and Thordis if any disagreement arose between them. When everyone had eaten his fill, Thorkel went aboard his own ship with twenty men and both parties set out.

Gamli's wife, Grima, had a large chair with a figure of Thor carved into the arms – a sizeable effigy – and the following morning, she said, 'Now, this is what I want done today. I will place my chair in the main room, and I want you, Thormod, to sit in it when they arrive. On no account must you stand up while Thordis is here. No matter what strange events you think you see, nor whether you think you are being attacked, you must not rise up from this chair. If it is time for you to die, there will be no escape wherever you run. Gamli will set up a pot and boil some seal meat, and he will put sweepings from the floor on the fire so that the house fills with smoke. I shall sit in the doorway and spin yarn, and receive them when they arrive.'

Grima's instructions were followed, and when Thorkel's and Thordis's ships were seen putting ashore, Thormod went and sat in the chair. Gamli hung up a pot and threw sweepings on to the fire, and the house filled with smoke so dark and dense that it obscured everything. Grima sat on the threshold, spun some yarn and hummed something that the others did not understand.

The ships were brought ashore and the party walked up to the farmhouse. When Thorkel arrived there, Grima greeted him and invited him to stay.

Thorkel said, 'Thordis from Longunes is with us and she is convinced that the outlaw Thormod is here with you. If you know where he is, hand him over. You'd have no hope of keeping such an outlaw away from Thordis and her son, Bodvar.'

Grima replied, 'I'm astonished that Thordis thinks me capable of harbouring an outlaw from people as powerful as those at Longunes when there's only the two of us here.'

'It is astonishing,' said Thorkel, 'but, even so, we're going to have to search the house.'

Grima said, 'There would be nothing wrong with your searching the house if there were not so many men with you. I always take great pleasure in your coming here, but I don't want these people from Einarsfjord trampling all over the place and damaging things.'

Thorkel said, 'Only Thordis and I will come in and search.'

That is what they did. They went inside and searched and they were not long at it because the place was so small. They opened the door to the main room, but the place was filled with smoke and they saw nothing remarkable. Moreover, the stench was everywhere, so they did not stay as long as they might have done if there had been no smoke. Then they came outside and the rest of the farm was searched.

Thordis said, 'I couldn't see whether there was anything in the main room for all that smoke. We'll go up on to the roof and take off the screens[40] to let the smoke out. Then we'll be able to see what's in the main room.'

So Bodvar and Thordis went up on to the roof and removed the screens, and the smoke poured out. That made everything in the room visible. They saw Grima's chair in the middle of the floor with the figure of Thor and his hammer carved into the arms, but they did not see Thormod, so they came down and went to the front door.

Then Thordis said, 'Grima still keeps to some of the old ways. She has a figure of Thor carved on the arms of her chair.'

Grima answered, 'I seldom go to church to hear the lessons of the wise because it is so far away and there's just the two of us here. What actually runs through my mind when I see the wooden figure of Thor is the thought that I can break it and burn it whenever I please. I also know that the Creator of heaven and earth and all things visible and invisible, who gives life to all things, is far superior to Thor, and that no man may vanquish his power.'

Thordis answered, 'Perhaps that is what runs through your mind, but I'm sure we'd make you say more if Thorkel wasn't here with all his men, for I suspect you know something of Thormod's whereabouts.'

Grima replied, 'It's just as the saying has it – "guessing often leads to error". And there's another saying, "if a man's time has not come, something will save him". What you sorely lack is a holy guardian so that the devil lead you not into the evil you are contemplating. It's excusable when people guess and are mistaken, but there's no excusing the man who rejects the truth once it's proven.'

After these words, they parted company. Thorkel went home to Brattahlid and Thordis to her own house. Skuf and Bjarni came in secret to Gamli and Grima. They brought them what provisions they needed and paid many times what it cost them for Thormod's keep.

24

When Thormod had fully recovered from the wound that Falgeir had inflicted, Skuf and Bjarni brought him back to Stokkanes and secretly sheltered him in one of the storehouses. That was Thormod's third winter in Greenland. The same year Skuf and Bjarni sold their farm at Stokkanes along with their other lands and livestock and intended to leave the country, and when spring came they made their ship ready to sail. Thormod was glad to leave the storehouse, and said that he had something to take care of in the north. So, he got a boat and had Egil the Fool go with him, and he sat at the oars while Thormod steered.

Egil was a good oarsman and a good swimmer. The weather was fair. It was a bright day, the sun shone and there was little wind, as they made their way into Einarsfjord. When they arrived in the fjord, Thormod became very agitated and rocked backwards and forwards so much that he began to tilt the boat.

Egil said, 'Why are you acting so foolishly? Are you mad? Do you want to capsize the boat?'

Thormod replied, 'I'm worried.'

Egil said, 'I can't row if you behave like a madman. If you don't stop you'll turn us over.'

But despite Egil's protests, Thormod finally tipped the boat over. Thormod dived away from the boat and swam in a series of plunges until he reached land. He had his axe with him.

Egil got up on to the keel of the boat, rested there and looked around for Thormod, but he could not see him anywhere. Then Egil righted the boat, sat down at the oars and rowed out of the fjord until he got home to Stokkanes. There he told Skuf and Bjarni what had happened, and added that he believed Thormod was dead. They were astonished at this news and doubted whether all of it was true. They were not convinced that Thormod had drowned.

Now our story turns to Thormod and what he did when he reached the shore. After wringing out his clothes, he began to walk and he continued on his way until he came to Sigrid's farm at Hamar late in the day. He knocked on the door and a woman came out to greet him, then she turned and went back into the main room. Thormod followed her in and sat down on the guests' bench near the door.

Sigrid began to speak, saying, 'Who are you?'

He answered, 'My name is Osvif (Bold).'

Sigrid said, 'A man is as he's named. Will you be staying the night?'

Thormod answered that he would like to.

The following morning, Sigrid spoke to him and asked the purpose of his journey.

Thormod said, 'It was true what I told you yesterday, my name is Osvif.'

She replied, 'I thought I knew who you were even though I've never seen you before. You are Thormod Kolbrun's Poet.'

He answered, 'There's no point in denying that you have guessed who I really am, so I'll tell you that I'm on my way to Longunes to Thorunn Einarsdottir to meet her son, Ljot. They have often spoken badly of me.'

Sigrid said, 'Then my son, Sigurd, shall go with you. Ljot and Thorunn have long caused us trouble.'

Thormod said, 'I don't think it's a good idea for Sigurd to come with me since you wouldn't be able to continue to support yourselves here if anything happens when we confront Ljot.'

'I would happily lose the farm,' said Sigrid, 'if Ljot was brought down.'

Then Sigurd went with Thormod to Thorunn at Langanes. They knocked on the door, and a woman came out and greeted them. Sigurd asked whether Ljot was at home.

She replied, 'He's in the main room.'

Sigurd said, 'Ask him to come out.'

So the servant went back inside and told Ljot to go to the door.

He said, 'Who's asking for me?'

'Sigurd from Hamar,' she said, 'and another man I didn't recognize.'

'This man you didn't recognize, what does he look like?'

She answered, 'He has dark, curly hair.'

Ljot said, 'That sounds like Thormod, our enemy.'

So Ljot left the main room, and the women in the house went with him. Then he took his spear and went to the door. He recognized Thormod and struck at his chest with his spear. Thormod deflected the blow with his axe, but the spear caught him on the calf and wounded him badly. Ljot thrust forward as he attacked Thormod, and as he did, Sigurd struck him full between the shoulder blades and made a great wound. Ljot ran inside and Thormod struck out at him, catching him on the thigh and scoring him down the length of his leg, before the axe fell out of his hand and lodged itself in the threshold. Ljot fell in the doorway and the women ran past him and closed the door. Thormod and Sigurd left.

Then Thormod told Sigurd to go home to Hamar.

'Tell your mother what has happened,' said Thormod. 'I'll make my own way.'

So they parted company, and Sigurd went home to Hamar and told his mother what had taken place.

Sigrid said, 'My advice is that you go to see Skuf and demand that he harbour you. Tell him that I want to sell my land and leave Greenland with him.'

So Sigurd went to meet Skuf and told him what he wanted. Skuf took him in, sold Sigrid's land and brought her belongings to his ship.

Thormod bound up his wound and went down to Thorunn's boathouse. He saw that a ship had been dragged out of the boathouse and assumed that Thorunn's men were out rowing. Then he went down to the shore and made himself a bed in some sea-weed and lay there for the day. When evening came, he heard the sound of oars and eventually Thorunn's farm-hands came ashore.

They said, 'There will be fine weather tomorrow, and we'll set out to row again. So, instead of putting the ship away, we'll moor it here in the harbour tonight.'

Having done that, they went home. By that time it was night. When they had gone, Thormod stood up and went to where the ship was moored, untied it and sat down at the oars. Then he rowed across the fjord to the farm at Vik.

That same evening, Thordis lay down to sleep at Longunes and she slept badly.

When she awoke, she said, 'Where is my son, Bodvar?'

He answered, 'Here I am, mother. What do you want?'

She replied, 'I want us to row out into the fjord. There's prey out there.'

Bodvar said, 'What kind of prey is that?'

Thordis answered, 'Thormod the outlaw is out in the fjord, alone in a boat. We're going out there to meet him.'

[From *Flateyjarbók*]

Sigurd went on his way and was not too far from home when he met Thormod, who had been waiting for him. The two of them went together to see Skuf and Bjarni and told them what had happened. Then Skuf sold Sigrid's land and moved her and all her belongings on to his ship.

One evening, Thormod left the house. He took a boat and rowed across Eiriksfjord through the night. Then he left the boat moored and walked from the ship until he came to Longunes. Then he went down to Thordis's boathouse and bedded down there in the expectation that Bodvar would row out to sea the following day, as he usually did.

When morning came he saw three men walk from the farmhouse to the boat. They were discussing whether Bodvar would return that day since he had gone to Ljot's house at Langanes to bind his wounds. Thormod lay where he was, for his wound made walking difficult. The farmhands rowed out to the catch that was waiting in the nets, and later that day Thormod saw them row back to land. He was in much pain from the wound on his leg.

There was a man named Kar, overseer of Thordis's farm, who had gone off fishing with the rest of the men. He was Bodvar's cousin.

The men gutted the catch, then put the boat away and covered it over, and went home when they had finished. The weather was becoming foggy and a fine rain began to fall. Thormod overheard them say that Bodvar had returned home. Thormod wanted to take the ship and row across the fjord to Vik.

When Kar and the others reached the farm, Kar said, 'I left my wood-axe behind. I'm going back to get it.'

They offered to go with him but he did not want them to, and he walked off briskly. Thormod had come down to the boat by then and set it afloat. Kar saw Thormod and recognized him, then turned back intending to tell Bodvar about it. Thormod saw that Kar had turned back and was about to pursue him, but his leg was so stiff that he could hardly move it. Instead, he threw his axe at Kar. It caught him just below the knee and cut a piece of flesh from his calf. Kar limped home, and it took him quite some time. Thormod picked up his axe, ran to the boat and rowed out away from the shore in the direction of the farm at Vik.

Thordis had been asleep that night and when she awoke, she was breathing heavily.

She said, 'Has Bodvar returned or not?'

He answered, 'I am here, mother. What do you want of me?'

She replied, 'The fish would bite on the hook now if we had the strength to drag it in. Thormod the outlaw has been in our boathouse all day long and he has wounded your cousin Kar, taken your boat and rowed across the fjord. I think he is in pain from the wound that Ljot dealt him, and he'll have difficulty getting across the fjord because of the fog. I think it would be a good idea for us to go out and meet him.'

Bodvar sprang to his feet and said, 'I am ready to make this journey.'

As they left the house they saw Kar limping, for he had reached the farm by then. But they could not see Thormod anywhere because the fog was so dense.

Five of Thordis's farmhands went with her and they rowed across the fjord through the night. Thormod heard the sound of the oars and people talking, and he guessed that it was Thordis and her farmhands. He knew he would not have much hope if they found him. There was a small, low-lying island close by which flooded over if there was a very strong current, but not at other times. Thormod capsized his boat and made his way to the island. It was covered all over with sea-weed. Thormod dug himself in between two rocks and spread sea-weed over himself.

Thordis and her party rowed through the darkness and saw a black shape in the water which they could not identify. So they rowed towards it and saw that it was an overturned boat with the oars in the rowlocks.

Then Thordis's men said, 'Thormod must have hit a rock while he was rowing. It's more than likely that he's drowned.'

Thordis said, 'Thormod has not drowned. Rather, he heard our approach and capsized the boat himself in order to have us believe that he is dead. He must have swum out to the island and hidden himself there. So we'll row there and search for him. Make sure you stab around the entire area with your spearheads, and more than once.'

They did as she instructed them, but they did not find him and did not believe there was much hope of doing so.

Thordis said, 'I still think he's here on the island even though you have not discovered him. Now, if Thormod can hear what I'm saying then he ought to answer me – that is, if he has a man's heart and not a mare's.'

Thormod heard what Thordis said and wanted to reply but he could not speak. He felt as if his mouth had been held closed.

Then Thordis and her men left, taking with them the boat that Thormod had rowed out on. When they had gone, he stood up from the pile of sea-weed, and then swam for the nearest part of the coast. He stopped at a number of skerries on the way to rest, but when there was only a short distance left to the shore he climbed up on to a skerry and was so exhausted that he could go no farther.

That night, Grim, the farmer at Vik, dreamt that a man came to him. He was a handsome, dignified man of medium height, thick-set and broad-shouldered. He asked Grim whether he woke or slept.

Grim answered, 'I'm awake. Who are you?'

The man in the dream said, 'I am King Olaf Haraldsson, and I have to come to you because I want you to go to Thormod, my follower and poet, and assist him so that he may escape from where he lies on a skerry close to the shore. To prove what I say is true, I will tell you that Gest, the foreigner who has been staying with you this winter, is actually Steinar, known as Helgu-Steinar. He is an Icelander who came to Greenland to avenge the death of Thorgeir Havarsson.[41] Yet, though Steinar is a great champion and an excellent warrior, he is not ordained to take much part in avenging Thorgeir. His courage will be evident elsewhere.'

When King Olaf had spoken these words, Grim awoke. Then he roused Gest from his sleep and asked him to get up. Gest did so, then picked up his axe and left with Grim.

They sat down outside and Grim said, 'What did you say your name was?'

Gest said, 'You remember what I told you it was.'

Grim said, 'Of course I remember what you said your name was. That's why I'm asking whether it's your real name.'

Gest said, 'Why shouldn't it be?'

Grim said, 'Because your name is Steinar and you are known as Helgu-Steinar in your country.'

Gest said, 'Who said this was so?'

Grim replied, 'King Olaf.'

Gest said, 'When did you meet with King Olaf?'

Then Grim answered him and told him what he had dreamt.

Gest replied, 'What your dream told you of me is true.'

Then Steinar and Grim went to look for Thormod and found him where King Olaf had said he would be. They took him back to Vik, watched over him there in secret and healed his wounds. And when Thormod had recovered from the wounds that Ljot had inflicted, Steinar took him to their ship. Skuf was not on board. Steinar was ready to set sail from Vik, but waited on the ship with Thormod. Skuf was greatly delayed at the assembly, and had to stay there until it was over. Thordis's son, Bodvar, had had Sigurd, the son of Sigrid, outlawed for wounding Ljot.

After the assembly, Skuf was ready to leave. But on the morning he was about to set sail, Thormod and Gest left the ship without asking him and went down into Einarsfjord to Thorunn's farm. There, they saw four men sitting in a boat, fishing, and recognized one of them as Thorunn's son, Ljot. They confronted and fought with him, and the encounter ended with Ljot and the three other men on the boat being slain.

Thormod and Gest returned to their ship, where Skuf was ready to set sail. Thormod and Skuf stepped aboard, but Steinar remained behind and went to stay with Thorkel at Brattahlid. Skuf and Bjarni set off to sea and because the winds were favourable they were not long reaching Norway. After mooring their ship they divided their wealth so that Bjarni took the ship and Skuf took the movable goods. Then Bjarni went south to Denmark and then to Rome on a pilgrimage to the tombs of Saint Peter and Saint Paul the Apostles. It was on that pilgrimage that Bjarni died.

Sigrid and her son, Sigurd, bought some land in Norway and lived there for the rest of their lives, and Skuf and Thormod went to see the king and remained with him till their dying day.

The king paid Thormod little attention at first, for an Icelander named Grim had come to him, claiming to have avenged Thorgeir Havarsson before Thormod, and the king honoured him and gave him gifts. Thormod had heard that Grim was an evil man, who had secretly murdered someone in Iceland.[42]

Thus Thormod went before the king and spoke this verse:

26.

Great bounty of wealth you have given
to Grim, king, but to me
much less than I deserve –
many scathing verses are made.
He has done a dog's work –
only a thief does that.
Yet I, king, have doubled
both my honour and your own.

The king said, 'Do you believe, Thormod, that you have won greater fame in Greenland than Grim in Iceland?'

Thormod answered, 'I'm afraid I have.'

Then King Olaf said, 'What great deeds did you accomplish in Greenland?'

Thormod answered:

27.

I slew Thorgrim Troll
– a mighty man fell there –
before that, warrior, undaunted,
I dealt Lodin his death.
Thorkel's life I took, and Thord
was the fourth to give up the ghost.
Falgeir, their famous champion,
I laid low on the ground.

King Olaf said, 'In terms of numbers slain, you have done more in Greenland than the fisherman does as penance for his catch. He regards himself absolved if he pulls in one fish for himself, a second for his ship, a third for his hook and a fourth for his tackle. You have gone further than that. Why did you slay so many?'

Thormod answered, 'I did not take kindly to their likening me to a mare. They said I was among men like a mare among stallions.'

The king said, 'It's understandable that you took displeasure at what they said. Your great deeds have spoken for you.'

Then Thormod spoke a verse:

28.
A great mark I have branded
on the dwellers in Greenland,
brought harm to the sea-king's   *sea-king's hail*: battle
    hail-makers,
those who had me outlawed.
That mark will be slow
to fade from the backs
of those warlike sword-wielders
unless they do me to death.

'I doubt it not,' said the king. 'It will be a long time before the ground you have scorched begins to grow again.'

Now Thormod was greatly honoured by the king and proved himself more than equal to all tests of strength. He left the country with King Olaf and remained with him the whole time the king was in exile. When Olaf returned to Norway, so too did Thormod, for he thought it better to die at the king's side than to outlive him.

When the king came to a valley named Veradal in the district of Trondheim, he knew that the people there were planning to besiege him.

So he asked Thormod, for the sake of amusement, 'What would be your instructions if you commanded our party?'

Thormod answered with a verse:

29.
Put flame to every house
we find inland from Hverborg.
Up swords to defend
the land for king's sake.
In Trondheim may they all
find their homes as cold ashes.
If my advice you follow,
light yew's harm in the forest.   *yew's harm*: fire

King Olaf said, 'There's some chance that your plan may work, but we shall find some other means than setting fire to our own lands. I do not doubt, though, that you would do as you have said.'

On the day of the Battle of Stiklestad, King Olaf requested some entertainment of Thormod, and he responded by reciting the old poem, Bjarkamal.[43]

The king said, 'A fitting poem for what is about to take place today. I shall rename it Huskarlahvot (That-which-spurs-on-the-soldiers).'

It is said that Thormod was in low spirits the day before the battle, and the king sensed this and asked, 'Why are you so quiet, Thormod?'

He answered, 'Because, my lord, I am not certain that we shall be resting in the same place tonight. Promise me now that we shall be and I will be glad.'

King Olaf said, 'I don't know whether it is within my power to decide, but if it is, then tonight you shall go where I go.'

Then Thormod was glad again, and he spoke a verse:

30.
Sprayer of arrows, now
the sea-king's hail approaches.   *sea-king's hail*: battle
We must not tread warily,
the age of swords draws near.   *age of swords*: (decisive) battle

Tree of the cove-steed, either   *cove-steed*: ship; its *tree*: seafarer
we escape or lie slain here
but it will not fail that we
will feed the greedy ravens.

The king replied, 'It may well be as you say, poet. The men who have come here will either leave or be left lying here.'

Then Thormod spoke a verse:

31.
At your knee I shall stoop,
brave lord and true king,
until you procure other poets.
But when do you expect them?
By your side I wish to live and die.
Wise and mighty groomer   *shield's serpent*: sword;
of the shield's serpent, we stand   its *groomer*: warrior, king
ready on the plank of the sea.   *plank of the sea*: ship

King Olaf said, 'Poet, your remarks about Sighvat[44] are cutting and unnecessary, for he would be here if he knew what was happening – and he may yet prove of great use to us.'

Thormod replied, 'That may be so, but there would be few gathered around the royal standard today if many had elected to go with him.'

Thormod won great acclaim for his bravery in battle at Stiklestad, where King Olaf fell, because he had neither shield nor armour. Always holding his broad axe two-handed, he hacked his way through the ranks of the enemy, and no one in his path had the least desire to be dispatched for the night with its blade.

It is said that when the battle was over Thormod had no wounds.

This he regretted bitterly, saying, 'Since I shall not be resting in the same place as the king tonight, living seems worse than dying.'[45]

And as he said that, an arrow flew towards him and struck

him in the chest. He knew not whence it came but he was glad
of the wound because he knew it would prove fatal. He made
his way to a barley barn where many of the king's men lay
injured. A woman there was heating some water in a pot to
cleanse their wounds. Thormod went over to a wicker wall and
leaned against it for support.

The woman said to him, 'Are you one of the king's men, or
from Trondheim?'

Thormod spoke a verse:

32.
It is plain to see that I
was battle-keen with Olaf.
I, at least, was wounded sorely
by sword's edge and saw little peace.
This poet suffered a cold blast –
signs of it show on my shield.
The spear-wielders have almost
rendered me left-handed.

The woman said, 'Why don't you have your wounds bound
if you're hurt badly?'

Thormod answered, 'The only wounds I have need no
binding.'

The woman said, 'Who fought best alongside the king
today?'

Thormod said:

33.
Battle-glad Harald fought
fiercely alongside Olaf.
Hring and Dag, too, made
hard play with their swords.
Those four kings stood with courage
bearing their red shields.
Then the carrion fowl
had dark beer to drink.   *dark beer*: blood

Then the woman questioned him once more, 'How did the king himself fare?'

Thormod spoke a verse:

34.
Olaf was stout of heart.
Steeped in blood, this king
surged forward at Stiklestad,
urging his men to war.
Damascened swords bit hard.
Save the king, I saw all
the trees of Odin's hailstones   *Odin's hailstones*: battle; its *trees*: warriors
seek shelter; most grew battle-seasoned.

The barn was filled with men, many of whom were gravely hurt, and from their gaping wounds issued that terrible sound that comes with such deep cuts to the flesh.

When Thormod had spoken these verses, one of the men from Trondheim came into the barn, and when he heard this howling of wounds, he said, 'It's no surprise that the king has not fared better against us if his men are as feeble as this. As far as I can see, the men in here can hardly bear their wounds without screaming.'

Thormod said, 'So you think the men in here have no courage?'

He answered, 'This is a great gathering of weaklings, if ever I saw one.'

Thormod said, 'It may well be that someone in here lacks courage. Perhaps my wound doesn't seem too bad to you?'

As the man went up to Thormod to look at his wound, Thormod swung his axe at him and wounded him badly. He let out a scream, then a loud groan.

Then Thormod said, 'I knew that someone in here was spineless. You're a hypocrite, looking for courage in other men when you lack such courage yourself. Here are many who are severely wounded and not one of them groans. They cannot help the sound their wounds make. But you moan and wail over one small injury.'

Thormod said this as he stood by the wicker wall in the barley barn, and when the two men had finished talking, the woman who was heating the water said to him:

[From *Hólmsbók*]

'Why are you so pale?'
Thormod spoke this verse:

35.
The oak of the hawk's perch wonders   *hawk's perch*: arm, wrist;
why we were so pale and wan.   its *oak*: woman
Few are made fair by wounds.
Woman, I felt the rain of arrows,
their dark metal drove through
my body with great force.
Sharp and dangerous iron bit
close to my heart, I expect.

The woman said, 'I thought you were wounded because you look so pale. Now have your wounds bound if you want to be helped.'

Thormod spoke a verse:

36.
My cheeks are not red, yet she,
the slim woman, has a hale man.
That ancient iron stands fast   *ancient iron*: arrowhead
in my marsh of wounds
and makes me look pale,
wearer of golden wave-fire.   *wave-fire*: gold; its *wearer*: woman
Deep marks from Danish swords
at Dagshrid[46] are full sore.

And when he spoken these words standing by the wicker wall, he expired and fell down to the ground, dead.

Harald the Stern[47] completed the verse that Thormod composed by adding: ' "are full sore" – that's what he would wanted to have said: "at Dagshrid are full sore".'

Thus ended the life of Thormod Kolbrun's Poet, and here too ends all we know of Thormod, the champion of Saint Olaf.

* * *

[The following is a variant ending to the saga, found in *Flateyjarbók*]

As mentioned earlier, on the night that Olaf lay resting with his army, he remained awake for a long time and prayed to God both for his own sake and the sake of his men. He had little sleep, except just before daybreak when weariness overcame him – and when he awoke it was dawn. The king thought it was too early to wake his men, so he asked Thormod the poet, who was close by, whether he was awake. Thormod asked the king what he wanted of him.

The king said, 'Let us hear some poetry.'

Thormod sat up and spoke so loudly that the whole army heard him, and it was the old poem Bjarkamal that he recited.

But before he began, he asked why Sighvat the poet did not provide entertainment and thus pay for the gold-hilted sword 'that the king gave him last Christmas as a gift'.

The king said, 'Don't you know that Sighvat is not here? No one will be more important to us now than he, for he is praying for us on his way to Rome.'

Thormod answered, 'To each as befits him. I'll be putting my manhood to the test and providing entertainment while he's enjoying himself in Rome.'

This is the beginning of the poem:

37.
Day has risen up,
the cockerel beats its wings.
Now it is time for Vikings
to awaken and set to work.
Awaken, awaken,
lift your heads, friends
and all the chieftains
of Adils and the Swedes.

38.
High, the hard-handed man
Hrolf the Shooter.
Men of high blood
who do not flee.
I wake you neither from wine
nor from women's whispers.
Instead I wake you to play
at Hild's hard game.   *Hild's* (valkyrie's) *game*: battle

Then the king's men awoke, and when Thormod had finished reciting the poem they thanked him. They said how much they enjoyed it, told him how fitting it was for the occasion, and named it Huskarlahvot (That-which-spurs-on-the-soldiers). The king also thanked Thormod for the entertainment, and then he took a gold ring and gave it to him.

Thormod thanked the king for the gift and said, 'We have a good king, but it remains to be seen how long his life will be. It is my prayer, king, that you let neither life nor death divide us. I would like to be sharing the same sleeping place as you tonight.'

'And so it shall be,' said the king, 'if we both leave Stiklestad alive.'

'If so, I would not think it so pressing a matter,' said Thormod. 'The truth is that I do not wish to outlive you. I have searched my mind and it seems to me that ever since I was seven years old, the only thing that has been of any help in my life has been following you and being your companion – I believe I have not proven unworthy.'

'I know you do not desire to outlive me,' said the king, 'but I do not know whether we are equally prepared to share the same sleeping place. How old are you, and how many men have you slain in single combat?'

Thormod answered, 'I am just a little over thirty-five, and I believe I have slain fourteen men.'

'That doesn't seem very old to me,' said the king, 'but I promise that you will find rest after your seven days' wake.

That means you will have to spend one day or one night in the fires of purification for each man you have slain.'

'But I requested, my lord, never to part company with you.'

The king answered, 'If I have any say in the matter – and because you do not wish to part with me – then we shall all go together.'

Then Thormod said, 'My lord, it is my hope, whether there be peace or war, and no matter who emerges victorious, that I may stand by your side as long as it is within my power.'

Then Thormod spoke a verse:

39.
At your knee I shall stoop,
brave lord and true king,
until you procure other poets.
When do you expect them?
Tree of the cove-steed, either   *cove-steed*: ship; its *tree*: seafarer
we escape or lie slain there
but it will not fail that we
will feed the greedy ravens.

[. . .] It is said that Thormod Kolbrun's Poet was wearing a red tunic the day he went to battle, and that he folded up the front of his tunic under his belt and let it hang low behind. One of the king's men asked why he had done that.

Thormod answered, 'Because I intend to go farther forwards than backwards.'

He was girded with a sword that King Olaf had given him and carried his axe in his hand, but he had no shield. The king asked him why he was not dressed for battle like the other men and why he carried no shield.

'Do you think the men of Trondheim don't know how to fight?' asked the king.

Thormod answered, 'They shall discover today that my axe is both my shield and my armour.'

For ever will it be remembered and praised how bravely Thormod fought that day. He hacked away with his axe in both hands in the first fray and then, when its head flew from the shaft, he fought with his sword for the whole of the final assault known as Dagshrid. So many men fell by Thormod's hand that naming them all would take far too long. [. . .] Thormod Kolbrun's Poet was hardly wounded, but so weary he could not fight on. Even so, he chose to stand fast by his companions. That he was not hurt, or barely so, was not due to his protecting himself more than the others. It was because the enemy found it easier to attack anywhere else than where he stood.

One man asked Thormod, 'Have you seen the shield that I cast away earlier?'

'What need have you of a shield, you coward?' said Thormod. 'I could have such a shield if I wanted one, but not the generous friend I have lost.'

[. . .] It is said that when the battle was over, Thormod went to where Dag Hringsson and his men were positioned. Night had fallen and there was not enough light to continue fighting. The people from Trondheim had surrounded Dag and his men to prevent them from escaping during the night and intended to attack them by first light.

Dag said, 'Is there any man among my company who can suggest how we might escape, and thus prevent these people from Trondheim from attacking us? If we stay here, I know they will come at us as soon as it grows light.'

No man answered him, and when Thormod saw that none of them had a plan to offer, he said, 'Why can no plan be found?'

Dag asked, 'Which man speaks so boldly?'

He answered, 'His name is Thormod.'

Dag said, 'Are you Thormod Kolbrun's Poet?'

'The very same,' said Thormod.

Dag said, 'And what way can you see to get us out of here with all our men?'

Thormod answered, 'Cut down the woods and use the branches to build several large fires, then place as many of the trunks as possible in front of them. Four men will position themselves by each fire – three to keep walking around it while the fourth keeps the fire going. When you have done that for a while, douse all the fires at once, then be on your way and do not stop – neither today nor tomorrow. When the people from Trondheim see all those fires, they will think that many more men have arrived. By tomorrow they will realize that they have been tricked, and I fully expect them to give chase, but by then you will be so far ahead of them it will be of no avail.'

Dag said, 'Are you wounded at all, Thormod?'

He answered, 'Far from it.'

Dag said, 'Come east to Sweden with me and I will treat you well. There is nothing to be gained by staying here.'

Thormod answered, 'It is not my fate to serve any other ruler now that King Olaf has fallen.'

Then Thormod left while Dag and his men employed his plan and escaped.

[. . .] Now Thormod was sorely disappointed that he was hardly wounded, and he was steeped in regret – for he believed that the evil he had done had prevented him from dying alongside the king.

So he prayed eagerly to King Olaf to take pity on him, and on his own he spoke out loud, 'Will you not, King Olaf, grant me the end you promised? You said you would not forsake me, if it were within your power.'

And the next thing he heard was the sound of a bow-string being plucked, and an arrow flew and pierced him deep under his left arm.

He was greatly pleased at being wounded thus and said, 'This man has drawn a more auspicious bow than any other and struck where it was most deserved.'

Then Thormod went over to the king's body, sat down beside it and broke the shaft from his axe.

[. . .] Naturally, Thormod was in great pain from his injury. He walked towards the camp, coming to a barley barn where the wounded among King Olaf's party had been placed. He had his sword drawn, and as he walked inside a man came towards him. Thormod asked him his name. He said it was Kimbi.

Thormod asked, 'Were you at the battle?'

'I was,' said the man, 'with the better side, the people from Trondheim.'

'Are you wounded?' asked Thormod.

'Scarcely,' said Kimbi. 'Were you at the battle?'

Thormod replied, 'I was on the victors' side.'

Kimbi saw that Thormod had a gold ring on his hand and said, 'You must be one of the king's men. Give me the ring and I will hide you. The people from Trondheim will make you pay dearly if you run into them. Are you wounded?'

Thormod answered, 'My wounds are such as need no healing. You may have the ring if you wish. I have lost so much now that I have begun to take less pleasure in gold than before.'

Kimbi stretched out his hand and, as he was about to take the ring, Thormod lashed out with his sword and cut off Kimbi's hand, saying that it would never steal again. Kimbi bore the pain badly. Thormod said that now he knew what it was like to suffer being wounded. Then Kimbi left while Thormod remained.

Then a man ran out of the barn to fetch some firewood. A woman heated some water in a pot to cleanse the men's wounds. Thormod went over to a wicker wall and leaned against it for support.

The woman then said to him, 'Who are you? Are you one of the king's men, or from Trondheim?'

Then Thormod spoke this verse:

40.
It is plain to see that I
was battle-keen with Olaf.
I, at least, was wounded sorely
by sword's edge and saw little peace.
This poet suffered a cold blast –
signs of it show on my shield.
The spear-wielders have almost
rendered me breathless.   *breathless*: dead

The woman said, 'Why don't you have your wounds bound up if you are hurt so badly?'

Thormod answered, 'The wounds I have need no binding.'

The woman said, 'Then you can resolve for me a matter that we have been discussing all night – which side has fared better in this battle and which has proven braver?'

Then Thormod spoke a verse:

41.
Olaf was stout of heart.
Steeped in blood, this king
surged forward at Stiklestad,
urging his men to war.
Damascened swords bit hard.
Save the king, I saw all
the trees of bow-storm's hailstones   *bow-storm's hailstones*: battle;
seek shelter; most grew battle-seasoned.   its *trees*: warriors

Then one of the Trondheim yeomen came into the barn
as Thormod and the woman spoke together. He was curious
to learn about the king's men. Many of them were sorely
wounded, and from those wounds to the innards or the head
issued that terrible sound that comes from such deep cuts to
the flesh.

The yeoman stopped at the entrance to the barn and listened
to them from there, and when he heard the groaning wounds,
he said, 'Considering the weaklings he has as followers, it's no
wonder that the king hasn't fared better in this battle against
the people from Trondheim. As far as I can see they can hardly
bear their wounds without screaming. They're not brave men –
they're spineless.'

Thormod answered, 'So, my friend, you think the men in
here lack courage?'

'Yes,' said the man, 'a great gathering of weaklings, if ever I
saw one.'

Thormod answered, 'If one were to search, perhaps one
might find a coward. You probably wouldn't consider my
wound too serious if you thought about it.'

The yeoman answered, 'It would be better if you had larger
wounds and more of them.'

Then the yeoman turned and was about to leave the barn,
and as he did, Thormod struck at him. The blow caught him on
the back and cut off both of his buttocks.

'Let's hear no groaning from you now.'

The man screamed out loudly and felt for his buttocks with both hands.

Then Thormod said, 'I knew I could find a man in here who would prove to lack courage. You are a hypocrite, looking for courage in other men when you lack such courage yourself. Here are many who are severely wounded, and not one of them complains. But you bleat like a she-goat in heat and whinny like a mare over one small flesh wound.'

After this event, a woman came into the barn with two pails of milk to give the wounded men a drink. She said to Thormod, 'Who is this who stands by the wicker wall?'

He answered, 'My name is Thormod.'

She said, 'Have you been at the battle today?'

Thormod answered, 'I would like some of these yeomen to go home to their wives tonight and tell them that Thormod Kolbrun's Poet had been at the battle today, but I doubt that many of them will be able to.'

The woman said, 'Who was bravest among the king's men?'

Thormod spoke a verse:

42.
Battle-glad Harald fought
fiercely alongside Olaf.
Hring and Dag, too, made
hard play with their swords.
Those four kings stood with courage
bearing their red shields.
Then the carrion fowl
had dark ale to drink.   *dark ale*: blood

The woman said, 'You must be badly wounded. Will you have some milk to drink? It gives strength to the wounded.'

Thormod answered, 'I don't need to drink milk; I am as full as if I had just eaten some Icelandic curds, and I'm not badly wounded.'

The woman said, 'If you're so little hurt, then why are you so pale?'

Thormod spoke a verse:

43.
The oak of the hawk's perch wonders   *hawk's perch*: arm, wrist;
why we were so pale and wan.   its *oak*: woman
Few are made fair by wounds.
Woman, I felt the rain of arrows,
their dark metal drove through
my body with great force.
Sharp and dangerous iron bit
close to my heart, I expect.

The woman said, 'I thought you were wounded because you look so pale. Now have your wounds bound like the other men, and let me attend to them.'

Then he sat down and took off his tunic. When the healing-woman saw the wound in his side, she suspected that he had been struck by an arrow, but she could not see which way the iron head of the arrow was turned in the wound. She had been boiling some onions and herbs together in a stone pot, which she gave the wounded men – if their wounds were deep they emitted the smell of the onions. She brought some gruel to Thormod and asked him to eat.

He answered, 'Take it away, I have nothing that herbs will cure.'

Then she took a pair of tongs and tried to pull out the arrowhead, but it was stuck fast and she could not move it. Only part of it showed because the wound was so swollen.

Then Thormod said, 'Cut to the arrowhead so that it is easier to reach with the tongs, then give them to me and let me pull it out.'

She did so. Then Thormod took the gold ring from his hand and gave it to the healing-woman, and bade her do as she wished with it.

'The gift is good,' said Thormod. 'King Olaf gave me the ring this morning.'

Then Thormod took the tongs and pulled at the arrowhead,

but it was barbed and the barbs lay on the nerves of his heart, some of which were red and others white, yellow and green.

And when Thormod saw this, he said, 'The king has nourished us well. The roots of this man's heart are white.'

Then he spoke a verse:

44.
My cheeks are not red, yet she,
the hawk's rest bright and slim,   *hawk's rest*: woman
has a hale man; few
tend to my wounds.
Something else makes me look pale,
foe to the troll's beaten gold: *foe to ... gold*: generous man
deep marks from Danish swords
at Dagshrid are –

When he had thus spoken, he breathed his last standing by the wicker wall and fell not to the ground until he was dead. King Harald Sigurdsson completed the verse that Thormod had composed.

' "At Dagshrid are full sore",' he said; 'that's how the poet would have wanted it to end.'

And the life of Thormod ended with these events, as they have been told here.

Translated by MARTIN S. REGAL

OLKOFRI'S SAGA

I

Ale-hood was the name of a man who lived at Thorhallsstadir in Blaskogar.[1] He was wealthy and getting on in years when this story took place. Small and ugly, he was a man of no great prowess, but he had a knack with iron and wood. He had a profitable business supplying ale at the Thing and through this business he soon got to be on speaking terms with all the great men, because they bought most of the ale. As often happens, the ale was not always liked and thus neither were the men who sold it. No one called Thorhall a generous man; he was, in fact, rather stingy. His eyesight was poor. It was his frequent custom to wear a hood; at the Thing he wore it always, and since he was a man whose name was not well known, the thing-men gave him a name that stuck: they called him Ale-hood.

The story goes that one autumn Ale-hood went to the woods that he owned, intending to make charcoal as was his wont. The woods were beyond Hrafnabjorg and east of Longuhlid. He stayed there several days, preparing for the charcoal-making, and afterwards burned the wood, watching over the fire pits at night. But in the course of the night he fell asleep and the fire escaped from the pits and spread to nearby branches, which soon caught fire. Next the fire reached the woods, which then began to burn. Then a sharp wind arose. Now Ale-hood awoke and was glad just to be able to save himself. The fire spread through the woods. First it burned all the part that Ale-hood owned, but then it raced through all the woods nearby, and in many places around the lava field it burned the woods, which are now known as Svidning (the Singed).

One of the woods to burn there was called Godi Woods. It was owned by six godis:[2] the first of these was Snorri the Godi, the second Gudmund Eyjolfsson, the third Skafti the Lawspeaker, the fourth Thorkel Geitisson, the fifth Eyjolf, son of Thord Gellir, the sixth Thorkel Scarf, son of Red-Bjorn. They had bought the woods to have them available for their use at the Thing.

After this charcoal-making Ale-hood went home. But the news became widely known in the district, reaching Skafti first among those who had suffered loss. During the autumn he sent word north to Eyjafjord with men who were travelling between districts and had Gudmund told of the fire, and that there was a possibility of a good profit from the case. Similar messages also went west to the districts of the other men who shared the ownership of the woods. During the winter messages passed among all of them, to the effect that the six godis should meet at the Thing to undertake a common action, but Skafti should prepare the case because he lived the closest.

When spring came, and with it Summons Days, Skafti rode over with many men and summoned Ale-hood for burning the wood, on pain of full outlawry. Ale-hood stormed and blustered, saying Skafti would not act so grandly at the Thing, where his own friends would be present. Skafti made little answer and rode away.

During the following summer the six godis who owned the woods came to the Thing and at once had a meeting together, where they decided to proceed with the case and demand a lot of money or else self-judgement.

Ale-hood came to the Thing and had ale to sell. There he met his friends who were in the habit of buying ale from him. He asked them for help and offered to give them ale, but they all answered in the same way, that they had not enjoyed any concessions in their previous dealings together. They said that they would not prod the bear to anger by participating in his case against such powerful men, and no one would promise him help or buy his wares. It seemed to him that the case was becoming rather difficult. He went from booth to booth and got no response, though he begged men for help; it put an end to his pride and arrogance.

One day Ale-hood came to the booth of Thorstein Sidu-Hallsson[3] and approached him to ask for his help. Thorstein gave him the same answer as the others.

2

There was a man named Broddi Bjarnason, Thorstein's brother-in-law, who was sitting beside him. Broddi was then in his twenties. Ale-hood left the booth after Thorstein had refused him help.

Broddi then spoke: 'It seems to me, brother-in-law, that this man is ill-suited to be an outlaw, and it is meanness in those who think themselves great to try to sentence him to outlawry. The decent thing to do would be to give him help, as you must admit, brother-in-law.'

Thorstein answered: 'Give him help if you are so eager to, and I will give you the same support in this as in other things.'

Broddi told a man to go after Ale-hood. He did so – went out and found Ale-hood, who was standing beside the wall of the booth, weeping wretchedly.

This man told him to go into the booth and to stop his wailing, 'and don't sniffle when you approach Thorstein'.

Ale-hood was so pleased he could have cried, but did as he was told.

When they came into Thorstein's presence, Broddi began to speak: 'I think Thorstein wants to help you because this seems to him an underhanded suit. You could not watch out for their woods when your own were burning down.'

Ale-hood spoke: 'Who is the worthy man who is now speaking to me?'

'My name is Broddi,' said he.

Then Ale-hood spoke: 'Would that be Broddi Bjarnason?'

'It would,' said Broddi.

'Not only are you a man more noble in appearance than other men, you also have the family for it,' said Ale-hood, and he went on about it, growing braver as he talked.

'The time has come, Broddi,' said Thorstein, 'if you're

willing, to provide him with some help, seeing that he praises you so much.'

Broddi then stood up and with him many men. He left the booth, then took Ale-hood aside for a talk and chatted with him. Afterwards they went over to the Thing fields. Many men were there already who had been to the Law Council. After the other men had left, Gudmund and Skafti stayed behind and talked law.

Broddi and his companions strolled through the Thing fields, but Ale-hood went to the Law Council.

He fell prostrate on the ground at the feet of the two godis and said, 'How lucky I am to have found you two honourable men, my chieftains, both of you good men. Will you help me – weak though I am – for I will be in deep trouble unless you support me?'

It would take a long time to relate all the words Ale-hood said in making himself out to be in every respect the most miserable of men.

Then Gudmund said to Skafti, 'How wretchedly this man carries on!'

Skafti answered, 'What has happened to your pride now, Ale-hood? How unlikely it seemed to you in the spring, when we came on our summoning trip, that your best choice would be to submit your case to me. Whatever became of the support of those godis with whom you threatened me in the spring?'

Ale-hood said, 'I was crazy then – or worse – not wanting you to have the judgement in my case. And don't mention chieftains, for they all lose heart the moment they see you two coming. Happy would I be, if I could submit my case to you both. But have I any hope of that? It is quite understandable, Skafti, that you were so angry with me that there is now no chance of that. I was a fool and a simpleton when I rejected your arbitrated settlement! Now I dare not look at these fierce men, who will kill me without hesitation if you two don't help me.'

He said the same thing again and again, claiming that he would think himself happy if they should judge his case: 'It seems to me that my money would be safest, if you two have it.'

Gudmund said to Skafti: 'I do not think this man worthy of outlawry. Would it not be more advisable to make him happy and let him choose men to arbitrate in this matter? But I do not know whether this will please the others involved in the case against him.'

'Now then, good men that you are,' said Ale-hood, 'you will surely grant me some assistance after this.'

Skafti spoke: 'It's up to me to conclude this case since I am prosecuting it. Gudmund and I will take the risk, Ale-hood, of naming the settlement and concluding the case. I think our help will do the trick for you.'

Then Ale-hood stood up and shook each by the hand, at once naming witnesses, one after another, and when word of the witness-naming spread, men crowded about. Ale-hood named Broddi and his companions first.

Skafti spoke: 'Our adversary in this case asks Gudmund and me to arbitrate it, and, though it was agreed among all of us who suffered losses that we would have self-judgement, Gudmund and I now wish to agree to his request that we, rather than other men, will name the settlement, if he, Thorhall, will accept this arrangement. You shall be witnesses that the case will be settled with damages and not outlawry. I confirm with my handshake that the charge on which I summoned him in the spring is hereby dropped.'

After they had finished shaking hands, Skafti said to Gudmund, 'Would it not be just as well to get this over with?'

'It would, indeed,' said Gudmund.

Ale-hood spoke: 'Don't be in such a hurry, because I have not decided to choose you rather than other men.'

Gudmund spoke: 'It was decided that we should name the settlement, unless you would rather choose others who share with us the case against you.'

Ale-hood said, 'I never agreed that they should arbitrate. We shook hands on the agreement that I should choose the two men I want.'

The issue was then referred to the witnesses to the handshake; the thingmen of Gudmund and Skafti disagreed completely as to what had been decided, but Broddi and his companions were quite clear that it had been decided as Ale-hood said, that he should choose the men to name the settlement.

Then Skafti spoke: 'Where did this wave come from,[4] Ale-hood? I see you bear your tail higher than you did a little while ago. Which men will you choose to name the settlement?'

Ale-hood spoke: 'No need to think long on that. I choose Thorstein Hallsson and Broddi Bjarnason, his brother-in-law, and I think the case will turn out better than if you two had decided it.'

Skafti said that he thought that the case would be properly dealt with even if they acted as arbitrators, 'because the grounds of our action are clear and valid, and these men are wise enough that they will be able to see how harshly you deserve to be treated'.

Ale-hood then joined Broddi's followers, and the men went back to their booths.

3

The next day the settlement was to be announced. Thorstein and Broddi took counsel together. Thorstein wanted to set higher damages, but Broddi said that it would be simplest if Thorstein did as he wished and announced a settlement himself. Broddi told him to choose whether he would announce the settlement or be the spokesman if anyone should challenge the settlement. Thorstein said he would rather announce the settlement than trade insults with the godis. Next Thorstein said that Ale-hood would not need to wait long for the outcome; he said that he should pay all the money then and there at the Law Rock.

After that they went to the Law Rock and, when the legal proceedings there finished, Thorstein Hallsson asked whether the godis might be at the Law Rock who had the case to plead against Ale-hood. 'I am told that Broddi and I are to name the settlement in the case. We will now declare the terms, if you are willing to hear them.'

They said that they fully expected that they would be justly treated in the settlement.

Then Thorstein spoke: 'It seems to us that the woods belonging to the six of you were worth little. They were of poor quality and too distant to benefit any of you. It was great selfishness on the part of men who had land enough to choose from to claim them along with their other property, whereas Ale-hood could not protect your woods while his own were burning down. Furthermore, such accidents happen. But because this has been put to arbitration, some compensation is called for. You six owned the woods. We will now award six ells of cloth to each of you, and that shall be paid here and now.'

Broddi had prepared for this and measured out pieces of homespun cloth. He himself then threw a piece to each of them and spoke: 'Queer payment, I call it.'

Skafti said, 'It is clear, Broddi, that you are eager to have us as enemies. You have involved yourself much in this case, and have hardly trod reluctantly in seeking our enmity. Other cases may prove more to our liking.'

Broddi answered: 'You will need, Skafti, to get more from other suits if you hope to start filling the gap left when your kinsman Orm tore a piece out of you for the love poem you composed about his wife. An evil deed that was, and repaid with evil.'

Then Thorkel Scarf spoke: 'For such a man as Broddi this is a big mistake. Either for Ale-hood's friendship, or for some bribe, he's willing to pay by making enemies for himself of such men as he has taken on here.'

Broddi said, 'It is no mistake to be true to one's convictions though there may be differences of rank between you and Ale-hood. But it was a blunder you made last spring when you were riding to the Spring Assembly and were not on the lookout for Steingrim's seal-fat stallion, which mounted you from behind, while the bony mare you were riding collapsed under you. I have not heard for a fact which of you he nailed, but men saw you pinned for a long time, because the stallion had its feet over your cloak.'

Eyjolf Thordarson spoke: 'It's true enough that this man has plucked off our prey, and then he hectors us to boot.'

Broddi said, 'I haven't plucked off any prey of yours. But

your prey was certainly plucked from you when you went
north to Skagafjord and stole oxen from Thorkel Eiriksson,
and Starri of Guddalir rode after you, and you saw the pursuit
when you came to Vatnsdal. You became so afraid then that
you turned into the likeness of a mare, which was a real abom-
ination. Starri and his men drove the oxen back, so it's true that
he plucked off your prey.'

Then spoke Snorri the Godi: 'Anything would profit us more
than exchanging insults with Broddi, but it's likely that we will
call to mind the enmity Broddi has shown us if we have a
chance to attack him.'

Broddi said, 'You have a twisted sense of honour, Snorri, if
you concentrate on taking vengeance against me but do not
avenge your father.'

Then Thorkel Geitisson said, 'It looks as if all you have got
from your namesake is his willingness to deal unjustly with
everyone; like him you may find that men will not put up with
it and you'll be killed some day.'

Broddi said, 'We gain no honour, kinsman, from holding
up in front of everyone the ill luck of our kindred. One cannot conceal the well-known fact that Brodd-Helgi was slain.
I have also been told that your father in the end had to accept
the same recompense, but I think that, if you try, you'll be
able to feel with your fingers where my father scarred you in
Bodvarsdal.'

After that they parted and went home to their booths.

Ale-hood is now out of the story.

4

The following day Broddi went over to the booth of Thorkel
Geitisson and then entered it and addressed Thorkel, who
answered little and was very angry.

Broddi said, 'I've come here, kinsman, because I see that
I was wrong in what I said to you. I want to ask you to blame
it on my youth and folly, and not let our kinship suffer. I have
here an ornamented sword that I want to give to you. I want to
follow it up by having you visit me in the summer, where I'll

make it clear that there are no things in my possession more costly than those you will receive.'

Thorkel accepted this gratefully, and said that he was eager that they make good their kinship. Then Broddi went home to his booth.

On the final evening of the Thing, Broddi went west across the river and at the end of the bridge met Gudmund. No greetings were exchanged.

But as they parted, Gudmund turned back and spoke: 'By which route will you ride home from the Thing, Broddi?'

He turned back and said, 'If you are curious to know, I will ride by Kjol to Skagafjord, then to Eyjafjord, then to Ljosavatn pass and so on to Myvatn and afterwards Modrudal heath.'⁵

Gudmund spoke: 'Keep your word and ride over Ljosavatn pass.'

Broddi said, 'I will keep it, but do you mean, Gudmund, to close the pass to me? It would be a serious mistake on your part if you close Ljosavatn pass to me so that I may not travel there with my companions, yet you couldn't keep the little "pass" between your own buttocks decently closed.'

This said, they parted and these words became known throughout the Thing.

But when Thorkel Geitisson came to hear of this, he went to meet Broddi and asked him to ride the Sand route or else the more easterly one.

Broddi said, 'I will ride the way that I have told Gudmund, because he will think me faint-hearted if I don't do so.'

Thorkel spoke: 'Then we will ride together, kinsman, along with our little band.'

Broddi said that he thought it an honour to be in his company and that it would please him very much.

Afterwards Thorkel and Broddi rode together with their bands north to Oxnadal heath. Thorkel's father-in-law, Einar Eyjolfsson, was with them on the journey. Broddi and Thorkel rode to Thvera with Einar and spent a night there. After that Einar rode along with them with a large company and they did not part until they reached the Skjalfandi river. Einar then rode home but Thorkel and Broddi continued on their way until they got to their farms east in Vopnafjord.

That summer Thorkel went to a feast at the home of Broddi his kinsman and there received excellent gifts. They enjoyed then the warmest of kinships and maintained it throughout their lives.

And with that ends the Saga of Ale-hood.

Translated by JOHN TUCKER

THE SAGA OF THE
CONFEDERATES

I

There was a man named Ofeig who lived in the west in Midfjord, at the farm called Reykir. He was the son of Skidi, and his
mother's name was Gunnlaug; her mother was Jarngerd,
daughter of Ofeig Jarngerdarson[1] from Skord in the north.
Ofeig was a married man; his wife was named Thorgerd, Vali's
daughter, a woman of good family and very strong character.
Ofeig was a very wise man and a shrewd adviser. He was a man
of distinction in every respect, but was not well off financially,
because he had extensive lands but not much cash. Although it
was quite a struggle to supply the needs of his household, he
denied no one hospitality. He was a thingman of Styrmir from
Asgeirsa, who was considered the most important chieftain in
the west at that time. Ofeig and his wife had a son called Odd,
who was a good-looking man and showed ability from an early
age, but he got little affection from his father; he was disin-
clined to work.

A man named Vali grew up in Ofeig's home, a handsome
and popular man. Odd grew up in his father's house until he
was twelve. Ofeig treated Odd coldly most of the time and
cared little for him, but the opinion spread that nobody in the
district had more ability than Odd.

One day Odd came to talk to his father and asked him to
fund him: 'I want to leave here. It's this way,' he said. 'You give
me little status, and I'm of no use to your household.'

Ofeig answered, 'I'll give you no less than you have earned,
and I'll do it right away, and then you'll see what support that
gives you.'

Odd said that he would not be able to support himself very far on that, and they broke off the conversation.

The next day Odd helped himself to a fishing line and all the tackle from the wall and twelve ells of homespun cloth, and went away without saying goodbye to anyone. He went north to Vatnsnes and there joined a group of fishermen, borrowing or hiring from them what equipment he most needed, and because they knew he was from a good family and he himself was well-liked, they took the risk of lending to him. So he bought everything on credit, and for the rest of that year he worked with them in the fishery, and it is said that the group Odd was with had the best catches of any. He stayed there three winters and three summers, and by then he had repaid everyone what he owed and had still built up a good trading capital for himself. He never visited his father and they both behaved as if there were no bond between them, but Odd was popular with his business partners.

At this point he got involved in cargo trips north to Strandir and bought a share in a ferry; he made money at this too. Now he quickly earned so much that he became sole owner of the ferry, and kept up this trade between Midfjord and the Strands for several summers. He was beginning by now to be a rich man. Then he grew tired of this occupation too, bought a share in an ocean-going ship and went abroad, spending some time in trading voyages. In this too he succeeded ably, profiting both in money and in reputation. He kept up this business until he owned the whole knorr and most of the cargo; he went on trading, becoming very prosperous and famous. When he was abroad he often stayed with men of rank and other leading people, and was highly regarded wherever he went. Now he became so wealthy that he owned two knorrs; it is said that no other trader sailing at that time was as rich as Odd. He was also a luckier sailor than others, never making land in Iceland further north than Eyjafjord or west of Hrutafjord.

2

It is reported that one summer Odd brought his ship into Hrutafjord at Bordeyri, intending to spend the winter in Iceland.

Then he was urged by his friends to settle down here and he did as they asked, buying land in Midfjord at the place called Mel. There he started farming on a large scale and living in grand style, and it is said that this enterprise was thought no less impressive than his former voyages, so that now Odd had no equal in the north of the country. He was more generous with his money than most, good at helping out people who needed it in his neighbourhood, but he never gave his own father any assistance.

He laid up his ship in Hrutafjord. It is said that not only was there no one else in Iceland as rich as Odd, but he was no less wealthy than the three next richest men put together. He was well off in every respect, in gold and silver, lands and livestock. His kinsman Vali was always with him, whether at home or abroad. Now Odd settled down on his farm with all the prestige described.

There was a man named Glum, who lived at Skridinsenni; that is between Bitra and Kollafjord. He had a wife called Thordis, daughter of Asmund Grey-locks the father of Grettir Asmundarson. Their son was called Ospak. He was a big, strong man, overbearing and very assertive, who started young in the cargo business between the Strands and the north country, an able man who grew immensely strong. One summer he put into Midfjord to sell his goods. He borrowed a horse one day and rode up to Mel to meet Odd. They exchanged greetings and general news.

Ospak said, 'It's like this, Odd: people speak well of your circumstances and praise you highly, and all your employees think themselves well placed. Now, I hope that it would turn out like that for me too; I'd like to join your household.'

Odd answered, 'You have no very good reputation and you're not well-liked; you're reckoned to be a tricky customer, like the rest of your family.'

Ospak answered, 'Trust your own experience rather than hearsay, because reputation rarely flatters. I'm not asking you to make a gift of it – I'd like you to house me but I would feed myself, and then see how you feel about it.'

Odd replied, 'You and your kinsmen are big men and difficult to cope with if it suits you to turn against anyone, but since you challenge me to take you in, we may as well chance it for one winter.'

Ospak accepted with thanks, moved to Mel that autumn with his belongings and quickly proved loyal to Odd, busying himself about the farm and doing the work of two men. Odd was very pleased with him. That winter passed, and when spring came Odd invited him to be fully part of his household, saying he thought that would be best. Ospak was very willing; he took charge of the farm and it prospered greatly. People were very impressed with how this man was turning out, and he was also personally popular. The farm was flourishing, and Odd seemed to be established more admirably than anyone. People thought only one thing detracted from his complete distinction, that he lacked a godord. At that time it was very common to set up new godords or to purchase them,[2] and Odd now did so. Thingmen quickly flocked to him, all eager to join him, and for a time everything was peaceful.

3

Odd was well pleased with Ospak and gave him a free hand with the estate. He was both skilful and hard-working and an asset to the farm. Another winter passed, and Odd was even more pleased with Ospak, because he was undertaking more tasks. In the autumn he rounded up the sheep from the hills and did so very successfully, with not a single sheep missing.

Now the next winter passed and spring came. Then Odd announced that he intended to go abroad that summer, and said that his kinsman Vali should take over the running of the farm.

Vali answered, 'The fact is, kinsman, that I'm not used to that, and I'd rather take care of our money and trade goods.' Then Odd turned to Ospak and asked him to take over the farm.

Ospak answered, 'That's too much for me, though things go well enough while you are on the spot.' Odd pressed him, but Ospak made excuses, although he was really mad keen for the job, and in the end he told Odd to have his own way, as long as he promised him his help and support. Odd said he was to manage his property for his own advancement and popularity, and said that he had proved by experience that there was no one else who could or would take better care of his possessions. Ospak said it should be as he pleased, and they broke off their conversation.

Now Odd prepared his ship and had his cargo loaded. The news of this spread and was much talked about. It did not take Odd long to get ready. Vali was to travel with him, and when everything was ready, people saw Odd on his way to his ship. Ospak went with him further than most, because they had much to discuss.

When they were only a short way from the ship, Odd said, 'Now there is just one thing that has not been settled.'

'What's that?' said Ospak.

'Nothing has been arranged about my godord,' said Odd, 'and I'd like you to take it over.'

'There's no sense in that,' said Ospak, 'I'm not up to the job. I've already taken on more than I'm likely to cope with or tackle well. There is nobody as suitable for the godord as your father; he's an expert in law and very wise.'

Odd said he would not entrust it to him – 'I want you to take it on.'

Ospak made excuses, but was very keen to do it. Odd said he would get angry if he did not accept, and when they parted Ospak took over the godord. Odd now went abroad and had a successful voyage, as he usually did. Ospak went home, and this matter was much discussed; Odd was thought to have put a lot of power into this man's hands.

Ospak rode to the Althing in the summer with a group of supporters, and succeeded ably. He knew how to discharge successfully all the duties the law required of him, and he rode away from the Althing with honour. He supported his thing-men enthusiastically, so that they held their own in everything and were not imposed on at all, and he was generous and help-ful to all his neighbours. In no way did the splendour and hospitality of the estate seem less than before; there was no lapse in management, and the household affairs flourished. Now the summer passed. Ospak rode to the Autumn Meeting and protected it by law, and as autumn drew on he went into the hills at round-up time and made a good job of gathering the sheep; it was pursued with energy, and not a single sheep went missing, either of his own or Odd's.

4

During the autumn Ospak happened to go north into Vididal to Svolustadir, where a woman named Svala lived. He was offered hospitality there. Svala, who was a good-looking young woman, talked to Ospak and asked him to manage her affairs.

'I've heard that you're a good farm manager,' she said.

He responded positively, and they talked about many things. Each was attracted to the other and they exchanged warm glances. Their discussion ended with him asking who was responsible for finding her a husband.

'No one of any importance is more closely related to me,' she said, 'than Thorarin the Wise, the Godi of Langidal.'

Ospak then rode to visit Thorarin, who welcomed him without enthusiasm. He explained his errand and asked for Svala's hand.

Thorarin answered, 'I don't find you a desirable in-law; your doings are much talked about. I can see that it's necessary to deal unambiguously with people such as you: either I'll have to confiscate her farm and move her in here, or the two of you will do as you please. Now I'll have nothing to do with this, and I declare it to be no affair of mine.'

After that Ospak went back to Svolustadir and told Svala how things stood. Then they settled their marriage themselves, with Svala declaring her own betrothal; she moved with him to Mel, but they kept the farm at Svolustadir and employed people to run it. Ospak now kept house at Mel in grand style, but people nonetheless found him very overbearing.

Now another winter passed, and in the summer Odd made land in Hrutafjord, having yet again done well in terms of both money and reputation. He came home to Mel and looked over his property; he thought it well cared for, and approved of it. As summer passed, one day Odd raised the matter with Ospak that it would be proper for him to take back his godord.

'Of course,' said Ospak. 'That was the thing I was least willing and fit to deal with. I'm quite ready to hand it over, but I think such transfers are most usually made either at autumn assemblies or at Things.'

Odd answered, 'That's fine with me.'

Summer passed and it was time for the Autumn Meeting. When Odd woke up on the assembly morning, he looked about him and saw few people in the hall. He had slept long and deep. He leapt out of bed and realized that all the men had left the hall. He thought this was strange, but said little; he got dressed and rode to the assembly, taking several men with him. When they arrived there was a crowd of people there, but they were nearly ready to leave, and the assembly had been completed by law. Odd was taken aback, and thought this behaviour strange.

Everyone went home, and some days passed. Then one day when Odd was sitting at table with Ospak opposite him, without any warning Odd leapt up from table, threatening Ospak with a raised axe, and ordered him to hand over the godord now.

Ospak answered, 'There's no need to pursue the matter with such vigour – you can have your godord whenever you want. I had no idea you were serious about taking it over.'

Then he stretched out his hand to Odd and with their handshake transferred the godord to him.

Things were now quiet for a time, but there was no love lost between Odd and Ospak. Ospak was savage tempered, and people suspected that he must have been intending to keep the godord for himself and not give it back to Odd, if it had not been forced from him in a way he could not escape. Now his management of the farm came to nothing; Odd gave him no orders, and they never exchanged a word. One day Ospak got ready to leave. Odd pretended not to notice, and they parted without either saying goodbye. Ospak now went to his farm at Svolustadir. Odd behaved as if nothing had happened, and things were now quiet for a time.

It is reported that when men went to the hills in the autumn, there was a striking difference in Odd's success in collecting his sheep compared with previous years. In the round-up he was forty wethers short, all the best of his stock; they were searched for far and wide in the hills and mountains but could not be found. People thought this strange, because Odd was reckoned to be luckier with his livestock than other men. So much effort was put into the hunt that the sheep were searched for both locally and in other districts, but without success. In the end this tailed off, but there was still a lot of discussion as to what could be behind it.

Odd was not cheerful that winter. His kinsman Vali asked him why he was so gloomy.

'Does the disappearance of the wethers prey on you so much? You're not a very high-minded man if such a thing can get you down.'

Odd replied, 'It's not the loss of the wethers which bothers me so much as not knowing who stole them.'

'Are you sure that's what has happened to them?' said Vali.

'Whom do you most suspect?' Odd said. 'There's no hiding the fact that I think Ospak is the thief.'

Vali answered, 'Your friendship has gone downhill since the time when you put him in charge of all your property.'

Odd said that that had been a very stupid thing to do, and it had turned out better than might have been expected.

Vali said, 'Many people said at the time that it was strange. Now I don't want you to rush into making a serious accusation against him; if it is thought ill-founded, there's a danger to your reputation. Now we two shall do a deal,' said Vali, 'that you leave it to me to decide how to go about this, and I shall find out the truth for certain.' They agreed on this.

Vali now got ready for a journey and rode on a trading trip north to Vatnsdal and Langidal, selling his merchandise. He was a popular man, helpful with advice. He went on his way until he came to Svolustadir, where he was warmly received. Ospak was in very cheerful mood. Next morning, when Vali prepared to leave, Ospak saw him off from the farm, asking for all the news of Odd. Vali said he was doing well.

Ospak spoke approvingly of Odd and praised his magnificent lifestyle: 'But didn't he suffer some losses last autumn?'

Vali said that was true.

'What are people's guesses about the disappearance of his wethers? Odd has been so lucky with his livestock up to now.'

Vali replied, 'Opinions vary, but some people think it was no accident.'

'Unthinkable!' said Ospak. 'Few men would be capable of such a thing.'

'Just so,' said Vali.

Ospak said, 'Has Odd himself any views?'

Vali said, 'He doesn't talk about it much, but there's plenty of speculation from other people about what was behind it.'

'That's to be expected,' said Ospak.

'It's like this,' said Vali, 'since we're speaking of the matter: some people seem to suggest that you might very probably be responsible. They put two and two together about your cold parting from Odd and the disappearance of the sheep not long after.'

Ospak answered, 'I never expected to hear you say such a thing, and if we weren't such good friends I would make you pay bitterly for that.'

Vali replied, 'There's no point in trying to deny this, or in getting so worked up about it. It won't clear you of the charge; I've been looking over the state of your supplies, and I can see that you have much more than you would be likely to come by honestly.'

'That will not prove true,' Ospak answered, 'and I don't know what my enemies can be saying, if this is how my friends are talking.'

Vali replied, 'I'm not saying this out of enmity towards you, and you are the only one hearing it. Now if you do as I want and come clean with me, you'll get off lightly, because I have a plan. I have been selling my goods all over the countryside: I'll say that you bought them all and used them to buy meat and other things. Nobody will disbelieve it. In this way I can contrive that you get out of this without dishonour, if you follow my advice.'

Ospak said he was not confessing anything.

'Then it will be the worse for you,' said Vali, 'and it will be your own fault.'

Then they parted, and Vali went home.

Odd asked what he had discovered about the disappearance of the sheep, but Vali had little to say.

Odd said, 'There's no point in denying that Ospak is the thief, because you would be quick to clear him if you could.'

The rest of the winter was uneventful, but in the spring when the Summons Days came, Odd set out with twenty men.

When they got near the farm at Svolustadir, Vali said to Odd, 'Now you let your horses graze, and I'll ride up to the house and meet Ospak, and see if he is willing to come to terms. Then the case will not need to go further.'

They did as he said.

Vali rode up to the house. There was nobody outside, but the door was open, so Vali went in. The house was dark. Without any warning, someone leapt from the benches and struck Vali between the shoulders so that he fell at once. It was Ospak.

Vali said, 'Run for it, you miserable wretch. Odd is almost at the farm and he means to kill you. Send your wife to tell Odd that we have come to terms and you have confessed to the charge, but that I have ridden north to the valleys about my business affairs.'

Then Ospak said, 'This act has turned out very badly; I meant this for Odd, not you.'

Svala now went to meet Odd and told him that Ospak and Vali had come to terms: 'Vali said that you should go home.'

Odd believed her and rode home, but Vali died, and his body was taken to Mel. Odd thought this terrible news. He received dishonour from the affair, which was considered to have turned out disastrously for him.

Ospak now disappeared, so that no one knew what had become of him.

5

To return to Odd, he prepared to take this case to the Althing by summoning a panel of neighbours from his home district. Now it happened that one of the panel died, and Odd summoned another man in his place. Then men went to the Althing, and nothing happened until the courts were in session. When the courts sat, Odd began an action for a killing, and it went smoothly for him until the defence was invited to speak.

A short distance from the court two chieftains, Styrmir and Thorarin, were sitting with their supporters.

Then Styrmir said to Thorarin, 'The defence has just been invited on the killing charge; do you want to offer any defence in this case?'

Thorarin answered, 'I'll have nothing to do with it. Odd seems to me more than justified in bringing a suit following the killing of such a man as Vali, and I regard the accused as a thoroughly bad lot.'

'Yes,' said Styrmir, 'the fellow is certainly bad, but you do have some duty towards him.'[3]

'I couldn't care less,' said Thorarin.

Styrmir said, 'But you have to look at the fact that he is going to be your problem, and a worse and more complicated one if he's outlawed. I think it is worth considering what steps we can take in the case, because we both can see a legal defence.'[4]

'I spotted that long ago,' said Thorarin, 'but I don't think it a good idea to hinder this case.'

Styrmir said, 'But this affects you most, and people will say that you have acted feebly if the case goes through when there is an unanswerable legal defence. The fact of the matter is that it would also do Odd good to realize that he's not the only person of consequence around. He tramples over all of us and our thingmen, so that he gets all the attention. It will do him no harm to discover just how skilled in law he really is.'

Thorarin answered, 'Have it your own way, and I'll back you up, but no good is likely to come of it, and it will end badly.'

'We can't let that influence us,' said Styrmir, jumping up and going over to the court.

He asked what case was in progress, and was told.

Styrmir said, 'The situation is, Odd, that there is a legal

defence against your charge. You have prepared the case incorrectly, in summoning a tenth panel-member at home. That is a legal error: you should have done that at the Althing and not in your home district. Now you can either leave the court as the case stands, or we shall move this defence.'

Odd was dumbstruck and thought the matter over. He realized it was true, left the court with his supporters and went back to his booth. When he reached the passage between the booths, there was a man coming towards him. He was an elderly man in a black-sleeved cape; it was threadbare and had only one sleeve, hanging down the back. He had a metal-pointed staff in his hand. He wore his hood low over his face, peering sharply out from under it. He walked with a stoop, jabbing his stick down for support. It was old Ofeig, his father.

'You're early leaving the court,' said Ofeig. 'You can boast more than one talent, when everything goes so promptly and decisively for you – or hasn't Ospak been outlawed?'

'No,' said Odd, 'he has not been outlawed.'

Ofeig said, 'It's not acting like a great man to make fun of me when I'm old. Why would he not be outlawed? Wasn't he guilty of the crime?'

'Of course he was guilty,' said Odd.

'What is it then?' said Ofeig. 'I thought the charge ought to stick – or did he not kill Vali?'

'No one's denying that,' said Odd.

'Then why isn't he outlawed?' said Ofeig.

Odd answered, 'A defence was found in the case and it collapsed.'

Ofeig said, 'How can there be a defence in a case brought by such a rich man?'

'They said it was wrongly prepared in the first place,' said Odd.

'That can't be so, when you were the prosecutor,' said Ofeig, 'though perhaps you are better at moneymaking and voyages than the perfect management of lawsuits. But I still think you are not telling me the truth.'

'I don't give a damn whether you believe me or not,' Odd replied.

'That may well be,' said Ofeig, 'but I knew before you set out from home that the case had been wrongly prepared, but you thought yourself all-sufficient and wouldn't ask anyone's advice. Now you will still be self-sufficient in the matter, I suppose. It's bound to turn out well for you, but it is a demanding situation for such as you, who look down on everyone else.'

Odd answered, 'It's more than plain that there will be no help from you.'

Ofeig said, 'The only hope in your situation is for you to make use of my help. How reluctant would you be to pay out if someone rectified your case?'

'I would spare no money,' Odd replied, 'if someone would take over the case.'

'Then hand over a reasonably plump purse to this old man,' said Ofeig, 'because many eyes squint when there's money around.'

Odd gave him a heavy purse. Then Ofeig asked, 'Was the defence formally made or not?'

'We walked out of the court first,' said Odd.

Ofeig answered, 'The only useful step you made was taken in ignorance.'

Then they parted, and Odd went back to his booth.

6

Now to go back to old Ofeig, he went up to the upper fields of the Thing site and to the courts. He came to the court for the North Quarter and asked how people's cases were going. He was told that some had been judged and some were ready for summing up.

'What about the case of my son Odd? Has that been dealt with?'

'As far as it ever will be,' they said.

Ofeig asked, 'Has Ospak been outlawed?'

'No,' they said, 'he hasn't.'

'For what reason?' asked Ofeig.

'A legal defence was found,' they said, 'that the case had been wrongly prepared.'

'Ah yes,' said Ofeig. 'Will you permit me to enter the court?'

They agreed, so he went into the judgement circle and sat down.

'Has the case of my son Odd been judged?' said Ofeig.

'As far as it ever will be,' they said.

'For what reason?' asked Ofeig. 'Was Ospak falsely accused? Didn't he kill Vali, an innocent man? Was the impediment that the case was not important?'

They said, 'A legal defence was established and the case collapsed.'

'What sort of defence was it?' asked Ofeig.

They told him.

'Quite so,' he said. 'Did there seem to you any kind of justice in paying attention to such a triviality instead of condemning a thoroughly bad man, a thief and a murderer? Isn't it a serious responsibility to acquit someone who deserves death and thus judge in contradiction to justice?'

They said that they thought it unjust, but that it was required of them by law.

'Maybe so,' said Ofeig. 'Did you swear the oath?'

'Of course,' they said.

'You must have done,' he said. 'And what form of words did you use? Wasn't it on these lines, that you would judge as truthfully and fairly and lawfully as you knew how? You must have said that.'

They agreed that he was right.

'But what could be truer or fairer,' said Ofeig then, 'than to condemn a thoroughly bad man to outlawry, to be killed with impunity and denied all help, when he has been clearly proved guilty of theft and of killing an innocent man, namely Vali? As to the third point in the oath, that may be bending things a bit. But think seriously for yourselves what is more important, the two terms touching truth and fairness or the one referring to the law? Then you'll see things as they are, because you must be able to see that it is a heavier responsibility to acquit someone who deserves death, when you have sworn an oath to judge as fairly as you knew how. One might consider that this responsibility will fall heavily on you, and you can't wriggle out of it.'

From time to time Ofeig let the purse slip down below his cape and then pulled it up again.

When he saw that they were following the purse with their eyes, he said to them, 'You'd be better advised to judge fairly and truly, as you have sworn, and so get in return the thanks and gratitude of all prudent and right-thinking men.'

Then he took the purse and emptied it out and counted the silver in front of them.

'Now I want to show you a token of friendship,' he said, 'though I can see more in this for you than for me. I'm doing this because some of you are my friends and some are related to me, though not so closely but that each should look to his own advantage. I intend to give an ounce of silver to every judge sitting in this court and half a mark to the one who sums up in the case, and then you will both have the money and rid yourselves of the responsibility and, most important of all, avoid breaking your sworn word.'

They considered the matter and found his arguments plausible, and thought they had been in danger of breaking their oaths, so they chose to accept Ofeig's offer. Then they sent at once for Odd, and he came, but Styrmir and Thorarin had gone back to their booths by then. Now the case was immediately resumed and Ospak was sentenced to outlawry; and then witnesses were named to testify that sentence had been delivered. At this juncture people went home to their booths.

News of this did not spread that night, but next morning Odd stood up at the Law Rock and announced loudly: 'A man called Ospak was declared an outlaw last night in the North Quarter court for the killing of Vali. This is the outlaw's description: he is a big, manly-looking man, with brown hair and strongly marked cheekbones. He has dark eyebrows, big hands and thick legs. His whole build is uncommonly big and he has a thoroughly criminal appearance.'

People were taken very much by surprise, for many had had no news of this beforehand. Odd was thought to have pressed his case with determination and to be lucky in the outcome, seeing the turn it had taken.

7

It is said that Styrmir and Thorarin had a talk together.

Styrmir said, 'We've been badly shamed and humiliated by this case.'

Thorarin said it was to be expected: 'And crafty men must have manipulated it.'

'Yes,' said Styrmir. 'Can you see any way of putting it right?'

'I don't know that we can do it quickly,' said Thorarin.

'What's the best way?' asked Styrmir.

Thorarin answered, 'If those who bribed the judges were prosecuted, the charge should stick.'

'That's a pleasant prospect, if we can get our own back,' said Styrmir.

Then they walked away and back to their booths. Now they called together their friends and relations for a meeting. One of these was Hermund Illugason, the second Gellir Thorkelsson, the third Egil Skulason, the fourth Jarnskeggi Einarsson, the fifth Beard-Broddi Bjarnason and the sixth Thorgeir Halldoruson,[5] plus Styrmir and Thorarin. These eight men now conferred together. Styrmir and Thorarin explained the situation and how the case then stood, and also how much of Odd's wealth was up for grabs and that they would all get very rich out of it.

Then they all made a firm agreement to support one another in the case, so as either to get Odd outlawed or to win self-judgement against him. Then they swore a formal covenant, reckoning that this could not be broken and that no one would have the confidence or skill to challenge them. With this settled, they parted.

People rode home from the Althing, and at first the plot was kept secret. Odd was very pleased with his journey to the Althing, and his relationship with his father was better than it had been. Nothing much happened that winter.

In the spring Odd and his father met at the warm baths, and Ofeig asked the news. Odd said he had none and asked in his turn. Ofeig told him that Styrmir and Thorarin had gathered supporters and intended to ride to Mel to summons him.

Odd asked what the charge was, and Ofeig told him all their plans.

Odd replied, 'This doesn't look too serious to me.'

'Maybe it won't be too much for you,' said Ofeig.

Time passed, and at the Summons Days Styrmir and Thorarin arrived at Mel with a large following. Odd too was well supported. They stated their case and summonsed Odd to the Althing for having caused money to be unlawfully brought into court. Nothing else happened there, and they rode away with their supporters.

It happened again that Odd and his father met and talked.

Ofeig asked whether he still thought it an unimportant matter.

Odd replied, 'The case doesn't look serious to me.'

'That's not how it looks to me,' said Ofeig. 'How clearly do you understand the situation?'

Odd said he knew what had happened so far.

Ofeig answered, 'It seems to me that there will be more to follow, because six of the other most important chieftains have come into the case with them.'

'They must think they need a lot of help,' said Odd.

Ofeig asked, 'What do you plan to do now?'

Odd answered, 'What else but to ride to the Althing and muster support?'

'That doesn't seem to me a good idea as matters stand,' replied Ofeig. 'It's not good to have your reputation dependent on too many people's help.'

'What do you suggest then?' asked Odd.

Ofeig said, 'I suggest that you should fit out your ship during the Althing and be ready to leave with all your movable property by the time men ride away from the Althing. And which money do you think will be in better hands, what they will confiscate from you, or what I hold?'

'I think it the lesser of two evils that you should have it.'

So Odd handed his father a bulging money bag full of silver, and with this they parted.

Odd fitted out his ship and hired a crew, and these arrangements were made quietly so that few got to know about them. The time for the Althing drew near.

8

Now the chieftains rode to the Althing, taking a very large following with them. Old Ofeig was in Styrmir's party. The confederates, Egil, Gellir, Styrmir, Hermund and Thorarin, had agreed to meet on Blaskogar heath; from there they all rode south to Thingvellir together. Beard-Broddi and Thorgeir Halldoruson from Laugardal rode from the east and Jarnskeggi from the north, and they met at Reydarmuli. Now all the parties rode down to the fields and so to the area of the Althing.

The chief topic of conversation there was the case against Odd. It seemed certain to everyone that nobody would be found to defend him, since they thought few would dare, and in any case it would get them nowhere, seeing what important men were on the other side. The confederates too were confident of success and swaggered a lot, and no one said a word against them. Odd had not asked anyone to defend his cause; he began preparing his ship in Hrutafjord as soon as men left for the Althing.

One day old Ofeig walked away from his booth with a lot on his mind. He could see no one likely to help him and thought he had a great deal to contend with, for he could scarcely see how he could cope on his own against such powerful men, when there was no legal defence to be made in the case. He walked bent at the knees, wandering and stumbling between the booths for a long time, until he came at length to the booth of Egil Skulason. There were some men there who had come to talk to Egil, so Ofeig went past the booth door and waited there until the men left. Egil showed them out, and when he was going back indoors, Ofeig stepped in front of him and greeted him. Egil looked at him and asked who he was.

'Ofeig is my name,' he said.

Egil said, 'Are you Odd's father?'

He said he was.

'Then you will be wanting to talk to me about his case, but it's no use discussing it with me; things have gone much too far for me to be able to do anything. Anyway, there are others more responsible for the case than I am, namely Styrmir and

Thorarin. It's chiefly their concern, though the rest of us support them.'

Ofeig answered with a verse:

1.
Before, I could speak
of my son with pride,
though I never came
in Odd's company.
Little heed to laws
the loud-mouth paid,
though money he has
more than enough.

Then he added another:

2.
An old stay-at-home
finds satisfaction
in talking chiefly
with intelligent men.
You won't refuse
to confer with me,
because worthy men
call you wise.

'I'll find something more entertaining to talk about than Odd's affairs,' Ofeig went on. 'Time was when they were rather better than now. You won't refuse me a chat; it's an old man's chief pleasure to pass the time by talking with people like you.'

Egil replied, 'I won't refuse you a talk.'

They walked off together and sat down.

Then Ofeig began: 'Are you a good farmer, Egil?'

He said he was.

'Do you farm at Borg?'

'That's right,' said Egil.

Ofeig said, 'I've been told good and agreeable things about you; they say that you begrudge food to nobody and live in lavish

style. We're not unalike: we are both men of good family and
generous with what we have, but find ourselves in financial difficulties; and I'm told that you like to help your friends.'

Egil answered, 'I would like to think I was as well spoken of as
you, because I know that you are of good family and also wise.'

Ofeig said, 'There is one difference between us: you're an
important leader and fear nothing, whatever happens, and
never fail to defend your rights against anyone at all, but I am
a nobody. But still we are alike in temperament, and it is a great
pity that men like us, who are so high-minded, should be short
of money.'

'That may soon change,' said Egil, 'and then I'll be better
off.'

'How so?' asked Ofeig.

'It seems to me,' said Egil, 'that if Odd's money comes our
way, we won't go short of much, considering the great tales we
have heard of his wealth.'

Ofeig answered, 'They won't have been exaggerated, even if
he was said to be the richest man in Iceland. But you must be
curious to know how large your share will be, seeing that you
need the money so badly.'

'That's true,' said Egil. 'You're a good fellow and intelligent
with it. You must know precisely how rich Odd is.'

He replied, 'I don't suppose anyone knows more about it
than I do, and I can tell you that he is richer than anybody has
ever said. But I have already been calculating what your share
will come to.'

And then he spoke this verse:

3.
Injustice, I grant you, has engaged
eight gold-greedy men.
These gods of wealth   *gods of wealth*: (noble) men
make words worthless.
You battle-windswept warriors,
I wish you'd suffer
loss of giant's laughter   *giant's laughter*: gold
and good fame both.

'What's that?' said Egil. 'That's not likely to happen, but you are a good poet.'

Ofeig said, 'I won't hold back from you just what a fortune you will come in for: a one-sixteenth share of the Mel lands.'

'What's this I hear?' said Egil. 'Then the fortune can't be as great as I thought. How can this be?'

Ofeig answered, 'No, the fortune is there all right, but I think this is pretty well exactly what you will get of it. Haven't you agreed that you and your allies should have half of Odd's fortune and the men of his quarter the other half? I reckon from that, that if there are eight of you confederates, you will each get a one-sixteenth share of the Mel lands, for these must be the terms you have planned and agreed. Even though you entered on this business for the most scandalous reasons ever heard of, you must have had this kind of agreement. But did you really expect my son Odd to sit still and wait for you to ride north and attack him? Oh no,' said Ofeig, 'Odd is not going to be short of a plan to outwit you, for well supplied as he is with wealth, he is no less blessed with intelligence and planning ability, when he finds he needs it. And though you may name him outlaw, I suspect that his knorr will glide no less smoothly with him across the Iceland Sea for that. Anyway, you can't call it outlawry when it arises from such an unjust charge, which will rebound on the men who brought it. I expect Odd will be at sea by now with all his possessions except the lands at Mel – that's all he means you to get. He had heard too that it would be only a short walk from the sea to Borg, should he happen to put in to Borgarfjord. This case is going to end as it began, with you all being shamed and disgraced and condemned by everybody – which is only what you deserve.'

'That's plain as daylight,' said Egil, 'and now the matter is getting tricky. It's obvious that Odd wasn't going to sit around doing nothing, and I for one don't blame him. There are some people involved in this case whom I wouldn't mind seeing humiliated, like Styrmir or Thorarin or Hermund, and they have been pressing it hardest.'

'It will all turn out for the best,' Ofeig said. 'They will get their deserts and be widely condemned for this affair. But I think it would be a shame if you didn't come out of this well, because I like you better than any of your confederates.'

As he spoke he let a well-rounded money bag drop into sight below his cape. Egil spotted it at once, and when Ofeig saw that, he quickly pulled the bag back up out of sight.

'As I was saying, Egil,' he said, 'I think things will turn out pretty much as I've told you. Now I'd like to offer you a token of my respect.'

Then he pulled out the money bag and emptied the silver out into the lap of Egil's cloak; it came to two hundred of the finest silver obtainable.

'This is for you as a little token of my regard – if you don't oppose me in this business.'

'You're no average rogue!' replied Egil. 'You can't expect me to be willing to break my oath.'

Ofeig said, 'You and your allies are certainly not what you make yourselves out to be: you want to be called chieftains, but as soon as you land in any difficulty, you have no idea how to get out with advantage. Now you mustn't let that happen to you, for I shall hit on a way for you to keep your oath.'

'What way?' said Egil.

Ofeig said, 'Haven't you agreed that you will press for either outlawry or self-judgement?'

Egil confirmed it.

'It may well be,' said Ofeig, 'that we, Odd's kinsmen, are granted the privilege of deciding which it shall be. Now it might also chance that you, Egil, were asked to pronounce the settlement, and in that case I'd like you to arrange it.'

'You're quite right,' said Egil. 'What a sly and intelligent old fellow you are! But I'm still not prepared to do this for you, because I have neither the strength nor the manpower to stand alone against all these chieftains, since anyone who opposes them is bound to face their enmity.'

Ofeig said, 'How about if someone else joined you in the matter?'

'That would be more like it,' said Egil.

Ofeig asked, 'Which of the confederates would you soonest have, supposing me to have the pick of all of them?'

'There are two possibilities,' said Egil. 'Hermund lives closest to me, but we are on bad terms; but the other is Gellir, and
I would prefer him.'

'It's a lot to ask of me,' said Ofeig, 'because I would like to
see them all come badly out of this case – except you, of course.
But Gellir will have the wit to see which is the better choice,
getting money and honour, or losing money and being shamed.
So you are willing to undertake this and reduce the settlement,
if the matter is referred to your judgement?'

'That's my firm intention,' said Egil.

'Then let this be a definite agreement between us,' said Ofeig,
'and I'll get back to you in a short time.'

9

Now they parted, and Ofeig went away. He wandered shuffling
among the booths, but he was not as dejected in mind as he
was tottering on his feet, nor so haphazard in his plans as
he was feeble in his gait. In the end he came to the booth of
Gellir Thorkelsson and had him called outside. He came out
and, being an unpretentious man, greeted Ofeig first and asked
what he wanted.

'I just wandered over this way,' answered Ofeig.

Gellir said, 'You'll be wanting to talk about Odd's case.'

'I don't want to talk about that,' said Ofeig. 'I've washed my
hands of it, and I'm looking for other entertainment.'

Gellir said, 'Then what do you want to talk about?'

Ofeig said, 'I'm told that you are a wise man, and I enjoy
talking to such people.'

Then they sat down and began talking together.

Ofeig asked, 'What young men are there in your west country who seem to you likely to become important chieftains?'

Gellir said there were plenty to choose from, and mentioned
the sons of Snorri the Godi and the men of Eyri.

'That's what I've been told,' said Ofeig, 'but now I am indeed
well placed to get news, since I'm talking to a man who is both
truthful and obliging. But which of the women there in the
west are the best matches?'

Gellir named the daughters of Snorri the Godi and those of Steinthor of Eyri.

'That's what I've been told,' said Ofeig. 'But how's this, haven't you some daughters too?'

Gellir said he had indeed.

'Then why didn't you mention them?' said Ofeig. 'To judge from probability, none can be prettier than your daughters. They're not married, are they?'

'No,' said Gellir.

'Why not?' asked Ofeig.

Gellir said, 'Because no suitors have come forward who are both rich enough and well established, of powerful family and good personal qualities. I may not be wealthy myself, but I am still choosy about sons-in-law, for the sake of my ancestry and reputation. But I mustn't let you ask all the questions. What men up there in the north are promising as chieftains?'

Ofeig replied, 'There are plenty to choose from. I reckon Einar the first, the son of Jarnskeggi, and then Hall Styrmisson. Some people say too that my son, Odd, is a promising man – and that brings me to the message he asked me to give you, that he would like to become your son-in-law and marry your daughter Ragnheid.'

'Yes, well,' said Gellir, 'there was a time when my answer would have been favourable, but as things stand I think we'll have to put the matter off.'

'On what grounds?' said Ofeig.

Gellir said, 'There seems to be a cloud over the prospects of your son, Odd, as things are now.'

Ofeig replied, 'I can tell you as a fact that you will never find her a better husband than him, because everyone agrees that Odd is the most accomplished man around, and he certainly lacks neither money nor good family. But you are much in need of money, and you might find him a source of strength to you, because he is a man generous to his friends.'

'That would be worth thinking about,' said Gellir, 'if this lawsuit were not impending.'

Ofeig answered, 'Don't mention that silly nonsense. There's nothing in it but folly and the dishonour of the people pressing it.'

'It's likely to turn out quite otherwise,' replied Gellir, 'so I'm not willing to agree to your proposal. But if this problem could be solved, I'd be glad to accept.'

Ofeig answered, 'It may be, Gellir, that you are all about to make a fortune here, but I can tell you what your share of it will amount to, because I know precisely. At very best, you confederates will get half the Mel lands between you. Your share won't be much good though: you'll get little of the money and lose your honour and integrity, when you have been known before as one of the most decent men in the country.'

Gellir asked how this might be.

Ofeig replied, 'I think it most likely that Odd is now at sea with all his possessions except the lands at Mel. You can't have expected him to sit there helplessly while you divide up his property and share it between you. No,' said Ofeig, 'on the contrary, he said that if he came to Breidafjord he would find his way to your farm, and then he could take his pick of a wife from your family, and he said he would have enough firewood with him to burn down your house if he wanted. So too if he came to Borgarfjord, he had heard that it was only a short walk from the sea to Borg. He mentioned as well that if he came to Eyjafjord, he might find Jarnskeggi's farm, and in the same way, if he came to the East Fjords, he would find where Beard-Broddi lived. Now it doesn't matter to him if he never comes back to Iceland, but you will all have got what you deserve from this, namely shame and disgrace. I think it a pity that such a good chieftain as you have been should come by such a bad fate, and I would gladly spare you this.'

'You must be right,' replied Gellir, 'and I don't much mind if some trick is tried to escape the confiscation. I let myself be talked into this by my friends, rather than being set on it myself.'

Ofeig said, 'You'll see, as soon as you are under less pressure, that it would be a more honourable part to marry your daughter to my son, Odd, as I said in the first place. Take a look at the money he has sent you! He said that he would provide her dowry himself, since he knew you were hard up, and this is two hundred of a silver that can hardly be matched.

Consider who else could make you such an offer, marrying your daughter to such a husband, who will provide her dowry himself. You will probably never go short again, and your daughter will have fallen into the lap of luxury.'

Gellir answered, 'This is such a splendid offer that it is hard to put a valuation on it, but on no account will I betray those who put their trust in me, even though I see that nothing is to be had from this case but ridicule and scorn.'

'How wise you chieftains are!' replied Ofeig. 'Who said anything about betraying those who trust you, or breaking your oath? On the other hand, it could happen that the settlement is put into your hands, and then you could reduce the amount and still keep your oath.'

'That's true,' said Gellir. 'What a crafty old man you are, and so cunning! But I can't take on the whole lot of them on my own.'

Ofeig said, 'How would it be if I could get another man in on it? Would you help me out then?'

'I'm willing,' said Gellir, 'if you can bring it about that I decide the terms.'

Ofeig asked, 'Who would you choose to have with you?'

Gellir answered, 'I'd choose Egil; he lives nearest me.'

'I never heard anything like it!' said Ofeig. 'You pick the worst of the whole bunch. It goes against the grain for me to offer him a share in the honour, and I don't know whether I can bring myself to do it.'

'That's up to you,' said Gellir.

Ofeig said, 'If I persuade him to join you, will you take the matter on? He'll be shrewd enough to see that it's better to gain some honour than none at all.'

'Since I stand to gain so much from it,' said Gellir, 'I think I'll take the risk.'

Then Ofeig said, 'Actually, Egil and I have already talked it over, and the matter doesn't look too difficult to him, so he's committed. Now I'll advise you how to handle this. You confederates and your supporters are all going about as one party, so no one will be suspicious if you and Egil get to talking as much as you want while you are going to evensong.'

Gellir accepted the money, and the matter was settled between them. Then Ofeig went away and back to Egil's booth, walking neither slowly nor uncertainly, nor yet with a stoop. He told Egil how things had gone, and he was delighted. Later in the evening, when people went to evensong, Egil and Gellir had a talk and agreed the matter between them, without anyone having any suspicion.

10

Now it is said that the next day men gathered in large numbers at the Law Rock. Egil and Gellir mustered their friends about them, and Ofeig helped Styrmir and Thorarin to gather their supporters.

When everyone who was expected had arrived at the Law Rock, Ofeig called for silence and said, 'I have stayed out of the case against my son, Odd, up to now, even though it was begun in such a scandalous fashion that no one can think of a parallel, is continuing like that and looks like ending in the same way. I know that all the men who have been pursuing the case are now present, and I'd like to call on Hermund first: I want to ask whether there is any possibility of a settlement out of court.'

Hermund answered, 'We will be satisfied with nothing less than self-judgement.'

Ofeig said, 'You'd be hard put to it to find a precedent for one man conceding self-judgement to eight opponents in a single lawsuit, though there are examples enough of a one-to-one agreement. But even though this case has been prosecuted with more shocking irregularity than any other, I am willing to concede that two of your party should act as arbitrators.'

'Naturally we'll agree to that,' replied Hermund, 'and we don't mind which two they are.'

'Then you'll grant me the petty privilege,' said Ofeig, 'of selecting from among you confederates the two I want.'

'Yes, certainly,' said Hermund.

Then Thorarin said, 'Mind you don't agree today to what you'll regret tomorrow.'

'I'm not going back on my word,' said Hermund.

Then Ofeig sought guarantors, and they were easy to find, because the money looked to be easily recoverable. They shook hands on the pledge that the guarantors would pay over whatever sum was awarded by the men Ofeig picked, and the confederates pledged themselves to drop the outlawry suit. Now it was agreed that the confederates and their supporters should move up to the fields; the parties of Gellir and Egil stuck close together. They sat down in a circle at a certain place, but Ofeig went into the ring, looked around him and put back the hood of his cape. He straightened up and stroked his arms. Then his eyes sparkled as he spoke:

'There you sit, Styrmir, and people will think it strange if I don't choose you for a case which concerns me, since I am one of your thingmen and have a right to expect support from you. You've accepted plenty of good gifts from me too – and all of them ill rewarded. It seems to me that you have been the first of anybody to show enmity to my son, Odd, in this matter and the most responsible for getting the case prosecuted. So I'll count you out.

'There you sit, Thorarin,' said Ofeig. 'There's no question of your lacking the intelligence to judge this case, but your contribution to this matter has been to damage Odd, and you were the first person to join Styrmir in prosecuting the case. So I won't choose you.

'There you sit, Hermund, an important chieftain, and I think it could be a good idea to refer the case to you. But nobody has got so worked up about the case since it all started, and it's plain that you want to make this dirty business public. Nothing but dishonour and avarice has drawn you into it, since you are not short of money yourself, and therefore I count you out.

'There you sit, Jarnskeggi. You don't lack the pride to judge this case, and it wouldn't displease you to have it referred to you. Indeed, your pride is so great that you had a banner carried before you at the Vodla Assembly, as if before a king; yet you shall not be king over this lawsuit, and I count you out.'

Then Ofeig looked around and said, 'There you sit, Beard-Broddi. Is it true that when you were with King Harald

Sigurdsson he said that, of all the men in Iceland, he thought you best fitted to be a king?'

Broddi answered, 'The king often spoke graciously to me, but it's not certain that he meant everything he said.'

'You can king it over other things than this lawsuit,' said Ofeig, 'and I count you out.

'There you sit, Gellir,' Ofeig went on, 'and nothing but avarice has drawn you into this case. Still, you have some excuse, since you're short of money and have large responsibilities. Now, although I think you all deserve a bad outcome from this case, I don't know but that someone will have to get some credit from it. There are few of you left now, and I don't care to pick any of those I've already turned down, so I'll choose you, Gellir, because you have never before been known for injustice.

'There you sit, Thorgeir Halldoruson,' said Ofeig, 'and it's common knowledge that no case of any importance has ever been referred to you, because you don't know how to judge cases and have no more brains for it than an ox or an ass. So I count you out.'

Then Ofeig looked around him and spoke this verse:

4.
It's ill for men
to endure old age;
it snatches from them
sight and sense.
I'd the option just now
of able judges:
now the one thing left
is the wolf's tail.

wolf's tail: i.e. worst choice

'I've ended up the same way as the wolves – they devoured one another, and didn't notice it until they got down to the tail. I had the choice of many chieftains, and now the only one left is a man from whom everyone expects the worst. He is known to be guilty of more injustice than any of the others, and he doesn't care what he does for money as long as he gets more than he had before. But he has an excuse for being unscrupulous in this case, when so many others have got tangled in it who previously had a reputation for fairness, but have abandoned honour and integrity in exchange for injustice and greed. Now it would never occur to anyone that I would choose a man of whom everyone expects the worst, when there isn't a craftier man to be found in your party, but that's what it comes down to, since all the others have been counted out.'

Egil grinned and said, 'It's not the first time I've ended up with an honour which other people didn't want me to have. What we must do now, Gellir, is stand up and withdraw to discuss the case.'

This they did: walked away from there and sat down.

Then Gellir said, 'What shall we say about this?'

Egil said, 'It's my advice that we impose a small fine, and I don't see what else can be done. But we're not going to win much popularity by this.'

'Wouldn't it be quite sufficient if we settled for thirteen ounces of scrap silver?' said Gellir. 'Seeing that the whole charge was based on a great injustice, the worse they like it, the better. But I'm not keen to announce the settlement, because I expect it to be badly received.'

'Choose which you'd rather do,' said Egil. 'Either announce the settlement or field the criticism.'

'I prefer to make the announcement,' said Gellir.

Then they went back to the confederates.

Hermund said, 'Let's rise and listen to this disgraceful business.'

Then Gellir spoke: 'We two won't be any wiser for putting it off, and it will all come to the same thing in the end. Egil and I have decided to award to us, the confederates, thirteen ounces of silver.'

'Did I hear that right?' said Hermund. 'Did you say a hundred and thirty ounces of silver?'

Egil answered, 'Come now, Hermund, you can't have been sitting on your ear when you were standing up. Thirteen ounces was what we said, and of such silver as no one would accept who wasn't wretchedly poor: it's to be paid in broken brooches and bits of rings and all the poorest stuff that can be found, to please you least.'

Then Hermund said, 'You've cheated us, Egil!'

'Oh really,' said Egil. 'You think you've been cheated?'

'Yes, I think myself cheated, and it's you who've cheated me.'

Egil answered, 'I'm glad I have managed to cheat a man who trusts no one, not even himself. I can prove what I say of you: you went and hid your treasure during such a thick fog that you thought you could never find it again if it crossed your mind to look for it.'

'That's another of your lies, Egil,' answered Hermund, 'like the one you told last winter, when you came home after I had invited you from your wretched hovel to spend Christmas with me. You were glad of the invitation, as one might expect, but when Christmas was over you got depressed, of course, about going home to starvation rations. I realized that and invited you to stay on, with one companion, and you accepted gladly. But in the spring, after Easter, when you got back to Borg, you said that thirty of my horses, which were wintering outside, had died – and that we'd eaten them all.'[6]

Egil replied, 'I don't think it's possible to exaggerate the poor state of your livestock, but I think that few or none of them got eaten. But everyone knows that I and my household never go short of food, even if my financial state is not always easy, but the conditions at your home don't bear speaking about.'

'I would like to think,' said Hermund, 'that we shall not both be alive to attend next year's Althing.'

'Now I'm going to say words which I never expected to speak,' said Egil. 'Namely, "may your words be fortunate!" – because it's been prophesied of me that I shall die of old age, but I think the sooner the trolls take you the better.'

Then Styrmir spoke: 'Whoever speaks worst of you, Egil, is nearest the truth, if he calls you underhanded.'

'Now things are going nicely,' said Egil, 'and I'm the better pleased the more you insult me and back your insults with proof, because I'm told that when you were all amusing yourselves over your ale by choosing men to compare yourselves with, you claimed me as your equal. Now it's true, of course,' he continued, 'that you have some nasty vices, which others may not know about but you most certainly do. But there's one difference between us – when each of us promises to back other people, I do all I can and spare no effort, but the moment black-handled axes are raised, you take to your heels. And it's true that I generally have difficulty making ends meet, but I turn no one away hungry, while you are miserly with food. As a token of that, you own a bowl called "Food-in-plenty", but no visitor to your farm has ever seen what's in it – only you know. Now it's no disgrace to me if my household have to tighten their belts when there's nothing in the larder, but it is shameful for someone to starve his household when there's no shortage. You can guess whom I mean!'

Now Styrmir was silenced, but Thorarin stood up.

Then Egil said, 'Sit down and shut up, Thorarin. Don't say a word, or I'll accuse you of such shameful things that it would be better for you to keep silent. I don't find it funny, though your servants laugh about it, when you sit with your legs tight, rubbing your thighs together.'

Thorarin answered, 'Wisdom is welcome, wherever it comes from.'

Then he sat down and kept quiet.

Then Thorgeir said, 'Everyone can see that this settlement is pointless and silly, awarding no more than thirteen ounces of silver in a case on this scale.'

'But I thought,' said Egil, 'that you at least would see the point of this settlement, and so you will if you think it over. Then you'll remember how, at the Ranga Assembly, some poor smallholder raised thirteen lumps on your skull, and you accepted thirteen ewes with their lambs in compensation. I thought this would be a good reminder for you.'

Thorgeir fell silent. Neither Beard-Broddi nor Jarnskeggi wanted to bandy words with Egil.

Then Ofeig spoke up: 'Now I want to recite you a verse, so that more people will remember this Althing and the outcome of this case:

5.
Many a metal-tree   *metal-tree*: warrior
of much less has boasted:
I record it in the pledge   *pledge*: poetry, the mead that reconciled
that appeased dwarf and giant.   Am (giant) and Austri (dwarf)
In rings I'm not rich, but –
I revel in telling it –
I hoodwinked those heroes,
hurling dust in their eyes.'

Egil answered, 'Well might you pat yourself on the back! No
one man can ever have taken the wind out of the sails of so
many chieftains.'

After this people went back to their booths.

Gellir said to Egil, 'I want us both to stick together, with all
our men.'

This they did. There was a great deal of hostility during the
remainder of the Althing, and the confederates were very unhappy
with the outcome of the case. None of them would touch the
money awarded, and it got scattered all over the upper fields.
Then people rode home from the Althing.

11

Odd was all ready to put to sea when he and his father met,
and Ofeig told Odd that he had conceded the confederates self-
judgement.

'You miserable creature, you abandoned the case!' said Odd.

'The full story has not been told yet, kinsman,' replied Ofeig,
and related the whole course of events, with the fact that a wife
was betrothed to him.

Then Odd thanked him for all his help, saying that he had
pursued matters far beyond anything that had occurred to Odd
as possible, and he should never go short of money again.

'Now you must sail as you planned,' said Ofeig, 'and
your wedding will take place at Mel six weeks before winter
begins.'

After that, father and son parted on the best of terms.

Odd put to sea, and got a favourable wind north as far as Thorgeirsfjord, where there were merchants lying at anchor. Then the breeze failed and the ship lay there becalmed for several days. Odd grew impatient waiting for a wind, so he climbed a certain high hill and saw that out beyond the fjord the weather was quite different. He went back aboard his knorr and ordered his men to put out of the fjord under oars.

The Norwegian merchants mocked them and said that it would be a long row to Norway.

Odd said, 'Who knows whether you'll still be waiting when we get back?'

When they got clear of the fjord, they picked up a favourable wind and did not lower their sail until they reached the Orkneys. There Odd purchased malt and grain, and spent a short while preparing his ship. Just when he was ready, an easterly wind rose, and they set sail before it. They made an excellent voyage, and put in to Thorgeirsfjord to find the merchants still there. Odd sailed on west along the coast and put in at Midfjord, having been away seven weeks.

Then preparations were made for the wedding feast, and good provisions were all in plentiful supply. A great crowd of guests came, including Gellir and Egil and many other important men. The feast went off well and indeed magnificently, and people thought they had never attended a better wedding in Iceland. When the party was finally over, the guests were seen off with splendid presents, the costliest falling to Gellir's share.

Gellir said to Odd, 'I hope you are going to be generous to Egil. He deserves it.'

'It seems to me,' said Odd, 'that my father has been pretty generous to him already.'

'You can improve on it though,' said Gellir.

Then he rode away with his supporters.

When Egil left, Odd saw him on his way and thanked him for his help: 'I can never do as much for you as you deserve, but yesterday I had sixty wethers and two oxen driven south to Borg, and they'll be waiting for you when you get home. And I'll never be ungenerous to you as long as we both live.'

Egil was very pleased at this, and they pledged friendship. Then they parted and Egil went home to Borg.

12

That same autumn Hermund gathered his forces and went out to the Hvamm Assembly, intending to go on to Borg and burn Egil in his house. When they came level with Valfell, they heard a sound like a bow-string twanging up on the hillside, and at the same moment Hermund felt a sickness and a stabbing pain in his armpit, so they had to turn back from their expedition. Hermund's sickness increased, and when they had come by Thorgautsstadir, they had to lift him from his horse. They sent to Sidumuli for a priest, but when he came, Hermund could not speak, so the priest stayed by him.

One time when the priest bent over Hermund, his lips moved, and he mumbled, 'Two hundred in the gully, two hundred in the gully.'[7]

Then he breathed his last, and his life ended just as reported here.

Odd now lived on his farm in lordly style and was well content with his wife.

All this time nothing had been heard of Ospak. A man called Mar Hildisson married Svala and moved into the farm at Svolustadir. He had a brother called Bjalfi, half imbecile and extremely strong.

There was a man called Bergthor, living at Bodvarsholar; he had summed up the case when Ospak was outlawed. It happened one evening at Bodvarsholar when people were sitting by the fire, that someone came and banged on the door and asked the farmer to come out. The farmer realized it was Ospak who had arrived, and he refused to go out. Ospak kept taunting him to come out, but he was not to be moved and he forbade his men to go out either, and so they parted. But in the morning when the women went into the cowshed, nine cows had been mortally injured. This news spread widely.

Some time later it happened at Svolustadir that someone walked into the room where Mar was sleeping. It was early morning. The man went across to the bed and thrust at Mar with a short-sword, right into his belly. It was Ospak, and he spoke a verse:

6.
Sharp from the sheath
my short-sword I drew
and stabbed it into
the stomach of Mar.
I hate the thought
that Hildir's heir
should share the embrace
of shapely Svala.

As he turned to the door, Bjalfi jumped to his feet and drove a wood-working knife into him. Ospak walked to the farm called Borgarhol and declared the killing, and then went away, and nothing was heard of him for some time. The news of Mar's killing spread and was widely condemned.

The next item of news was that the best five stud horses which Odd owned were all found dead, and people held Ospak to blame for that.

Now for a long time nothing was heard of Ospak. Then in the autumn, when some men went to round up the wethers, they found a cave in some crags, and in it a dead man. Beside him stood a basin full of blood, and it was as black as pitch. It was Ospak, and people reckoned that the wound Bjalfi dealt him must have weakened him, so that he then died for lack of food and help. That was the end of him. It is not reported that any case was ever brought over the killings of Mar and Ospak.

Odd lived at Mel until old age and was thought a most outstanding man. Many important men in Midfjord are descended from him, including Snorri Kalfsson. The friendship and good family feeling between Odd and his father lasted the rest of their lives. And there this saga ends.

Translated by RUTH C. ELLISON

THE SAGA OF HAVARD
OF ISAFJORD

I

This saga begins with a man named Thorbjorn,[1] the son of
Thjodrek. He lived in Isafjord on a farm named Laugabol. He
had the godord in Isafjord. He was a well-born man and a
powerful chieftain and a very unjust man, so that there was no
one in Isafjord who had the strength to oppose him. He took
people's daughters and kinswomen and kept them for a while,
and then sent them home. He took the possessions of others or
drove them off their land. Thorbjorn had taken a woman named
Sigrid into his household. She was a young woman from a prominent family. She had a lot of assets for her own upkeep that were
not to be increased while she was with Thorbjorn.

There was a man named Havard who lived on a farm named
Blamyri. He was a high-born man and was by this time infirm
with age. Early in life he had been a great Viking and fighter,
and in one battle he had been severely wounded, receiving an
injury to his knee, and from then on he walked with a limp.
Havard was married, and his wife was named Bjargey. She was
a woman of firm character from a good family. They had a son
named Olaf. He was in his youth and very promising. He
was large and handsome. Havard and Bjargey loved Olaf very
much. In return he was obedient and compliant.

There was a man named Thormod. He lived on a farm
named Bakki in Isafjord. His wife was named Thorgerd. There
was something decidedly eerie about Thormod. He was by this
time somewhat infirm with age. It was said that he was a shape-
shifter. Everyone found him most unpleasant to deal with.

There was a man named Ljot who lived on a farm named

Manaberg in Isafjord. Ljot was big and strong. He was Thorbjorn's brother and like him in all respects. There was a man named Thorkel who lived on the island of Aedey. He was wise but mean spirited, and although of a good family, he was quite irresolute. Thorkel was the lawspeaker in Isafjord.

Two men come into the saga, one named Brand, the other Vak. They belonged to Thorbjorn's household at Laugabol. Brand was tall and very strong. It was Brand's job to travel around in summer and transport what was needed to the farm, but in winter he looked after the old livestock. He was popular and unassuming. Vak was the son of Thorbjorn's sister. He was small and puny, abusive and foul-mouthed, and repeatedly goaded his uncle Thorbjorn, who behaved even worse. Vak became unpopular because of this, and people spoke of him as he deserved. He did no work other than to go around with Thorbjorn or run his errands, especially when Thorbjorn wanted some nasty business performed.

There was a woman named Thordis who lived on a farm named Hvol in Isafjord. She was Thorbjorn's sister and Vak's mother. She had another son named Skarf. He was big and strong. He lived with his mother and looked after their farm. There was a man named Thoralf who lived on a farm named Lonseyri. He was popular but not influential. He was closely related to Thorbjorn's housekeeper. Thoralf had offered to take Sigrid in and to increase her assets, but Thorbjorn would not hear of this and once more showed his overbearing manner and told him never to speak of the matter again.

2

To go back to Olaf, he was growing up at Blamyri and had become a promising young man. People say that Olaf Havardsson had bear-warmth,[2] because never was there such frost or cold that Olaf put on more than a pair of trousers and a shirt tucked into them. Never did he leave the farm dressed in more clothes. Thorhall was the name of a young man. He was a kinsman of Havard's and Bjargey's, and a member of their household and very fleet of foot. He saw to the provisions on their farm.

One autumn the people of Isafjord went to round up their livestock from the upper pastures but they found very few sheep. Thorbjorn from Laugabol was short sixty wethers. The Winter Nights passed, and not one was found. A little before winter Olaf Havardsson left the farm and walked all over the mountains through the upper pastures, searching for the sheep, and finding a good many of them: those that belonged to Thorbjorn and others, and to his father and himself. He then drove the livestock home and returned the sheep to the farmers. Olaf became very popular for this, and everyone wished him well.

Early one day Olaf drove Thorbjorn's wethers down to Laugabol. He arrived just as everyone was eating, so that no one was outside. Olaf knocked on the door, and a woman came to answer it. It was Sigrid, Thorbjorn's housekeeper, and she greeted him warmly. She asked what he wanted.

Olaf answered, 'I have brought the wethers that Thorbjorn was short last autumn.'

When Thorbjorn heard someone knocking on the door, he told Vak to see what had happened. He did so, and went to the door. He then saw that Olaf and Sigrid were talking to each other. He then leapt up on to the crossbeam of the door and stayed there while they talked.

Then Olaf said, 'Now I don't need to go any farther. Tell someone about the sheep, Sigrid.'

She said she would and said goodbye to him. Vak ran shrieking into the main room. Thorbjorn asked why he was carrying on so and what had happened.

'I think,' he said, 'that Olaf the fool from Blamyri, Havard's son, has arrived. He has driven the wethers here that you were short in the autumn.'

'That was well done,' said Thorbjorn.

'I think something no less important was behind his visit,' said Vak, 'because he and Sigrid talked to each other the whole morning. I saw how delighted she was to put her arms around his neck.'

Thorbjorn said, 'Although Olaf is a courageous man, it is still foolhardy of him to pay us such an insulting visit.'

Olaf went home. Time passed, and it was said that Olaf

often went to Laugabol and visited Sigrid, and they got on well together. It was soon rumoured that Olaf was seducing Sigrid.

The next autumn people once again went to round up live-stock in the upper pastures but gathered very few sheep. Again Thorbjorn was short the most. And when the round-up was over, Olaf set off from home alone and walked from heath to highland over all the upper pastures, and once more he found many sheep and drove them back to the settlement and returned the sheep to the farmers. Now he became so popular with the local people that everyone wished him well except for Thorbjorn. He was angry with him both because others praised him and because he heard of his visits to Sigrid spoken of all over the settlement. Vak never failed to slander them both to Thorbjorn.

Now it happened that Olaf arrived at Laugabol with the wethers, as many as before, and when he arrived, no one was outside. He entered the house and went into the main room. Thorbjorn, his nephew Vak and many farmhands were there in the room. Olaf went well into it. He carried his axe in front of him. When he came to the cross-bench, he set the shaft of his axe on the floor and leaned upon it, but no one greeted him, all keeping their silence.

And when he saw that no one spoke to him, he recited this verse:

1.
I resolve to request
of the reticent men:
why do all stay silent,
the steadfast companions?
No one tenders a toast
to timid voiceless men;
here have I long stood still,
sounds I hear from no one.

Then Olaf said, 'My business in coming here, Thorbjorn, is that I have driven your wethers home.'

Then Vak spoke: 'It is known to everyone by now, Olaf, that

you have become quite the model sheep drover here in Isafjord. We also know your business in coming here, to demand a share of the sheep. That's a beggar's share, and it is fitting to remember it, though it be but a pittance.'

Olaf answered, 'That is not my business, but I won't be driving sheep here a third time.'

He then turned away, but Vak leapt up and shrieked at him. Olaf paid no attention but went home, and that year passed. And in the autumn the round-up went well except for Thorbjorn. He was short sixty wethers, and they were not found. The kinsmen spread the word that Olaf once again intended to claim a share or even to steal them.

One evening Olaf and his father were sitting at table, and on a plate in front of them lay a leg of mutton.

Olaf picked it up and spoke: 'This is a very large, fat leg.'

Havard spoke: 'But I imagine, my son, that it comes from one of our sheep and not from Thorbjorn's. It is hard to endure such injustice.'

Olaf laid the leg down on the table, and his face flushed. Only those who sat nearby saw him press the leg on the table so hard that it broke apart with such force that one piece flew against the gable end and stuck fast. Havard looked up and said nothing, but smiled all the same.

At that moment a woman walked into the room, and it was Thorgerd from Bakki. Havard greeted her warmly and asked her the news. She reported the death of Thormod, her husband.

'And yet we are not well off, because every night he returns to his bed. So I would be thankful for whatever help you might offer, Havard, because although my farmhands always found Thormod troublesome, they are now all on the point of leaving.'

Havard answered, 'I am not getting any younger and am not up to such things, but why don't you go to Laugabol? It is to be expected that chieftains will quickly lend a hand in community matters.'

She answered, 'I do not expect any good from there. I am happy enough if he does me no harm.'

Then Havard said, 'You should ask my son, Olaf, for it is up to young men to prove their manhood. Such a thing would have seemed a lark to us in the old days.'

She did so. Olaf promised to come and invited her to stay overnight, and the next day Olaf went home with Thorgerd. There all the people were in low spirits, and in the evening they went to bed. Olaf lay in a bed by the gable end just inside the door. A light was burning in the hall. Higher up it was light, but below it was dark. Olaf lay down in his shirt and trousers, because he never wore more clothes. He covered himself with only one pelt. After sunset, Thormod walked into the hall, wagging his head back and forth in the light. He saw that the bed, normally empty, was occupied. He was not exactly hospitable – he reached forward and grabbed hold of the pelt. Olaf would not let go and held on to it until they tore the pelt in two. When Thormod felt the strength in the man before him, he leapt on to the bench beside the bed. Olaf leapt up and reached for his axe, intending to strike him a blow, but not quickly enough, for Thormod slipped under his grasp and clutched him around the waist. Olaf countered, and the most furious struggle commenced. Thormod fought so hard that he tore Olaf's flesh wherever he grabbed hold. Everything in their way was smashed, and suddenly the light went out. Olaf found this scarcely better. Thormod then attacked in earnest, and finally they found themselves outside. In the field lay a large piece of driftwood, and it chanced that Thormod caught his heels on the log and fell on to his back. Olaf drove his knee into his groin, and, when he got the chance, dealt with him in a manner he found fitting.

Everyone was silent when Olaf went inside. The moment he said something, they all got up at once, brought light and rubbed him from head to toe. He was covered with injuries from his fight with Thormod. Every living soul capable of speech thanked him. He said he thought that they would come to no more harm from Thormod. Olaf remained there a few nights, then went home to Blamyri. He became famous throughout Isafjord and in every quarter of the land for this deed, and because of this, the ill will between Thorbjorn and him grew even greater.

3

The next thing to be told is that a whale was stranded in Isafjord. Thorbjorn and Havard had drift rights[3] on both sides. The first report was that the whale belonged to Havard. It was a splendid finback whale. Both went there and decided to accept the lawspeaker's verdict. A lot of people were assembled. It seemed clear to everyone that the whale belonged to Havard. Thorkel the lawspeaker arrived. He was then asked to whom the whale belonged.

Thorkel answered, rather faintly, 'The whale belongs to them, of course,' he said.

Thorbjorn then walked up to him with drawn sword and spoke: 'Who is *them*, you simpleton?' he said.

Thorkel answered immediately, and lowered his head, 'You, you, of course,' he said.

Then Thorbjorn proceeded in his overbearing way to claim the entire whale. Havard then went home very dissatisfied. Everyone thought that Thorbjorn had once again acted unjustly and dishonourably.

One day Olaf went to his sheep sheds because the weather had been very bad that winter, and men had to keep close watch on their livestock. The weather had been very bad that night. And when he was about to go back, he saw a man walking towards the shed. It was Brand the Strong. Olaf greeted him warmly, and Brand returned his greeting cordially. Olaf asked him why he was out so late.

He answered, 'It is hardly worth telling. I went to my sheep early today, but they had all wandered down to the beach. It is possible to drive them up in two places, but every time I tried to do so, a man stood in the way and waved his arms at the sheep so that they ran back towards me, and it has gone like that all day until now. Now I would like both of us to go there together.'

Olaf answered, 'I will do as you wish.'

Then they both went down to the beach together. But when they attempted to drive the sheep up, they saw that Thormod, Olaf's wrestling partner, was in the way and flailing his arms at the sheep, so that they ran back towards them.

Then Olaf spoke: 'Which would you prefer, Brand, to drive the sheep, or to attack Thormod?'

Brand answered, 'I will choose the easier, to drive the sheep.'

Olaf walked to where Thormod stood opposite and above him. A lot of snow lay on the face of the ridge. Olaf suddenly ran up the ridge towards Thormod, who gave way to him. When Olaf arrived at the top, Thormod suddenly ducked under his grasp and clutched him round the waist. Olaf countered with all his might, and they struggled for a long time. Olaf found Thormod no more tractable after his beating. Finally, they both fell down the slope, and they turned over and over as they tumbled through the snow. First one, then the other, was on top until they reached the beach. Then it chanced that Thormod was on the bottom. Olaf took advantage of this, and broke his back. He then made such preparations as seemed fitting, swam out to sea with him far from land and sank him in the deep. The place has seemed unhallowed ever since to men who sail close by.

Olaf swam back to shore. By then Brand had got all the stock up on to the ridge, and received Olaf warmly. Then they both went home. When Brand got home, it was late at night. Thorbjorn asked what had delayed him. Brand told what had happened and how Olaf had helped him.

Then Vak spoke: 'You must truly have been terrified if you praise that fool. His greatest renown seems to be wrestling with revenants.'

Brand answered, 'You would have been even more afraid, for you wag your tongue as a fox waves his tail. In nothing can you match him.'

They talked back and forth until both were excited.

Thorbjorn told Brand not to make so much of Olaf: 'It won't do you or anyone else any good to put Olaf ahead of me or my kinsmen.'

The winter passed. And when spring came, father and son, Havard and Olaf, had a talk. Havard said, 'It has reached the point, my son, where I do not feel like living so close to Thorbjorn any longer, because we just do not have the strength to hold our own against him.'

Olaf answered, 'It is little consolation for me to run away from Thorbjorn, but still I want you to decide. Where are you thinking of going?'

Havard answered, 'Farther out in the fjord on the other side are large green pastures and a lot of land that no one owns. I would like us to build a farm there, and then we will be closer to our kinsmen and friends.'

They agreed on this plan, moved all the livestock and goods they owned there, and built an excellent farm. Ever since it has been named Havardsstadir. They were the only farmers in Isafjord in those days who settled unclaimed land.

4

Thorbjorn Thjodreksson rode every summer to the Althing with his men. He was a powerful chieftain, of noble birth, who had many kinsmen. In those days Gest Oddleifsson[4] lived on a farm named Hagi on Bardastrond. He was a great sage, wise and popular, and a very prophetic man, and he had a position of authority. The same summer that Havard and Olaf moved their farm, Thorbjorn rode to the Althing and asked for the hand of Gest's sister in marriage. Gest regarded this suit coolly and said he cared little for Thorbjorn because of his unjust acts and violent behaviour, but because many were supportive of Thorbjorn's suit, Gest declared that the marriage would take place, but only if Thorbjorn promised with a handshake to leave off his unjust acts and wrongdoing, to give everyone his due and to abide by law and order. If he did not keep to this agreement, Gest could annul the betrothal and cause their separation. Thorbjorn agreed to this, and they settled on those terms. Then Thorbjorn rode home with Gest from the Althing to Bardastrond, and there the wedding took place that summer. The wedding feast was very fine.

When this news became known in Isafjord, Sigrid and her kinsman Thoralf decided to summon the neighbouring farmers and have all of Sigrid's assets at Laugabol appraised. She went to Thoralf's at Lonseyri. And when Thorbjorn returned to Laugabol, he became extremely angry that Sigrid was gone and promised the farmers who had valued her assets that they would feel his anger and contempt, and then at once began acting in a vicious way. He felt even grander as a result of his marriage.

Havard's sheep were very restless during the summer, and early one morning a shepherd came home, and Olaf asked him how things were going.

'Things are going like this,' he said, 'many sheep are missing. I cannot do two things at once: look for the ones that are missing, and tend those that have been found.'

Olaf answered, 'Cheer up, my friend, take care of those that have been found, and I will look for the missing ones.'

He was becoming a very promising and handsome man, and he was both big and strong. He was then eighteen years old. He now took his axe in his hand, then walked out along the fjord until he came to Lonseyri. He saw where all the sheep were and that they had been driven there. Olaf then turned towards the farm. It was early in the morning. He knocked on the door. Then Sigrid came to the door and greeted Olaf warmly. He returned her greeting affectionately.

When they had chatted a while, Sigrid spoke: 'A boat is coming from the other side of the fjord, and I see clearly that Thorbjorn Thjodreksson and his kinsman, Vak, are in it. I see that their weapons are lying forward in the bow. There is also Gunnlogi (War-flame), Thorbjorn's sword, and either he has done an evil deed or he intends to do one, and I do not wish you, Olaf, to meet him. There has long been little love lost between you two, and I think there has been no improvement since you and the others valued my possessions at Laugabol.'

Olaf spoke: 'I have nothing to fear from Thorbjorn as long as I have done him no harm. And I will not run very far from him alone.'

She answered, 'This is bravely spoken, that you at eighteen would not flee from one who is the equal to any man in a fight. He also has the sword which never fails to hit its mark. I also think that if they are looking for you, as I suspect is the case, the despicable Vak will not sit idly by while you two fight.'

Olaf answered, 'I have no business with Thorbjorn. I shall

not seek them out, but if we should chance to meet, you will hear of courageous exploits, should they be called for.'

Sigrid answered and said she would not hear of them. Olaf leapt up quickly and wished her well, and she wished him farewell. He then went down to the spit where the sheep were. Thorbjorn and Vak were just landing. He went down to the boat and took hold of it and pulled them ashore. Thorbjorn greeted Olaf warmly. Olaf returned his greeting and asked him where he was heading.

He said he intended to visit his sister, Thordis: 'We could all go together.'

Olaf answered, 'That is not possible, because I must drive my sheep home. Besides, it would truly be said that sheep drovers were coming up in the world around Isafjord if you so lowered yourself.'

'I do not care about that,' said Thorbjorn.

There was a large stack of wood on the spit and on top of it lay a large boathook broken off at the end. Olaf picked it up and held it in his hand and prodded the sheep forward. They all walked along together. Thorbjorn spoke with Olaf and was in the best of spirits. Olaf noticed that they kept slowing down, but he was on his guard, and they moved along all together until they reached the hill. There the paths divided.

Thorbjorn then turned around and spoke: 'Vak, my nephew, there is no need to delay what is planned.'

Olaf then saw what they intended. He ran up the hill, and they attacked from below. Olaf defended himself with the boathook, but Thorbjorn hacked hard and often with his sword Gunnlogi and whittled the boathook down as if it were a reed. Even so they received many sharp blows from the boathook as long as anything was left of it. But when it was cut to pieces, Olaf took his axe and then defended himself so well that they were uncertain how things would turn out. They all received many wounds.

Thordis, Thorbjorn's sister, walked outside on the morning they fought and could hear them without being able to see them. She sent her servant-boy to investigate. He did so and told Thordis that her brother, Thorbjorn, and her son Vak were fighting against Olaf Havardsson. She darted into the house, found her son Skarf, told him the news, and ordered him to go and help his kinsmen.

He spoke: 'I'd rather fight with Olaf against them. It seems shameful to me for three to go against one man, because the two of them have as much of a chance as four others. I will not be going anywhere.'

Thordis answered, 'I thought I had two courageous sons. It is true what people say, much remains hidden. Now I see that you are a daughter rather than a son when you dare not defend your kinsmen. Now it will be put to the test whether I am a more courageous daughter than you are a son.'

She then left, but he became extremely angry, and leapt up and grabbed his axe. He ran outside and down the hill to where they were fighting. Thorbjorn saw him and attacked furiously, but Olaf did not see him. And when Skarf got into striking range of Olaf, he struck him two-handed between the shoulder blades so that the axe bit deep. Olaf had been about to strike Thorbjorn, but when he received the blow, he turned around quickly. Skarf no longer had his axe, but Olaf already had his axe raised, and he struck Skarf in the head, so that it stuck fast in his brain. At that moment Thorbjorn came up to them and struck him in the chest. That too was a sufficient death blow, and they both fell. Thorbjorn then went to Olaf and struck him across the face, so that his top and bottom teeth popped out.

Vak asked, 'Why do that to a dead man?'

Thorbjorn said they would come in useful later. He then took a cloth and wrapped the teeth in it and kept it. Afterwards they walked up to the farm and told Thordis the news. Both of them were heavily wounded. She was very distressed by this account and lamented that she had egged her son on so much. Still, she took them in and nursed their wounds.

This news spread all over Isafjord, and everywhere people felt a keen sense of loss when they heard of the defence Olaf had put up. Thorbjorn behaved well in that he told just how things had gone and gave Olaf his due in the account. They went home as soon as they thought they were well and their weakness had subsided. Thorbjorn went to Lonseyri and inquired after Sigrid. He was told that she had not been seen since she went away with Olaf on that morning. She was searched for far and wide, and the story goes that she was never seen again. Thorbjorn then went home and remained quietly on his farm.

5

To go back to Havard and Bjargey, they heard the news of the fall of their son Olaf. Havard sighed deeply and took to his bed. And it was said that for the next twelve months he lay in his bed and did not once get up. Bjargey resolved to row to sea with Thorhall every day and to do whatever chores were necessary by night. And so the year passed, and nothing happened. There was no prosecution for Olaf. Most people thought it unlikely that any restitution would ever come to his kinsmen, because Havard was considered helpless. Also there was not much hope of justice from such powerful men, and so the year passed.

One morning Bjargey went in to see old Havard and asked him whether he was awake, and he said he was awake and asked her what she wanted.

'I want you,' she said, 'to get up and go over to Laugabol and pay a visit to Thorbjorn and request compensation for your son Olaf. It is a manly thing for him who is incapable of heroic deeds not to hold his tongue and to speak when it might do him some good. Don't be too demanding if he behaves well.'

He said, 'I do not expect good to come of this, but you decide.'

Thereupon Havard got ready and rowed until he arrived at Laugabol. Thorbjorn greeted him warmly. Havard returned his greeting.

Then Havard said, 'Matters have arrived at a point, Thorbjorn,' he said, 'that I have come to demand compensation for my son Olaf, whom you killed without cause.'

Thorbjorn answered, 'It is well known, Havard, that I have killed many a man. Although people have considered I acted without cause, I have never paid compensation for any of them. But because you had a courageous son and your loss is so great, I think it advisable to give you something, though it be but a pittance. There is a horse whom the hands call Old Nag just outside the hayfield wall. He is grey, very old and broken down, and up to now has been unable to get up off the ground, but since he has been feeding on chaff for a few days, I think he is on the mend. Take the horse home, if you like, and keep him.'

Havard flushed red, unable to say anything, and to Vak's jeers he left in a rage. He went down to his boat walking very stooped over. Thorhall had waited for him in the meantime. Then they rowed home. Havard went in to bed and lay down, not getting up once in the next twelve months. This became known, and Thorbjorn was thought once again to have shown his overbearing and ill nature with this response. The year thus passed.

6

In the summer Thorbjorn rode to the Althing with his men from Isafjord. One day Bjargey again went in to talk to Havard. He then asked what she wanted.

She answered, 'I think that you should now ride to the Althing and find out whether there has been any change in your case.'

He answered, 'This is very much contrary to my inclination. Don't you think I have already been humiliated enough by Thorbjorn, the killer of my son, or do you think he would not humiliate me even more where all the chieftains are assembled?'

'It won't be like that,' she said. 'I think there will be a few supporters of your case and that Gest Oddleifsson, for one, will do so. And if things go as I imagine and he achieves a settlement between Thorbjorn and you, so that he will have to pay you a lot of money, then I imagine that he will have a lot of men present and a ring will be formed around you, and there will be only a few of you inside the ring when Thorbjorn pays the money. And if it turns out, before the money is paid, that Thorbjorn does anything that is offensive or painful to you, then you should hurry away as fast as you can. And if you feel better

than you expected, you should not settle the case, because then
there is a hope, as unlikely as it might seem, that Olaf, our son,
will be avenged. But if you do not feel better, then you should
not leave the Althing without a settlement, because then there
will be no revenge.'

He said he did not know where this was heading, 'but if
I knew that revenge for my son, Olaf, were possible, then
I would stop at nothing to achieve that end'.

7

After that she prepared him for his journey, and he rode on his
way. The old man was rather bent over when he arrived at the
Althing. The booths were already tented over and the people
had all arrived. He rode to a large booth owned by Steinthor of
Eyri, a powerful man and a great chieftain and a great and fearless warrior. Havard dismounted and went into the booth.
Steinthor was sitting there with his men. Havard went up to
him and greeted him warmly. He returned his greeting and
asked who he was. Havard told him his name.

Steinthor spoke: 'Are you the one who had the renowned
son whom Thorbjorn killed and whose defence men praise so
highly?'

He said that he was the same, 'And I would like you, sir, to
allow me to stay in your booth during the Althing.'

He answered, 'I will certainly permit that, but be quiet and
keep to yourself. My lads are great pranksters, and you are still
grieving. Besides you are in a bad state, old and helpless.'

It is said that old Havard took a bed somewhere in the
booth, lay down there and never left his bed. He never mentioned his case to anyone, and the Althing drew to a close.

One morning Steinthor went to Havard and spoke: 'Why
did you come here to lie around like the heir to a fortune or a
cripple?'

Havard answered, 'I had intended to seek compensation for
my son Olaf, but I am very reluctant. Thorbjorn is unsparing of
abuse and dishonourable behaviour.'

Steinthor spoke: 'Take my advice, go and find Thorbjorn

and plead your case. I expect that if Gest goes along with you, you will get your rights from Thorbjorn.'

He got up and went out very bent over. He went to Gest and Thorbjorn's booth and entered it. Thorbjorn was there, but not Gest. Thorbjorn greeted Havard and asked him why he had come.

He answered, 'The slaying of Olaf is so fresh in my memory that it seems only yesterday, and it is my purpose to ask you for compensation for the killing.'

Thorbjorn answered, 'Now I can give you some good advice: come to me at home in the district, and I will have something for you, but now I have a lot to attend to and don't want you snivelling about here.'

He answered, 'Experience has shown me that if you do nothing now, then you will certainly do nothing at home in the district. I had thought that some men would support my case.'

Thorbjorn spoke: 'Listen to this nonsense,' he said. 'He intends to turn men against me. Go away and don't ever mention this matter to me again if you wish to stay healthy.'

Havard flew into a rage and tore out of the booth, saying, 'I have become old, but there was a day when I would have thought it unlikely that I would put up with such an injustice.'

And as he went away, men came walking towards him, Gest Oddleifsson and his followers. Havard was so angry that he scarcely paid attention where he was going. Nor did he wish to see anyone. He went back to his booth. Gest looked at the man who walked past him. Havard went to his bed and lay down and sighed heavily. Steinthor asked how things had gone. Havard told what had happened.

Steinthor answered, 'Such an injustice is disgraceful and will very likely cause him great shame when the day of reckoning comes.'

When Gest came into the booth, Thorbjorn greeted him warmly. Then Gest spoke: 'Who was the man who just walked out of the booth?'

Thorbjorn answered, 'Why do you ask such strange questions, wise man? Many more people go in and out than we can keep track of.'

Gest answered, 'This man was unlike other men. He was large and getting on in years and just shuffled along, yet was manly and, so I thought, deeply sad, aggrieved and put upon, and so angry that he paid no heed where he was going. I also thought he appeared fortunate and not a man for just anyone to tangle with.'

Thorbjorn answered, 'That will have been old Havard, my thingman.'

Gest asked, 'Was that not his son whom you killed unjustly?'

'That is indeed correct,' he said.

Gest spoke: 'How well do you think you have kept to what you promised me when I married my sister to you?'

Thorgils Holluson was the name of a man who was named after his mother Halla. He was a fine, courageous man. He was then staying with Gest, his kinsman, and his reputation was at its peak. Gest told Thorgils to go after Havard and ask him to come back. Thorgils went to Havard's booth and told him that Gest wanted to see him.

Havard answered, 'I am not eager to go and be forced to endure Thorbjorn's injustice and abusive language.'

Thorgils asked him to come: 'Gest will support your case.'

Havard reluctantly went along, and they arrived at Gest's. He got up to receive him, welcomed him and seated him beside himself.

Gest then spoke: 'Now, Havard, start at the beginning and tell us about your dealings with Thorbjorn.'

He did so. And when he had spoken, Gest asked Thorbjorn whether any of this were true. Thorbjorn said nothing had been exaggerated.

Gest spoke: 'Has anyone ever heard of such injustice? There are now two choices: either I cancel our agreements, or you allow me to arbitrate in the matter involving the two of you.'

Thorbjorn agreed. They then went out of the booth. Gest called many men together, and the men stood round in a ring, and there in the ring a few men came together and spoke about the case.

Then Gest spoke: 'Thorbjorn, I cannot award the proper amount, because you have not got that much. But I am going to award three wergilds[5] for the killing of Olaf. And for the other injustice that you have done Havard and his family, I am going to make you this award, Havard, to invite you to come to me every autumn and spring, and I will honour you with gifts and promise never to treat you meanly as long as we both are alive.'

Then Thorbjorn spoke: 'I will agree to this and will pay promptly at home in the district.'

Gest answered, 'All the money will be paid immediately here at the Althing and paid fully and honourably. I will contribute one wergild myself.'

He immediately laid it out, all paid in full. Havard sat down and scooped it up into the hood of his cloak. Thorbjorn then walked forward and handed it over bit by bit and came up with one wergild and said that was all he had with him. Gest told him to stop stalling.

Thorbjorn then took out the knotted cloth and untied it. 'It is certain that he will not consider himself underpaid if this is included.'

He then struck Havard on the nose so that blood splattered all over him. 'There are the top and bottom teeth,' Thorbjorn said, 'of your son Olaf.'

Havard watched them tumble into his hood. He leapt up so enraged that the coins scattered in all directions. He had a staff in his hand and ran at the ring and struck one man on the chest so that he fell backwards and lay unconscious for a long time. Havard leapt over the ring of men, not touching anyone and landing far on the other side, and thus home to his booth like a young man. When he got there, he was unable to speak to anyone and threw himself down and lay as if he were ill.

After that Gest spoke to Thorbjorn: 'You are like no other man for malice and injustice. I am no judge of men if you or your kinsmen do not live to regret this.'

Gest was by then in such a fury that he immediately rode from the Althing to Isafjord and declared the separation of Thorbjorn and Thorgerd. Thorbjorn, as well as all his kinsmen, regarded this as a disgrace, but they could do nothing about it.

Gest said that something worse and more befitting his character awaited him. Gest rode to Bardastrond with his kinswoman and all her possessions.

It is said that after the Althing Havard prepared to go home. He was by then very stiff.

Steinthor said, 'If you ever need a little help, Havard, then come to me.'

Havard thanked him, then rode home, and lay down in his bed and stayed there a third year. He was by then all but crippled with stiffness. Bjargey continued her tasks as usual, and rowed to sea every day with Thorhall.

8

One day in the summer when they were at sea, they saw a boat coming out of the fjord. In the boat they recognized Thorbjorn and his followers.

Then Bjargey said, 'Let's take up our lines now and row towards Thorbjorn. I want to talk to him. You row up to the bow of the smack, and I will talk to Thorbjorn a bit while you row in a circle around it.'

They did so, rowing towards the smack. Bjargey called out to Thorbjorn in greeting and asked where he was going.

He said he was travelling west to Vadil: 'My brother Sturla has just arrived there with his son Thjodrek. I am going to take them home with me.'

She asked, 'How long are you going to be away, sir?'

'About a week,' he said.

Thorhall had by then rowed around the smack. Bjargey had a bag in her hand and waved it around the smack. And when she had done what she wanted, they set to on the oars and rowed away as fast as they could.

Then Thorbjorn spoke: 'That damned witch, let's row after them and kill him and maim her.'

Then Brand spoke: 'Now you are proving once again what people say about you, that there is no evil deed you would not commit, but I am going to help them all I can. It will cost you dearly.'

And at Brand's insistence and because they had got far away, Thorbjorn let the matter rest and went on his way.

Then Bjargey said, 'It is not likely, but yet it is my belief that my son Olaf will be avenged. Let's not go home.'

'Where do you want to go?' said Thorhall.

'Now we shall go,' she said, 'and find my brother Valbrand.'

He lived on a farm named Valbrandsstadir. He was a very old man, but had been a very good man. He had two sons, both promising men. One was named Torfi, the other Eyjolf. They were then in their youth. They did not stop before they got there. Valbrand was out in the hayfield with a lot of men. He went to meet his sister and welcomed her warmly and invited her to stay, but she said she did not want to.

'I must return home this evening.'

He asked, 'Then what is it you want, sister?'

'I would like you to lend me your seal nets.'

He answered, 'Here are three nets, and one is very old and no longer reliable, although it used to be dependable. But two are new and untested. Take what you want, two or three.'

She answered, 'I want to have the new ones, for I do not want to risk the old one. Have them ready for me to be picked up.'

He said he would. After that they went away.

Then Thorhall spoke: 'Where are we going now?'

She answered, 'Now we shall go and visit my brother Thorbrand.'

He lived on a farm named Thorbrandsstadir. He was then very old. He had two young sons. The one was named Odd, and the other Thorir. They were promising men. When they got there, Thorbrand greeted them warmly and invited them to stay. She said she was not able to.

'Then what do you want, sister?' he asked.

'I would like you,' she said, 'to lend me your fishnets.'

He answered, 'I have three at hand, and one is very old, but two are new and have not been used. Take whatever you want, two or three.'

She said she wanted to have the new ones, and they parted at that. Then they went away.

Thorhall asked, 'Where are we going now?'

'Now,' she said, 'we shall go to visit my brother, old Asbrand.'

He lived on a farm named Asbrandsstadir. He was the oldest of the brothers. He was married to the sister of old Havard. He had a son who was named Hallgrim. He was young, but big and strong, unattractive in appearance, but nevertheless manly. And when Bjargey got there, Asbrand greeted her warmly and invited her to stay. She said that she had to return home that evening.

He asked, 'What do you want, then, you who so seldom come to visit your kinsmen?'

'It is a small matter,' she said. 'We are so in need of peat-cutting tools that I would be very pleased if you lent me your peat-cutting axe.'

He answered smiling, 'Here are two, the one a large rusty lance, old and nicked and probably of no use now, the other is new and large and has never been used at all.'

She said she wanted to have the new one: 'When I have it sent for.'

He answered that she should decide. Then Bjargey and Thorhall both returned to Havardsstadir that evening.

9

A few days passed until she thought it likely that Thorbjorn would be returning from the west. And one day she went to Havard's bed and asked whether he was asleep.

He sat up and recited this verse:

2.

No sleep settled my brow
since he who said pledges   *he*: Olaf
to spear-man of surf-plough   *surf-plough*: ship;
succumbed to blade's edges;   its *spear-man*: Viking, Havard
since the cove of corpses'   *cove of corpses*: shield; its *conifers*: warriors;
conifers took a hard toll,   *took a hard toll*: killed
that man unkindly killed
innocent Olaf our son.

'It is certain,' she said, 'that it is a very big lie that you have not slept in three years, but yet it is now time to get up and gird up your loins if you wish to avenge Olaf, your son, because he will never be avenged in your lifetime if not tonight.'

And when he heard her speech, he leapt forward out of the bed on to the floor and recited this verse:

3.
Old age mocks us most as we –
men, all of you there, then,
render me rapt esteem! –
relate our deeds of fame;
now that Njord of weapons   *Njord* (god) *of weapons*: Olaf
kneels down on battle plain,
our son, our noble stave
and staff, is grim death's gain.

Havard was then very sprightly and walked without a limp. He went to a large chest. It was full of weapons, and he opened it up, put on a helmet and a strong coat of mail. He then looked up and saw a gull flying past the window.

He recited this verse:[6]

4.
Hail-stippled, shrieking gull
of the slaughter heap's gulf   *slaughter heap's gulf*: blood; its *gull*: raven
flies to the firth of the dead;   *firth of the dead*: blood
flagged, it screams for dawn's   *dawn's part*: breakfast portion, i.e.
     part.   dead warriors
Thus war-waders of yore   *war-waders*: birds of prey
warbled of men's decay,
callous cuckoo of Gauk's
concoction screamed of doom.   *Gauk's* (Odin's) *concoction*: battle

He armed himself quickly and deftly. He also outfitted Thorhall with good weapons. And when they were ready, he turned to Bjargey and kissed her and said it was not certain when they would meet again.

She wished him farewell: 'I do not need to goad you to avenge our son, Olaf, because I know that courage and manliness will follow you wherever you go.'

After that they parted. Havard and Thorhall went down to the sea, pushed out a six-oared boat, started rowing and did not stop until they came to Valbrand's farm. There was a long spit of land that went out into the sea. There they beached their boat. Havard asked Thorhall to guard the boat, and he went up to the farm. He had a spear in his hand, an excellent weapon. And when he came up to the home field, father and sons were there. The brothers were undressed and were raking hay. They had taken off their boots and set them aside in the field. They were high boots. Valbrand walked towards Havard and greeted him warmly and invited him to stay.

He said he could not stay there: 'I have come to collect your nets that you promised your sister.'

He walked to his sons and spoke: 'Your kinsman Havard has come, and he is dressed as if he intended some great deeds.'

And when they heard this, they threw down their rakes and ran to their clothes. And when they tried to put on their shoes, the leather had shrunk. They pushed their feet into them so hard that the skin on their heels was stripped off, and when they came home their boots were full of blood.

Valbrand gave his sons good weapons and said, 'Give Havard good support. Think more on vengeance than on what might come after.'

After that they went to Thorbrandsstadir. They were also quickly ready, Odd and Thorir. They now continued on to Asbrandsstadir. Havard there requested the peat axe. Hallgrim, his kinsman, got ready to go with him. There was a man named An, who was a farmhand in Asbrand's household. He was Hallgrim's foster-father and got ready to go with them. And when they were ready, they walked to the boat. Thorhall greeted them warmly. They were eight all together, and each one more warlike than the next.

Then Hallgrim said to his kinsman Havard, 'Why did you leave home, kinsman, with neither sword nor axe?'

He answered, 'If it chances that we run into Thorbjorn

Thjodreksson, then you will speak otherwise after our parting,
for I intend the sword Gunnlogi, the best of weapons, for myself.'

They wished that his words would prove true: 'It is very
important that we act courageously.'

It was very late in the day. They pushed the boat out and got
in and began rowing. They saw a big flock of ravens flying in
front of them over the spit of land that lay in front of them.

Havard recited this verse:

5.
First I fashion my vow,
to feed the greedy birds;
the awful gulls of gore   *gulls of gore*: ravens
glide over fallow plain.
Grimly, I gauge our cause,
gain we will their downfall;
may hale heroes crush foe,
hazard battle on field.

They rowed across the sound. There was rough weather in
the fjord, and they shipped a lot of water. They rowed courageously and did not stop before they came to Laugabol. They
found a calm berth because Thorbjorn had built a magnificent
harbour, deep and clear and dredged far inland. A smack or
even a bigger boat could anchor there at will. Large whale ribs
were buried in the ground as rollers, their ends made fast with
stones, so that no one needed to wade to or from a ship,
whether large or small. And up above was a high pebble ridge.
Above the ridge stood a large boathouse with doors, very finely
built. On the other side behind the ridge was a large lagoon.
From the boathouse the beach could not be seen, but from the
ridge one could see both the boathouse and the beach. When
they reached land, they leapt out of the boat.

Then Havard spoke: 'Let us now carry the boat up over the
ridge to the lagoon. We will also stay on top of the ridge so that
they are not able to see us right away. We should not be too
eager. No one is to leap up until I give the word.'

It was then very dark.

10

Now we go back to Thorbjorn and nine companions heading from the west in the smack. Sturla was there and Thjodrek his son, Thorbjorn and Vak, Brand the Strong, and two farmhands. The smack was heavily loaded. That same evening they arrived at Laugabol before dark.

Then Thorbjorn said, 'Let's not be in a hurry, and let's leave the smack here for the night and not take anything except our weapons and clothes. The weather is good and dry. Vak, you carry our weapons.'

He first took their swords and spears and carried them up to the boathouse.

Then Torfi said, 'We ought to take their swords and the man in front.'

'Let's wait a while,' said Havard.

He told Hallgrim to go and take the sword Gunnlogi and bring it to him. And after Vak walked down, Hallgrim ran and took the sword and brought it to Havard. He raised it aloft, and shook it by the hilt. Vak went up a second time and had the shields loaded on his back, but he carried the stacked up steel helmets in his arms. He had a helmet on his head. And when he had come up to the lagoon, they leapt up intending to take him. When he heard their noise, he sensed trouble in the air. He tried to hurry back with the weapons. But as he moved quickly, his feet slipped out from under him on the edge of the lagoon so that he landed on his head. It was very slippery and the water shallow, and he was weighed down with all the weapons. He was not able to stand up, and as none of them made any effort to help him, Vak's life ended there. Havard and his men then ran down to the ridge. When Thorbjorn saw them, he threw himself into the water and set out from land. Old Havard saw this and quickly dived into the water after Thorbjorn.

It is told next that Brand the Strong ran up and tore up a launching roller – it was a large whale rib – and drove it into the head of Hallgrim's foster-father. Hallgrim had just come down from the ridge and saw that An had fallen. He ran at Brand with a raised axe and struck him in the head and split it

down to his shoulders, just as Thorbjorn and Havard leapt into
the sea. He then leapt in after them. Torfi Valbrandsson ran up
to Sturla. He was both big and strong and a very able fighter.
He also had all his weapons with him. They fought long and
courageously.

11

Now we go back to Thorbjorn and Havard, who had set
off from shore. It was a long swim before Thorbjorn came to
a skerry which lies at the mouth of the sound. And as he was
getting up on to the back of the skerry, Havard was just
approaching from the front. When Thorbjorn saw that and
because he had no weapon, he picked up a large stone intending to dash it into his head. When Havard saw that, it occurred
to him that he had heard it said that a different faith was propa-
gated abroad from the one in the north, and if anyone could
tell him that this belief was better and fairer, then he would
believe it if he defeated Thorbjorn. And then he renewed his
efforts to reach the skerry. Just as Thorbjorn was on the point
of releasing the stone, his feet slipped out from under him on
the slippery rocks and he fell on to his back, the stone landing
on his chest and knocking him senseless. At that moment Havard
managed to climb up on to the skerry and ran him through with
the sword Gunnlogi. Hallgrim had just then got to the skerry.
Havard then struck Thorbjorn across the face and hacked out
his top and bottom teeth. Hallgrim asked why he had done that
to a dead man.

Havard answered, 'I was reminded just then that Thorbjorn
struck me in the nose with his knotted cloth. The top and bottom teeth that he had hacked out of my son Olaf with this same
sword fell out.'

Then they headed back towards land. It seemed to men
who later spoke of it that Hallgrim had acted courageously
when he set out into the fjord without knowing that the skerry
was there. It was indeed a very long swim. When they got to
shore, everything was very quiet. As they got to the ridge, a
man ran at them with a raised axe. He wore a black shirt tucked

into his trousers. They turned towards him, and when they
neared each other they recognized Torfi Valbrandsson, and they
greeted him warmly. Torfi asked whether Thorbjorn was dead.

Havard recited this verse:

6.
I carved the skirmish-scrub,   *skirmish-scrub*: inferior man
the scoundrel, to his chops;
And with hard blow I bashed
brow of the wretched man.
No slack in shiny blade,
snake-carved edge took no rest;
dagger-dealt battle's woes;   *dagger*: the sword Gunnlogi
death took the man from here.

Havard asked what they had done. Torfi said that Sturla and
the farmhands had fallen, 'and An is dead'.

Havard recited this verse:

7.
We eight quelled the quartet
– quitted their deed of blood –
who butchered Bjargey's son,
battered her lad to death.
Of our host, Hallgrim says,
he was cut down by blows;
weapon-woman swelled up,   *weapon-woman*: valkyrie
workman swiped with a plank.

Then they went up to the boathouse. Their companions
were there and greeted them warmly. Then Eyjolf Valbrandsson asked whether the slaves should not be killed.

Havard said that his son, Olaf, would not be more avenged if
they killed the slaves: 'They are to stay here tonight and keep
watch that no one steals any driftwood.'

Then Hallgrim asked what they were going to do next.

Havard answered, 'Let's take the smack and everything we
think necessary and set out for Manaberg and seek out Ljot the

warrior. It would be rather good revenge on such a man, if we are so fortunate.'

Then they took the smack and many of the treasures which the kinsmen had owned and rowed out along the fjord to Manaberg.

Then Havard spoke: 'Now we must proceed with deliberation: Ljot is always on his guard because he is forever fighting someone. Every night he posts armed guards around him, and he sleeps in a bed closet. There is a chamber under the floor of the bed closet, and the other end of the chamber is behind the house. He also has a lot of men with him.'

Then Torfi Valbrandsson spoke: 'It is my advice that we set fire to the house and burn every last man inside.'

Havard said that this was not to be: 'You and your kinsman Hallgrim will climb up on to the roof of the house and guard the exit to the underground chamber. I trust you two best for this. There are two doors on the front of the house, and there are also two doors to the hall. Now Eyjolf and I will go in through the front doors and the brothers Odd and Thorir through the others into the hall, but you stay here, Thorhall, and guard the smack. You are to defend it valiantly, if the need arise.'

And when he had arranged everything as he desired, they went up to the farm. There was a large shed in the hayfield, and an armed man was sitting on the ground resting against the wall. And when they got very close to him, he saw them and leapt up running, intending to make their arrival known. Hallgrim was walking ahead of the group. He threw his spear at him, and it went through him, pinning him to the wall. He met a quick death at the point of the spear. Afterwards they went to where they had planned, Torfi and Hallgrim to the farmhouse exit.

12

It is said that Havard swiftly went into the hall. Higher up it was light, but below it was dark. He went immediately to the bed closet. As it happened, the woman of the house had not yet gone to bed and was in the main room along with her women. The bed closet was not locked. Havard struck the flat of his sword blade against the door. Ljot awakened and asked who was making such a noise. Havard told him his name.

Then Ljot spoke: 'Why are you here, old Havard? We were told yesterday that you had met your death.'

Havard answered, 'You will sooner hear of another's death. I can tell you of the killing of your brothers, Thorbjorn and Sturla.'

And when he heard this, he leapt up in the bed and took down a sword that hung above him. Ljot ordered his men in the hall to get up and take up arms. Havard then leapt up into the bed closet and struck Ljot on the left shoulder, but Ljot moved very quickly and the sword merely glanced off his shoulder, flaying the skin on his upper arm and cutting it off at the elbow. Ljot leapt forwards out of the bed with drawn sword, intending to strike at Havard. By then Eyjolf had come and struck off his right arm at the shoulder, and they slew Ljot then and there. Then there was a great commotion in the hall. Ljot's farmhands wished to get up and take up arms. The sons of Thorbrand had by then come inside. Some of them were lightly injured.

Then Havard spoke and ordered the farmhands to be still and not to resist: 'Otherwise we will kill every last man of you, one by one.'

It seemed to them best to lie as quietly as possible. Ljot was mourned by few, even by those who had been of his household. After that they went outside. Havard wished to do nothing more there. Then Torfi and Hallgrim came towards them. They had intended to go in and asked what had happened.

Havard recited this verse:

8.
Geirdis's son strode in stealth,   *Geirdis's son*: Eyjolf?
struck him who lived in wealth;
I saw him hew swiftly,
his slashing blade aloft.
Eyjolf played with edges,   *played with edges*: made battle
eager, he sought sedges,   *sedges*: men
repaid reeds of slaughter,   *reeds of slaughter*: warriors
revenge he sought toughly.

Then they went down to the smack, and Thorhall greeted them warmly. Then Torfi Valbrandsson asked what they were going to do next.

Havard said, 'Now we are going to look for some support. Although the revenge is not as much as I had desired, we still cannot be confident of protecting ourselves after these deeds. Many formidable kinsmen of Thorbjorn's are still left. It seems to me best to look towards Steinthor of Eyri. He most of all promised me support if ever I needed any.'

They all requested him to arrange things and said they would do what he wanted, and that they would not separate until he thought it advisable. After that they set out into the fjord. They began to strain at the oars, and Havard sat at the helm. Then Hallgrim spoke and requested Havard to recite a verse.

Havard then recited this verse:

9.
Our troop has just taken
our toll on Thjodrek's sons
– Hallgrim, I feel no guilt –
grievous were their misdeeds.
The strong men were struck down,
seekers of blades' rainfall;   *blades' rainfall*: battle
vengeance for vile Thorbjorn
will visit death to men.   *death to men*: i.e. Havard

13

Now there is nothing to tell about their trip before they reached Eyri. It was the time of day when Steinthor ate with his men. They went into the main room, all four of them fully armed. Havard went up to Steinthor and greeted him. Steinthor returned his greeting and asked who he was. He said his name was Havard.

'Were you in our booth last summer?'

He said this was so.

Steinthor spoke: 'Lads, have you ever seen anyone more unlike his former self than this man now is? It seemed to me that he could scarcely hobble between booths without a staff, and so great were his troubles that he seemed on his last legs, but now he seems to me a most accomplished man of arms, but can you tell us any news?'

Havard answered, 'We report the killing of Thorbjorn Thjodreksson and his brothers, Ljot and Sturla Thjodreksson, Brand the Strong, and seven of their men.'

Steinthor answered, 'This is news indeed, and who are they who have killed these great warriors and mighty men?'

Havard spoke and said that he and his kinsmen had done it. Steinthor spoke and asked whether Havard intended to look for support after such a great deed.

Havard answered, 'I had intended, as I am doing now, to look to you. I thought that you said last summer at the Althing that if I needed a little help, I should come to you rather than to other chieftains.'

Steinthor answered, 'I can't imagine when you'll need a lot of help if now you need only a little. But still if I held back now, you would not expect me to be a good host in a future time of need. And such will not be the case. I want to invite you, Havard, to remain here with your companions until this case is concluded. I will also promise to plead your case, because you strike me as men who bring good fortune to those who help you, and it is not certain that there are men as valiant as you are. So far the case has proceeded justly if unexpectedly.'

Havard recited this verse:

10.
Thus should savvy warriors
of surf-sun venture forth,   *surf-sun*: gold; its *warriors*: chieftains
they who strive to support
surging guiders of boats.   *guiders of boats*: Havard and his men
I say that the splendour
of sages of Icefjord   *Icefjord*: Isafjord
shall roundly be smitten,
sorely hacked by the blade.

They thanked Steinthor for his generous offer. He had their clothes and weapons taken away and had them provided with dry clothes. And when Havard took off his helmet and removed his coat of mail, he recited this verse:

11.
The sword-trees then snickered,   *sword-trees*: warriors, men
sniggering at my fall;
may the doom dealt on my son
do much harm to them all.
Since malicious mockers
were murdered with swift blades,
stones weeping in water
whisper sonorous tones.

Steinthor requested that Havard come to the bench and sit opposite him, 'and place your companions next to you'.

Havard did so, placed Hallgrim, his kinsman, on the inside next to him, and next to him sat Thorir and Odd Thorbrandsson, but on the other side of Havard sat Torfi and Eyjolf Valbrandsson, then Thorhall, then the farmhands who had already been seated.

And when they were all seated, Havard recited this verse:

12.
I command that we calmly
the cowards at home await
– I long to tell the truth –
the test is yet to come.
The battle-cares we waged
will be wasted away;
I have no plans to pay
for those pointers of spears.   *pointers of spears*: warriors

Then Steinthor spoke: 'It is now easy to hear, Havard, that things are going your way; and this might continue if no prosecution were taken up for such valiant and powerful men as these brothers were and if there were not such mighty survivors to take up the prosecution.'

Havard said he was not worried about prosecution. He said

that from now on he would never have any sorrow or grief in his heart nor be dissatisfied with the way his case turned out. He was as happy and delighted as a young man with every living soul. This news spread widely, and was thought most incredible. They remained there at Eyri with farmer Steinthor. There was no shortage of men, and all were well treated. There were no fewer than sixty able-bodied fighters. We turn now from them as they dwell with Steinthor at Eyri in good cheer and at great expense.

14

There was a man named Ljot.[7] He lived at Raudasand. He was called Ljot the Dueller. He was both big and strong and the greatest of duellers. He was a brother of Thorbjorn Thjodreks-son. It is said that Ljot was a very unjust man, and sank his axe in the head of every man who would not let go of whatever he wanted, and no one's head in Raudasand or anywhere else was safe around him.

There was a man named Thorbjorn. He lived on a farm named Eyri. He was wealthy but mean spirited, and getting on in years. He had two sons, one named Grim, the other Thorstein. It is said that Ljot and Thorbjorn jointly owned a trenched meadow, a most valuable piece of land. It was agreed that each was to have use of the pasture on alternate summers, and the stream that ran into the pasture in the spring passed below Ljot's farm. There were sluice gates in it, all well con-structed. It always happened that when Thorbjorn was supposed to have the pasture, he never got any water, and things came to the point that Ljot spread the word that Thorbjorn had no rights to the pasture and should not dare to claim ownership. And when Thorbjorn heard of this, he was certain that Ljot would keep his word.

Their farms were close together, and one day they met. Thorbjorn asked whether Ljot intended to take the pasture away from him.

Ljot answered and told him not to mention the matter: 'It won't do you any more good than others to complain about how I want to have things. Do one of two things: be content with what I choose to do, or I will drive you off your land, and then you will have neither the pasture nor anything else.'

And when Thorbjorn recognized Ljot's injustice and because he had a lot of money, he bought the pasture at the price that Ljot set and paid twenty hundred pieces of silver on the spot, and at that they parted. And when Thorbjorn's young sons heard of this, they became very angry and called it a great robbery of their estate, to buy what they already had owned. This news spread far and wide. People thought that a great injustice had occurred.

The brothers tended their father's sheep. Thorstein was twelve years old, and Grim ten. One day at the beginning of winter the brothers went to the sheep sheds. The weather had been bad, and they intended to see whether all the stock had come home. It happened that Ljot had gone that morning to see to his driftwood. He was very industrious around the farm. Just as the boys came to the shed, they saw Ljot walking up from the beach.

Then Thorstein said to Grim, his brother, 'Do you see Ljot the Dueller coming up from the beach?'

'Why should I not see him?' said Grim.

Then Thorstein spoke: 'This Ljot does us and many others much injustice, and I feel like taking revenge, if I can.'

Grim spoke: 'It is foolish to say that you are going to show your hostility to such a fighter as Ljot, who is mightier than four or five others, no matter how big they might be, and no child is a match for him.'

Thorstein answered, 'Don't try to stop me. I am going to resolve matters once and for all, but you can be like your father and be Ljot's victim, like so many others.'

Grim answered, 'Since you are so minded, brother, you will have very little use for me, but I will give you everything in my might, such as it is.'

'May you prosper, then,' said Thorstein, 'and it might be that things will turn out justly.'

They were carrying hand-axes, small but sharp. They stood and waited until Ljot got near the shed. He hurried past them.

Ljot had a wood-axe in his hand. He went on his way and pretended not to see the boys. And as he passed them, Thorstein
struck Ljot on the shoulder. The axe did not bite, but the blow
was still so forceful that the shoulder was put out of joint.
When Ljot saw that the boys were intent on pestering him, he
turned quickly and raised his axe, intending to strike Thorstein.
And just as he raised his axe, Grim ran at him and cut off his
hand above the wrist. The hand fell to the ground with the axe.
Then they did not hesitate between blows, and strange as it
may seem they killed Ljot the Dueller then and there without
being injured themselves. They buried him in the snow and
went on their way.

When they arrived home, their father was standing in the
doorway and asked what had kept them and why their clothes
were bloody. They told of the killing of Ljot. He asked whether
they had killed him. They said that it was so.

Then he said, 'Go away, you unfortunate creatures! You
have committed the most unfortunate deed and killed a very
great chieftain and our leader. You have done something that
will deprive me of my land and all that I own, and you two will
be killed, and that will serve you right.'

Thorbjorn then ran away from the farm.

Grim spoke: 'Let us not pay any attention to this shameful
creature, who acts so tediously. It is no ordinary coward who
carries on so.'

Thorstein answered, 'Let's go after him, for I suspect that he
is not as angry as he pretends.'

After that they went out to him. Thorbjorn spoke cheerfully
to them and asked them to wait for him there. He then went
home and was away only a short time. He came back with two
horses well provisioned.

Then Thorbjorn said that they should get on their horses: 'I
will send you to Eyri to my friend Steinthor. Ask him to take
you in. Here is a gold ring, a great treasure, which you should
give him. He has often offered to buy it and has never got it,
but now I shall turn it over to you in your time of need.'

After that the old man kissed his sons and wished them well
and a safe return. Nothing is told of their journey before they

arrived at Eyri. It was early in the day. They walked into the main room and it was hung round with curtains, and the benches were occupied on both sides. There was no lack of merriment or good cheer. They walked up to Steinthor and greeted him warmly. He returned their greetings warmly. He asked who they were. They told him their names and that of their father.

Then Thorstein said, 'Here is a ring that my father sends you with his greetings, and he requests that you provide us with a place to stay during the winter or even longer, should we need it.'

Steinthor accepted the ring and spoke: 'Do you have any news?'

They then told of the killing of Ljot and that they had killed him.

Steinthor answered, 'This is yet another marvel, that two boys have been the downfall of such a fighter as Ljot, and what was the reason?'

They related matters as they saw them.

Then Steinthor spoke: 'It is my advice that you two go over to Havard, the grey-haired man sitting opposite me. Ask him whether he will take you into his troop.'

They did so and walked up to Havard. He received them warmly and asked the news and pretended that he had not been listening, and they related their story in very great detail.

And when their tale was over, Havard leapt up opposite them and recited this verse:

13.
Dear to me for this death,
to dagger-tree be true;   *dagger-tree*: warrior, Havard
may thickets of terror   *thickets of terror*: champions, heroes
tread long days on the earth.
Ljot's fain fall to the earth
filled my men with great joy;
hear, west men, these words drear,
woe-bringing to your hearts.

Havard seated the brothers between him and the door. They sat there in good cheer.

News of these events spread all over Raudasand and beyond. Ljot was found buried at the base of the wall. Thorbjorn was visited and questioned. Thorbjorn did not deny that his sons had killed Ljot. But because Ljot was unpopular in Raudasand and because Thorbjorn said that he had become angry and driven them away – and his farmhands supported him – no prosecution was undertaken at that time. Thorbjorn remained quietly on his farm.

15

Now to go back to them all as they sat together at Eyri in fine style. It was very expensive for Steinthor, given the many men that he had, the large amount that he was required to lay out and the lavishness that he showed.

There was a man named Atli who lived in Otradal, and he was married to Steinthor of Eyri's sister, Thordis. Atli was the tiniest and most miserable-looking of men, and, so it was said, his appearance was in keeping with his temperament, in that he was a great miser, and yet he was of a good family and so rich that he scarcely knew the extent of his wealth. Thordis had been married to Atli for his money. It is said that his farm in Otradal was far from the highway. It was out on the other side of the fjord from Eyri. Atli was too stingy to keep any farm-hands. He worked both day and night as hard as he could. He was also so stubborn that he wanted nothing whatever to do with other people, for better or worse. He was a very skilful farmer. He had a large storehouse; it contained all sorts of choice things. There were large stacks of provisions, all kinds of meat, dried fish, cheese, and everything else he needed. Atli had put his bed there, and he and his wife slept there every night.

So it is said that one morning Steinthor was awake early and went to Havard's bed and grasped him by the feet and asked him to get up. Havard leapt up quickly and moved forward on to the floor. When he got up, each of his companions got up one after the other, for it was their custom that all went wherever one of them needed to go. When they were all ready, they went out into the hayfield. Steinthor was there with some of his men.

Then Havard spoke: 'We are ready, sir, to go wherever you wish to have us go. We will gladly follow you, whether on a long or a short journey. But it is a matter of pride with me that I will go nowhere when I do not know where I am going.'

Steinthor answered, 'I intend to visit my brother-in-law, Atli, and I want you to give me some assistance.'

They walked down to the sea. The smack that they had taken from Thorbjorn was there. They pushed it out and took to the oars and rowed across the fjord. Steinthor thought that the companions did everything efficiently.

That morning Atli woke up early and got out of bed. Atli was dressed in a white shirt, short and very snug fitting. He was an awkward man, both wretched and ugly in appearance, and bald with deep-set eyes. He went outdoors and checked on the weather. It was cold and well below freezing. He saw that a smack was coming from the other side across the fjord and was nearing the shore and in it he recognized Steinthor the farmer, his brother-in-law, and was not pleased. At some distance from the farmhouse there was an enclosure in the hayfield. Inside the enclosure was a huge, top-heavy haystack. Atli quickly dashed inside the enclosure and pulled the haystack down on top of him, and he lay underneath it.

Now to go back to Steinthor and the companions as they reached land and walked up to the farm. When they got to the storehouse, Thordis leapt up and welcomed her brother and everyone else and said that he was seldom seen there. Steinthor asked where Atli his kinsman was. She said that he had gone somewhere a short while ago. Then Steinthor ordered a search to be made for him. They looked for him all over the farm but did not find him, which they then told Steinthor.

Then Thordis spoke: 'What brings you here to us, kinsman?'

He answered, 'I had thought that Atli might have given or sold me some provisions.'

She said, 'I do not think I have less to say on this than Atli. I want you to have such as you wish.'

He said he would gladly accept. After that they emptied the

storehouse and carried everything down to the smack until it was loaded. There were all kinds of provisions.

Steinthor spoke: 'Now you are to go home in the smack, but I will remain here with my sister. I am curious to see how my kinsman, Atli, acts when he comes back.'

She answered. 'I think this is unnecessary, my kinsman,' said Thordis. 'You will not find it amusing to listen to him, but still it is your decision. But you must promise me not to be less a friend to Atli than before, whatever he says or does.'

Steinthor agreed to this. She put him behind a curtain out of sight while the others headed back home in the smack. They had stormy weather in the fjord, and they shipped a lot of water before they reached land.

16

Now to go back to Atli lying under the haystack. When he saw that they had left his land, he crawled from under the haystack, and he was then so stiff and cold that he could scarcely stand up. He dragged himself back to the storehouse. And when he came in, he was shaking so much that every tooth in his head clicked and clacked. He raised his eyes and saw that the storehouse had been emptied.

Then he said, 'What robbers have been here?'

Thordis answered, 'No robbery has occurred here, but my brother Steinthor was here with his men, and I gave him the things that you say are stolen.'

Atli answered, 'I most rue the day I married you, for I am bereft of all my wealth. I do not know a worse man than Steinthor, your brother, nor greater robbers than they who were with him, and now everything that was here has been taken from me and stolen and I have been robbed so that we will soon have to go begging.'

Then Thordis spoke: 'We are never going to lack money, but get into your bed now and let me warm you up a bit. You look nearly frozen to death.'

And with that he crawled under the bedcovers next to her. Steinthor thought his brother-in-law a pitiful figure, with nothing on his feet and his shirt thrown over his head and covering very little of him. Atli snuggled down next to her, cursing and insulting Steinthor and calling him a robber. Then he was silent for a while.

And when he had warmed up, he said, 'But there is this to say, that in you I have a great treasure. It is also true to say that such a splendid fellow as my kinsman, Steinthor, is scarcely to be found. And it is just as well that he took what he did. It is the same as if I still had it.'

His praise for Steinthor went on for a long time. Steinthor then approached the bed, and when Atli saw him, he stood up and greeted him.

Then Steinthor spoke: 'How do you like it, Atli my kinsman, that your storehouse has been emptied?'

Atli answered, 'If the truth be told, it seems to me best, after all, that you have the provisions. I also want to offer you everything from my goods that you want, for nothing is lacking. You nobly decided to take in those men who have avenged the wrongs done them. You now will be intending to conclude things honourably. May you for this reason prosper most magnificently.'

Then Steinthor spoke: 'I would like to request, Atli my kinsman, that you do not behave so miserably as you have done up to now. Behave well and take some farmhands, and be sociable with others. I know that you are not mean spirited, even though you sometimes act that way because of your temperament.'

Atli then promised this. Steinthor went home the same day. The kinsmen parted very warmly, and Steinthor arrived home at Eyri and considered everything well done. They sat now at home, and the winter passed. They were in good spirits during the winter and played games that tested their manhood.

17

There was a man named Svart. He was a slave at Eyri, big and so strong that he had the might of four men. He was very useful on the farm, and did a lot of the work.

One day Steinthor had the slave brought to him and spoke

to him: 'They want you to be in the game with us today, for we lack one man.'

Svart answered, 'There is no need to ask this of me, for I have a lot of work to do. I also wager that your champions won't do my work, but all the same I will comply with your wishes.'

So it is told that Hallgrim had to play against Svart. The long and short of the matter is that each time they clashed, Svart fell down, and after each fall, his shoes came off and he had to pause a long time to tie on his shoes. This continued the whole day, and people whooped and laughed about it a lot, but Havard spoke this verse:

14.
The laced shoes were not long
unlashed upon the feet
of victors, Valbrand's sons,
I venture to mention.
When stalwart men were sought,
the storm-tossed wave rose up,
sanctioned the shield's oar handle,   *shield's oar handle*: warrior
my son, last year, at last.

The play was of the best. Hallgrim was then eighteen years old and thought capable of valiant accomplishments when fully grown.

So it is said that the winter passed and nothing eventful happened until they prepared for the Althing. Steinthor said he did not know what to do with the companions. He did not want to have them along at the Althing, but thought it unwise to let them stay at home.

And a few days before the Althing, Atli and Steinthor met. Atli asked what he was going to do with the companions during the Althing.

Steinthor said he did not know for sure where he could put them so that he would not be anxious about their safety, 'Unless you take them.'

Atli spoke: 'I promise to take in these men.'

'Then you are doing right,' said Steinthor.

Atli spoke: 'I will do everything in my power to do what you want.'

Steinthor spoke: 'I trust you completely in this.'

18

After that Havard and his companions went home with Atli to Otradal. He took them in with open arms. There nothing that was needed was lacking. He gave them fine hospitality. Ten warlike men were there. Atli had the storehouse cleared and put their beds there and hung up their weapons, and everything was very fine.

Steinthor assembled his men. Neither friends nor kinsmen were lacking. He was also related by marriage to chieftains. He rode to the Althing with three hundred men – his thingmen, friends, kinsmen and in-laws.

19

Thorarin was the name of a man. He was a godi out west in Dyrafjord, a great chieftain and rather old. He was a brother of the sons of Thjodrek and the cleverest and wisest. He had heard the news, the killing of his brothers and kinsmen. He thought that the blows had landed very near to him and that he would not be able to sit idly by in such matters where the prosecution depended mainly on him. And before he rode to the Althing, he summoned men from Dyrafjord and wherever else he had friends and kinsmen.

Dyri was the name of a man, the second great chieftain there, and a great friend of Thorarin the godi. Thorgrim was the name of his son. He was a grown man when these events took place. It was said that he was big and strong, and very knowledgeable in many kinds of black magic, which he practised a lot. Thorarin took up the matter with his friends, and it was their unanimous decision that Thorarin and Dyri should ride to the Althing with two hundred men, but Thorgrim offered to kill Havard and all his kinsmen and companions. He said that he had heard that Steinthor from Eyri had kept them all winter and had promised to support their case to the full letter of the law against those plaintiffs opposing the companions.

Thorgrim said he knew that Steinthor had ridden from home with a great many men, but that the kinsmen and companions had gone to Steinthor's brother-in-law, Atli the wretch, in Otradal, 'and nothing stands in the way of killing them, one after another'.

It was decided that Thorgrim should ride from home with eighteen men. Nothing about their trip is told until they arrived at Atli's farm in Otradal. It was early morning, and they rode into a little depression so that they could not be seen from the farm. Thorgrim ordered them to dismount, and said that he was so sleepy that he was on no account able to sit up. They did so and let their horses graze, but Thorgrim fell asleep and spread a skin over his head and tossed in his sleep.

20

Now we turn to what was happening back in Otradal. It was their custom to sleep in the storehouse at night. On that morning they woke up because Atli was tossing so in his sleep that no one else could sleep, for he thrashed around and sighed, and banged his feet and hands against the bed until Torfi Valbrandsson leapt up and waked him, and said that no one was able to sleep because of him and his noise. Atli sat up and rubbed his bald head. Havard asked whether he had dreamt anything strange.

He said this was true: 'I dreamt that I walked out of the storehouse and I saw eighteen wolves running together from the south into the field, and in front of the wolves ran a vixen. It was such a cunning animal that I have not seen its like before. It was very awful and evil. It looked around carefully, taking in everything, and all the animals seemed to me very fierce. And just as they reached the farm, Torfi waked me, and I know for certain that they were the spirits of men. Let us get up immediately.'

Atli did not change his habits, leapt up and put on his tunic, and ran out like an arrow shot from a bow. The others took their weapons and dressed and prepared themselves nobly. And when they were nearly ready, Atli came back dressed in a sturdy coat of mail with a drawn sword in his hand.

Then Atli said, 'It is most likely that this will turn out as many a man has said, that it would not benefit Steinthor, my brother-in-law, to have you come here. Now I request this, that you let me decide our plan of action. First, it is my plan that we go out and stand by the wall of the house and not let ourselves be cut down inside. I assume that you are of a mind not to flee, no matter what befalls us.'

They said this was true.

21

Now the tale turns to where Thorgrim was waking up. He had become warm. Then he said, 'I have just been up to the farmhouse for a while, and everything was such a muddle that I do not see matters clearly, but still we will go up to the farmhouse. I think we should burn them inside the house. It seems to me the quickest way of resolving matters.'

They took their weapons and went into the field.

When Atli and the others saw the men, Atli spoke: 'It is my belief that the men of Dyrafjord have come here and that Thorgrim Dyrason, the worst man in all Dyrafjord and a great magician, is their leader. They are the closest friends of Thorarin, who is obliged to take up the action over his brothers. I myself intend, although it is unexpected, to go against Thorgrim, and I want you, Havard, an experienced and a great fighter, to take on two. I have reserved two of the toughest for Hallgrim, your kinsman. I have set aside four for the sons of Valbrand, Torfi and Eyjolf, and for the sons of Thorbrand, Odd and Thorir, I also have allotted four. I think that the sons of Thorbjorn, Grim and Thorstein, can handle three, and that Thorhall and my farmhand can deal with one each.'

And just as Atli had arranged things as he desired, Thorgrim and his men walked from the south towards the house, and saw now that things were shaped otherwise than they had expected: armed men were there ready for an encounter.

Then Thorgrim spoke: 'Who knew but that Atli the coward is more cunning than we thought, but all the same let's attack them at once.'

They ran at each other as planned. In the first rush little Atli ran at Thorgrim and struck at him with both hands on his sword, but it did not bite. They struck at each other for a while, but Thorgrim remained unscathed.

Then Atli spoke: 'You are like a troll, Thorgrim, not like a man, for no iron bites you.'

Thorgrim answered, 'How dare you speak of such a thing, for I struck at you as often as I could just now, and nothing bit into your miserable bald head.'

Atli saw that he was getting nowhere fast. He then threw away his sword and slipped under Thorgrim's grasp and threw him to the ground. Now he was unarmed and knew that the odds were much against him. He decided to bend over and bite through Thorgrim's windpipe, then dragged him over to his sword and cut off his head. After that he focused his beady eyes on Havard and saw that he had killed one of the men he was fighting. Atli charged the other one, and they did not exchange many blows before he fell. Hallgrim had killed both of those he had fought, and Torfi also. Eyjolf had killed one of those men he had fought, Thorir and Odd had killed three, but one was left. Thorstein and Grim had killed two, but one was left. Thorhall had killed the one he had fought. The farmhand had not killed the one intended for him. Havard ordered them to stop.

Then Thorstein Thorbjarnarson spoke: 'My father will not hear in Raudasand west of here that we brothers did not do our part as others have.'

He ran at one of them with a raised axe and drove it into his head, so that he died immediately. Atli asked whether he should not kill them all. Havard said there was no reason for that. Atli sat down and ordered them led before him. He shaved their heads bald and tarred them. Then he took his knife out of its sheath and cut off their ears, and ordered them thus marked to go and find Dyri and Thorarin. He said they would more readily be able to remember that they had met Atli the Short. Three

of them, all told, departed, but eighteen of them had come,
strong, valiant looking and well armed.

Havard recited this verse.

15.

Wondrous word must have come
– wet the oar-blade of wounds –   *oar-blade of wounds*: sword
from the east to Icefjord,   *Icefjord*: Isafjord
to arrow-showers' lords,   *arrow-showers*: battle; its *lords*: commanders
that the battle-breeders   *battle-breeders*: warriors
bandied the spears' chatter.   *spears' chatter*: battle play
Out east the sons of Valbrand
yielded nothing to their foes.

After that they went on their way and buried those who had
been killed, and then they took rest and leisure as they required.

22

Now we turn to the Althing, where a great many people had
assembled, among them great chieftains of high standing: Gest
Oddleifsson, Steinthor from Eyri, and Dyri and Thorarin. Their
lawsuit was discussed in detail. Steinthor defended Havard and
his men. He offered a settlement for them and proposed Gest
Oddleifsson as arbitrator, saying he was the best informed
about the case. And because Dyri and Thorarin already knew
how they had contrived matters, they gladly agreed.

Then Gest spoke: 'As it is the will of both parties that I say
something here, there will be no delay. I will first take up the
killing of Olaf Havardsson, as it was spoken of last summer: I
awarded three wergilds. This is cancelled by the killings of
Sturla, Thjodrek and Ljot, who were killed in complete inno-
cence, but Thorbjorn Thjodreksson is deemed to have fallen
without right to compensation because of his injustice and
many unspeakable acts that he committed against Havard and
many others. Vak and his brother Skarf also fell without right
to compensation. But the killings of Brand the Strong and An,
Hallgrim's foster-father, are to be weighed against each other, and

one wergild shall be paid for the follower of Ljot from Mana-berg, whom Havard and his men killed. Likewise for the killing of Ljot I cannot award any compensation. His injustice towards Thorbjorn and all the others with whom he had dealings is apparent to everyone. It is only just that two children should have killed such a fighter as Ljot. In addition, Thorbjorn shall have sole ownership of that meadow that they owned jointly. But as consolation for Thorarin, these men shall be banished: Hallgrim Asbrandsson, Torfi and Eyjolf Valbrandsson, Thorir and Odd Thorbrandsson, Thorstein and Grim Thorbjarnarson. Because you, Thorarin, are an elderly man, they will not be able to return before they learn of your death. And Havard will move his farm and not be in this quarter, and this applies also to his nephew Thorhall. I want you now to settle your differences once and for all, and may it be without deceit on both sides.'

After that Steinthor went forward and accepted the settle-ment for Havard and all the companions with the conditions that Gest had previously stated. Steinthor also paid the hun-dred pieces of silver he owed. Thorarin and Dyri agreed to everything honourably and expressed their complete satisfac-tion with everything that had been done. But just as the case was concluded, the earless men arrived at the Althing and as all could hear told the news of their expedition. Everyone thought this news indeed, but that they had got what they deserved. Everyone thought that Thorgrim had committed an act of hos-tility and had been justly repaid.

Then Gest spoke: 'It can truly be said that you kinsmen have no equals in nasty and dishonourable behaviour, for how could you have pretended to have settled the dispute and practised such deception? Now, because I have just spoken in a manner to bring your suit to a balanced conclusion, I will now let it stand, according to how it was formerly arbitrated and announced. It would serve you two right, Thorarin and Dyri, if your case were destroyed by your own deceit. Instead, I shall never again sup-port any of your lawsuits. But for you, Steinthor, be satisfied that from now on I shall support you in any lawsuits that you may have against anyone. You have behaved well and honour-ably in this.'

Steinthor said that Gest should have the most to say about this: 'It seems to me that they now have had the worst of it, for they have lost many men and their honour to boot.'

With that the Althing came to an end. Gest and Steinthor parted in great friendship, but Thorarin and Dyri were very dissatisfied. And when Steinthor arrived home in Eyri, he sent men over to Otradal for the others. And when they met, each told the others what had happened. It seemed to them that everything had turned out as well as could be expected. They thanked Steinthor for his help and also related how well his brother-in-law, Atli, had treated them and how bravely he had behaved, and they said he was the most resolute of men. Then the best friendship developed between the two kinsmen. From that time on Atli was held to be a man of honour wherever he went.

23

After that Havard and all the others went home to Isafjord. Bjargey was extremely pleased with them, and likewise the fathers of the brothers, and they seemed to have become young a second time.

Now Havard decided to prepare a great feast. The farm there was large and magnificent. Nothing at all was lacking. Then he invited Steinthor of Eyri and his brother-in-law, Atli, Gest Oddleifsson, and all his brothers-in-law and kinsmen. A lot of people were present, and the feast was very fine. They remained there all together for a week, happy and merry. Havard was a rich man in all kinds of goods, and at the end of the feast Havard gave Steinthor thirty wethers and five oxen, a shield and a sword and a gold ring, a fine treasure. He gave Gest Oddleifsson two gold rings and nine oxen. He also gave Atli the farmer good gifts. He gave the sons of Valbrand and Thorbrand and Thorbjorn and the others fine gifts – to some, good weapons and other things. He gave his nephew Hallgrim the sword, Gunnlogi, and along with it the entire kit. He thanked them all for their excellent support and manly conduct. He gave good gifts to everyone he had invited there, for in no way was gold or silver lacking.

And after this feast Steinthor rode home to Eyri, Gest to Bardastrond and Atli to Otradal. All of them parted now in the warmest of friendship. But they who had to go abroad travelled west to Vadil and from there abroad in the summer. They had favourable winds and arrived in Norway. At the time Earl Hakon ruled over Norway. They were there during the winter, but in the spring they got a ship and went raiding and became the most renowned of men. They pursued this occupation for several years. Then they returned home to Iceland, and Thorarin was then dead. They become excellent men. There are many stories of them here in the land and in other places far and wide. This is the conclusion of their story.

24

So it is said of Havard that he sold his property, and they moved north to Svarfadardal and up into a valley named Oxadal. He built his farm and lived there some winters, and Havard named the farm Havardsstadir. A few winters later Havard heard the news that Earl Hakon was dead and that King Olaf Tryggvason had come into the land and become sole king over all Norway and preached another, true faith. And when Havard learned this, he gave up his farm and with Bjargey and Thorhall, his nephew, travelled to Norway. They went to meet King Olaf, and he received them well. Havard and Bjargey and Thorhall were baptised, and they were there for the winter in high favour with King Olaf. That same winter Bjargey died, but Havard and his nephew, Thorhall, went to Iceland the next summer.

Havard took some very good wood for a church. He established his farm in the lower region of Thorhallsdal and did not live there very long before he became ill.

Then he called his nephew, Thorhall, and said, 'It happens that I have the sickness that will cause my death. I want you to have my wealth. I hope that you enjoy it to the full, for you have served me well and given me excellent support. You are to move your farm to the upper part of Thorhallsdal. You are to build a church there, and I want you to have me buried there.'

And when he had said all that he wanted, he died soon after. Thorhall acted quickly and moved his farm up into the valley and built a magnificent farmhouse there and named it Thorhallsstadir. He made a good marriage, and many good men are descended from him. He lived there until old age. It is also said that when Christianity came to Iceland, Thorhall had a church built on his farm from the wood which Havard had brought with him. It was a magnificently decorated building, and Havard was buried next to the church and was considered to have been a great man. And so with this matter we end the story for now.

Translated by FREDRIK J. HEINEMANN

THE SAGA OF
REF THE SLY

I

In the days of King Hakon, the foster-son of King Athelstan,[1] a
man named Stein was living in Breidafjord, Iceland, at the farm
at Kvennabrekka. Thorgerd, his wife, was Oddleif's daughter,
Gest of Bardastrond's[2] sister. Stein was rich and an outstanding
farmer. He was very old when the story begins.

They had a son, Ref. He was big for his age, good-looking
and hard to manage. No one realized how strong he was. He
stuck close to the fire and did no useful work but lolled under-
foot where people had to walk. The couple felt that it was a
great misfortune that their son was so unwilling to behave like
other people. Most people said that he was a fool.[3]

There was a man named Thorbjorn who was rich, overbearing, a great fighter and a troublemaker. He had lived in every
quarter of the country but the chieftains and the public had
expelled him from each district in turn because of his unfair-
ness and killings. He had not paid damages for any man he had
killed. His wife was called Rannveig; she was stupid and dom-
ineering. It was generally felt that Thorbjorn would have
committed fewer outrages if she had not driven him on. Now
Thorbjorn bought land at Saudafell mountain. Many of those
who knew his reputation beforehand were apprehensive about
his coming.

Stein's and Thorbjorn's farmsteads were not far apart; the
river which ran between their farms was the boundary separating their lands.[4] When Thorbjorn had lived there a while, his
livestock began straying on to Stein's land because Thorbjorn
had many grazing animals.[5]

In due course, Stein went to confer with his neighbour, Thor-bjorn, and said, 'The situation is this: you've lived in the neighbourhood with me for two years and our relationship has been good rather than bad, though it's generally said that you are not a popular man. Up until now I've suffered no harm because of you or yours, but now your livestock are straying into my fields and grazing on them. Now, I wish that you would improve matters in response to this request of mine and have your livestock watched more closely than has been the case up till now. It could fall out, since I am no liar, that people who may have a quarrel with you will believe what I say. And in a case like that, I shall be able to testify that you have not dealt unfairly with me or wrongly desired what is mine.'

Thorbjorn said that no one had ever spoken so moderately and reasonably with him, and said that he thought that, if more people had spoken to him about matters that seemed out of order, he would have committed fewer impulsive killings: 'This matter will certainly improve as you ask.'

After this they parted. Thorbjorn had changes made for the better so that his livestock caused Stein no further damage, as he had requested.

2

Some time later Stein fell ill. He declared that he would not have any more illnesses, saying that this one would single-handedly be his death.

He said to his wife, Thorgerd, 'I want you to sell your land after my death and move west to Bardastrond where your brother, Gest, lives. I have an inkling that Thorbjorn won't be a quiet neighbour for you, even though the two of us have got on well. I expect that your land will seem more convenient to him for grazing now than when I was around.'

Then Stein died.

Now Thorgerd did not have the heart to let the land go because it seemed beautiful and good in every respect. And before very long, Thorbjorn's watch over his livestock wors-ened. Now his animals went into Thorgerd's pastures night and day. The result of this overgrazing was that Thorbjorn's stock devastated Thorgerd's hayfields, and for two winters she had to slaughter livestock for want of hay. Thorgerd often spoke of this with Thorbjorn, requesting that he should watch his livestock better, but it did no good. Then she looked to see if people were interested in buying her land, but no one admitted to being keen on living close to Thorbjorn. So the land was not sold.

It is said that there was a man named Bardi in the district, a very small man. He was called Bardi the Short. He was very swift-footed and could run as fast as the best horses. He was sharp-sighted and observant. He herded livestock in summer and was reliable and honest in everything. Thorgerd sought this man out at the Spring Assembly and asked if he would go to work for her watching over livestock and said that he could have what wages he pleased. She made it clear to him that more often than not he would have to watch out for Thorbjorn's straying livestock and told him the long and the short of the conflict between the two farms.

Bardi answered, 'I would not choose any job other than the one with you, given the way you tell it. It doesn't seem too much for me to protect your land from grazing by other people's livestock.'

So Bardi went home with Thorgerd and began tending the livestock. He built himself two sheds, one at the foot of the mountain and the other in the meadows along the river which ran between the houses. He quartered in that one every night and kept Thorbjorn's livestock from Thorgerd's land so that they never got over the river. He stayed on the bank and from there he kept the livestock away. He never crossed the river.

3

Thorgerd's livestock now gave lots of milk which they had not done the previous summers.

On her part, Rannveig, mistress of the other house, felt that her summer's production was poor. One day she spoke with Thorbjorn and asked where the livestock were put to pasture. He said that they grazed along the river every day.

'Is it at all fitting,' she said, 'that that man should be with Thorgerd to bar our livestock from the pasture they have had past summers? You've done the wrong thing and left the right undone, Thorbjorn, since you've attacked and killed wholly inoffensive men but allow this nitwit to carry on to our shame by barring our livestock from the pasture they want.'

'Who is this man?' said Thorbjorn.

'His name is Bardi,' said Rannveig. 'He's a miserable, tiny wretch and he sleeps outside every night and prevents our livestock from crossing the river.'

After that Thorbjorn took his horse and rode across the river and came to the shed where Bardi was.

Then Thorbjorn said, 'Is it true that you keep our livestock from this pasture and beat them so that they don't dare graze near the river? That way we're not getting any milk.'

Bardi answered, 'It's no lie that I never let your livestock come on to our land. But it is not true that I beat them or prevent them from grazing on your own land. I think that you won't have any less production than you had your first summer here. And you're getting it more honestly.'

Thorbjorn said, 'It seems to me more likely that you are acting unlawfully than I, because you can be declared an outlaw if our autumn round-up goes short. Now I want you to leave off this work yourself or it just won't do.'

Bardi answered, 'I have often undertaken tending livestock and I do my job, and so it's always been and will be.'

Then Thorbjorn struck Bardi his death blow and dragged him into the shed and rode home afterwards and reported what had happened. It seemed to Rannveig that the matter was nicely settled and immediately she had the livestock driven on to Thorgerd's land. The herd went right into the hayfield, pulled down Thorgerd's haystack and did a lot of damage. She came out and saw the cattle standing around the whole farmyard. It seemed to her that this meant something terrible had happened and she sent people to drive the cattle off; they found Bardi lying slain in the shed and reported this news to Thorgerd. Then she went into the fire room and saw Ref, her son.

Then she said, 'I shudder in my heart whenever you are

before my eyes, you disgrace of a son, and how luckless I was when I bore you, you cretin. It would have been better if my child had been a daughter. I might have married her to a man we could rely on. Even if our land is eaten up or haystacks broken down or our people killed, you, you coward, lie about and act as if we had nothing to attend to.'

Ref got up and said, 'The rest will make hard hearing, mother, if your scolding begins like that.'

Then he took down a big halberd. Stein had had a good many weapons. Then he walked from the farmyard and went along the road, throwing the spear ahead of him and running after it. Thorbjorn's men were at work and saw Ref on his way, knew who he was and jeered loudly. Ref went straight to Thorbjorn's farmhouse and when he got to the door he saw no one outside. He heard the women in the main room and they were asking if Thorbjorn had awakened. He had lain down to sleep. Ref broke off the lower part of his spear-shaft, then walked in quickly and went along the hall. Thorbjorn heard someone coming and asked who was moving there.

Ref said, 'I'm moving here now.'

'Who are you?' said Thorbjorn.

'Someone from another farm,' said Ref.

'But you've got to have a name,' said Thorbjorn.

'My name is Ref.'

And in that instant, Ref slipped into the bed closet.

Thorbjorn had thrown off the bedclothes and said, 'Age is really getting to me when I don't recognize you. You're very welcome, Ref, but what is your business here?'

Ref said, 'What that will be depends entirely on you.'

'How so?' asked Thorbjorn.

Ref answered, 'I have come to ask compensation for the killing of Bardi, my farmhand. I'll be modest about it and accept what is very little for you to pay and yet honourable for me to receive. It will be to my honour that you value my request since you have killed a humble man.'

Thorbjorn got dressed quickly and said, 'Your request is good and it might be that I will pay some compensation, but it's no less likely that I will neither pay damages for him nor for any other.'

Ref said, 'It's more appropriate that you pay something.'

Thorbjorn said, 'You speak so well that something has to be forthcoming.'

He was all dressed then and reached down beneath the bed frame and brought up a large single-edged knife with a whetstone.

Then Thorbjorn took a sword in one hand and offered the knife and whetstone to Ref saying, 'One should offer an untempered blade to a softy.'

At that instant, Ref thrust his spear through Thorbjorn's midsection. Thorbjorn fell backwards. He had not been able to draw the sword because the safety band was still fastened and it all happened quickly. Ref closed the door to the bed closet and headed for the front door. At that moment, the door to the main room opened. There was a large pile of driftwood in front of the main door. Ref decided to jump into the woodpile because he knew Thorbjorn's men were near the road and would notice him at once if he went home. The women had heard men talking and were curious. Then they saw blood running along the floor. They called for the farmhands and when they arrived, they saw Thorbjorn had been killed. They searched for Ref and did not find him. No one thought they had seen him going home. The search was given up that evening.

Then Ref got out of the woodpile and went home. He awakened his mother and asked her to come outside. When they were out of the house, she asked if Thorbjorn had paid any compensation for Bardi's killing.

Ref spoke in verse:

1.

The squanderer of the sea's fire   *sea's fire*: gold;
today offered me a broad untempered   its *squanderer*: generous man
blade and a whetstone with it that was
too little to take as compensation.
So, with the wounding serpent   *wounding serpent*: spear
in my hand, I probed the path
to his heart and killed   *path to his heart*: chest
that free-spending man.

'Well said and bravely done,' she replied. 'Now take two horses from here, beside the farmyard, and bring them to me.'

One horse was saddled and the other fitted with packs full of valuable goods. Then Ref took good clothes. Now he seemed like a very valiant man.

Then Thorgerd said, 'There's a man called Grim who lives near here in a valley on our land. He'll be your guide. I will send you west to Bardastrond to my brother. I want you to stay there until this killing has been settled.'

4

Ref set out and did not stop until he reached Hagi where he got a hearty welcome. When the two kinsmen began talking, Gest asked if he had any news to report. Ref said he had not.

'But do you know any?' Gest asked.

Ref said it was not unlikely that he did and told what he was involved in. Gest said that he would certainly shelter him and asked if he were a master in some skill. Ref said that was not the case at all.

Gest said, 'I can see that you are potentially a master of something and I'll soon see what it is.'

Ref stayed there for some time.

In due course, Gest came to Ref and said, 'Now I know what your gift is. You could be a master craftsman if you wished. I've noticed when you started cutting a bobbin for yarn, it was always cut true, neither twisted nor rough. And of the things you've put your hand to, that carving was the most adroitly done.'

'That could be,' said Ref, 'but I've never built anything.'

Gest said, 'I'd like to put this to the test. I want you to make me a boat for seal hunting.'

Ref said, 'Get more than enough tools and material because lots of people, when a project doesn't turn out well, blame the outcome on inadequate supplies. Moreover, I don't want anyone to know about this project, because if it turns out well people will probably say that somebody came and taught me how to do it.'

Then Gest had a big boat shed built and a great deal of timber brought up. A knorr had been wrecked on Gest's beach and he had bought all the ship's timbers. Gest had all this timber brought to Ref's shed along with the ship nails. Gest also had a supply of unwrought iron and Ref said he wanted that brought and said he would forge ship nails for himself. Gest had all kinds of tools brought there as well as a forge and charcoal.

Then Gest said, 'Now I have had everything taken to your shed so that nothing more would be needed, even if you built a cargo vessel capable of sailing to other lands.'

Ref said that Gest could do no more however the project turned out.

Then Ref started work. He rose early and came home late and this went on for three months.

One morning, Gest sent his most trusted man to the shed telling him to find out how the seal-hunting boat was going – he said that it was probably ready, though he knew little about it. The man who was sent got there without Ref's noticing and looked the work over thoroughly. Then he went home and told Gest that a seal-hunting boat like that would seldom be seen: 'Because a bigger ship than that has never come here to Iceland.'

Gest told him to say nothing about it. Two months passed.

5

One morning when Gest had got up, he saw that Ref was lying in bed.

Gest reached out to him and said, 'You're sleeping late, nephew. Is the seal-hunting boat ready?'

'You could say,' said Ref, 'that she'll float, and I won't do any more until you've seen her.'

'We'll go there today,' said Gest, 'and look at this job.'

Gest went to the shed with only a few people because he did not want it generally known if the project was bungled. When he got there, there stood a thoroughly seaworthy cargo vessel. Gest inspected the ship very carefully and Ref's skill seemed all the more remarkable to him since Ref had never built a ship before.

Gest thanked Ref for the shipbuilding then and said, 'Now I want to pay you for the ship by giving it to you.'

Ref said that he would gladly accept it.

Word that Ref Steinsson had built an ocean-going cargo vessel went round. This seemed extraordinary news since Ref was generally regarded as a simpleton. It had happened that a Norwegian and his son had once lodged with Ref's father. Ref and the visitor's son were of the same age. The boy had, as a plaything, a Norwegian toy ship made exactly like an ocean-going vessel. When the Norwegian's son went away, he gave Ref this ship, which Ref had for amusement in the fire room and as a model for his shipbuilding.

Then the winter passed and the games began.

There was a man named Gellir. He was very much a traveller and spent alternate years in Norway and Iceland. He was very boisterous and much given to good times. His mother lived nearby at a farm called Hlid. Her name was Sigrid and she was very rich. Her husband was dead, hence Gellir was called Sigridarson. Gellir was very active in sports and was the most competitive of those involved. One day, Gellir went to play with some men at Hagi. Gellir asked if Ref would like to go with him. Ref said he was not suited for sports and would not go. Gellir asked if Ref wanted to excuse himself from going by wrestling with him. Ref said that he would not do that.

Gellir leapt from the saddle and attacked Ref saying, 'For shame! You say you won't wrestle when I want to. Now you'll have to wrestle even though you don't want to.'

He tried every way to throw Ref and could not get him down. Ref fended him off while Gellir pressed his attack with all his strength. But when Gellir went at him less strongly, Ref grasped Gellir with one hand on his belt and the other between his shoulder blades and threw him on to the frozen ground a short distance off. Gellir came down on his elbows and skinned them both; his brow went livid. He sprang up at once, jumped into the saddle, grasped his spear, raised the shaft and struck at Ref. The blow landed on his shoulders and bounced off and hit him on the head. He was not injured. Gellir and his companions galloped off and bragged a lot about it. Gellir claimed that he had struck Ref two great blows and went around telling the story, saying that Ref would not avenge it. Ref acted as if he did not know about this. Gest was not home when this happened.

6

After the Yule celebrations, Ref tarred his ship and readied it. Gest brought him all the rigging. It is said that Gellir was on the way from home and his road lay next to the shed, and he stopped to look at the ship. One man was travelling with him. Ref heard that Gellir had come by and ran out from under the ship with his adze and went for Gellir.

Ref said, 'Now I'll repay you for two blows with one.'

The blow caught him in the side and went into the body. Gellir fell dead to the ground and his companion rode away.

Ref went home and met with Gest, who said, 'You look like fortune's favourite, nephew, what's the news?'

Ref spoke in verse:

2.

The goddess of shields was reddened   *goddess of shields: ogress, i.e. axe*
in Gellir's gore.
The stroke this day was struck,
I felled the famous man.
I reckon two blows revenged
and hot blood won for the raven.
Such deeds are told in stories,
related by wise men.

'Very well done,' said Gest. 'When I heard it widely reported that Gellir had struck you two blows, I would have preferred that you respond like this. And what are your plans now?'

Ref said, 'I intend to steer my ship to Greenland.'

Gest said, 'You've chosen to do as I would wish because there would be no peace for you in Norway when this killing becomes known. Now I'll supply you with a crew for your ship and give you the goods you'll need. And later your mother and I will divide things up as seems good to us.'

Then Ref got his ship ready and manly farmers' sons came forward to follow him. Gest sent him on his way generously.

When they parted, Gest said, 'If it turns out you are not destined to come back to Iceland, I wish that you would have a story written about your journey,[6] because it will seem noteworthy to some people since I think you are the second wise man to appear in our family. And surely you are destined for great achievements. And I call on the One Who Made the Sun to strengthen you for good ends now and in the future.'

Ref thanked Gest for his words.

Then they parted and Ref put out to sea. The voyage went well until they caught sight of Greenland, but then they were tossed about and driven north along the coast. In time they came to a fjord in the uninhabited north. On both sides of the fjord, glaciers reached south and out into the sea. Because they had been tossed about at sea, they were keen for land. They cast anchor. Ref rowed ashore and went up the highest mountain to look around. He saw that where they had come the fjord reached far into the land and two headlands ran into the fjord from the opposite shores. He went back to his ship. In the morning, he commanded the crew to take the ship in as far as the fjord reached. They did so and when they reached the headlands, they saw a big and long fjord started there. When they reached the end of it, there was a good harbour. The hillsides were covered with forests and the shores were green. Glaciers girded it on both sides.[7] There was plenty of game, driftwood on every shore and good fishing. At that time, they could not continue to the settlement. They built a large hall and settled comfortably into it. Ref built a large ferry and got it ready for the voyage to the settlement in the spring and then they made a shelter for the trading vessel.

Then they sailed to the settlement and came into a little bay. Not far from there was a farm. A man named Bjorn lived there. He was married and had one daughter, who was called Helga. She was attractive and intelligent and was accounted the most desirable match in that settlement. Ref did not sell his goods but took up building. Bjorn met Ref and asked if he would contract to put up buildings on Bjorn's farm. Ref agreed to that and they fixed the terms. Then Ref set to work and built a splendid farmhouse. That farm is called Hlid.

On the other side of the headland stood the farm called Vik. A man named Thorgils lived there. He was nicknamed Vikarskalli (Baldy from Vik). He was malicious, slanderous and cunning. He was a very difficult person and people thought it was bad to have dealings with him. He was old and married. His oldest son was named Thengil, the second Orm, the third Thorstein, the fourth Geir. His daughter was called Olof. She was married to a man called Gunnar. Thengil had asked for the hand of Helga, but she did not want to marry him.

At this time, Ref was with Bjorn and constructing buildings for his farm, and then he asked for the hand of Helga. Bjorn was agreeable. Thormod was one of Bjorn's workers and Helga's foster-father. He was eager to see the match made and so it came about that the woman was engaged to Ref and the date for the wedding feast was set. The match was made with the condition that Ref and Helga would take over the farm and Bjorn would live with them without any control over the property.

The next spring, Ref took over the farm and acquired many possessions very quickly. He made a great deal of money from his building. Helga was a woman with a mind of her own. When Ref and Helga had been together a short time, Bjorn died. Soon afterwards Ref and Helga were granted children. They had a son named Stein. Two years later they had a second named Bjorn. The brothers were very promising.

Ref lived in Greenland for eight years at the same homestead. During those years, he had a ship, a large ferry, under construction: the boat shed was out on the headland separating Vik and Hlid. He went out to the boat early and came home late. Each night he locked up his adze in the boat shed and went home unarmed.

7

One evening he went home like that as usual. Ref was able to see there was a polar bear up ahead on the headland. The bear quickened his pace when he saw a single man. Then it seemed to Ref that he had acted imprudently. There was new-fallen snow on the ground and it was easy to follow tracks wherever they led. Ref did not see that he had the means to take the bear on unarmed. He turned back to the boat shed and took his adze, locked the boat shed up and then went to the place where the bear had been and it was dead. The brothers, Thorgils's sons, had killed the bear when they came in from fishing. Ref went on home then.

At this point in the story, Thorgils's sons came home. Their father asked them how the fishing had gone. They said they had got no fish: 'But we got a polar bear'.

Thorgils said, 'You made a wonderful contribution to the support of our household – few would have made a catch like that.'

Thengil said, 'We probably wouldn't have got anything at all if Ref the Timorous hadn't revealed his manliness. I don't think that a fainter heart has come to Greenland than the one in his breast, because a man's tracks run from the boat shed to the headland and then turn back, and there was piss splattered in the footprints.'

Thengil then said many slanderous things about Ref. Thorgils, his father, was silent.

Thengil then asked why he did not reply: 'Father, don't you know who Ref the Effeminate is?'

Thorgils said, 'It's bad even to speak of such things and Greenland will always have to blush when it hears Ref named; when he first came here, I saw that Greenland had already been affected by a great scandal. I've had little to do with him because when I was in Iceland he was not like other men in his nature. On the contrary, he was a woman every ninth day and needed a man, and for that reason he was called Ref the Gay, and stories of his unspeakable perversions[8] went around constantly. Now I'd like for you to have nothing to do with him.'

And then they left off this talk and went to butcher the bear. But Thorgils's sons repeated this slander everywhere they went and also invented a story that Ref had been sent away from Iceland because of his homosexuality and had been paid a sum of money to leave. They talked up this slander so much that it became a commonplace and Ref heard of it. He acted as if he did not know, but he got the ship that he had under construction ready and in the best order possible. He had much of his livestock slaughtered and sold some for Greenland wares. He held a great autumn feast and invited his friends and quietly sold his land for cash. He agreed that he would vacate the land within six months and would give the buyers notice. He had many strong followers, twelve at least. Ref had become very rich. All this happened at hay-time.

8

One day Thormod came to talk with Ref and he said, 'Nearly everyone credits a vicious story about you, and Thorgils and his sons started it. And when I urged that the match between you and Helga be made, it seemed to us that we were marrying her to a capable man, and so I think you are. But it seems to me that you almost confirm the story spread by bad men when you leave them in peace. And now I ask that you make them blame themselves for their slander.'

Ref answered, 'A man should have his plans worked out before he enters into great undertakings or incites others to them.'

Then they broke off this talk and Ref set to work and forged himself a huge spear. One could cut or thrust with it. He fitted it with a short shaft which he covered with iron. Then he sharpened it to an edge that would cut whiskers.

When much of the day had passed, Ref left home alone. He had no weapon other than the spear. He went to Vik and arrived there late in the day. Thorgils was in the kitchen cooking. Ref went there and Thorgils asked who was coming. Ref announced himself.

Thorgils said, 'There's a lot of smoke in my eyes so I don't recognize you, but you are welcome.'

Ref said, 'Thanks for that.'

Thorgils said, 'What's your business here?'

Ref said, 'I've come to ask compensation for the slanders you've uttered about me.'

Thorgils said, 'When have we spoken ill of you and what is the slander you blame on us?'

Ref repeated the words.

Then Thorgils said, 'I won't deny that we say many things as jokes, but in this case it isn't lying because I believe that every word in this is true.'

Then Ref struck at him with the spear and split him open down to the shoulders. Then he yanked the spear out and walked down to the shore and sat down in the boathouse belonging to the brothers, Thorgils's sons. It had got quite dark. Then he heard the sound of oars. When the brothers reached the shore, Thengil leapt from the boat, walked ashore and was about to look for rollers in the boathouse. But when he got there, Ref struck off his head. Thorstein leapt from the boat knowing nothing of this because it was so dark that he could not see to the boathouse. Thorstein took the oars and carried them ashore. When he got to the boathouse, Ref thrust the spear through him.

At that moment Thorstein called out: 'Save yourselves, boys! Our brother Thengil has been killed and I'm run through.'

Orm grasped the oars from the other boat and pushed their ship out. They rowed off and around the headland to Ref's boat shed, went ashore and thought that Ref would not look for them there. But when they had dragged the ship ashore, Ref came and killed them both.

After that, Ref went home and ordered his men to carry goods and provisions to his ship. Then he had his ferry loaded. It was broad daylight the next morning by the time all the goods Ref wanted to take with him were loaded on to the ship. Then he chose gifts for the young men who had been with him and asked them to be ready to accompany him when he called on them, whenever that should be. They agreed wholeheartedly to that. Ref then sent word to those who had bought his land that they should take possession of it.

Then Ref, his wife and his sons went aboard the ferry. Stein was nine at the time and Bjorn was seven. The third was named Thormod, and he was three then. Helga's foster-father Thormod was also to go. When the wind stood from the land, Ref ran up the sail, so they put out to sea that day.

For a time, they are out of the story.

9

And now the story turns back to the point when the people of Thorgils's household grieved long and loudly over him when he was killed. In the evening, they went to the shore and found Thengil and Thorstein slain there, and in the morning they found the other two slain. This news went all round and few grieved for Thorgils or his sons. It was regarded as quite a job to be done by one man in one evening and Ref was thought to have avenged the slander sharply.

Gunnar, Thorgils's son-in-law, heard this news and had watches set at every headland around both settlements in case anyone should catch sight of Ref in the autumn. The property could not be seized because it had all been sold. Gunnar was the leading man in the Western Settlement. There was no news of Ref anywhere. In the spring, Gunnar sent men north into the wilderness to search for Ref, but he was not found and nobody had heard anything of him. Gunnar began to think that Ref had perished, since he had taken a ship with only six people, none of them able-bodied. Now four years passed without any word of Ref and the search for him was abandoned. People thought that surely he had been lost at sea or had driven his ship into the wilderness.

And now we will leave this matter for a while.

10

While these events – and Ref's upbringing – were going on, many changes took place in the rule of Norway. King Harald Sigurdarson had succeeded to the kingdom.[9]

In the king's retinue was a man called Bard. He was a follower of the king's. In summers he made trading voyages to various lands, Iceland or the British Isles, and so he did the summer we are speaking of now. He got his ship ready and intended to go out to Iceland. The king had Bard summoned to him and asked where he intended to steer his ship.

'To Iceland,' said Bard.

The king said, 'I want you to proceed otherwise. You are to sail out to Greenland and bring us walrus ivory and ship ropes.'

Bard said that the king would decide.

After that, Bard put out to sea and his voyage went extremely well. He reached Greenland and arranged to winter with Gunnar. And when he had been there a while, Bard brought the matter up and asked Gunnar how much truth there was in the story he had heard that an Icelander had single-handedly killed a father and four sons in one evening and so avenged the slander regarding him they had made up. Gunnar said something like that had happened. Bard asked what had become of this man.

'We think,' said Gunnar, 'that he was lost because he was so frightened that with six others he sailed into the open sea at the onset of winter.'

Bard asked what had gone on among those involved. Gunnar then told what he knew.

Bard said, 'I would be astonished if that man who escaped your clutches by the power of his good luck would have sunk. It seems to me that his luck left him sooner than was to be expected if that happened. Now, have you searched the wildernesses?'

Gunnar said that they had searched wherever it seemed possible for people to stay, and still further.

Bard said, 'How could he go out on the open sea at the beginning of winter with only a few people in a ferry? I suppose it seems better to you to say something like that when Thorgils and his sons are unavenged. I want you to get a ship ready for us in early spring and we'll travel the wildernesses, and if I don't find him, I'll surely confirm that he was lost.'

Gunnar said that it should be so. Now winter passed. As soon as the ice broke up, Gunnar got ready for his expedition. Bard and Gunnar had a ferry and seven men. They steered for the wildernesses and searched in every hidden bay and found nothing that seemed to have been a human habitation. Bard was a very sharp-sighted man.

One evening, they came to a large fjord which wound its way inland with many turns. Then it ended. They anchored for the night in a bay. Bard rowed ashore in a boat. He walked up the headland at the mouth of the fjord and looked all around. It was a bright clear night. A breeze was blowing from the sea down the fjord. He saw a raft of kelp driven down the fjord to its head, but then it completely disappeared. Bard wondered about that and he walked all the way down the lip of the headland and there he saw another fjord, which was wide and long, begin there. And there he saw a large and beautiful valley running up to the mountains. Then he went back to the ship and lay down.

That morning, Bard asked Gunnar if they had explored the whole fjord. Gunnar said they had. Bard said that he wanted to go all the way to where it ended. And so they did, and then they came to the place where the two headlands jutted out from the opposite sides of the fjord. A sound ran between the headlands. It was quite narrow but very deep. Then the fjord opened up again and that inner fjord was very long. They came into a bay late in the evening. The crew didn't want to explore the land and they all lay down except for Bard. He quickly launched a boat and made for shore and then walked along the water's edge alone until he came to a great pile of shavings. He picked up a shaving and took it with him and then went back to the ship.

In the morning, Bard showed Gunnar the shaving and said, 'I've never in my life seen a shaving cut so skilfully. Was Ref something of a craftsman?'

Gunnar answered, 'He was a master craftsman.'

Bard said, 'I would think, in that case, that we must look for Ref as if he were alive.'

Now they and some others left the ship. Soon they were able to see a fortification standing near the edge of the shore. They went up to it and walked around it and considered it carefully, and they thought that they had never seen such a beautiful building. It was large and strongly built, untarred, and with four corners. They did not see one board overlapping another anywhere; it seemed to be made all of one plank.

And while they were surveying the fortification, a man appeared on the wall. He was of large stature. He greeted Gunnar, who acknowledged the welcome. They recognized him as Ref. He asked where they intended to go.

Bard answered, 'No farther this way.'

Ref asked the news. Bard said that no one would tell him. Then Ref said that one should not ask more than would be thought fitting.

Bard ordered them to drag wood up to the fortification. When the wood was piled all around it, they set it on fire. The wood kindled quickly. But they saw that it promptly went out. They dragged up wood to the fortification anew. Then they saw that a great stream of water came from the fortification and put the fire out. They searched all around the fortification and found no source for the water. They built a fire up to the top of the fortification, but as much water came from the top as from the bottom.

Ref appeared on the wall and spoke: 'Is the assault on the fortification going badly?'

Bard spoke: 'You can certainly boast about your witchcraft because we will go back for now. But I promise that if you dare to stay here for another spring, Gunnar and I will have your head at our feet.'

Ref spoke: 'It isn't your destiny nor the destiny of the men of Greenland to guard my corpse, even if I stay here as many years as I have already, unless you have the help of wiser men than yourselves.'

11

After that, Bard and Gunnar went to their ship with their men and made for the settlement. In the autumn, they reached the Western Settlement and Bard spent a second winter with Gunnar.

The summer after, Bard fitted out his ship for Norway and Gunnar gave him gifts. Gunnar sent three valuable possessions to King Harald. The first was a full-grown and very well-trained polar bear. The second was a board game skilfully made of walrus ivory. The third was a walrus skull with all its teeth. It was engraved all over and was extensively inlaid with gold. All the teeth were fast in the skull. That was a splendid treasure.

12

Bard put out to sea and his voyage went well. He came to the ports he would have chosen to visit. He brought many excellent Greenland wares to King Harald.

One day, Bard came before the king and said, 'Here is a board game which the most honourable man in Greenland sent you. His name is Gunnar and he wants no money for it; rather than that he wants your friendship. I spent two years with him and he was good to me. He is very eager to be your friend.'

The board game was both for the old game with one king and the new with two.

The king examined the set for a time and ordered him to thank the one who sent him such a gift: 'We certainly must reciprocate with our friendship.'

Not long after this, Bard had the polar bear led into the hall and before the king. The king's followers were delighted with the bear.

Bard spoke: 'My lord,' he said, 'this animal has been sent to you by Gunnar of Greenland.'

The king spoke: 'This man's gifts are splendid, but what does he want from us in return?'

'Quite simply, my lord, your friendship and wise counsel.'

'Why would that not be appropriate?' said the king.

One day in the course of that winter, Bard requested that the king go to his meeting room. The king did so.

When they were there, Bard brought the head with all its splendour before the king and spoke: 'That very noble man, Gunnar of Greenland, sends this treasure to you.'

The king inspected the head carefully and said that the gift seemed excellent to him and ordered Bard to take care of it.

Then the king spoke: 'Now, Bard, tell me what is behind these gifts – now I know that there is more to it than a matter of friendship only.'

Bard spoke: 'It's just as I said to you, my lord. He wishes to have your friendship and your wise counsel on taking a fox[10] who has done the people of Greenland great harm.'

The king asked what sort of a fox that might be.

Bard said, 'There's an Icelander who killed a father and four sons in a single evening, and then sailed into the wilderness with six others and there he built a fortification out of large timbers. We found him and fired his fortification, but water gushed from all parts of the fortification and put out the fire. There was as much water at the top and the middle as at the bottom. But we found no source for the water.'

The king spoke: 'Is this the Ref – or Fox – who built a trading vessel out in Iceland though he had never seen one and in that ship sailed to Greenland, and when he had been living there for some years, a great slander regarding him was made up, and he avenged it so boldly that he killed five men in a single evening?'

Bard answered, 'We're both talking about the same man.'

The king asked what the lay of the land was there and Bard described it in exact detail.

'Whatever else, such are real men,' the king said.

Bard spoke: 'At our parting, he said that no one would be able to drive him away from there.'

'That could be,' said the king, 'but it could be that he said something quite different. But I will advise you,' said the king, 'not to go there again, because if you do, you won't be coming back.'

Bard answered, 'I have promised Gunnar I would and I can't break my promise.'

Then they ended this talk. The winter wore on.

13

In the spring, Bard fitted out his ship and when it was ready, he went to meet with the king and spoke: 'My lord,' he said, 'have you considered Gunnar's necessity?'

The king spoke: 'I have considered the necessity that you not go to Greenland because you are under no obligation to anger a man who has done you no evil that you should avenge. I have a premonition that the outcome will be bad for you if you go.'

Bard answered, 'You will prophesy more accurately in other matters, my lord.'

The king spoke: 'On the contrary, I think that if this one fails, I shall seldom prophesy rightly. But if you really intend to go, then I shall give you two some advice, if you and Gunnar think it is really important.'

'I am not the one to decide that,' said Bard.

'Then,' said the king, 'I will suppose that in the little valley that runs up to the glacier there is a lake. Ref probably made a conduit by laying down timber pipes, one after another, until the water reached the lowest-lying corner of the fortification. There, I suppose, are two timber pipes and the water will flow from the one into both, which then fill both sectors of the fortification with water. The whole fortification is made of hollow timbers and every timber connects with the one below and with the one above so that they fill the whole wall, from top to bottom, with water. In this way, I believe, the system supplies the water. And it seemed to you that there were no joins in the wood of the wall where the water gushed out everywhere around the fortification because, I believe, he has drilled holes in the timbers and these are so small that only the wood that can be shaved thinnest can close them and I surmise that he has used this wood for all the timbers of the wall. And I suppose that all of these twig-like plugs are connected to and withdrawn by a mechanism that he moved only a little when he wanted water to flow from the wall. All these plugs have been skilfully made and one kind of wood will have been used in making the plugs and timbers.

'Now my advice for Gunnar is that you should go north in two ships, twelve in each. One crew should dig a ditch as long as the fortification is wide, north of it, and quite deep enough to reach up to a man's armpits and then they will probably find the arrangement for the stream of water. And if it is as I said, they will cut off the flow so that it does not supply water to the fortification. The other twelve men should carry wood to the fortification. After that it would seem likely to me that you can burn the fortification because of [cutting off] the water. And now that I have given such advice I promise Gunnar that either Ref will flee the fortification and Greenland or Gunnar will be able to capture him. I am unable to see how he can get away if all this is done, unless he has great cunning in his heart. But I would not wish that you go, Bard, because I don't know what you will bring back from Ref's place.'

Bard said that it could not be otherwise and thanked the king for his advice and cast off from his moorings.

14

To go back to him, Ref was living in the wilderness. His sons became very capable men. This same spring, Ref sent them south to the settlement to meet with those men who had promised him their support as was told before. The brothers went secretly and Gunnar got no intelligence of their movements. When his friends received Ref's messages, they were glad to help and went at once to meet with him. Then Ref proceeded to have the ship he had sailed from Iceland launched. The boat shed and tar had protected it so well that it was as tight as a bucket. Then, Ref had the ship loaded with Greenland goods, walrus-hide ropes, walrus ivory and furs. As soon as the ship was ready, they sailed it north into the next fjord and anchored it in a hidden bay. On board were Helga, Ref's wife, Thormod, her foster-father, and Thormod, their son, and the twelve men who came from the settlement. Ref said that he and his older sons would stay in the fortification for a while.

It should be reported that Bard's voyage went extremely well. He made his landfall in Greenland exactly where he would have chosen. Gunnar welcomed Bard joyfully. They immediately assigned men to attend to Bard's cargo, and set off at once for the wilderness with the number of men the king had specified. Now they were familiar with the territory and quickly found their way to the fjord where Ref's fortification stood. Gunnar landed his ship in the outer reach of the fjord because it was loaded with their provisions and awkward to row. It seemed to them easier to walk in along the fjord. Bard and his crew rowed hard all the way to the fortification. Then Gunnar and his crew arrived. They all walked up to the fortification. As far as they could see, nothing was changed except that a ditch had been dug as wide as the part of the fortification facing the water. The ditch reached to the edge of the shore. The water was very deep at the shore even at low tide. The ditch was no deeper than up to a man's belt.

Just then, a man came towards them, walking on the wall. They recognized this man; it was Ref. He greeted them and asked the news.

Bard said he would tell him no news: 'Other than that the legs you're standing on in the fortification are doomed.'

'That is,' he said, 'hardly news.'

Bard proceeded at once to have a ditch dug and they soon found timbers which were wrapped with birch bark. They chopped into the timbers and a great stream of water gushed out. Gunnar and his crew dragged wood up to the fortification and set it afire. At first a great flow of water gushed from the fortification, but it soon dried up. Ref went out on the wall and asked who had given them this advice. Bard said that did not matter.

Ref spoke: 'I know,' he said, 'that none of you would have hit on this plan unless you profited from the counsel of wiser men than yourselves.'

Bard answered, 'Whoever taught us this plan, we shall master you and your possessions today and hang you up where you can overlook this homestead of yours – otherwise you'll have to burn.'

Then Ref spoke in a verse:

3.
He who makes blades bound,
the warrior wont to rule, supposes
our fate's in his two strong fists;
that's to be expected.
But I guess that before he gets me,
the ring-giver, craver of sword-crashing,   *ring-giver*: man; *craver of*
will meet with tricks – there'll be   *sword-crashing*: warrior
a victory ode for me.

Ref went back into the fortification. They built up the fire and at this point there was a great bed of coals and only a little steam. In that instant, they heard a great crash in the fortification and quite unexpectedly the part of the wall facing the water fell down. It was so well aimed that the wall fell into the ditch running to the shore. The wall was as smooth as a single plank. And just when the wall fell, a ship on wheels ran along it and down to the water. Ref and his sons hoisted the sail.

There was a bit of wind blowing along the mountains from the north. Four of Bard's men were under the part of the fortification that fell and they were killed instantly.

15

Then Bard called to his men. The eight of them ran to the ship. They raised their sail at once and rowed as hard as they could under the sail. Bard gained quickly on Ref and his sons.

Gunnar explored the fortification but what was left, no one cared to have. Then, with his men he headed out along the inner reach of the fjord to the ship.

Ref saw that Bard would quickly overtake them.

Then he spoke: 'Now, first, we'll run our sail down. I'm sure, because their ship goes quickly, that they can't slow it down easily and they don't expect that we'll wait for them, so their ship will run on past us on the other side. Then, Stein,' said Ref, 'you must cut their mast ropes and, Bjorn, you must splash with the oars so that it seems to them that we are rowing away smartly, but do it so that the ship moves as little as possible.'

Then Ref cut the wheels off his ship and thereupon took up a small spear and sharpened it vigorously.

Now it should be reported that Bard and his men both sailed and rowed; they had no inkling that Ref would wait for them. Their ship ran on past Ref's. At that moment, Ref threw his spear at Bard. It flew right through him and nailed him to the ship's side. Stein cut through all their ropes, the sail went overboard with all its rigging, and at that moment the ship seemed likely to capsize. Ref and his sons raised their sail and their ship was quickly far ahead, and they held their course until they sailed out of the fjord. Bard's crew managed to save their rigging and landed beneath a headland.

Gunnar and his men saw that Ref was sailing seaward down the fjord. Then he thought that the outcome of the encounter between Ref and Bard was certainly one that Bard could not report. He ordered his men to hasten to the ship and get in front of the mouth of the fjord. They did so. At this point, the day was drawing towards its close.

When Ref and his sons came out of the sound and the fjord opened up again, they saw that Gunnar and his men were rowing away from the land as hard as they could. It grew dark as night fell and there was little moonlight.

Then Ref spoke: 'We must row as hard as we can, but, Bjorn, you must lower our sail little by little and after a while drop it.'

And so they did.

Then Gunnar addressed his men: 'You're rowing like weaklings. Just now we were so close to them that I thought we'd overtake them quickly and now they've got so far away from us their ship looks like a tuft of marsh grass.[11] There's probably more wind there so they'll get away from us. Now we'll head back for land and not be driven on the open sea at night chasing Ref.'

And so they did.

In the morning, Bard's men came to Gunnar and said their course had not been smooth. They had Bard's body with them. Gunnar went back to the settlement and was displeased with his expedition. Everyone said the same thing, that seldom would revenge attempted on just one man turn out so badly.

The sailors who had been with Bard exchanged their goods quickly, and in the autumn they sailed to Norway and there's no report of Gunnar's sending any treasures to King Harald. His crew told the king about Bard's death and his encounter with Ref. It seemed to the king that the outcome was not very unlike his prediction.

16

Then Ref and his sons sailed to the other ship and both groups were glad to see the other. They prepared for a sea voyage and, as soon as they were ready, they sailed into the open sea. They had a long, easy voyage. They reached Norway in the autumn and landed first at the island of Edoy. The people there asked who commanded the ship. He gave his name as Narfi and said he was an Icelander. Narfi asked where in the country the king was and the Norwegians said that he was in Trondheim. Edoy is six knots from Trondheim. Narfi sailed in to the mainland

and anchored his ship in a hidden bay; he left his companions there and rented himself a six-oared boat and hired a guide. His sons and wife went with him; his men were to watch over the ship there.

Nothing is reported about Narfi's trip before he reached the market town of Nidaros and rented a hut. They stayed there for some days. Narfi commanded them very strongly never to leave Helga alone there. Narfi had a black hooded cape made for himself. He always had a walrus-hide rope round his waist. He had a white beard tied on and said that he was an old merchant; then he went around the town dressed in this way. He carried a spear with a short, iron-bound shaft in his hand.

The king was in the town with a great company. One of the king's men was named Grani and was called Sheath-Grani, a handsome man who loved fine weapons and clothing. He liked women and love-making. In this way he grieved many, but people put up with it because he enjoyed the king's favour.

It happened that one day the king held a large assembly and the public was summoned by a blowing of horns. Narfi went to the assembly with his sons Stein and Thormod. Bjorn was left behind with his mother. He was no less curious than the others about what was being talked about at the assembly and he went there. Narfi noticed Bjorn and asked him who was with Helga. He said no one. Then Narfi started back towards the hut.

Shortly after Bjorn set out, a man came into the hut. He was dressed in black clothing and acted very grandly. Helga greeted him and asked his name. He said his name was Grani and that he was one of the king's men.

'I've come here,' he said, 'to buy a woman.'

She told him to go elsewhere for that. Grani said that it was a shame that an old man had a young woman so fair and beautiful. She said that, for all of him, she would decide that herself. He said he was not going to be fastidious and reached for her. She sprang up and defended herself. It turned into a wrestling match, and at that moment Narfi came to the window and looked in. When Grani saw a shadow falling on the window, he tore himself free of Helga and made for the door. Narfi wanted to get in front of the door, but Grani got there and out first, and ran for it.

Helga ran to the door and wanted to lay hold of Narfi.

'Let Grani go,' she said; 'he hasn't harmed anything of yours.'

Narfi tore himself away from Helga and ran after Grani and called on him to stop running. Nonetheless, Grani ran until he came to a wooden fence. There was not much distance between them and Grani saw that he was going to be caught.

He turned around and spoke: 'Consider what you are doing. Even if you kill me, it will be the death of you. But as long as you are in the town, I will never do you any harm.'

He tried to talk his way out of it as well as he could.

Narfi spoke: 'It's true that you are ill-disposed in every way. You're an extravagant fop, you think you're a man of great ability and power, you bring shame on many people – and now you are so frightened you don't know what to do or how to conduct yourself. Now prepare yourself because asking for peace will do no good.'

Narfi thrust at him with the spear. Grani had an axe in his hand and parried the thrust. So it went several times. Narfi was too tough for him, and it ended with him driving the spear right through Grani. Narfi dragged him up under the fence while he was in his death-throes and there covered up his corpse.

It occurred to Narfi that it was not a good idea to keep the killing secret and so be guilty of murdering the man, and it seemed best to announce the killing to the king himself.[12] First Narfi went home to the hut and asked Helga to take their things and get them to the ship along with their guide.

Then Narfi went to the assembly. There was a great crowd of people there. Narfi pressed his way between people until he came before the king. At that moment, the king was talking about urgent public matters.

For all that, Narfi spoke up like this:

'My lord king,' he said, 'the two of us, Sword-house Grani and I, had a soup-understanding today when he told my wife he wanted to buy a swamp. I lady-pigged him through the wall's eye. Then he searched it thoroughly and then I searched it thoroughly. Then I nest-balled him and he many-horsed at that. Then I cloak-stuffed him, my lord, and at that he tarred like a ship, and then I wild-swined him, my lord, to a wooden fence not far off and at the end I counterpaned him.'[13]

Narfi immediately left and went to his boat and made his trip as quickly as he could. They kept going through the evening and the night until they reached Narfi's cargo vessel. Then they put out to sea at once.

17

To return to King Harald, he was at the assembly, as was reported earlier. While Narfi made his announcement, the king did not interrupt his own speech and no one noticed that he paid any attention to what Narfi was saying.

When he finished his speech, the king had a signal for silence blown and afterwards he spoke: 'Who was this man, unknown to us, who stood before us for a time dressed in his black hooded cloak, and belted with a great walrus-hide rope and with his spear in his hand, and whence did he come?'

People said that they had never known where he was from; they said he had been in town for a few days and had rented a hut and given his name as Narfi.

The king spoke: 'What did it seem to you he was saying?'

They said that they never knew that was anything other than silliness and folly.

'So it might be,' said the king, 'but this did not seem an insignificant man to me, and where is our follower, Sheath-Grani? Call him into my presence.'

They did so, but did not find him.

Then the king spoke, 'This matter has taken a turn for the worse. This man said, "We two, Sword-house Grani and I, had a soup-understanding today. He told my wife he wanted to buy a swamp." I guess,' said the king, 'that he encountered my follower, Sheath-Grani, because a sheath is the house of a sword. He probably went around the inns looking for women. It may be that he encountered this Narfi's wife. There's a drink in Iceland called "mysa", but "mysa", or soup, is much the same.

So, they had a "mys"-understanding. He said that Sheath-Grani told Narfi's wife he wanted to buy a swamp, but a swamp is a moor and an amour is intercourse, which Grani wanted with her. Then, Narfi said that he "lady-pigged him through the wall's eye", and that's an apt expression since a "lady-pig" is a sow. And you know that a window in a house can be called an eye in its wall, so Narfi "saw" him through the "window" of the room the couple shared. "Then I searched all round, king," he said, "and he searched all round." But when you search something thoroughly, you ransack it, so both of them ran. Narfi must have run along the outside wall of the hut when he saw what was going on between Grani and his wife. Grani probably heard that and broke off the work he had in hand. He tried to save himself by running. "Then I nest-balled him," Narfi said. He must have egged Grani on to take a stand because an egg is a nest-ball. "And he many-horsed at that." But if many horses are always together, they are called a stud of horses, so Grani stood. Then Narfi said he "cloak-stuffed him" and Grani "tarred like a ship". The stuff for making cloaks is wool, so Narfi woolled or walloped him – ran him through with his spear. "And at that he tarred like a ship", but tar is pitch, so Grani pitched like a ship in a storm in his death-throes. "Then I wild-swined him to a wooden fence," said he, "not far off." A wild swine is called a boar, thus Narfi bore Grani's body to a wooden fence. Then he said that he counter-paned him afterwards. A counterpane is a quilt or bedcover, thus Narfi covered Grani's body at the end. Now I wish,' said the king, 'that you search for these men, both him who has been slain and the slayer.'

Men did as the king commanded. Then they found Grani dead and Narfi nowhere.

The next morning, the king had the signal for an assembly blown and said this, 'Events that should not be repeated took place here yesterday and therein our follower was slain. I did not expect that any Icelander would dare to do that within our domain. But now I will guess at this man's identity: that same Ref who caused the people of Greenland so much woe has been here.'

And after that the king appointed men to search for this man both by land and by sea. They proceeded according to the king's orders.

18

To turn to Ref's voyage, they sailed directly to Denmark without stopping. Ref immediately sought an audience with the king and told him all the circumstances of his coming and asked to be taken in.

The king said that it seemed to him that necessity had often driven Ref to act harshly: 'You and your sons impress me as persons in whom I would find good service. Now because you have sought to meet with us, and because you have brought those goods – such as walrus-hide ropes for our ships – to our country which for some time have not been easy to obtain because of our enemies, we will take you in. I shall obtain a farmstead and estates for you as seems good to us, but your sons, Stein and Bjorn, are to stay here with us. Their advancement will depend on my judgement of their qualities when they are put to the test. And your son Thormod is to stay with you.'

Ref said that it was good that the king should make these provisions by himself: 'But, my lord, we will first take care of our business dealings and then prepare the brothers for your service.'

The king said that so it should be.

Ref and his sons went to their ship. It became known that they had great wealth in walrus-hide ropes, walrus ivory and furs, and that they had many kinds of Greenland wares which were seldom seen in Denmark. They had five polar bears, and fifty falcons, including fifteen white ones.

19

To go back to the ship which Bard had commanded, it came to Norway that autumn. Then the king learned of the death of Bard and all its circumstances.

Then the king had the signal for an assembly blown and

announced publicly the death of Bard, his follower from
Greenland.

'From this and the events,' said the king, 'which took place
here in the killing of Grani, I now know for certain that this
Narfi was Ref Steinsson. Now, I shall grant him an addition to
his name and call him Ref the Sly. Now, even though he is a
powerful and strong man, we must preserve our dignity and
make others fear to slay our followers, and therefore, we here
today make this man an outlaw the length and breadth of
Norway and as far as our realm extends.'

After that, the king appointed Eirik, Grani's brother, and with
him sixty men, to go south to Denmark and assassinate Ref.

20

Eirik and the men who were to accompany him got ready for
their expedition. They sailed directly to Denmark without
stopping and lay at anchor for some days at a good harbour in
Jutland.

As soon as they arrived, an old man wearing a tattered cape
and hood, with two walking sticks and a hoary white beard,
came down from the countryside. They greeted him warmly
and asked the old man's name. He said that he was Sigtrygg.[14]
They asked where his family roots were. He said that he was
Norwegian by ancestry, but had then been for some time in
Denmark where he had become very poor. They said that he
must be a good old fellow who could tell them many things. He
asked what they wanted to learn. They said that they wanted to
inquire about a man who was called Ref, and who, with some
others, would have come there that summer in a ship.

Sigtrygg asked, 'Is there something in it for me if I tell you
what you want to know?'

They said he would not be short of food for days.

Sigtrygg spoke: 'I won't tell you where to find Ref just for
food, because I know from the people's talk that you will make
an attempt on his life. These are my terms for leading you to
where you will see Ref and his sons and the twelve men who
accompanied him this summer: from each of you I will have an

ounce of silver, and in addition a valuable item from your ship, and you, moreover, will be obligated to take me to Norway at your expense if I choose. And you must let me direct our expedition until we find Ref.'

They struck this bargain.

Sigtrygg spoke: 'Now we must take down the ship's tent and row out around the headland.'

They did so and anchored offshore.

'Now I'll go ashore,' said the old man, 'and two of you with me, and we'll see what we can find out.'

Then they did so. There was a forest nearby. When they had gone a short distance into the forest, armed men ran up to them. These were Ref's sons and the twelve followers all together. Both of the Norwegians were captured. Sigtrygg threw off his rags and his beard as well. They walked to the sea by another way. There before them were two longships at anchor with two hundred men. King Svein had sent this force to Ref as soon as he heard that spies had been sent against him. Ref and his men armed themselves and attacked Eirik and his men at sea. When they met, the outcome was quick: all but ten of Eirik's men were killed and those were captured.

Then Ref spoke: 'It has turned out, Eirik, that Sigtrygg, your partner and companion whom you met yesterday evening, has come. Now, I have done what I promised you, so that you can see Ref and his sons here. Now, because I killed your brother, I will grant you your life if you swear that you will never make an attempt on my life or the lives of my sons. And you must tell King Harald the whole truth about our encounter. And tell him that now I have repaid him a little for plotting against me when he advised those who wished to take my life. But King Harald is probably not destined to have me killed. And in Denmark only he who has more power than I will be more dangerous to him than I.'

After that, Eirik swore to do all this. Then Ref gave him a twelve-oared boat and those things he needed to have. Ref took the longship they had brought with them and sent it to King Svein.

The king praised Ref's actions highly, saying they were both valiant and magnanimous: 'And now you shall have this name,' said King Svein, 'here in our realm, and be called Sigtrygg, because the other name isn't common in this country. And at your name-giving, we wish to give you this gold ring which is worth one mark. And therewith you shall have twelve farms out west in Vendil, and those you will choose yourself because I see that you are a very wise man.'

Ref thanked the king eloquently for his princely gifts and the honour which he gave him. Ref and Helga, his wife, and Thormod his son now went to his farms which the king had given Ref. Sigtrygg became a great man.

And when he had been there for some years, he went on a trip to Rome and visited the holy apostle Peter. And in that journey, Sigtrygg contracted the illness which caused his death and he is buried in a rich monastery out there in France.

Stein and Bjorn were with King Svein a long time, and he valued them so greatly that he arranged fine marriages for them in Denmark and both of them stayed there and were considered excellent men. From Stein was descended Bishop Absalon who lived in the days of King Valdimar Knutsson.[15] Ref's son Thormod returned to Iceland after the death of King Harald and took over the land at Kvennabrekka and married in Iceland and many excellent men are descended from him.

And with that we close the saga of Ref the Sly.

Translated by GEORGE CLARK

TALES

TALES

HREIDAR'S TALE

I

There was a man named Thord. He was the son of Thorgrim, the son of Hreidar whom Glum killed.[1] Thord was a short, good-looking man. He had a brother called Hreidar, who was ugly and barely intelligent enough to care for himself. Hreidar could run faster than other men, was strongly built, had a good disposition and always stayed at home. Thord travelled abroad as a merchant. He was a follower of King Magnus[2] and was highly regarded.

One time when Thord was in Eyjafjord getting his ship ready, his brother Hreidar appeared. When Thord saw him he asked why he had come.

Hreidar said, 'I wouldn't be here, except that I have some business to take care of.'

'What do you want, then?' asked Thord.

'I want to go abroad,' said Hreidar.

Thord said, 'I don't think you are suited for travelling. Instead I want to offer you the inheritance from our father, which is worth twice as much as I have in merchandise.'

Hreidar answered, 'Then I would not be very smart,' he said, 'if I accepted this unequal share but voluntarily gave up your supervision. Everyone would get our money from me, since I don't know how it should be managed properly. And you will be no better off if I beat people up or get into some other difficulties with those who are looking for a chance to wheedle money out of me, or if in return I am beaten or injured for my actions. And, what is more to the point, it will be hard for you to keep me here when I want to go.'

'That could be,' said Thord, 'but don't speak about your trip in front of other people.'

He promised him that he would not. But when the brothers had parted, Hreidar told everyone who would listen to him that he was going abroad with his brother. And everyone blamed Thord for taking a fool abroad.

2

When they were ready, they put out to sea and had a good voyage. They landed at Bergen, and right away Thord asked about the king. He was told that King Magnus had come to town shortly before, but would not allow himself to be disturbed that day, thinking that he needed rest when he was newly arrived.

People soon noticed Hreidar standing out from other men. He was big and ugly and talkative with those he met.

Early in the morning, before people were awake, Hreidar stood up and called, 'Wake up, brother. He learns little who sleeps. I have some news: I just heard a strange noise.'

'What was it like?' asked Thord.

'Like some creature makes,' said Hreidar, 'a loud shrill whistling, but I don't know what it was.'

'Don't carry on so foolishly,' said Thord; 'it was probably a trumpet being blown.'

'What does it mean?' asked Hreidar.

'A trumpet is always blown to call people to an assembly or to the launching of a ship.'

'What is an assembly for?'

'Often judgements are rendered in difficult cases,' Thord said, 'or things announced that the king thinks should be brought before the people.'

'Will the king be at this assembly?' Hreidar asked.

'I should certainly think so,' Thord answered.

'Then I have to go there,' said Hreidar, 'because the first thing I want to do is to be where I can see a large number of people all at once.'

'Then we disagree completely,' said Thord; 'it seems better

to me that you shouldn't go where there are big crowds, and I certainly won't go.'

'There's no point in talking like that,' said Hreidar; 'we both have to go. You will like it better than my going alone, and you can't keep me from going.'

Hreidar set off running. Thord realized that he would have to go too, and went after him, with Hreidar running far ahead and a long distance between them.

And when Hreidar saw how slowly Thord was moving, he said, 'It's really true that being small is bad, because then one isn't strong enough. And yet one could have speed, but I don't think you've been given much of that. It wouldn't hurt you to be less good-looking and to move as fast as other men.'

Thord answered, 'I don't think my weakness is any worse for me than your strength is for you.'

'Then let's join hands, brother,' said Hreidar.

They did so and went on for a while, until Thord's hand began to grow numb. He let go, thinking that it was unpleasant being pulled by the hand while Hreidar ran on so foolishly.

Hreidar raced ahead and stopped on a hill, staring fixedly from there at the crowd which had formed where the assembly was.

And when Thord caught up to him he said, 'Let's now go together, brother.'

And Hreidar did so.

3

When they got to the assembly, many people recognized Thord and greeted him warmly, and the king became aware of his arrival. Thord went directly into the king's presence and addressed him appropriately. The king received his greeting graciously.

The brothers had been separated as soon as they got to the assembly, and Hreidar found himself being pushed and shoved, and handled roughly. He was talkative and laughed a lot, making it all the more fun for people to tease him. And then it was impossible for him to make his way.

The king asked Thord the news, and then asked him which of the men whom he had brought with him did he want to stay with him.

'My brother is with me on the trip,' said Thord.

'He must be a good man,' said the king, 'if he is like you.'

Thord said, 'He is not like me.'

The king said, 'Even so, he may still be a good man. In which ways are you most unlike?'

Thord said, 'He's a very big man, ugly and somewhat like a criminal in looks. He is a strong man, but with a good disposition.'

The king said, 'Still, he may be a good man in many ways.'

Thord said, 'He wasn't called a genius when he was young.'

'I care more,' said the king, 'about here and now. Is he able to take care of himself?'

'Not entirely,' said Thord.

The king said, 'Why did you bring him abroad?'

'My lord,' said Thord, 'he owns everything jointly with me, but he has no use for the money and takes no interest in property. He asked only one thing for himself, to travel abroad with me, and it seemed unreasonable not to permit him this one thing, when he allows me to have my way in so many other ways. And I also thought that you would probably bring him good luck if he came into your presence.'

'I would like to see him,' said the king.

'You shall,' said Thord, 'but just now he is somewhere being treated roughly.'

The king then sent for him. And when Hreidar heard that the king wanted to meet him he strutted about haughtily, shoving anything that was in his way, so unaccustomed was he to being invited to attend upon a king. He was dressed in ankle-length trousers with a grey cloak. When he came into the king's presence, he knelt before him and greeted the king courteously.

The king responded by laughing and said to him, 'If you have some business before me, then tell me at once what it is you want. There are others who still need to speak to me.'

Hreidar said, 'My business seems more urgent to me. I wanted to look at you, your highness.'

'Are you now happy to have seen me?'

'I certainly am,' said Hreidar, 'and yet I still don't think I've looked at you very carefully.'

'What should we do about that?' said the king. 'Would you like me to stand up?'

Hreidar answered, saying, 'I would like that.'

When the king had stood up he said, 'Now do you think you are able to see me well?'

'Still not really well,' said Hreidar, 'but moderately so.'

'Would you like me, then,' said the king, 'to take off my cloak?'

'I certainly would,' said Hreidar.

The king said, 'First, however, we have to discuss the matter a little. Many of you Icelanders are clever, and I don't know whether or not you are playing a trick on me. Now I want to be sure that this is not the case.'

Hreidar said, 'Your highness, no one is able to trick you or to lie to you.'

The king then took off his cloak and said, 'Examine me now as closely as you want to.'

'I will,' said Hreidar.

He walked in a circle around the king, mumbling the same thing over and over.

'Excellent, excellent,' he said.

The king said, 'Have you now seen me as much as you want?'

'Yes, indeed,' he said.

The king asked, 'Then what do you think of me now?'

Hreidar answered, 'My brother, Thord, has not exaggerated your good points.'

The king said, 'Can you find some fault with what you see now, something that is not common knowledge?'

'I don't want to find fault,' he said, 'and I am not able to. Anyone would want to be just as you are, if they were free to choose.'

'You're going pretty far,' said the king.

'It would be dangerous to others,' he said, 'to have praised you, if you were not truly the way I think you are and have just said.'

The king said, 'Point out something, even a little thing.'

'Well, if there is something, my lord,' he said, 'it is that one of your eyes is a bit higher than the other.'

'Only one man has mentioned that before,' said the king, 'and that was my kinsman King Harald.[3] Now, to be fair, I should have a turn,' said the king. 'Stand up and take off your cloak, because I want to look at you.'

Hreidar flung off his cloak. He had filthy paws – a large-handed, ugly man – and washed rather carelessly. The king examined him carefully.

Then Hreidar spoke. 'My lord,' he said, 'what fault do you think you can find in me?'

The king said, 'I doubt whether an uglier man than you was ever brought up.'

'That's what people say,' Hreidar said. 'Is there anything,' he said, 'that is a good point about me in what you have observed?'

The king said, 'Your brother, Thord, said that you are even-tempered.'

'And it's true,' said Hreidar, 'but I don't like being that way.'

'You will get angry though,' said the king.

'Bless you for saying so, my lord!' Hreidar said. 'How long until that happens?'

'I don't know exactly,' the king said. 'Probably this winter, from what I can guess.'

Hreidar said, 'May you say this in good health!'

The king said, 'Are you skilled at some craft?'

Hreidar said, 'I've never tried, and so I don't know.'

'It seems not unlikely,' said the king.

'May you say this in good health,' said Hreidar. 'It will turn out to be true, because you are saying it. But I think I'll need some place to stay over the winter.'

'You are welcome in my household. But I think it would be better for you to stay where there are fewer people.'

Hreidar answered, 'Well, yes, that's so. But no matter how few people there are, something that's been said can be repeated, especially if it strikes people as funny. I am not a man careful about what I say, and I always talk a lot. Now it could happen that they spread my words around to other people, and mock me, and make something outrageous out of words that were spoken in fun. So to me it seems wise to be around someone who keeps an eye on me, like my brother, Thord, even if there are a lot of people, rather than to be somewhere less crowded where there is no one to smooth things over.'

The king said, 'Then you decide, and both brothers come and join my followers if you like that better.'

Hreidar immediately rushed off when he heard the king say this, and told anyone who would listen that his visit to the king had been a great success, and especially he told his brother, Thord, that the king had given him permission to stay with him.

Then Thord said, 'Get yourself some fine clothes and weapons, because they are essential, and we can easily afford it. Many people improve with nice clothing, and indeed it requires more care to dress in the king's quarters than elsewhere. You would be less likely to become the butt of the king's men's jokes.'

Hreidar answered, 'You've got it all wrong if you think I'll allow myself to be dressed in fine clothes.'

Thord said, 'Then we'll have them made of homespun cloth.'

Hreidar said, 'That's more like it.'

Thord's advice was then followed, and Hreidar set aside his objections. When he had on his clothing of homespun and had thoroughly cleaned himself up, he seemed like a completely new man. He looked ugly and grimacing, but a man of courageous bearing. Still, there was something about him that caused Hreidar at first to be teased a lot by the king's men when he and Thord joined them. They made all sorts of remarks to him and discovered that he was an untiring talker. There was no telling what he would come out with, and they had great fun in their exchanges with him. And he was always laughing at what they said and getting the better of them; he loved so much to prattle and [. . .]. Because he was very strong and they found him apparently impervious to injury, the king's men completely lost interest [. . .] with the king's men.

4

At this time both King Magnus and King Harald ruled the country. A dispute arose [. . .] one of King Magnus's followers killed a follower of King Harald's. A meeting was arranged to reach a settlement, and at it the kings themselves would look into the matter and resolve it.

When Hreidar heard that King Magnus was to go to a meeting with King Harald, he went to King Magnus and said, 'There is something that I would like to ask of you.'

'What is that?' said the king.

Hreidar said, 'To go to the settlement meeting. I am not widely travelled, and I have a great curiosity to see two kings together in one place.'

The king answered, 'You're telling the truth when you say that you are not widely travelled, and yet I will not give you permission for this journey, because it would not do for you to fall into the clutches of King Harald's men, in which case you or someone else could be injured. I am afraid that you could lose your temper, as you are wishing to do, and it seems best to me to avoid that.'

Hreidar answered, 'Now you're saying something good. I shall certainly go if I can expect to lose my temper.'

The king said, 'Would you go if I didn't permit it?'

Hreidar answered, 'That would have no effect.'

'Do you imagine that you can deal with me in the same way you do with your brother, Thord, when you always get your way?'

Hreidar said, 'It will be easier dealing with you by as much as you are smarter than he.'

The king saw then that Hreidar would go even if he forbade it and he did not travel in his retinue, and he did not think it was any better if Hreidar went in another party. He was uncertain how he would be protected if he went by himself, so instead he gave him permission to go with him, and Hreidar was given a horse to ride. And as soon as they were on their way, he galloped hard, without slowing, until the horse was exhausted under him.

When the king learned of this, he said, 'Well, that's fortunate. Take Hreidar home – he shouldn't go.'

He said, 'It won't keep me from travelling if the horse gives out. My running ability wouldn't amount to much if I couldn't keep up with you.'

They went on then, and many of them pulled up beside him on their horses, thinking it would be fun to test his speed as a runner, so boastful had he been about it. But it turned out that he exhausted every horse that tried to pass him, and he said that he did not deserve to go to the meeting if he could not keep up with them. On account of that, many of them had to get off their horses and stay behind.

5

And when they arrived at where the kings were to meet, King Magnus said to Hreidar, 'Accompany me now, sit next to me and don't leave me. But I have an uncomfortable feeling about what will happen when King Harald's men come and see you.'

Hreidar said it would be as the king asked, 'And the closer I am to you the better I like it.'

Then the kings met, went into their talks and discussed the case. King Harald's men could see where Hreidar walked. They had heard about him and thought this was an excellent opportunity. While the kings were meeting, Hreidar joined a group of Harald's men. They took him to a woods nearby, grabbed at his clothing and pushed him around for a while. The sport took various forms: at times he flew before them like a wisp of straw, and at others he was as solid as a wall and they bounced off him. But then the game intensified to the point that they were being very rough with him. They threw axe handles and scabbards at him. The studs on the metal tip of a scabbard hit him on the head and scratched him. Still he pretended that he was having fun and laughed constantly.

When this had gone on for a while, they did not ease up in their game.

Then Hreidar said, 'Well, we've had fun for some time, but

now it would be best to stop. I am beginning to get tired of it. Let's go to your king. I'd like to see him.'

'It will never happen,' they said, 'as much of a devil as you are, that you will look at our king. We will send you to Hell.'

He did not like that, and thought he could see that it might happen. And then he became angry and lost his temper. He grabbed the man who had attacked him most fiercely and played with him most roughly, lifted him in the air, and dashed him down on his head so that his brains came out and he died.

With that, they thought he was scarcely human in his strength. They fled from the fight and went to tell King Harald that one of his followers had been killed.

The king answered, 'Then kill the man who did it.'

'That's not so easy,' they said. 'He has escaped by now.'

Meanwhile Hreidar met King Magnus.

The king said, 'Do you know now what it's like to lose your temper?'

'Yes,' he said, 'I know now.'

'How did you like it?' asked the king. 'I noticed how curious you were about it.'

Hreidar answered, 'I didn't like it. It made me want to kill them all.'

The king said, 'It occurred to me clearly that it would be bad when you lost your temper. I am going to send you to Oppland, to my landholder Eyvind, so that he can keep you from King Harald. I can't be sure that you can be protected here in my retinue while we kings are meeting with each other. My kinsman Harald is cunning, and difficult to handle. Come back to me when I send for you.'

Then Hreidar travelled to Oppland, and Eyvind received him in accordance with the king's instructions.

The kings had come to an agreement in the matter that was between them earlier and were reconciled. But now they could not agree. Magnus thought that Harald's men had of their own accord forfeited any claim to compensation. They started the trouble, and he thought that the king's man had died without the law's protection. But King Harald asked for compensation for his follower. And they parted, unable to agree.

6

It was not long before King Harald learned what had become of Hreidar. He assembled a party of sixty men and went to Eyvind in Oppland. He got there early in the morning, hoping to surprise them. But that did not work, because Eyvind had expected that he would come and was at no time unprepared for it. He had secretly summoned forces, and they were in the woods that lay near the farm. Eyvind was to give them a signal if King Harald came and it looked as though he needed help.

It is said that once, before King Harald came, Hreidar asked Eyvind to provide him with silver and a little gold.

'Are you a craftsman?' he asked.

Hreidar answered, 'King Magnus told me that I am, but otherwise I can't tell, because I have never looked into it. He would only say it because he knew it, and therefore I believe what he said.'

Eyvind said, 'You are a strange man. I will get you the material. You must return the silver if the work is not good for anything; otherwise you may keep it for yourself.'

Hreidar was locked in a building where he went to work. But before the piece he was making had been finished, King Harald came.

And then, as I mentioned earlier, Eyvind was in no respect unprepared, and he gave the king a great feast.

As they sat drinking, the king inquired whether Hreidar was present: 'And you will have my friendship in return if you hand the man over.'

Eyvind answered, 'He is not here now.'

'I know that he is,' said the king, 'and there's no need to conceal it.'

Eyvind said, 'Even if he were, I wouldn't favour you over King Magnus to the extent of giving you the man whom he wanted to have protected', and then went out of the room.

When Eyvind came outside, Hreidar pounded on the door and shouted that he wanted to get out.

'Be quiet,' said Eyvind. 'King Harald is here and wants to kill you.'

Hreidar beat on the door just as hard, saying he wanted to meet the king.

Eyvind could see then that he was going to break down the door. He went over, unlocked it and spoke.

'The devils will take you,' he said, 'when you go to your death.'

Hreidar went into the hall and up to the king, greeted him and said, 'My lord, let your anger against me pass, because I am well suited for a number of reasons to do what you want to have done, even though there is not much profit in the dangers associated with it, and I will be eager to carry out whatever you have me sent to do. Here is something valuable I want to give you.'

He laid it on the table before the king. It was a pig made of silver and gilt.

When the king had looked at the pig, he said, 'You are very skilful. I have rarely seen a thing like this made so well.'

It was passed around from hand to hand.

The king said that he would be reconciled with him: 'And it would be good to send you on great exploits. You are a strong and courageous man, as far as I can tell.'

When the pig had come back to the king, he picked it up and inspected the workmanship more carefully. Then he saw that there were teats on it and that it was a young sow.

He threw it away and, realizing that it had been made in mockery, he said, 'The trolls take you! Stand up and kill him.'

Hreidar took the pig, walked out of the hall and set off from there, until he came to King Magnus, and told him what had happened.

At the same time, the men got up and went out, intending to kill him. But when they came out, Eyvind blocked their way with a large body of men, so that they could not continue pursuing Hreidar. So Eyvind and the king parted on this footing, with the king very displeased.

When King Magnus and Hreidar met, the king asked how things had gone. Hreidar told the whole story and showed the king the pig.

When King Magnus had examined the pig, he said, 'This is

made with superb craftsmanship. My kinsman King Harald has punished far lesser mockery than this is. You're not lacking in great courage or in ingenuity either.'

7

Hreidar stayed then for some time with King Magnus.

And once he came to speak to the king and said, 'I want you, your highness, to grant me what I am going to ask for.'

'What is that?' the king asked.

'That you would listen, my lord, to a poem that I have composed about you.'

'Why not?' said the king.

Then Hreidar recited the poem, and it was most unusual, most peculiar at the beginning and better towards the end.

When the poem was finished, the king said, 'This poem seems strange to me, but good by the time it gets to the end. The poem follows the pattern of your life, which began in an odd and peculiar way, but will improve as it goes on. I will choose a reward for the poem that is in accordance with this. There is a small island off the coast of Norway which I will give you. It has good grass and it is good land, although it is not large.'

Hreidar said, 'There I shall unite Norway and Iceland.'

The king said, 'I don't know how that will go, but I do know that many people will be willing to buy the island from you and to pay you money for it. But I think it would be more sensible if I bought it for myself, to keep it from becoming a bone of contention between you and those who want to buy it. And your stay here in Norway should not continue much longer, because I am suspicious as to what King Harald wants to happen to you if he gets his way, and he will get his way if you stay for long in Norway.'

Then King Magnus gave him silver for the island, not wanting to put him in danger. Hreidar went back to Iceland and lived in Svarfadardal in the north at a place that has been called Hreidarsstadir ever since, where he became a powerful figure. His life went much as King Magnus had predicted, in that it got

better as it went on. For the most part he outgrew the foolishness which he had adopted in the first half of his life. He lived
to an old age in Svarfadardal, and many people are descended
from him. Here ends this tale.

Translated by ROBERT KELLOGG

THE TALE OF THORLEIF, THE EARL'S POET

1

The story that will now be told happened in the early days of Hakon, Earl of Lade.[1] It shows how he was shamed, and quite rightly, for magic arts, witchcraft and sorcery, because his wickedness and apostasy were both a great burden to many, and irreparably harmful to their body and soul. It befell him, as it does to many, that when the time of chastisement came he could not escape, for it is in the devil's nature to deceive the man over whom he thinks he has full control and who has no hope of God's mercy. He first puts him to shame with the crooked guile of his accursed cunning, causing him to live a hideous life, and at the end of his days in the world, drowns him in the dark dungeon of wretched torments, in misery and subjection without end.

2

Asgeir Red-cloak lived at Brekka in Svarfadardal at that time.[2] He was a powerful man from a great family. His wife Thorhild was intelligent, popular and had a mind of her own. They had three sons who were all promising. Their eldest son was named Olaf, known as Knuckle-breaker, the second one was called Helgi the Bold, and both of these play a greater part in other stories than this one.

Their youngest son was called Thorleif. He was fully capable at an early age, skilful and especially talented. He was a good poet. He lived with his mother's brother Skeggi of Midfjord at Reykir in Midfjord until he was eighteen years old.

Skeggi was very fond of Thorleif and brought him up lovingly. People said that Skeggi would teach Thorleif more about the magic arts than others could ever know.

Thorleif went home to his father's house. He killed Klaufi the Mauler with the help of his brother Olaf. It was Karl the Red's duty to prosecute, and the result was that Thorleif was outlawed and banished from Svarfadardal. The chieftain Ljot-olf lived with Thorleif's sister Yngvild Fair-cheek, and he got Thorleif on to a ship at Gaseyri,[3] but it was driven back by the weather. Thorleif spent the winter hiding, partly with Ljotolf and partly with his father, Asgeir. During this time he learned many magic arts from his father, who knew many things. Thorleif turned nineteen. Karl looked hard for Thorleif, and many noteworthy things happened that winter, as described in *The Saga of the People of Svarfadardal*.

The following spring, Thorleif went west to Skeggi, his foster-father and uncle, and asked him for protection, and for guidance with his problems. And with the support and advice of Skeggi of Midfjord and of Ljotolf, Thorleif went to buy himself a ship from some merchants up in Blonduos, and secured a first mate for it. He then went home to Brekka to see his father and mother, wanting wares to finance the journey, and he got as much money as he needed. In the first days of spring he packed his wares for the ship and set off from Brekka once and for all, wishing his father and mother and uncle Skeggi well.

3

Thorleif set out to sea and had a good wind, and arrived in Vik[4] in Norway when Hakon, Earl of Lade, was there. Thorleif disembarked and had his ship unloaded. He met the earl and greeted him. The earl welcomed him and asked for his name, family and origins, and Thorleif told him. The earl also asked many questions about Iceland, and Thorleif answered them willingly.

Then the earl said, 'Now, Thorleif, I'd like to buy some things from you and your mates.'

Thorleif answered, 'We have little in the way of wares, my

lord, and we need more useful customers, so please let us decide who to trade with.'

The earl thought this an arrogant thing to say, and they parted with the earl very displeased at this answer.

Thorleif went back to his men and slept through the night. When he got up in the morning, he went to the town and sought out good customers, and spent the day making bargains with them.

When the earl heard this, he took a large number of men to Thorleif's ship and had all the men captured and tied up. Then he stole everyone's money for himself and had the ship burned to ashes. After this, he rigged up some poles between the booths and hanged all of Thorleif's companions there. When the earl and his men left, he took Thorleif's cargo with him and divided it among his men.

In the evening, when Thorleif came home and looked for his men as usual, he saw the evidence of how his partners had been treated, and felt sure that Earl Hakon had perpetrated this evil deed, and asked exactly what had happened.

And when he had heard the full truth about what happened, he recited a verse:

1.

I'm shivering in my heart.
Lady, this lad's been hurt,
losing both ship and boat,
I see, out on the sand.
Who knows but I'll avenge
the ashes of my ship
on him who fired the poet's
elephant of the waves.   *elephant of the waves*: ship

4

It is said that after this Thorleif got passage on a ship with some merchants and sailed south to Denmark. He went to find King Svein[5] and spent the winter with him.

He had not been there long when one day Thorleif went to

the king and asked him to listen to a poem he had made about him. The king asked if he was a poet.

Thorleif answered, 'That's for you to judge, my lord, when you've heard it.'

The king told him to perform away. Thorleif then recited a drapa of forty stanzas, of which this is the refrain:

2.
Often, with lots of luck
from the Lord of Heaven's wheel,   *Lord of Heaven's wheel*: the sun
the splendid Jutland prince
reddened swords in England.

The king was very complimentary about the poem, and everyone who heard it said it was both well composed and excellently performed. As a reward for the poem, the king gave Thorleif a bracelet worth a mark, and a sword worth half a mark of gold, and asked him to stay for some time. Thorleif took his place in the hall and thanked the king graciously.

Some time passed, but it was not long before Thorleif became so unhappy that he could hardly be bothered to go and drink or talk with his bench mates.

The king soon noticed this and had Thorleif called before him and asked, 'What makes you so miserable that you can hardly keep to our customs?'

Thorleif answered, 'You must have heard, my lord, that he who asks another's problem must solve it for him.'

'Tell me first,' said the king.

Thorleif answered, 'I composed some verses this winter which I've called Woman Verses. They're about Earl Hakon, because the earl is called a woman in the language of poetry. I will be unhappy, my lord, unless you give me permission to go to Norway and deliver the poem to the earl.'

'Of course you can have permission,' said the king, 'but you must promise to return to us as soon as possible, because we can't do without your skills.'

Thorleif promised. He got himself some wares and went

north to Norway, without stopping until he reached Trondelag. Earl Hakon was then in residence at Lade.

Thorleif disguised himself as a beggar. He tied on a goat's beard and took a large leather bag which he hid under his beggar's gear, so that everyone would think he ate the food that he actually put into the bag, as its opening was up by his mouth under the goat's beard. He also took two crutches with spiked ends, and went to Lade.

It was the evening before the midwinter festival, and the earl had just taken his seat along with the many important people whom he had invited to his feast. The old man went quickly into the hall and, on entering, he stumbled badly, falling heavily on his crutches. He then turned to join the other beggars and sat down at the edge of the straw. He was tetchy with the others, and quite rough, and they were not happy at being knocked by his sticks. They drew back and this caused a disturbance and loud talking, which was heard by everyone in the hall. When the earl became aware of this, he asked what was causing the din. He was told there was a beggar who was so unpleasant and vicious that he stopped at nothing. The earl asked that he be brought before him and this was done. And when the old man came before the earl, he only mumbled a greeting. The earl asked him his name, his family and his home.

'My lord, my name is unusual, in that I am called Nidung,[6] Gjallandi's son (Scoundrel, son of Boomer), and I come from Syrgsdalir in Scythia the Cold. I am called Nidung the Pernickety. I have travelled widely and visited many chieftains. I am now getting so old that I can hardly remember my age. I have heard a lot about your nobility and your valour, your wisdom and your popularity, your legislation and your humility, your generosity and all your accomplishments.'

'Why are you so much harsher and more badly behaved than the other beggars?'

He answered, 'What else can you expect from someone who has never had anything but misery and wretchedness, who lacks the bare necessities and has long slept out in fields and forests, than that he should get angry at old age and everything else, when he was once used to honour and a life of enjoyment from the most glorious chieftains but is now hated by every worthless peasant?'

The earl asked, 'Is there anything you're especially good at, old man, since you say you've been with chieftains?'

The old man said it was possible that there had been something like that: 'When I was young. But as the saying goes, decrepitude comes to every man. It is also said that it is hard for a hungry man to swagger. I can't show off to you, my lord, unless you give me something to eat, since I am so overcome by age, hunger and thirst that I can hardly stand up any longer. It is hardly chieftainly to ask a strange person so many questions but to forget his requirements, for all are created so that they need both food and drink.'

The earl arranged for him to be given food properly, and as much as he needed, and this was done. When the old man sat at the table he ate quickly and cleared all the plates nearest him, forcing the servants to go and get him a second helping. He ate this just as greedily. Everyone thought he was eating, but actually he was throwing the food into the bag, as described above. People rocked with laughter at this old man. The servants agreed that there were two things about him, that he was both tall and broad, and that he could eat a lot. The old man did not react to this, and continued as before.

5

When the tables had been removed, the old man Nidung went to the earl and said, 'Thank you, my lord, for that but your servants are bad men who do everything less generously than you have ordered. But now, my lord, I would be glad if you would condescend to hear a poem I have composed about you.'

The earl said, 'Have you composed poems about chieftains before?'

'I have, my lord,' he answered.

The earl said, 'There may be something in the old proverb: "That which an old man recites is often good." So perform your poem, old fellow, and we'll listen to it.'

The old man began his poem and recited it to the halfway

point, and the earl thought he heard praise in every stanza, and the noble deeds of his son Eirik were mentioned too. But as the poem continued, the earl was very startled to feel a great itching uneasiness creep all the way around his body and especially around his thighs so that he could hardly sit still. This uneasiness was so strange that he had himself scratched with combs wherever they could reach. Where they could not reach, he had three knots made in a coarse cloth and two men pulled it between his thighs.

Now the earl began to think less well of the poem and said, 'Can't you recite something better, you hellish old man, because this sounds to me more like abuse than praise. You'd better improve it or you'll be paid back for it!'

The old man promised improvement and began the verses called Fog Verses which are in the middle of Earl Abuse, and this is the beginning of them:

3.
Fog spreads up the outside,
the blizzard grips the west,
the theft of the dragon's bed   *dragon's bed*: gold
has caused this cloud to come.

When he had finished the Fog Verses, it was dark in the hall and, when it was completely dark, he began on the Earl Abuse again. And as he recited the third and last part, every weapon in the hall moved of its own accord and many men were killed. The earl then fell unconscious and the old man disappeared through closed doors and undone locks.

At the end of the poem the darkness lifted and the hall became bright. The earl came to his senses and found that the abuse had come very close to him. There was further evidence in that his beard had fallen out, along with the hair on one side of his parting, and neither ever grew again. The earl had the hall cleared and the dead carried out. He had now worked out that this must have been Thorleif rather than an old man, and that he was paying him back for the loss of his men and money. The injuries kept the earl in his sickbed all that winter and much of the summer, too.

6

As for Thorleif, he set out on the journey south to Denmark, and for his provisions he had the food he had tricked out of them in the hall. However long the journey was, he did not stop until he reached King Svein, who received him with open arms and asked about his trip. Thorleif told him all that had happened.

The king answered, 'Now I will add to your name and call you Thorleif, the Earl's Poet.'

Then the king recited this verse:

4.

Before all, Thorleif slashed
the earl of Tronds' renown,   *Tronds*: people of Trondelag
huge abuse of Hakon
has been spread all over.
The profiteering poet's
poem, brought east to us,
grimly repaid the earl for
smashing the wave-lion.   *wave-lion*: ship

Thorleif told the king he wished to go to Iceland and asked his permission to travel as soon as spring came.

The king gave his permission, and 'I will give you a ship as a name-giving present, with crew and tackle and whatever cargo you need.'

Thorleif spent the winter there in great favour and at the beginning of spring he prepared his ship and set out to sea. He had a good wind and brought his ship to Iceland, into the mouth of the Thjorsa river.

People say that Thorleif got married that autumn, to a woman called Aud. She was the daughter of Thord of Skogar, at the foot of the Eyjafjoll mountains, who was a successful and wealthy farmer, descended from Thrasi the Old. Aud was a woman of firm character. Thorleif spent the winter at Skogar, but the following spring he bought land at Hofdabrekka in the Myrdal valley, where he lived thereafter.

7

Going back to Earl Hakon, he recovered from most of his injuries, but some people say that he was never the same again. As the earl was very keen to take revenge on Thorleif for this humiliation if he could, he called on his tutelary spirits, Thorgerd Altar-bride and her sister Irpa,[7] to perform whatever witchcraft in Iceland that would kill Thorleif. He took them many offerings and sought their support. When he had received the omens he wanted, he had a wooden figure made from driftwood, and, with his own witchcraft and spells, and with the sorcery and magic of the sisters, he had a man killed so that his heart could be put into this wooden figure. They then clothed it and named it Thorgard. With the strong power of the devil, they charmed it so that it could walk and talk, put it on a ship and sent it to Iceland with the task of killing Thorleif. Hakon equipped him with the halberd he had taken from the sisters' temple, and which had once belonged to Horgi.

Thorgard arrived in Iceland at the time people were at the Althing. Thorleif was there too.

One day Thorleif was leaving his booth when he saw a man crossing the Oxara river from the west. He was large and did not look pleasant. Thorleif asked this man what he was called. He said Thorgard, and spoke sneeringly to Thorleif. When Thorleif heard this, he meant to draw the sword King Svein had given him, which he happened to be wearing, but at that moment Thorgard thrust the halberd through his middle. When the blow hit Thorleif, he struck at Thorgard, but he disappeared down into the earth so that only the soles of his feet could be seen.

Thorleif twisted his tunic about him and spoke this verse:

5.
What happened to Thorgard?
The battle-bold one's gone,
chimera to the ground,
despite his derring-do.

The lord of battle-fire   *battle-fire*: sword
has magically melted
into the dust; he'll spend
many a year in Hell.

Thorleif went back to his booth and told people what had happened: they all agreed it was momentous news. Then Thorleif threw off his tunic and his guts spilled out. He died there with a good reputation, and everyone thought it a great loss. They worked out that this Thorgard had been nothing other than a magical spell of Earl Hakon's.

Thorleif was buried in a mound which stands to the north of the Law Council and can still be seen. His brothers were at the Althing when this happened and they gave Thorleif a fitting funeral. They gave him a funeral feast according to ancient custom, as their father Asgeir had recently died. People went home from the Althing and the momentous news spread right across Iceland.

8

A man named Thorkel lived at Thingvellir. He was wealthy, with a lot of cattle and a comfortable farm, but he was not a man of rank.

He had a shepherd named Hallbjorn, who had the nickname Tail. He often came to Thorleif's mound and spent the night there, keeping his flock nearby. It regularly occurred to him that he would like to compose a Praise Poem about the mound dweller, and he often said so when lying on the mound. But because he was not a poet and he did not have that gift, he was not able to compose anything, and never got any further in his poetry than this beginning:

6.
Here lies a poet.

He was unable to compose any more.
One night as usual he was lying on the mound and was still

trying to see if he could make his praise of the mound dweller any longer. Then he fell asleep and saw the mound opening up and a large and well-dressed man coming out of it.

He went up on to the mound and said to Hallbjorn, 'There you lie, Hallbjorn, and you would like to struggle with something not in your power, namely to compose in praise of me. And either you will become expert in this art, and you can get this from me more than most others, and it is likely that this will happen, or else there will be no point in your struggling with this any longer. I will now recite you a verse, and if you can learn it and remember it when you wake up, then you will become a great poet and will compose the praise of many chieftains, and you will be a great expert in this art.'

He pulled Hallbjorn's tongue and spoke this verse:

7.
Here lies a poet, who
was best of all poets.
I hear the skilful man
crafted abuse of Hakon.
No other man, before
or after, got to pay
him back for his thieving;
that's well known everywhere.

'Now you can begin your poetic career by composing a Praise Poem about me when you wake up. Make sure it is elaborate in both metre and diction, and especially in kennings.'

He went back into the mound and it closed behind him. Hallbjorn woke up and thought he saw the shoulders disappearing. He could remember the poem and went back to the farm with his flock after a while, and told what had happened. Then Hallbjorn composed a poem in praise of the mound dweller and became a great poet. He often went abroad and composed poems about many chieftains, and received honour and good gifts from them, and this wealth increased. There is a story about him that is well known both in Iceland and abroad, though it is not written down here.

Thorleif's brothers Olaf and Helgi travelled to Norway the summer after his death, intending to avenge his death. But they were not yet fated to have Earl Hakon's head at their feet because he had not yet done all the evil which was destined for his shame and harm. However, they managed to burn many of the earl's temples, and depleted his wealth through robbery and pillage and other disturbance.

And this is the end of what there is to say about Thorleif.

Translated by JUDITH JESCH

THE TALE OF
THORSTEIN SHIVER

I

It is said that the following summer King Olaf[1] attended feasts in the east around Vik[2] and elsewhere. He feasted at a farm called Reim with a large company of men. There was a man accompanying the king at that time named Thorstein Thorkelsson. His father, Thorkel, was the son of Asgeir Scatter-brain, who was the son of Audun Shaft. Thorstein was an Icelandic man, who had come to the king the previous winter.

In the evening while people were sitting at the drinking tables, King Olaf made a speech. He said that none of his men should go alone to the privy during the night, and that anyone who had to go must have his bedfellow accompany him, or else be guilty of disobeying him. Everyone drank heartily that night, and when the tables were taken down, they all went to bed.

Now in the middle of the night, Thorstein the Icelander woke up and had to go to the toilet. The man lying next to him was sleeping soundly, and Thorstein certainly did not want to wake him. So he got up, slipped his shoes on, threw on a heavy cloak and went out to the privy. The outhouse was big enough for eleven people to sit on each side of it. Thorstein sat on the seat nearest the door. When he had been sitting there a few moments, he saw a demon climb up on to the seat farthest in and sit down.

Thorstein asked, 'Who's there?'

The fiend answered, 'It's Thorkel the Thin who fell upon corpses with King Harald War-tooth.'

'And where did you come from?' asked Thorstein.

The demon answered that he had just arrived from Hell.

'What can you tell me about that place?' asked Thorstein.

He replied, 'What do you want to know?'

'Who endures the torments of Hell best?'

'No one endures them better,' replied the demon, 'than Sigurd Fafnisbani[3] (Killer of the Serpent Fafnir).'

'What kind of torment does he suffer?'

'He kindles the oven,' answered the ghost.

'That doesn't strike me as much of a torment,' said Thorstein.

'Oh yes, it is,' replied the demon, 'for he is also the kindling!'

'There is something in that then,' Thorstein said. 'Now who has the hardest time enduring Hell's torments?'

The ghost answered, 'Starkad the Old[4] takes it worst, for he cries out so terribly that his screaming is a greater torment to the rest of us fiends than almost anything else, and we never get any reprieve from it.'

'What torment is it,' asked Thorstein, 'that he takes so badly, as brave a man as he is said to have been?'

'He stands up to his ankles in fire.'

'Why, that doesn't seem like much to me,' replied Thorstein, 'as great a hero as he was.'

'Then you don't see it,' said the ghost. 'Only the soles of his feet are sticking up out of the flames!'

'That is something,' said Thorstein. 'Now let me hear you scream the way that he does one time.'

'All right,' said the demon.

He then threw open his jaws and let fly a great howl, while Thorstein pulled the fur trimming of his cloak up round his head.

He was not very impressed and asked, 'Is that the best he can scream?'

'Far from it,' replied the ghost, 'for that is the cry of us petty devils.'

'Scream like Starkad does once,' said Thorstein.

'All right,' said the demon.

He then began to scream a second time so terribly that Thorstein thought it monstrous that such a little fiend could howl so loudly. Again Thorstein wrapped his cloak around his head, but the crying paralysed him and he fainted.

Then the demon asked, 'Why are you so quiet now?'

When he had recovered, Thorstein replied, 'I'm silent because I'm amazed at what a horrible voice you have, as little a demon as you appear to be. Was that Starkad's loudest cry?'

'Not even close,' he answered, 'rather his quietest.'

'Stop beating about the bush,' said Thorstein, 'and let me hear the loudest cry.'

The demon agreed to it. Thorstein then prepared himself by folding the cloak, winding it around his head and then holding it there with both hands. The ghost had moved closer to Thorstein by three seats with each cry, so that there were now only three seats left between them. The demon then inflated his cheeks in a terrible manner, rolled his eyes and began to howl so loudly that it exceeded all measure for Thorstein.

At that very moment, the church bell rang out, and Thorstein fell unconscious to the floor. The demon reacted to the bell by tumbling to the floor. The sound could be heard for a long time down in the ground. Thorstein recovered quickly. He stood up and went to his bed and lay down.

2

Now in the morning everyone got up. The king went to the chapel and heard Mass. After that they sat down to eat. The king was not terribly cheerful.

He addressed his men: 'Did anybody go alone to the out-house last night?'

Thorstein came forth and fell down before the king, admitting that he had disobeyed his order.

The king replied, 'It was not such a serious offence against me, but you prove what is said about you Icelanders – that you are very stubborn. But did anything happen?'

Thorstein then told the whole story.

The king asked, 'What good did you think his crying would do you?'

'I want to tell you that, my lord. I thought that since you had warned all of us not to go out there alone and since the devil showed up, that we would not leave the place unharmed. But I reckoned that you would wake up when he cried out, my lord, and I knew I would be helped if you found out about it.'

'Indeed, it happened,' said the king, 'that I woke up to the sound, and I knew what was going on. I had the bell rung because I knew that nothing else could help you. But weren't you frightened when the demon began to scream?'

Thorstein answered, 'I don't know what it means to be frightened, my lord.'

'Was there no fear in your heart?' asked the king.

'I wouldn't say so,' Thorstein replied, 'because when I heard the last cry a shiver nearly ran down my spine.'

The king replied, 'You will now receive your nickname and be called Thorstein Shiver from now on. Here is a sword I'd like to give you in honour of the occasion.'

Thorstein thanked him.

It is said that Thorstein was made one of King Olaf's men and stayed with him thereafter until he fell on Olaf's longship, *The Serpent*, alongside the king's other champions.

Translated by ANTHONY MAXWELL

THE TALE OF
SARCASTIC HALLI

I

The beginning of this story is that King Harald Sigurdarson was ruling over Norway. That was in the period after the death of his kinsman, King Magnus.[1] It is said that King Harald was a very wise and very shrewd man. Almost everything that he counselled turned out well. He was a good poet and always mocked whomever he pleased. And when he was in a good mood, he was extremely patient even if abusive obscenities were directed at him. At this time, he was married to Thora Thorbergsdottir. Thorberg was Arni's son. Harald took great pleasure in poetry and always had people about him who knew how to compose poems.

There was a man named Thjodolf.[2] He was an Icelander whose family came from Svarfadardal. He was a well-mannered man and a great poet. He was on very warm terms with King Harald. The king called him his chief poet and honoured him above all his other poets. Thjodolf was of humble origins, well brought up and envious of newcomers.

King Harald loved Icelanders very much. He gave Iceland many valuable goods, including the good bell for Thingvellir. And when the great famine came to Iceland – and such another has not come – he sent four knorrs loaded with flour, one to each quarter, and he had a great many poor people transported from Iceland.

2

There was a man named Bard who was one of King Harald's followers. He sailed out to Iceland, landed at Gasir[3] and took lodgings there for the winter.

A man named Halli, nicknamed Sarcastic Halli, took passage to Norway with Bard. Halli was a good poet and a very impudent person. He was a tall man, long-necked, with narrow shoulders and long arms, and was rather ill-proportioned. His family was from Fljot.

They sailed as soon as they were ready and had a long passage. That autumn they reached Norway north of Trondheim at the islands called Hitra, and then sailed in towards Agdenes and lay up there that night. And that morning they sailed into the fjord with a light breeze. And when they reached Reine, they saw three longships rowing out down the fjord. The third was a dragon-ship. And when the ships were rowing by the trading vessel, a man dressed in scarlet and with a golden band round his forehead went out on the top deck of the dragon-ship; he was tall and of noble bearing.

This man spoke: 'Who commands your ship, and where were you this winter, and where did you first make land, and where did you lie up last night?'

The merchants were nearly struck dumb when so much was asked all at once, but then Halli answered, 'We were in Iceland for the winter, and sailed from Gasir, and made land at Hitra; last night we lay up at Agdenes (Agdi's Ness); and our skipper is called Bard.'

This man, who in fact was King Harald Sigurdarson, then asked, 'Didn't Agdi fuck you?'

'Not yet,' said Halli.

The king grinned and spoke: 'Is there some agreement that he will do you this service some time later?'

'No,' said Halli, 'and one particular consideration was crucial to our suffering no disgrace at his hands.'

'What was that?' said the king.

Halli knew perfectly well whom he was talking to: 'It was this, my lord,' he said, 'if you're curious to know it: in this matter

Agdi was waiting for nobler men than ourselves, and he expected your arrival there tonight, and he will pay you this debt fully.'

'You are being extremely impudent,' said the king.

What more they said at that time is not known. The merchants sailed on to Trondheim, unloaded their cargo and rented a house in the town.

A few days later the king returned to town; he had gone out to the islands on a pleasure trip. Halli asked Bard to take him to meet the king and said he wanted to ask to stay for the winter, but Bard asked Halli to stay with him. Halli thanked him but said that he wanted to be with the king if that option were open.

3

One day Bard went to meet the king and Halli went with him. Bard greeted the king. The king acknowledged his greeting warmly and made many inquiries about Iceland and also asked if Bard had brought any Icelanders to Norway.

Bard said he had brought out one Icelander: 'And his name is Halli and he is here now, my lord, and wishes to ask to stay for the winter with you.'

Then Halli went before the king and greeted him.

The king received him warmly and asked if he had answered him in the fjord: 'When we met you and your companions.'

'I'm the very man,' said Halli.

The king said that he would not withhold food from Halli and asked him to stay at one of his estates. Halli said that he wished to be a king's follower or look for a place elsewhere.

The king said that it always turned out: 'So that I get blamed if our friendship with you doesn't go well, even though that seems hardly likely to me. You Icelanders are stubborn and unsociable. Now stay if you wish, but you are responsible for yourself whatever happens.'

Halli said that so it would be and thanked the king. And then he was with the king's followers and everyone liked him. An old and agreeable follower called Sigurd was Halli's bench companion.

King Harald's custom was to eat one meal a day. The food was served first to him, as would be expected, and he was always very well satisfied by the time food was served to the others. But when he was satisfied, he rapped on the table with the handle of his knife, and then the tables were to be cleared at once. Many were not nearly satisfied.

It happened on one occasion that the king was walking in the street attended by his followers, and many of them were not nearly satisfied. And then they heard a noisy quarrel at an inn. It was a tanner and a blacksmith and they were almost attacking one another. The king stopped and watched for a while.

Then he said, 'Let's go. I don't want to get involved in this, but, Thjodolf, you compose a verse about them.'

'My lord,' said Thjodolf, 'that's hardly suitable considering that I am called your chief poet.'

The king answered, 'It's more difficult than you probably think. You are to make them into altogether different people than they really are. Make one of them into Sigurd Fafnisbani[4] (Killer of the Serpent Fafnir) and the other into Fafnir, but nevertheless identify each one's trade.'

Then Thjodolf spoke a verse:

1.
Sigurd of the sledge-hammer goaded   *Sigurd*: (legendary hero) of the hammer, blacksmith
the snake of the scary skin-scraper,   *snake of the . . . skin-scraper*: tanner
but the scrape-dragon of skins   *scrape-dragon of skins*: tanner
slithered away from the moor of socks.   *moor of socks*: floor
Folk feared the serpent, fitted out
with footwear, before the long-nosed king
of tongs set about him,   *king of tongs*: blacksmith
the serpent of ox-skin.   *serpent of ox-skin*: tanner

'This is well composed,' said the king, 'and now compose another verse and make one into Thor and the other into the giant Geirrod and nevertheless identify each one's trade.'

Then Thjodolf spoke a verse:

2.

Thor of the great bellows threw	*Thor of the . . . bellows*: blacksmith
from the malicious town	*town of taunts*: mouth;
of taunts jaw-lightning	*jaw-lightning*: abusive words
at the giant of goat-flesh.	*giant* (enemy) *of goat-flesh*: tanner
Gladsome Geirrod of the worn	*Geirrod of the . . . skin-scraper*:
skin-scraper from Thor's forge took	tanner; *forge*: mouth
with sound-grippers sparks	*sound-grippers*: ears
from that smithy of spells.	*smithy of spells*: mouth;
	its *sparks*: abusive words

'You're not over-praised,' said the king, 'when you're called a master poet.'

And they all applauded the verses as well composed. Halli was not present. And that evening when people sat drinking they recited the verses for Halli, and said that he could not compose like that even though he thought himself to be a very good poet.

Halli said that he knew he composed poetry worse than Thjodolf: 'I'll fall especially short if I don't try to compose a verse, and even more so if I am not present.'

This was reported to the king and represented as if Halli thought himself to be no less a poet than Thjodolf.

The king said that Halli probably would not be that: 'But it may be that we can put that to the test soon.'

4

One day when people were sitting at tables, a dwarf called Tuta came into the hall. He was Frisian by descent. He had been with King Harald for a very long time. He was no taller than a three-year-old child, but was very thick-set and broad-shouldered; he had a large, elderly-looking head, his back was not noticeably short, but below, where his legs were, he was cropped.

King Harald had a coat of mail which he called Emma. He had had it made in Byzantium. It was so long that it reached down to King Harald's shoes when he stood upright. It was all of double thickness and so strong that no weapon ever pierced it. The king had ordered the dwarf to be dressed in the coat of mail and had a helmet placed on his head, and he girded a sword on him. After that he walked into the hall, as was written above, and the man seemed a wonder.

The king called for silence and then announced: 'The man who composes a poem about the dwarf which to me seems well composed will receive this knife and belt from me' – and he laid the objects on the table before him – 'but understand clearly that if I think the poem is not well composed, he will have my displeasure and lose both possessions.'

And as soon as the king had made his announcement, a man on the outermost bench composed a poem, and he was Sarcastic Halli.

3.
A kinsman of the Frisians' clan
appears to me in chain mail clothed.
Decked out with a helmet, the dwarf
goes round the court in ring-mail.
At dawn he never flees the fire,
our Tuta, veteran of many kitchen raids.
I see swinging by the side   *rye-bread's waster*: one who
of the rye-bread's waster a sword.   eats rye bread, man

The king ordered the possessions to be taken to Halli: 'And you are to have them by right because the verse is well composed.'

One day when the king was satisfied, he struck the table with the handle of his knife and ordered the tables to be cleared. The servers did so. Halli was far from being satisfied and took a chop from the dish, kept it and spoke this verse:

4.
I don't give a damn
for Harald's hammering.
I keep my moustache munching on
and full-fed I go to bed.

In the morning, when the king and his followers had taken
their seats, Halli came into the hall and to the king. He had his
sword and shield slung over his back.

He spoke a verse:

5.
For butter I'll have to barter,
oh king, my sword and,
speeder of the clash of shields,   *clash of shields*: battle; its *speeder*: king
my red buckler for bread.
The helmsman's warriors hunger.   *helmsman*: ruler, king
We walk around really wanting food.
For sure my belt draws ever nearer
my backbone – Harald's starving me!

The king did not answer at all and acted as if he had not
heard, although everyone knew he was displeased.

One day a little later, the king was out walking in the street
with his followers. Halli was in the procession. He rushed on
past the king.

The king spoke this:

6.
'Where are you heading, Halli?'

Halli answered:

'I'm briskly running to buy a cow.'

'You've probably ordered some porridge,'

said the king.

'When buttered, it's the best of food,'

said Halli.

And then Halli ran into a house and thence to a kitchen. He

had ordered himself a stone kettle of porridge there and sat down and ate his porridge.

The king saw that Halli had gone into the house. He summoned Thjodolf and two other men to look for Halli. The king also went into the house. They found him where he was eating his porridge. The king came to him and saw what Halli was occupied with. The king was very angry and asked Halli if he had come from Iceland and visited chieftains in order to create scandal and gossip.

'Don't talk like that, my lord,' said Halli. 'I constantly see that you do not reject good food.'

Then Halli stood up and threw down the kettle and the handle rattled against it. Then Thjodolf recited this:

7.
The handle rattled and Halli
has pigged out on porridge.
A cow's-horn spoon better suits him,
I say, than something fine.

Then the king went away and was very angry.

And that evening food was not served to Halli as it was to the others. And when people had been eating for a while, two men came in carrying a large trough of porridge with a spoon and set it before Halli. He set to and ate as much as he wanted and then stopped.

The king ordered Halli to eat more. He said he would not eat more at that time. Then King Harald drew his sword and ordered Halli to eat the porridge until he burst. Halli said that he would not burst himself on porridge, but the king could take his life if he had made up his mind to that. Then the king sat down and sheathed his sword.

5

One day somewhat later, the king took a dish containing a roasted piglet from his table and ordered the dwarf, Tuta, to take it to Halli: 'And tell him that if he wants to preserve his life to compose a verse and deliver it before you reach him, and do not tell him this until you get to the middle of the floor.'

'I'm not keen on doing this,' said Tuta, 'because I like Halli.'

'I see,' the king said, 'that you think the verse he composed about you was good and you will know how to hear him fully. Now go at once and do as I command.'

Tuta took the dish and walked to the middle of the floor and said, 'Halli, compose a verse at the king's command, and have it composed before I reach you if you want to preserve your life.'

Halli stood up and reached his hand out for the dish and recited a verse:

8.
The poet received a dead piglet
from a ruler well-regarded.
The god of the ring-land sees a swine   *ring-land: shield; its god: warrior*
standing before him on the board.   *board: table*
The swine's red sides I see.
I recite a poem rapidly made.
A warrior has burnt the swine's snout off,   *warrior: i.e. the cook*
may you live in good health, king.

Then the king said, 'Now I shall give up my anger, Halli, because the verse is as well performed as it was quickly undertaken.'

6

It is said that one day Halli went before the king when he was cheerful and happy. Thjodolf and many other people were there. Halli said that he had composed a drapa about the king and asked for a hearing. The king asked if Halli had ever composed such a poem before. Halli said that he had not.

'Some people would say,' said the king, 'that you're taking on quite a job considering the calibre of poets who have previously composed poems about me for various reasons. But what seems advisable to you, Thjodolf?'

'My lord, I cannot give you advice,' said Thjodolf, 'but on the other hand I might be able to give Halli some sound advice.'

'What is that?' asked the king.

'First of all, my lord, that he should not deceive you.'

'What deception has he practised now?' said the king.

'He was being deceptive when he said that he had not composed a long poem before,' said Thjodolf, 'but I say that he has.'

'What long poem is that,' asked the king, 'and what is it about?'

Thjodolf answered, 'We call it Polled Cow Verses which he composed about cows he tended out in Iceland.'

'Is that true, Halli?' asked the king.

'That's right,' said Halli.

'Why did you say that you had not composed a long poem?' said the king.

'Because,' said Halli, 'it would not seem to be much of a poem if it were to be heard, and would hardly be praised.'

'We want to hear that first,' said the king.

'Then there will have to be more than one amusement,' said Halli.

'With what matter?' said the king.

'Thjodolf must then perform Food Trough Verses which he composed out in Iceland,' said Halli, 'and it's fine that Thjodolf should attack me or denigrate me because my eye teeth and molars have come in, so that I am quite able to answer him word for word.'

The king grinned at that and thought it fun to set them against each other.

'What is that long poem like and what is it about?' asked the king.

Halli answered, 'It's about his carrying out ashes with his siblings, and he was thought to be capable of nothing more because of his lack of intelligence, and moreover it was necessary to make sure there were no live coals in the ashes because he had no more brains than he needed at that time.'

The king asked if that was true.

'It's true, my lord,' said Thjodolf.

'Why did you have such contemptible work?' asked the king.

'Because, my lord,' said Thjodolf, 'I wanted us to get out to play quickly, and no work was assigned to me.'

'The cause of that,' said Halli, 'was that it was believed that you didn't have the brains to be a workman.'

'You two mustn't quarrel,' said the king, 'but we wish to hear both these poems.' And so it had to be and each of them performed his poem.

And when the poems were finished, the king said, 'Both poems are minor and moreover the subjects are trivial, but what you composed, Thjodolf, was even slighter.'

'That's so,' said Thjodolf, 'and, my lord, Halli is very sarcastic. But it seems to me he's more obligated to avenge his father than to engage in verbal duels with me here in Norway.'

'Is that true, Halli?' asked the king.

'It's true,' said Halli.

'Why did you leave Iceland to meet with chieftains given that you had not avenged your father?' said the king.

'Because, my lord,' said Halli, 'I was a child when my father was killed, and my relatives took over the case and settled it on my behalf. And in our country it's thought bad to be called a truce-breaker.'

The king answered, 'It's a duty not to violate truces or settlements. You've answered this very well.'

'So I thought, my lord,' said Halli, 'but Thjodolf may very well speak arrogantly in such matters, since I know no one who has avenged his father as grimly as he.'

'Certainly, Thjodolf is likely to have done that boldly,' said the king, 'but what in fact is the proof that he did more in this than other men?'

'Most of all, my lord,' said Halli, 'that he ate his father's killer.'

At this people set up an uproar and it seemed to them they had never heard such a monstrosity. The king grinned at this and ordered silence.

'Show that what you've said is true, Halli,' said the king.

Halli said, 'I think that Thorljot was Thjodolf's father. He lived in Svarfadardal in Iceland and he was very poor and had many children. It's the custom in Iceland that in the autumn the farmers assemble to discuss the poor people, and at that time no one was named sooner than Thorljot, Thjodolf's father. One farmer was so generous that he gave him a calf which was one summer old. Then he fetched the calf away and had a lead on it and a noose in the end of the lead. When he got to his hayfield wall, he lifted the calf up on to the wall, and it was extremely high and all the higher on the inner side because the turfs for the wall had been dug there. Then he went in over the wall and the calf rolled off the wall on the outside. The noose at the end of the lead tightened around Thorljot's neck and he couldn't reach the ground with his feet. Then each was hanging on his own side of the wall and both were dead when people came up. The children dragged the calf home and prepared it for food, and I think that Thjodolf ate his full share of it.'

'That would be very close to reasonable,' said the king.

Thjodolf drew his sword and wanted to strike Halli. Men ran in between them.

The king said that neither should dare do the other harm: 'Thjodolf, you went for Halli first.'

Then it was as the king would have it. Halli performed his drapa and it was highly regarded. The king rewarded him with a generous sum in cash.

Then the winter wore on and all was quiet.

7

There was a man named Einar who was nicknamed Fly. He was the son of Harek from Thjotta. He was a landholder and the king's envoy to Halogaland; he had the sole right to collect the king's tribute from the Lapps. At this time he was on very good terms with the king, though their relationship had its ups and downs. Einar was not at all straightforward. He killed men if they did not do everything he wanted, and paid compensation for no man. Einar was expected by the king for Yule.

Halli and his bench companion, Sigurd, fell into talk about Einar. Sigurd informed Halli that no one dared to oppose Einar or behave otherwise than he wished and that he paid no compensation for his killings or robberies.

'Men like that would be called bad chieftains in our country,' said Halli.

'Do speak carefully, companion,' said Sigurd, 'because he is quick to take offence at what is said if it displeases him.'

'Even though all of you are so afraid of him that you don't dare to say a word against him,' said Halli, 'I tell you that I would surely accuse him if he did me wrong and believe he would compensate me.'

'Why you more than others?' said Sigurd.

'That will be clear to him,' said Halli

They argued about the matter until Halli offered to make a bet with Sigurd on it. Sigurd put up a gold arm ring which weighed half a mark and Halli put up his head.

Einar came that Yule. He sat next to the king and his men sat farther out from him towards the door. He was given all the service that was given the king himself.

And on a Yule day, when men had eaten, the king spoke: 'Now we want to have more amusement than just drinking. Einar, tell us what news you have from your travels.'

Einar answered, 'I can't make up any sagas about it, my lord, even though we treated some Lapp farmers or fishermen roughly.'

The king answered, 'Tell the whole story because we are easily satisfied, and it all seems entertaining to us even though it seems trivial to you who are constantly engaged in battles.'

'At any rate, the main thing to report, my lord,' said Einar, 'is that last summer when we went north to Finnmark we encountered a ship and crew from Iceland, which had been driven off course and had lain up there for the winter. I charged them with having traded with the Lapps without your permission or mine. They denied it and would not admit it, but we thought they were not truthful and asked them to allow a search, but they flatly refused. I told them that then they would have what was worse for them but appropriate, and ordered my men to arm and attack them. I had five longships and we attacked them from both sides and didn't leave off until we had cleared the ship. One Icelander whom they called Einar defended himself so well that I have never encountered his equal. Surely that man was a loss and we would never have overcome that ship if everyone on board had been like him.'

'You did that badly,' said the king, 'when you killed men who were innocent even though they didn't do everything as you wished.'

'I won't run that risk,' said Einar. 'And, my lord, some people say you don't always act righteously. But they turned out to be guilty because we found many Lapp goods in the ship.'

Halli heard what they were saying and threw his knife down on the table and stopped eating. Sigurd asked if he were ill.

He said that was not so, but said this was worse than sickness: 'Einar Fly announced the death of Einar, my brother, whom he said he killed on the trading vessel last summer, and now it is appropriate to seek compensation from this Einar.'

'Don't say anything about it, companion,' said Sigurd; 'that's the most promising course.'

'No,' said Halli, 'my brother would not act like that in my case if he had to bring the suit following my killing.'

Then he jumped over his table and went up before the high seat and spoke: 'You announced news which concerns me greatly, Einar, in the matter of the killing of Einar, my brother, whom you said you struck down on the trading vessel last summer. Now I want to know whether you will pay me some compensation for my brother, Einar.'

'Haven't you heard that I don't pay compensation for anyone?' said Einar.

'I was not obliged to believe,' said Halli, 'that you were utterly wicked even though I heard that said.'

'Take a walk,' said Einar, 'or be the worse for it.'

Halli went to sit down. Sigurd asked him how it had gone. Halli replied that he had got a threat instead of monetary compensation. Sigurd told him not to raise the matter again and the bet would be off.

Halli said that Sigurd was behaving very well: 'But I shall raise the matter again.'

And the next day, Halli went before Einar and said, 'I want

to bring up the matter, Einar, and see if you are willing to compensate me in some way for my brother.'

Einar answered, 'You're persistent about this and if you don't get out of here you'll fare as your brother did, or worse.'

The king told him not to answer like that: 'It's extremely painful for the kinsmen, and one can't know what is in other people's minds. But, Halli, don't raise this matter again because bigger men than you have to endure such harm from him.'

Halli said, 'So it will probably have to be.'

Then he went to his place. Sigurd welcomed him warmly and asked how it had gone. Halli said that he had got a threat from Einar instead of compensation.

'So I thought it would be,' said Sigurd. 'The bet is off.'

'You are behaving very well,' said Halli, 'but I shall raise the matter a third time.'

'I'll give you the ring now,' said Sigurd, 'on condition that you let this lie quietly because I am partly responsible for this in the first place.'

'You make clear what kind of man you are,' said Halli, 'and you are not to blame no matter how this turns out. But I shall try one more time.'

And early the next day when the king and Einar Fly were washing their hands, Halli came up and greeted the king. The king asked what he wanted.

'My lord,' Halli answered, 'I want to tell you my dream. It seemed to me that I was quite another man than I am.'

'What man did you think yourself to be?' said the king.

'I thought myself to be the poet Thorleif and Einar Fly seemed to me to be Earl Hakon Sigurdarson.[5] I thought I had composed a slanderous poem about him and I remembered some of the slander when I awakened.'

Then Halli went along the hall towards the door and mumbled something in his mouth but people were not able to catch any of the words.

The king said, 'This was not a dream but rather he compared these two cases. And it will go with the two of you as it did with Hakon, the Earl of Lade, and the poet Thorleif. Halli is doing the same thing. He shrinks from nothing. We can both see how a slanderous poem has damaged more powerful men than you, Einar. Earl Hakon was one, and that will be remembered as long as the northern countries are inhabited. One short verse composed about a highly esteemed man, if it is remembered afterwards, is worse than paying a small bribe. Do, please, satisfy him in some way.'

'You shall decide, my lord,' said Einar, 'and tell him he may take from my treasurer the three marks of silver that I just gave him in a purse.'

This was reported to Halli. He went to meet the treasurer and told him. He said that there were four marks of silver in the purse. Halli said that he was to have three. Then Halli went to Einar and told him.

'You will have taken what was in the purse,' said Einar.

'No,' said Halli, 'you'll have to take my life in some other way than by my turning thief for your money. I saw that was what you had intended for me.'

And so it was. Einar had thought that Halli would have taken what was in the purse and that seemed to Einar an offence quite worthy of death.

Then Halli went to his seat and showed the money to Sigurd. Sigurd took the ring and told Halli that he had won it fairly.

Halli said, 'We are not equally good men then – keep and enjoy the ring, best of men. And to tell you the truth, I was not at all related to this man whom Einar killed, but I wanted to see if I could get money out of him.'

'You have no equal in trickery,' said Sigurd.

After Yule, Einar went off north to Halogaland.

8

In the spring, Halli asked the king for permission to go to Denmark on a trading expedition.

The king said that he could go as he wished: 'And come back soon because we find good entertainment in your company, but go warily on account of Einar Fly. He will be ill disposed towards you, and I hardly know of his having slipped up so badly.'

Halli took passage south to Denmark with some merchants and then went to Jutland. A man called Raud had the steward-ship there and Halli got food and lodging with him.

At some point it happened that Raud was to hold a large assembly, and when people were to plead their cases there was so much uproar and noise that no one could bring his case forward. With that people went home that evening.

And that evening when people came to the drinking, Raud said, 'It would be a cunning man who could find a plan so that all these people would be quiet.'

Halli said, 'I can manage it, whenever I wish, so that every mother's son here will be quiet.'

'You can't manage that, Icelander,' said Raud.

The next day people came to the assembly, and then there was as much shouting and noise as the day before and no settlement was reached in any case. At that, people went home.

Then Raud said, 'Halli, do you want to bet that you can manage to bring silence to the assembly?'

Halli said he was ready to do this.

Raud answered, 'You bet your head and I will bet a gold arm ring which weighs one mark.'

'So it shall be,' said Halli.

In the morning, Halli asked Raud if the bet was on. Raud said it was on. Then people came to the assembly, and there was as much shouting – or more – as on the preceding days.

And when people least expected anything, Halli jumped up and shouted as loudly as he could, 'Listen everybody! I need to speak. I've lost my hone and honing grease and my bag with all its tackle, which is better for a male to have than to lose.'

Everyone fell silent. Some men thought he had gone mad, others thought that he would announce some message from the king. And when all was silent, Halli sat down and took the ring. But when people realized that this was nothing but mockery, then there was uproar as before and Halli got away on the run, because Raud wanted to take his life and thought this had been an enormous cheat. Halli did not stop until he got to England.

9

Then Harold Godwin's son was ruling England.[6] Halli went straight to the king and said he had composed a drapa about him and asked for a hearing. The king had him given a hearing. Halli sat down at the king's knee and delivered his poem. When the poem was finished, the king asked his poet, who was with him, how the poem was. He said he thought that it was good. The king asked Halli to stay there with him, but Halli said that he was already prepared to go to Norway.

The king said then that it would go the same way: 'In rewarding you for the poem as it equals our benefit from it because no fame accrues to us from a poem no one knows. Now sit on the floor and I will have silver poured over your head. Keep what sticks to your hair. It seems to me the prospects look the same on both sides because we shall not get to learn the poem.'

Halli answered, 'It's true both that only small rewards are due and that the rewards will be small. But, my lord, you will surely allow me to go out and answer nature's call.'

'Go just as you wish,' said the king.

Halli went out to where the shipwrights were and put tar on his head and shaped his hair so that it would be like a dish, and then went inside and asked them to pour the silver over him. The king said that he was crafty. And now it was poured over him and he got a lot of silver.

Then he went where the ships were that were intended for Norway, but they had all left except for one, which was taken by many people with very heavy cargo. Halli had plenty of money and wanted very much to get away, because he had not composed a poem about the king but had just recited rubbish, and on that account he could not teach it. The skipper told him to find a device so that the people from southern lands would leave the ship and then he would gladly take him. At that time winter was at hand. Halli was there with them in common sleeping quarters for a while.

One night Halli was much troubled in his sleep, and it was a very long time before they could awaken him. They asked what he had dreamt.

He said that he was finished with asking for passage away from there: 'It seemed to me as if a terrible-looking man came up and recited this:

9.
There's roaring where I've grasped the tall
sea-weed since giving up my life.
It's very clear I'm residing with Ran.   *Ran*: sea-goddess
Some have lodgings with lobsters.
It's bright staying with the whitings.
I have lands beyond the sea-shore.
So now I sit, pale, in heaps of sea-weed.
Pale sea-weed undulates about my neck,
pale sea-weed undulates about my neck.'

And when the men from the southern lands knew about this dream, they left the ship and thought it would be their death if they sailed in it. Then Halli immediately took passage on the ship and said this was a trick of his and no dream.

They put out to sea as soon as they were ready and reached Norway in the autumn, and Halli immediately went to King Harald. He welcomed Halli warmly and asked if he had composed poems about other rulers.

Then Halli spoke this verse:

10.
I composed a thula   *thula*: mnemonic list in verse form
about an earl.   *an earl*: Harold Godwinson
Not among the Danes   *Danes*: regarded as unpoetic
has a poorer drapa appeared.
Fourteen mistakes in metre
and ten terrible rhymes.
It's obvious to anyone,
it goes upside-down.
So he has to compose
who knows how to badly.

The king grinned at this and it seemed to him that Halli was always entertaining.

10

In the spring, King Harald went to the Gulathing Assembly. And one day the king asked Halli how he was doing for women at the assembly.

Halli answered:

11.
This Gulathing's great,
we fuck whatever we fancy.

From there the king went north to Trondheim. When they sailed past Stad, Thjodolf and Halli were assigned the cooking and serving. Halli was very seasick and lay under the ship's boat, and Thjodolf had to serve alone. And when he was carrying the food, he fell over Halli's leg which was sticking out from under the boat.

Thjodolf spoke this verse:

12.
Sticking out from under the boat
is a sole-bucket. You're fucking now?   *sole-bucket*: shoe

Halli answered:

I made this servant into a waiter
and caused Thjodolf to cook the food.

And then the king continued on his way until he reached Trondheim.

Thora the queen was on the expedition and she disliked Halli, but the king liked him and thought that Halli was always entertaining.

It is said that one day the king was walking in the street and his followers were with him. Halli was in the procession. The king had an axe in his hand; its blade was inlaid with gold and the shaft was wound round with silver, and it had a large silver band on the upper part of the shaft and a precious stone was set into it. It was an excellent possession. Halli kept looking at the axe. The king noticed that at once and asked Halli if he liked the axe. Halli said he liked it very much.

'Have you seen a better axe?'

'I don't think so,' said Halli.

'Will you allow yourself to be fucked for the axe?' said the king.

'I will not,' said Halli, 'but it seems understandable to me that you should want to sell the axe for the same price that you paid for it.'

'So it shall be, Halli,' said the king. 'Take it and use it for the best – it was given to me and so shall I give it to you.'

Halli thanked the king.

That evening when people came to the drinking, the queen spoke to the king and said it was scandalous: 'And it's not a reasonable exchange to give Halli goods that are hardly meant for commoners' possession, to reward him for his obscene language when some men receive little in return for good service.'

The king said that he would decide to whom he would give his possessions: 'I don't wish to take those words of Halli's which are ambiguous in a bad sense.'

The king had Halli summoned and it was done. Halli bowed to him.

The king ordered Halli to make an ambiguous statement about Queen Thora: 'And I'll see how she endures it.'

Then Halli bowed to Thora and spoke this verse:

13.
You're the most fitting by far,
by a long mark, Thora,
to roll down from a rising crag
all the foreskin on Harald's prick.

'Seize him and kill him,' said the queen. 'I won't put up with his abusive obscenities.'

The king ordered that no one be so bold as to lay hold of Halli for this: 'But it can be changed, if you think that another woman is more suitable to lie beside me and be my queen – you hardly know how to listen to your praise.'

The poet Thjodolf had gone to Iceland while Halli was absent from the king. Thjodolf had shipped a good stallion from Iceland and intended to give him to the king, and Thjodolf had the stallion led into the king's courtyard and shown to the king. The king went to see the stallion, and it was big and fat. Halli was there when the horse stuck out his prick.

Halli spoke this verse:

14.
Always a young she-pig –
Thjodolf's horse has
wholly befouled his prick;
he's a master fucker.

'Tut tut,' said the king, 'he will never come into my possession at this rate.'

Halli became one of the king's men and asked permission to go to Iceland. The king told him to go warily because of Einar Fly.

Halli travelled out to Iceland and settled down. His money ran out and he took up fishing, and one time he and his crew had such great difficulty rowing back that they only just reached land. That evening the porridge was brought to Halli and when he had eaten a few bites, he fell backwards and then was dead.

Harald learned of the deaths of two of his men from Iceland: Bolli the Elegant[7] and Sarcastic Halli.

He said of Bolli, 'The warrior must have fallen victim to spears.'

But of Halli he said, 'The poor devil must have burst eating porridge.'

And so I conclude the story of Sarcastic Halli.

Translated by GEORGE CLARK

Notes

Sagas

The Saga of the Sworn Brothers

1. *Saint Olaf*: Olaf Haraldsson the Saint, King of Norway, 1014–30. He was also king of the Faroe Islands and Orkney Islands. The Norwegian chieftains revolted in the name of the Danish king Cnut (Canute) the Great, and exiled Olaf, who tried to regain power at Stiklestad (see note 46).

2. *Isafjord district*: In the West Fjords, the large peninsula that forms the north-west part of Iceland.

3. *Killer-Styr*: Chieftain in Snæfellsnes peninsula: see *The Saga of the People of Eyri*.

4. *Olaf Peacock*: Chieftain in Dalir district, of royal, Irish descent: See *The Saga of the People of Laxardal*.

5. *Grettir Asmundarson*: An outlaw and famous for his enormous strength. His saga is one of the greatest and best known, *The Saga of Grettir the Strong*; he is referred to in other sagas, including *The Saga of the Confederates* (in this volume).

6. *Thorgils Arason*: A well-known chieftain, appearing in a few sagas, including *The Saga of the People of Eyri*, *The Saga of Grettir the Strong* and *The Saga of the Confederates*.

7. *Sigurd Fafnisbani*: A famous, ancient Germanic hero, known from the Eddaic poems on which Wagner based his *Der Ring des Nibelungen*.

8. *barbed spear*: With sharp hooks on the socket.

9. *he had sent . . . to dine in Valhalla*: He had killed many men in armed fight. Those who were killed with weapons went to Valhalla.

10. *Vigfus*: A common name that means 'eager to kill'. Thormod also uses it as an alias in chapter 23.

11. *they always gave him valuable gifts*: There were mutual obligations of support and protection between the chieftains and their thingmen.

12. *The daughters of the sea-goddess, Ran*: The waves of the sea.

13. *one of the two benches*: The second bench from the master of the house, second in rank also.

14. *"Best to know bad company by report alone"*: I.e. better than meeting the bad company in person.

15. *Lady Hel*: The evil female deity of Hell in Old Norse mythology.

16. *three hundred pieces of silver as a settlement price*: This was 9.5 kilos, or triple the average price for a man of a hundred pieces of silver.

17. *to hunt whales*: Beached whales were a great asset, not least when the climate was as the saga describes, and fights over them were not an uncommon trigger of a feud.

18. *dead when he fell from the horse*: Riding another man's horse was regarded as a serious offence according to the law of the Icelandic Commonwealth. A similar episode starts the plot of *The Saga of Hrafnkel Frey's Godi*.

19. *the land of the Wends*: The south-western coast of the Baltic, now Poland and the lands south of it.

20. *Thorgeirshrof*: *Hróf* is a shed for a ship. See also chapter 12.

21. *Six*: The inconsistency between six and seven is in the original.

22. *as a troll on his doorstep*: I.e. a dangerous, if not insurmountable, obstacle.

23. *he formally accused Kolbak of grievously wounding his son*: A formal accusation was necessary if Kolbak was to be sentenced at the court of the Althing.

24. *recited occasional love songs*: Composing love songs to women could lead to a sentence of outlawry, according to early Icelandic law.

25. *Thormod, Kolbrun's Poet*: It was customary to give gifts as tokens of a name-giving, in order to fix or confirm the name (cf. *The Saga of Ref the Sly*, chapter 20). Therefore, it is strange that Thormod later gives the poem to another woman.

26. *pain in his eyes*: Such pain sometimes appears in sagas in connection with moral faults and deceit.

27. *Snorratoftir*: Snorri's ruins.

28. *nicknamed Helgi Hviti (the White), not to belittle him*: The nickname was often used to denote a lack of courage.

29. *Thorstein Egilsson*: He was the son of Egil Skallagrimsson, the

hero of *Egil Skallagrimsson's Saga*, who also appears in *The Saga of Gunnlaug Serpent's Tongue*.

30. *Bishop Magnus Gizurarson ... Skalholt*: Bishop in Skalholt, 1216–37. In indicating directions, conventional Icelandic usage is often illogical – cf. the location of Reykjaholar here and Map 1.

31. *Rognvald Brusason*: Earl of the Orkneys, killed there in 1046 or 1047.

32. *Selseista*: Means 'seal's testicle', which explains Illugi's taunts about his being frightened and lacking courage.

33. *two ... are named in those verses*: This has been regarded as a misunderstanding of verse 18, which states that Thorgeir killed thirteen men (and the prose text just before verse 17 says 'fourteen'), but this was the total killings of his lifetime. In this battle he killed only two.

34. *small heart ... less prone to fear*: It was not uncommon to connect the size of the heart to character.

35. *Thorgeir's head in a leather bag ... to show off his great victory*: Carrying a dead enemy's head occurs in other sagas, such as *The Saga of Grettir the Strong*, chapter 83.

36. *Gudmund the Powerful*: One of the most powerful chieftains in Iceland in the early eleventh century.

37. *He was a godi*: The author apparently assumed that there was the same power structure in Greenland as in Iceland.

38. *skin-throwing games*: Four men in their corners throw a piece of skin (crumpled into a ball) between themselves, and a fifth tries to catch it.

39. *the Gardar Assembly in Einarsfjord*: The assembly at Gardar in the Eastern Settlement of Greenland seems to have been similar to the assemblies in Iceland, including judging outlawry. Gardar is at the east of Einarsfjord, where Igaliko is now.

40. *the screens*: Semi-transparent frames that could be removed in order to let in light and for smoke to escape.

41. *avenge the death of Thorgeir Havarsson*: Helgu-Steinar was a distant relative of Thorgeir, but close enough to be obliged to take revenge for him.

42. *secretly murdered someone in Iceland*: A secret murder was a much more serious crime than a declared murder.

43. *Bjarkamal*: An ancient lay of which only some fragments are preserved, about the Viking hero Bodvar Bjarki.

44. *remarks about Sighvat*: Sighvat Thordarson (*c.* 995–1045) was St Olaf's leading court poet, but in July 1030 he was on a pilgrimage to Rome. See also p. 99.

45. *living seems worse than dying*: Thormod's wish alludes to Christ's words to one of the robbers on a cross next to his, that they would be together in paradise that day (Luke 23:43).

46. *Dagshrid*: 'Dag's battle' was the last part of the Battle of Stiklestad, taking its name from Dag Hringsson, St Olaf's kinsman who kept fighting after the king had fallen. Svein Knutsson (son of Canute the Great) became king and ruled until 1035.

47. *Harald the Stern*: See *The Saga of Ref the Sly*, note 9.

Olkofri's Saga

1. *Ale-hood ... Blaskogar*: The saga's title is derived from the main character's nickname, Olkofri, which means 'Ale-hood'. Blaskogar was a woodland with heath near Thingvellir, the site of the Althing.

2. *six godis*: These chieftains were well known and appear in other sagas. Snorri the Godi was the main 'hero' of *The Saga of the People of Eyri*, and Gudmund Eyjolfsson (the Powerful) a main character in *The Saga of the People of Ljosavatn*, while Skafti the Lawspeaker has a prominent role in *Njal's Saga*. Thorkel Geitisson appears in the sagas from the East Fjords, Eyjolf Thordarson plays an unheroic role in *Gisli Sursson's Saga* and Thorkel Scarf appears in *Hen-Thorir's Saga* and *The Saga of the People of Laxardal*.

3. *Thorstein Sidu-Hallsson*: A respected chieftain in the East Quarter. He fought in the Battle of Clontarf, as described in chapter 157 of *Njal's Saga*. There is a minor eponymous saga about him.

4. *Where did this wave come from*: The wave might refloat his stranded hopes.

5. *Kjol to Skagafjord ... Modrudal heath*: This route goes north across the highlands and eastwards north of the great Vatnajokul glacier.

The Saga of the Confederates

1. *Ofeig Jarngerdarson*: A well-known chieftain in the north who appears in a few other sagas. Styrmir Thorgeirsson from Asgeirsa (a few sentences later) is mentioned in only one other medieval source. Glum Ospaksson and his son (chapter 2) are mentioned in a few other sagas. Thorarin the Wise Thorvaldsson (chapter 4) is briefly mentioned in a couple of other sources.

2. *it was very common to set up new godords or to purchase them*: It is not entirely clear whether it really was possible to purchase

a godord at the time of the saga, but it had recently been decided that a godi was able to have more than one godord.

3. *you do have some duty towards him*: Thorarin's 'duty' towards Ospak arises from his kinship with Ospak's wife Svala, even though he had refused to countenance the marriage.

4. *we both can see a legal defence*: It is not known for certain whether these legal formalities really were built on rightful law. The legal matters of the saga are in fact rather unclear.

5. *Hermund Illugason . . . Thorgeir Halldoruson*: These chieftains are known from other sources, except for the last. Gellir Thorkelsson is in several sagas, and Beard-Broddi appears in a very different role (as Broddi Bjarnason) in *Olkofri's Saga* (in this volume).

6. *horses . . . that we'd eaten them all*: Accusing someone of eating horse meat was a serious insult after the conversion to Christianity, as it was forbidden. Horses were the main animals to be sacrificed in the former pagan system.

7. *two hundred in the gully*: The implication is that Hermund has buried two hundred of silver in the gully, so that Egil's insult in chapter 10 was at least partly right.

The Saga of Havard of Isafjord

1. *Thorbjorn*: He is mentioned in other sources but is not well known, and the 'historicity' of most of the other characters is rather uncertain and may be namedropping. For instance, Havard is only referred to by his first name in *The Book of Settlements*, and Thorkel the 'lawspeaker' is not mentioned in other sources. The topography is often inaccurate; the author was obviously not familiar with the area.

2. *bear-warmth*: It was generally believed that bears had exceptional body warmth.

3. *drift rights*: The rights to everything, e.g. wood, whales, that drifts in from the sea.

4. *Gest Oddleifsson*: A godi who appears in several sagas, he was respected for his humane wisdom. His sister is not mentioned elsewhere. The roles of Gest and Steinthor of Eyri, a well-known chieftain (chapter 7), are most likely fictitious.

5. *three wergilds*: This is an unlikely amount of compensation for a man who was not a chieftain (a wergild was a hundred of silver).

6. *He recited this verse*: The two halves of this verse occur, in separate poems, in the *Tale of Hromund the Lame*, where they are attributed to Hromund.

7. *Ljot*: At this point in the story, the author might have forgotten that one Ljot, Thorbjorn's brother, had been killed already. This character is somehow mixed up with the historical Ljot Thjodreksson who lived not far away from Raudasand.

The Saga of Ref the Sly

1. *King Hakon, the foster-son of King Athelstan*: King of Norway, r. *c*. 934–60; he was a foster-son of King Athelstan of England.
2. *Gest of Bardastrond's*: The saga is fictitious and the name of Gest hardly more than namedropping in order to create credibility. Stein, Thorgerd, Thorbjorn and Rannveig are not mentioned in any other sources.
3. *he was a fool*: Ref is a 'coal-biter': see Introduction.
4. *the river ... was the boundary separating their lands*: There is in fact quite a distance (2–3 kilometres) between these two farmsteads.
5. *Thorbjorn had many grazing animals*: Grazing animals on another's land was forbidden by law.
6. *have a story written about your journey*: Needless to say, nothing was written down in Iceland at that time.
7. *Glaciers girded it on both sides*: Although this description resembles a fjord in Greenland, the people in and near the settlement are not known from any other sources.
8. *and stories of his unspeakable perversions*: Accusations of homosexuality are not uncommon in the sagas, but were regarded as insulting, even against the law. They often initiated a series of revenge and counter-revenge.
9. *King Harald Sigurdarson had succeeded to the kingdom*: King Harald Sigurdarson the Stern (Hardradi) ruled Norway 1046–66. He is quite prominent in the Tales of Icelanders, such as *Hreidar's Tale* and *The Tale of Sarcastic Halli* included in this volume. The fictional nature of this saga is highlighted by the fact that King Harald came to power about 85 years after King Hakon (see note 1).
10. *taking a fox*: Ref means 'fox' in Icelandic.
11. *their ship looks like a tuft of marsh grass*: As Ref's crew slowly lowers the sail, it appears to Gunnar that the ship is disappearing quickly in the darkness.
12. *best to announce the killing to the king himself*: A self-defence killing that was not publicly acknowledged was regarded as murder, a more serious crime. Ref did not announce his night-time killings in Greenland.

13. *soup-understanding ... I counterpaned him*: This wordplay is based on the logic of the kennings in the *dróttkvætt* poetry. See A Note on Poetic Imagery. (King Harald explains in chapter 17.)

14. *Sigtrygg*: An ordinary name, but *sig* is related to victory, *tryggr* means 'faithful'.

15. *Bishop Absalon who lived in the days of King Valdimar Knutsson*: Archbishop Absalon (1128–1201), King Valdimar Knutsson of Denmark (r. 1157–82).

Tales

Hreidar's Tale

1. *the son of Hreidar whom Glum killed*: Although this most likely refers to Killer-Glum from *The Saga of Killer-Glum*, this episode is not mentioned in other sources and is probably fictional.

2. *King Magnus*: King Magnus the Good (r. 1035–47), son of King Olaf Haraldsson the Saint.

3. *my kinsman King Harald*: King Harald Sigurdarson the Stern (Hardradi) ruled in Norway 1046–66. He and King Magnus both ruled 1046–47.

The Tale of Thorleif, the Earl's Poet

1. *Hakon, Earl of Lade*: Earl Hakon Sigurdarson reigned in Norway 975(65?)–995.

2. *Asgeir Red-cloak lived at Brekka in Svarfadardal*: Most persons mentioned in this chapter appear in other sagas, especially *The Saga of the People of Svarfadardal*.

3. *Gaseyri*: A well-known trading post in Eyjafjord in the Middle Ages.

4. *Vik*: Oslo.

5. *King Svein*: King Svein Haraldsson, nicknamed Forked Beard (r. 986–1014).

6. *Nidung*: The name might indicate some scorn (*nið* = abuse, libel, defamation), and cf. below the poem entitled 'Earl Abuse'. Scythia, in the remote north-east, where the inhabitants had a reputation for sorcery and trolldom.

7. *Thorgerd Altar-bride and her sister Irpa*: Some kind of mythological female beings, related to the Hladir clan to which Earl Hakon belonged.

The Tale of Thorstein Shiver

1. *King Olaf*: King Olaf Tryggvason, the missionary king of Norway (r. 995–1000).
2. *Vik*: Oslo.
3. *Sigurd Fafnisbani*: See *The Saga of the Sworn Brothers*, note 7.
4. *Starkad the Old*: A character who appears in some kings' sagas and legendary sagas, especially *The Saga of Gautrek*.

The Tale of Sarcastic Halli

1. *King Harald ... King Magnus*: King Harald Sigurdarson the Stern (Hardradi) ruled in Norway 1046–66. King Magnus Olafs-son the Good ruled 1035–47.
2. *a man named Thjodolf*: According to Halli in chapter 6, Thjodolf was the son of Thorljot. But Thjodolf Arnorsson (son of Arnor) was among the best poets of the eleventh century.
3. *Gasir*: See *The Tale of Thorleif, the Earl's Poet*, note 3.
4. *Sigurd Fafnisbani*: See *The Saga of the Sworn Brothers*, note 7.
5. *the poet Thorleif ... Earl Hakon Sigurdarson*: See *The Tale of Thorleif, the Earl's Poet* and its note 1.
6. *Harold Godwin's son was ruling England*: Harold Godwinson was Earl of Wessex and for nine months in 1066 King of England; his tenure was unsuccessfully challenged by Halli's patron, Harald Sigurdarson, and successfully by William the Conqueror.
7. *Bolli the Elegant*: Probably Bolli Bollason, a hero in *The Saga of the People of Laxardal* and *Bolli Bollason's Tale*.

Maps

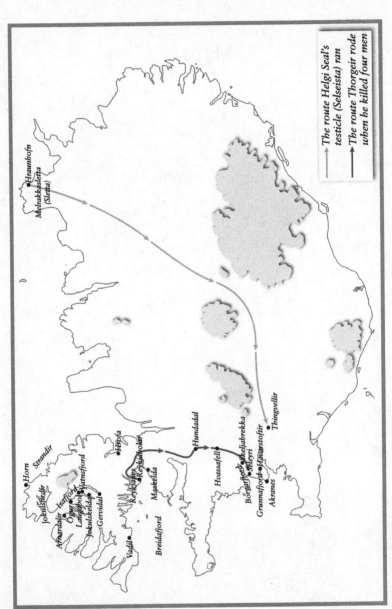

Map 1. The Saga of the Sworn Brothers

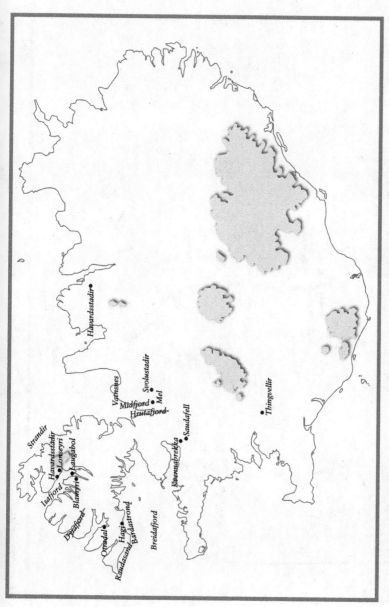

Map 2. The Sagas: Olkofri, The Confederates, Havard of Isafjord and Ref the Sly

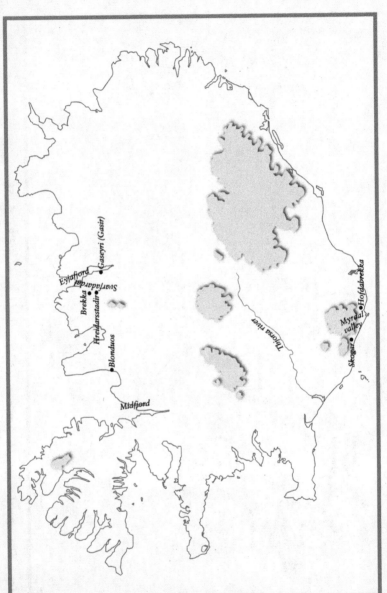

Map 3. The Tales

Map 4. *Norway in the Sagas and the Tales*

A Note on Poetic Imagery

The characteristic tightly-wrought poetry which is found in many of the Sagas of Icelanders is a genre in its own right, and occurs in other branches of saga literature (notably the kings' sagas) and elsewhere. It is enriched by the use of poetic diction (*heiti*): many synonyms, known only from verse, cover single terms such as sword, man, woman and so forth, some with very subtle distinctions of connotation, as when a 'sword' word also suggests 'flame'. Forged from this rich diction is one of the poetry's most distinctive features: the *kenning* (a stylized metaphor or association of images), an exuberant exercise in imagination and meaning which poses a special challenge to translators.

Inevitably, the translators engaged in this project have frequently had to simplify the verse. The range of synonyms within the poetic diction could not always be matched, and the choice of whether to cite the names of deities or merely call them 'god' or 'goddess' has been left to their discretion. Furthermore, the translations have often resulted in lengthy, complex or obscure kennings in order to render their essence.

ELEMENTS OF THE KENNINGS

The best key to understanding the kennings used in the verse is perhaps Snorri Sturluson's *Language of Poetry* (*Skáldskaparmál*), the very compilation of which in the early thirteenth century shows that the devices and thinking patterns underlying the kennings were becoming remote by that time. Snorri adorns his glosses of poetic diction and images with accounts of certain underlying myths, which means that his work not only has scholarly value but is also entertaining to read.

To simplify greatly, a kenning is a figurative expression in which two or more elements combine to denote an object or concept which in prose would be expressed by a simple noun. A straightforward example is when a *ship* is referred to as a *sea-steed*. The range of concepts referred to by kennings is quite limited, with only two dozen or so occurring very frequently, among them *ruler, man, woman, sword, battle, raven, poetry* and *mind*. The elements used to create the kennings, on the other hand, and the patterns in which they are combined, are very diverse, though always stereotyped to some degree. Most elements of the kenning are archetypal forces (sea, fire and the like) or emblems from a stylized world (such as gold and weapons), or are motifs originating in mythological events. As well as being named directly, using a term drawn from the rich variety of synonyms, a kenning-element can be identified by allowing a part to stand for the whole: for example, *wave* can be substituted for *sea*, so that *wave-flame* can stand for the *flame of the sea*, both referring to gold. As a further elaboration, an element of a kenning can itself be a kenning, so that *sea* can become *sea-steed's path*, and *gold* can therefore be called the *flame of the sea-steed's path*.

Whether the kennings have evolved from naming taboos or represent some kind of ritual glorification cannot be established; and the origins of individual kenning types are often obscure. Kennings such as *flame of the sea* which associate gold with water, for instance, may hint naturalistically at the extracting of gold from streams, or refer to the legend of the Rhinegold or to a myth involving the sea-god Aegir.

HYPERBOLE

Modern ethics make a poor yardstick for responding to the kennings. In these poems, an *enemy* or *waster of gold* (rings or bracelets) is not a derisory term, but one of praise, because a man who does not like gold gives it away, in other words is generous. Similarly, it is an honour rather than a psychological disorder to be a *feeder of corpses to ravens* (or *eagles* or *wolves*), that is, to leave dead bodies lying around after a successful battle, for carrion beasts to feast on. In some instances at least, poets seem to take a particular delight in overdrawing the gore and bloodshed, almost to the level of caricature. The tradition of referring to men as gold-givers or carrion-providers can extend to niggards, cowards or ordinary farmers (as often happens in the verses within the Sagas of Icelanders), and allowance has to be made for usage that may be hyperbolic, ironic, or merely an empty convention.

SOME COMMON CONCEPTS

The following points about the associations underlying the kennings may prove helpful in conveying their conceptual mechanisms. This is not an exhaustive list, but highlights many of the main ideas.

Human qualities: *Men* are largely identified with two character traits: prowess in battle and generosity, as in the examples given above. In satirical verses or ritual insults they may be identified with the opposite of these traits.

Battle can be represented symbolically as a shower of spears, clash of swords, an assembly of weapons and the like; stated in terms of its result (flowing blood and spread corpses); or lent a mythological dimension by invoking Odin or valkyries. *Weapons*, the tools with which men display their prowess in battle, are referred to in a variety of ways. Sometimes they are represented by their physical content (swords being described as *iron* or *steel*, spears as *ash*, bows as *yew*). Their impact is sometimes invoked in general (as in *wound-maker*), while specific images occur for specific types of weapon as well: missiles are called *hail*, *blizzard* and *rain*, swords are *snakes* and axes are *trollwomen* or *ogresses*.

Women are often called *goddesses*, with a 'conventionally feminine' attribute or association such as *goddess of cloth*, *ring* or *headdress*. Some indication of their stylized social role is given by the use of 'passive' kennings such as *prop*, *stand* or *wearer* of *gold* or *bracelets* (although similar expressions can be used of men), and by their identification with serving ale. The names of trees are often used and to some extent this may represent an elaboration of the notion of *prop* or *stand*.

Shape and physical quality are frequently invoked to draw comparisons between otherwise disparate objects. With reference, presumably, to their being taller than they are wide, men and women are termed *trees*, ships *skis* and swords *snakes*; shields are identified with circularity; the head, as a protrusion, is a *helmet-stand*, and so forth. Gold is often associated with *flame*, but so is any other form of glittering metal, for example, a sword.

MYTHICAL AND LEGENDARY BACKGROUND

Myths known from other old Icelandic literature provide a rich stock of motifs and elements for kennings. References to the complex myths about poetry and gold are particularly common, and two of the main ones are outlined here. The gift of *poetry* was originally transmitted by drinking mead which had been brewed by dwarfs from honey and the blood of Kvasir, the wisest of men (himself the product of the gods' spittle). The dwarfs handed over the mead of poetry as compensation to a giant called Suttung, who appointed his daughter Gunnlod to guard over it. Odin turned himself into a snake to 'worm his way' into her chamber, seduced her, stole the mead and flew off in the guise of an eagle to take it to the gods. This legend is told, in succinct but relatively straightforward language, in one of the Edda poems, *Hávamál* (*The Words of the High One*). Kennings invoke poetry with references – which are sometimes little more than obscure tags or catch words – to any of the various episodes in this tale.

Complex myths and legends also underlie *gold*, inviting numerous allusions. In the most extended story the gods, after wrongfully killing a man who was in the guise of an otter, paid compensation to his father and two brothers by filling and covering the skin with gold which Loki, the treacherous god, seized as a ransom from a dwarf. One ring within this gold was cursed. Fafnir, one of the brothers, took the gold from the others and made himself a lair where, in the guise of a serpent, he jealously guarded it. Sigurd the Volsung, who had been fostered by the other brother, Regin, killed Fafnir and took the gold, and the curse on it brought tragedy upon a whole cast of characters, including Attila the Hun. This myth is central to a cycle of Eddic poems and was synthesized by Snorri Sturluson, but is probably best known today through Richard Wagner's *Der Ring des Nibelungen*. In particular, the serpent figure is a prominent element in kennings for gold.

Gods and goddesses provide further motifs which adorn the kennings. They are often identified genealogically, as when Thor is referred to as a son of Odin or of the goddess Earth, but their individual attributes also form the basis of kennings. *Odin*, mightiest of the gods, is also the main god of battle, poetry and wisdom, with his two ravens Thought (Huginn) and Memory (Muninn) and his array of names and disguises. He has one eye, having given the other to gain wisdom, and is also associated with a gallows, because he sacrificed himself to himself by hanging, in order to learn the secrets of the runes (as recounted in *Hávamál*).

Thor is often invoked as a scourge of trolls and giants, and *valkyries* feature widely as overseers of battle, in the role of both cheerleaders and choosers of the slain. Names of deities are often twinned with words for weapons to mean warrior, and their personal attributes disappear under such associations. The gentle god *Balder*, for example, becomes ferocious when a warrior is identified as *sword-Balder*.

Outline of Medieval Icelandic
Literature

Writing, enabled by the advent of Christian learning *c.* 1000, flourished
in Iceland from the twelfth century onwards. Native traditions were
combined with materials and influences drawn from foreign literature,
especially medieval Latin and, later on, French, though the 'native'
strand predominates in the most famous branch of the literature, the
Sagas of Icelanders. The word *saga* in Icelandic derives from the verb
segja (say, tell) and denotes an extended prose narrative which may (to
modern perceptions) be located anywhere on the spectrum between seriously historical and wholly fictional, and various groupings of sagas
are customarily identified especially on the basis of content and degree
of apparent historicity. Some but by no means all of these saga genres
were recognized in medieval Iceland. Literacy also enabled poetry to
be recorded, some of it oral composition dating from the Viking Age
(approximately ninth to mid eleventh centuries). Some poetry, especially the earlier compositions, and certain prose genres had their
genesis in Norway, and for a few texts Norwegian or Icelandic origins
are equally possible.

SAGAS

Sagas of Icelanders or Family sagas (*Íslendingasögur*)

The sagas in this volume belong to this group. Composed from the early
thirteenth century to *c.* 1400 and beyond, based on characters and
events from the Icelandic past, especially from the settlement period
(*c.* 870–*c.* 930) to the early eleventh century. Most are concerned with
feuding in a pastoral setting, and feature, in varying proportions, both
exceptional individuals and neighbourhoods: hence titles such as *The
Saga of Grettir the Strong*, *Egil's Saga* and *The Saga of the Sworn
Brothers* on the one hand, and *The Saga of the People of Eyri* and *The*

Saga of the People of Vatnsdal on the other. *The Saga of the People of Laxardal* is unusual in featuring a woman, Gudrun Osvifsdottir, as its central figure. Many sagas, including *The Saga of Hrafnkel Frey's Godi* and *The Saga of the Confederates*, are concerned with chieftainly power. In *The Saga of Grettir the Strong* and *Gisli Sursson's Saga* the titular heroes spend long periods of outlawry in the Icelandic 'wilderness', and many depict episodes abroad, including *Bard's Saga*, a late work of *c.* 1400, which differs from the 'classic', feud-based, sagas in narrating adventures of an often fantastical kind.

Contemporary sagas (*Samtíðarsögur*)

Sturlunga Saga (*The Saga of the Sturlungs*): a compilation, from *c.* 1300, of sagas based on Icelandic events from the twelfth century to the end of the Icelandic Commonwealth in the 1260s with various authors. Sturla Thordarson's *Saga of the Icelanders* (*Íslendinga saga*) is the most substantial; shorter items include *The Saga of Thorgils and Haflidi*, which relates the dispute between these two men in the early twelfth century.

Sagas of Kings (*Konungasögur*)

Mostly about Norwegian kings and earls, but also Danish kings and earls of Orkney (*Orkneyinga saga*). Writing begins, in Latin and the vernacular, in Norway and Iceland, in the mid twelfth century. Some sagas concern individual kings, especially the two missionary Olafs, e.g. the sagas of Olaf Tryggvason by Odd Snorrason and Gunnlaug Leifsson, both written originally in Latin, or Snorri Sturluson's *Great Saga of St Olaf*. Others cover a broad sweep of reigns, including the anonymous *Morkinskinna*, *Fagrskinna* and Snorri Sturluson's massive *Heimskringla*, all from the first decades of the thirteenth century. *Flateyjarbók*, a huge manuscript compilation mainly from the late fourteenth century, contains many kings' sagas.

Short tales (*Thættir*)

Brief narratives, often of encounters between Norwegian kings and low-born but canny Icelanders; these are more or less independent stories, but are incorporated especially in major compilations of Sagas of Kings such as *Morkinskinna*, *Fagrskinna* and *Hulda-Hrokkinskinna*. Other tales, including some contained in *Flateyjarbók*, are in effect miniature Sagas of Icelanders or legendary sagas.

Sagas / Lives of Saints (*Heilagra manna sögur*)

Mainly translations from Latin; some fragments are preserved from the mid twelfth century, putting this among the earliest type of literature produced in Iceland.

Legendary sagas / Sagas of Ancient Times (*Fornaldarsögur*)

Usually set in remote times and locations, showing stereotypical heroes in racy though in some cases tragic adventures involving the supernatural, hence giving a generally unrealistic impression. These include *The Saga of the Volsungs* (*Völsunga saga*), *c.* 1260–70, *The Saga of King Hrolf Kraki* (fourteenth century) and *Fridthjof's Saga* (*c.* 1400).

Chivalric sagas (*Riddarasögur*)

Romances: some are adaptations of French originals, such as *The Saga of Tristram and Isond* (*Tristan and Isolde*, Norwegian *c.* 1226); others are original Icelandic compositions in a similar mode. The latter have sometimes been termed 'lying sagas' (*lygisögur*).

Translated quasi-historical works

Includes *The Saga of the Trojans* (*Trójumanna saga*, first half of thirteenth century), a retelling of the story of the Trojan Wars, mostly based on classical sources, especially the late Latin *De excidio Troiae historia* attributed to 'Dares Phrygius'.

POETRY

Skaldic poetry

Usually attached to named poets and specific occasions, skaldic poetry includes praise of princes, travelogue, slander, love poetry and, especially in the earliest surviving poetry (late ninth and tenth centuries), pagan mythology. Metre, diction and word order tend to be elaborate (see A Note on Poetic Imagery), though the style of later religious poetry (twelfth to fourteenth centuries) is simpler. This poetry tends to be preserved as fragmentary citations within prose works, including the sagas of poets. The names of 146 poets, and the rulers they composed for, are preserved in the *List of Poets* (*Skáldatal*), *c.* 1260.

Eddic poetry / The *Poetic Edda*

Poems mainly in older, simpler metres, but spanning the ninth to the twelfth or thirteenth centuries. Topics drawn largely from pagan mythology or legend. Composed in Norway, Iceland or the wider Nordic-speaking world, but preserved mainly (as complete or near-complete poems) in the Icelandic *Codex Regius*, *c.* 1270.

OTHER PROSE WORKS

Works on Icelandic history

The Book of the Icelanders (*Íslendingabók*): By Ari Thorgilsson *c.* 1122–33, on the Settlement and the establishment of Christianity.

Kristni Saga: a saga-narrative of the Christianization of Iceland, probably late thirteenth century.

The Book of Settlements (*Landnámabók*): names, also often genealogies and anecdotes, of over four hundred settlers, region by region.

Annals: lists of dates and events (Icelandic and foreign), existing in numerous versions, the oldest compiled in the late thirteenth century from older sources.

Legal writings

Grágás (*Grey Goose*): the laws of the Icelandic Commonwealth, as preserved in a range of mainly thirteenth-century manuscripts. These are Christian laws, but to some extent founded on the pre-Christian Norwegian laws brought by early settlers of Iceland.

Works on poetry, language or grammar

The *Prose Edda* of Snorri Sturluson (*Snorra Edda*, probably composed 1220s) comprises a prologue and three sections: on Nordic mythology (*Gylfaginning* (*The Deceiving of Gylfi*) – the most comprehensive medieval account we have); on the diction of skaldic poetry (*Skáldska-parmál* (*The Language of Poetry*)); and on metre (*Háttatal* (*List of Metres*), 102 illustrative verses with commentary).

The Third Grammatical Treatise: By Olaf Thordarson, mid thirteenth century: the fullest of four prose treatises to apply Classical grammar and rhetoric to Icelandic language and poetry; rich in poetic quotations.

Glossary

Althing *alþingi*: The holding of meetings or assemblies (*þing*) of free men for a variety of different purposes was fundamental to early Scandinavian society. The system of regular local and larger-scale assemblies had already been established in Norway, as can be seen in the description in *Egil's Saga*, chapter 57, of the annual Gula Assembly, which represented Sogn, Fjordane and Hordaland. The Althing was the equivalent general assembly in Iceland, but with some differences. Three *godis* in each area presided over each of the thirteen annual local *Spring Assemblies*. The *godis* appointed the judges who tried the cases presented at the assemblies, whose main task was to settle local disputes. The Althing was the national equivalent, and annually convened at Thingvellir for a fortnight around midsummer, when ten weeks of the old Scandinavian 'summer' had passed (see *Autumn Meeting*). Here, the thirty-nine *godis*, each accompanied by two free men to advise them, formed the *Law Council*, a form of legislative assembly, which met within a strictly defined area. The Law Council also elected the lawspeaker (*lögsögumaður, lögmaður*), who was responsible for the preservation and clarification of legal tradition. He had the role of reciting a third of the law code annually, perhaps at the *Law Rock*. Other important bodies at the *Althing* were the four Quarter Courts, which tried cases against individuals. In the early eleventh century, a Fifth Court was added to these, as a means of breaking legal deadlocks.

arch of raised turf *jarðarmen*: In order to confirm *sworn brotherhood*, the participants had to mix their blood and walk under an arch of raised turf: see *The Saga of the Sworn Brothers*, chapter 2.

assembly *þing*: See *Althing*.

Autumn Meeting *leiðarþing*: Small local meetings held in the early autumn, no later than eight weeks before the end of the old Scandinavian 'summer', which began in April (around the 20th) and ended the second half of October, so the Autumn Meeting took place mid August. The proceedings and decisions from the *Althing* were announced here.

bed closet *hvílugólf, lokrekkja, lokhvíla, lokrekkjugólf*: A private sleeping area used by the heads of better-off households. The closet was partitioned off from the rest of the house, and had a door that was secured from the inside.

black *blár*: Nowadays, *blár* means 'blue', but the closest translation at the time of the sagas is 'black', as can be seen from the fact that *blár* was used to describe (e.g.) the colour of ravens. It was impossible to create a dye that was jet-black then, and the nearest colour was a very dark blue-black. 'Blue' would create the wrong impression, especially when a man intending to slay somebody deliberately dresses in *blár* clothes (e.g. in *Havard*, chapter 11). (The Icelandic *svartur* which nowadays means 'black' seems in the saga world to have referred mainly to a brown-black colour, used (e.g.) to describe horses.)

bloody wounds *áverki*: Almost always used in a certain legal sense, that is with regard to a visible, most likely bloody wound, which could result in legal actions for *compensation*, or some more drastic proceedings such as the taking of revenge.

board game *tafl*: Probably refers to chess, which had reached Scandinavia before the twelfth century. In certain cases it might be another board game *hnefatafl*, whose rules are uncertain, though we know what the boards looked like.

booth *búð*: A temporary dwelling used by those who attended the various *assemblies*. Structurally, it seems to have involved permanent walls which were covered by a tent-like roof, probably made of cloth.

compensation *manngjöld*: Penalties imposed by the courts were of three main kinds: awards of compensation in cash; sentences of lesser outlawry, which could be lessened or replaced by the payment of compensation; and sentences of *full outlawry* with no chance of being compounded. In certain cases, a man's right to immediate vengeance was recognized, but for many offences compensation was the fixed legal penalty and the injured party had little choice but to accept the settlement offered by the court, an arbitrator or a man who had been given the right to self-judgement (*sjálfdæmi*). It was certainly legal to put pressure on the guilty party to pay. Neither court verdicts nor legislation, nor even the constitutional arrangements, had any coercive power behind them other than the free initiative of individual chieftains with their armed following.

cross-bench *pallur, þverpallur*: A raised platform or bench at the inner end of the *main room*, where women were usually seated.

dowry *heimanfylgja*: Literally 'that which accompanies the bride from her home', this was the amount a bride's father gave to his daughter at her wedding. It remained the property of the wife, and was her financial contribution to the new household.

drapa *drápa*: A heroic, laudatory poem in the complicated metre preferred by the Icelandic poets. Such poems were in fashion between the tenth and thirteenth centuries. They were usually composed in honour of kings, *earls* and other prominent men. On other occasions they might be addressed to a loved one, or composed in memory of the deceased or in relation to a religious matter. A drapa usually consisted of three parts: an introduction, a middle section including one or more refrains, and a conclusion. It was usually clearly distinguished from the *flokk*, which tended to be shorter, less laudatory and without refrains. For an example of a drapa, see *Egil's Saga*, chapter 61. See also *Sworn Brothers*, e.g., chapters 3 and 5; *Thorleif*, chapter 4; and *Sarcastic Halli*, chapter 9.

earl *jarl*: This title was generally restricted to men of high rank in northern countries (though not in Iceland), who could be independent rulers or subordinate to a king. The title could be inherited, or it could be conferred by a king on a prominent supporter or leader of military forces. The earls of Lade who appear in a number of sagas and tales (see the tales of *Thorleif, the Earl's Poet* and *Sarcastic Halli* in this volume) ruled large sections of northern Norway (and often many southerly areas as well) for several centuries. Another prominent, almost independent, earldom was that of Orkney and Shetland.

fire room *eldhús, eldaskáli*: In literal terms, the fire room or fire hall was a room or special building (as perhaps at Jarlshof in Shetland) containing a fire. Its primary function was that of a kitchen. Such a definition, however, would be too limited, since the fire room/fire hall was also used for eating, working and sleeping. Indeed, in many cases the words *eldhús* and *eldaskáli* seem to have been synonymous with the word *skáli*, meaning *hall*.

follower *hirðmaður*: A member of the inner circle of followers that surrounded the Scandinavian kings, a sworn *king's man*.

foster- *fóstur-, fóstri, fóstra*: Children during the saga period were often brought up by foster-parents, who received either payment or support in return from the real parents. Being fostered was therefore somewhat different from being adopted: it was essentially a legal agreement, and more importantly, a form of alliance. Nonetheless, emotionally, and in some cases legally, fostered children were seen as being part of the family circle. Relationships and loyalties between foster-kindred could become very strong. It should be noted that the expressions *fóstri/fóstra* were also used for people who had the function of looking after and bringing up the children on the farm, like Thjostolf and Thord Freed-man's son in *Njal's Saga*, chapters 9 and 39. See also, e.g., *Sworn Brothers*, chapter 15; *Havard*, chapter 9; *Ref the Sly*, chapter 1; and *Thorleif*, chapter 2.

full outlawry *skóggangur*: A term applied to a man sentenced to full outlawry was *skógarmaður*, which literally means 'forest man', even though in Iceland there was scant possibility of his taking refuge in a forest. Outlawry simply meant banishment from civilized society, whether the local district, the province or the whole country. It also meant the confiscation of the outlaw's property to pay the prosecutor, cover debts and sometimes provide an allowance for the dependants he had left behind. A full outlaw was to be neither fed nor offered shelter. According to one legal codex from Norway, it was 'as if he were dead'. He had lost all goods, and all rights. His children became illegitimate, and wherever he went he could be killed without any legal redress, and his body was to be buried in unconsecrated ground.

giant *jötunn, risi*: According to Nordic mythology, the giants (*jötnar*) had existed from the dawn of time; they can be seen as the personification of the more powerful natural elements, and the enemies of the gods and mankind. The original belief was that they lived in the distant north and east in a large mythical place called Jotunheim ('The world of the giants'), where they were perpetually planning the eventual overthrow of the gods. The final battle between the giants and the gods, Ragnarok ('The fate of the gods'), would mark the end of the world. These giants were clever and devious, and had an even greater knowledge of the world and the future than that which was available to Odin. *Risi* is a later term, coined when old beliefs were fading and the ancient giants were on the way to becoming the stupid *trolls* of later ages, and refers primarily to the physical size of these beings which lived in the mountains on the borders of civilization.

godi *goði*: This word was little known outside Iceland in early Christian times, and seems to refer to a particularly Icelandic concept. A godi was a local chieftain who had legal and administrative responsibilities in Iceland. The name in fact seems to have originally meant 'priest', or at least a person having a special relationship with gods or supernatural powers, and thus shows an early connection between religious and secular power. As time went on, however, the chief function of a godi came to be secular. The first godis were chosen from the leading families who settled Iceland in c. 870–930. Every free person was required to be a *thingman* of one godi. While the office of godi was predominantly hereditary, allegiance to him was more or less voluntary and could be transferred; if he neglected to look after the people for whom he was responsible, they could decide to withdraw their support when he needed it.

godord *goðorð*: The authority of a *godi* was partly geographical and partly social. It referred to the number of free men living in a certain region who were under the responsibility of the godi.

halberd *atgeir*: This weapon has not been found in archaeological excavations in Scandinavia, but on the basis of descriptions in the sagas seems to have most resembled the halberd which appeared elsewhere in the fourteenth century. The most famous halberd was that used by Gunnar Hamundarson of Hlidarendi in *Njal's Saga* (see chapter 30).

hall *skáli*: The word was used both for large halls like those used by kings and for the main farmhouse on the typical Icelandic farm.

hayfield *tún*: An enclosed field for hay cultivation close to or surrounding a farmhouse. This was the only 'cultivated' part of a farm and produced the best hay. Other hay, generally of lesser quality, came from the meadows which could be a good distance from the farm itself.

hayfield wall *túngarður*: A wall of stones surrounding the *hayfield* in order to protect it from grazing livestock.

hay-time *tvímánuður*, *heyannir*: The fourth month of summer; the month when haymaking took place.

high seat *öndvegi*: The central section of one bench in the *hall* (at the inner end, or in the middle of the 'senior' side, to the right as one entered) was the rightful high seat of the owner of the farm. Even though it is usually referred to in English as the 'high seat', this position was not necessarily higher in elevation, only in honour. Opposite the head of the household sat the guest of honour.

homespun cloth *vaðmál*: Iceland had a surplus of wool, and for centuries wool and woollen products were Iceland's chief exports, especially in the form of strong and durable homespun cloth. It could be bought and sold in bolts or made up in the form of homespun cloaks. There were strict regulations on homespun, as it was used as a standard exchange product and often referred to in *ounces*, meaning its equivalent value expressed as a weight in silver. One ounce could equal three to six ells of homespun, one ell being roughly 50 cm.

hundred *hundrað*: A 'long hundred' or one hundred and twenty. The expression, however, rarely refers to an accurate number. It more often means a generalized 'round' figure.

judgement circle *dómhringur*: The courts of heathen times appear to have been surrounded by a judgement circle, marked out with hazel poles and ropes (see the description of the court at the Gula Assembly in *Egil's Saga*, chapter 57), where judgements were made or announced. The circle was sacrosanct. Weapons were not allowed inside it, and similarly no act of violence.

king's follower or **king's man** *hirðmaður*: A member of the inner circle of followers that surrounded the Scandinavian kings, a sworn king's man.

knorr *knör*: An ocean-going cargo vessel, which was most often used by those travelling to Iceland and Greenland.

Law Council *lögrétta*: The legislative assembly at the *Althing*. See also *Althing*.

Law Rock *Lögberg*: The raised spot at the *Althing* at Thingvellir, where the lawspeaker may have annually recited a third of the law code, and where public announcements and speeches were made. See also *Althing*.

lawspeaker: See *Althing*.

leather sleeping sacks *húðfat*: A large leather bag used by travellers for sleeping at night and for storage by day.

longship *langskip*: The largest type of Viking warship.

main room *stofa*: A room off the *hall*. See also *cross-bench*.

mark *mörk*: A measurement of weight: eight *ounces*, approximately 216 grams.

Moving Days *fardagar*: Four successive days in the seventh week of 'summer' (in May) during which householders in Iceland could change their abode.

ounce *eyrir*, *aurar*: A unit of weight which varied slightly through time, but roughly 27 grams. Eight ounces were equal to one *mark*.

outlawry for life *skóggangsmaður*: See *full outlawry*.

quarter *fjórðungur*: Administratively, Iceland was divided into four quarters based on the four cardinal directions. Each quarter (except for the northern) had nine *godis*, who shared among themselves the control of three *Spring Assemblies*. The more densely populated northern quarter had four assemblies and twelve godis. The four Quarter Courts at the *Althing* reflected the idea of the four quarters, and were the next stage for a case after the *Spring Assembly*.

self-judgement: See *compensation*.

shape-shifter, **shape-changer** *hamrammur*: Closely associated with the berserks, those who were *hamrammir* were believed to change their shape sometimes at night or in times of stress, or leave their bodies (which appeared asleep) and take the physical form of animals such as bears or wolves. There are again faint associations with shamanistic activities and figures known in folklore throughout the world, like the werewolf. The transformation was not necessarily intentional. Three of the best examples in Icelandic literature are the figures of Kveldulf (literally, 'Night Wolf') in *Egil's Saga*, chapter 1, and Sigmund and Sinfjotli in the legendary *Saga of the Volsungs* (*Völsunga saga*), chapter 8. See also *Havard*, chapter 1.

single combat *einvígi*: Used for the less formal single fights in the sagas to differentiate them from the formally organized duel (*hólmganga*) which was fought according to defined rules and rituals.

slave *þræll*: Slavery formed a high proportion of Viking Age trade. A large number of slaves were taken from the Baltic nations and the west European countries that were raided and invaded by Scandinavians between the eighth and eleventh centuries. In addition, the Scandinavians had few scruples against taking slaves from the other Nordic countries. Judging from their names and appearance, a large number of the slaves mentioned in the sagas seem to have come from Ireland and Scotland. Stereotypically they are often presented as being stupid and lazy, an image emphasized by the Eddic poem *The Chant of Rig* (*Rígsþula*), which describes the origins and characteristics of the four main Scandinavian classes: slaves, farmers, aristocrats and kings. By law, slaves had hardly any rights at all, and they and their families could only gain freedom if their owners chose to free them, or somebody else bought their freedom. In Iceland, a slave who was wounded was entitled to one-third of the *compensation* money; the rest went to his owner.

Spring Assembly *vorþing*: The local *assembly*, held each spring, at the end of the fourth week of the old Scandinavian 'summer' (see *Autumn Meeting*). See also *Althing*, *godi* and *quarter*.

Summons Days *stefnudagar*: The days during which someone could be summonsed to appear at a given *assembly* for a legal case.

sworn brothers/sworn brotherhood *fóstbræður/fóstbræðralag*: This was seen as another form of foster-brotherhood, but instead of being arranged by the parents (see *foster-*), this was a relationship that was decided by the individuals themselves. Sworn brothers literally were a form of 'blood-brother': they swore unending loyalty to each other, sealing this pact by going though a religious ceremony involving a form of symbolic rebirth, in which they joined blood and passed beneath an *arch of raised turf*. See *Gisli Sursson's*

Saga, chapter 6, and in this volume *The Saga of the Sworn Brothers*, chapter 2.

thingman/men *þingmenn*: Every free man and landowner was required to serve as a thingman ('assembly man') by aligning himself with a *godi*. He would either accompany the godi to assemblies and other functions or pay a tax to cover the godi's costs of attending them.

troll *tröll*: Trolls in the minds of the Icelanders were not the huge, stupid figures that we read about in later Scandinavian wonder-tales and legends. At the time of the sagas, they were essentially evil nature spirits, a little like large dark elves. It is only in later times that they come to blend with the image of the Scandinavian *giants*.

Viking *Víkingur*: Normally has an unfavourable sense in the sagas, referring to violent seafaring raiders, especially of the pagan period. It can also denote general bullies and villains.

Winter Nights *veturnætur*: The period of two days when the winter began, around the middle of October. This was a particularly holy time of the year, when sacrifices were made to the female guardian spirits, and other social activities like games meetings and weddings often took place. See, for example, *Gisli Sursson's Saga*, chapter 15. It was also the time when animals were slaughtered for storage over the winter. See also *Havard*, chapter 2.

Index of Characters

THE STORY OF PENGUIN CLASSICS

Before 1946 ... 'Classics' are mainly the domain of academics and students; readable editions for everyone else are almost unheard of. This all changes when a little-known classicist, E. V. Rieu, presents Penguin founder Allen Lane with the translation of Homer's *Odyssey* that he has been working on in his spare time.

1946 Penguin Classics debuts with *The Odyssey*, which promptly sells three million copies. Suddenly, classics are no longer for the privileged few.

1950s Rieu, now series editor, turns to professional writers for the best modern, readable translations, including Dorothy L. Sayers's *Inferno* and Robert Graves's unexpurgated *Twelve Caesars*.

1960s The Classics are given the distinctive black covers that have remained a constant throughout the life of the series. Rieu retires in 1964, hailing the Penguin Classics list as 'the greatest educative force of the twentieth century.'

1970s A new generation of translators swells the Penguin Classics ranks, introducing readers of English to classics of world literature from more than twenty languages. The list grows to encompass more history, philosophy, science, religion and politics.

1980s The Penguin American Library launches with titles such as *Uncle Tom's Cabin*, and joins forces with Penguin Classics to provide the most comprehensive library of world literature available from any paperback publisher.

1990s The launch of Penguin Audiobooks brings the classics to a listening audience for the first time, and in 1999 the worldwide launch of the Penguin Classics website extends their reach to the global online community.

The 21st Century Penguin Classics are completely redesigned for the first time in nearly twenty years. This world-famous series now consists of more than 1300 titles, making the widest range of the best books ever written available to millions – and constantly redefining what makes a 'classic'.

The Odyssey continues ...

The best books ever written

PENGUIN (🐧) CLASSICS

SINCE 1946

Find out more at www.penguinclassics.com